# Grief
# Cottage

# Grief Cottage

*a novel*

# GAIL GODWIN

B L O O M S B U R Y

NEW YORK · LONDON · OXFORD · NEW DELHI · SYDNEY

Bloomsbury USA
An imprint of Bloomsbury Publishing Plc

1385 Broadway        50 Bedford Square
New York             London
NY 10018             WC1B 3DP
USA                  UK

www.bloomsbury.com

BLOOMSBURY and the Diana logo are trademarks of Bloomsbury Publishing Plc

First published 2017
© Gail Godwin, 2017

ISBN:    HB:    978-1-63286-704-9
         ePub:  978-1-63286-706-3

Library of Congress Cataloging-in-Publication Data
Names: Godwin, Gail, author.
Title: Grief cottage : a novel / Gail Godwin.
Description: New York : Bloomsbury USA, an imprint of
Bloomsbury Publishing Plc, 2017.
Identifiers: LCCN 2016036527| ISBN 9781632867049 (hardback) |
ISBN 9781632867063 (ebook)
Subjects: | BISAC: FICTION / Literary. | FICTION / Romance / Gothic.
Classification: LCC PS3557.O315 G75 2017 | DDC 813/.54—dc23 LC record
available at https://lccn.loc.gov/2016036527

2 4 6 8 10 9 7 5 3 1

Typeset by RefineCatch Limited, Bungay, Suffolk
Printed and bound in the U.S.A. by Berryville Graphics Inc., Berryville, Virginia

To find out more about our authors and books visit www.bloomsbury.com. Here
you will find extracts, author interviews, details of forthcoming events and the
option to sign up for our newsletters.

Bloomsbury books may be purchased for business or promotional use. For
information on bulk purchases please contact Macmillan Corporate and Premium
Sales Department at specialmarkets@macmillan.com.

*Grief Cottage is dedicated
to my three nephews
Trey and Cam Millender
&
Justin Cole*

*and to my great-nephew
Matthew Millender*

Not everybody gets to grow up. First you have to survive your childhood, and then begins the hard work of growing into it.

# *1.*

Once there was a boy who lost his mother. He was eleven years, five months, four days—and would never know how many hours and minutes. The state troopers came to the apartment around midnight, but the accident had happened earlier. A part of him believed that if he had known the exact moment her car slid on a patch of black ice and somersaulted down the embankment, he could have sent her the strength to hold on. *Please, Mom, you're all I've got.* And she would have heard him and held on. She had gone out to buy them a pizza. They were going to watch one of their favorite old movies on TV, the one where Alec Guinness and his band of thieves pretend to be musicians. They rent a room in a nice old lady's house, shut the door, put a string quartet on the gramophone, and she is never the wiser. Before the movie is over, she is helping them move their stolen goods and she is still none the wiser. The star of this movie had special meaning to the mother and son because they had read an article about how Alec Guinness never knew who his father was because his mother had refused to tell him, but he had still grown up to be famous anyway.

★   ★   ★

AUNT CHARLOTTE WAS my mother's aunt, which made her my great-aunt. I had only heard tales about her before I went to live with her. Even the tales weren't much. She had run away from home early, married several times, and then gone to live by herself on an island. At some point she had taken up painting and had become a successful local artist. She wasn't a letter writer but whenever Mom wrote to her she sent back a post-card with one of her paintings. I was always mentioned by name. Mom stuck the postcards up on the refrigerator, paint-ings of storm clouds over waves, orangey light on wet surf, a gloomy ruin of an old beach cottage. The paintings had names: *Storm Approaching, Sunset Calm, Abandoned Cottage.* My late grandmother had referred to her as "Crazy Charlotte," or "my Bohemian baby sister." She painted under the name of Charlotte Lee. "It could have been the name of one of her husbands," Mom said. "Or maybe she chose it for herself."

I DID NOT get to Aunt Charlotte's island until late spring. The wheels of the law had to turn first. A person from Social Services stayed with me the rest of that night and helped me pack my things. She asked about my next of kin and I showed her Mom's life insurance policy. "We've got to get you a guardian ad litem quickly," she said. "That's someone who will be your voice in legal matters." When I asked what legal matters, she said, "Determining who will be your permanent guardian and how your estate will be managed." When I asked what estate, she said, "The estate from this insurance policy." Our belongings from the apartment were put into storage and I was sent to live with a foster family and finished seventh grade from their address. I was a year ahead of my age because I had skipped sixth grade. The boy I shared a room with in the foster home had had the left side of his face crushed by his stepfather while his mother was out at work. From his right profile he looked like a normal boy, but from the front and left it looked like his cheek had melted. There was much plastic surgery ahead. At night I could hear him whacking off under the covers.

I liked my guardian ad litem, William. He was the one who got me into the hospital morgue to see my mom and helped me decide on burial arrangements. William was so tall he had to stoop to get through ordinary doorways, and he wore a flowing dark beard. He could have been a stand-in for Abe Lincoln, though he had a shiny bald dome. He had grown up in the high mountains of western North Carolina and had a mountain twang so thick it sounded like it was making fun of itself.

The foster parents had Bible study for us every night. It was called "Parable Party," and they made it a competitive game. Even the little kids could quote chapter and verse from the gospel parables and I soon became a whiz at it myself. I was a fast learner and a good memorizer and I enjoyed a mental challenge. Mom and I had read the King James Bible aloud to each other because she wanted me to be grounded in its stories and language. Sometimes we used it as our augur, opening it at random to see what we should do about something. But it didn't take precedence over everything the way it did in the foster home.

Then one day I was told to pack my things. It was all set up legally and I was going on my first plane ride to live with my great-aunt at her beach cottage in South Carolina. "You are one lucky boy, Marcus," the foster mom said. William stayed with me at the gate until I had a nametag hung around my neck and was escorted onboard by a flight attendant. William's last words to me were, "Live long and prosper," and we gave each other the Spock hand-blessing from *Star Trek*.

Aunt Charlotte was waiting just on the other side of the security gate, a very thin lady in white slacks, loose white shirt, and scuffed brown sandals. She had stern, beaky features and a frosty mannish haircut. At that time she was fifty-seven, but she appeared elderly to me. Though she was my late grandmother's younger sister by six years, she looked at least a generation older than that stylish, coiffed lady who had visited Mom and me several times. The flight attendant who had escorted me checked her papers. Then he handed me over and wished us good luck. I had steeled myself for a theatrical hug like the foster mother's or some display of aunt-ish emotion, but she simply gave me a firm handshake and said, "Well, Marcus, here we are."

While we waited for my suitcases down in baggage claim, she told me "my boxes" had arrived and were stored in her garage, to unpack when I was ready. It took me a minute to realize she meant Mom's and my stuff from our apartment.

We went out into the suffocating heat and she had me heave the suitcases into the trunk of her old Mercedes sedan. The leather seats were boiling, but she said they would cool down in a minute. She wasn't much of a talker. "Are you hungry? Do you like shrimp? We'll go to a place where they serve all the shrimp you can eat."

The shrimp were very small and fried in batter and I ate three helpings. There were also these sweet fried bread balls called hush puppies. Aunt Charlotte picked at her salad and had two glasses of red wine. The waitress kept urging me to go back and refill my plate. Her name was Donna, which was stitched on her uniform, and she smiled a lot. Her teasing-affectionate tone with me reminded me a little of Mom and I went back for the third mostly to make her smile some more. Aunt Charlotte had not smiled once. Looking back on that first day, I realize she must have been as apprehensive as I was. I doubt if I smiled that day, either.

When I threw up in my aunt's car, she pulled over. "No problem, the seats are leather and most of it's on the rubber mat." She set me up with an eight-ounce bottle of spritzer water, a roll of paper towels, and gallon of windshield wiper fluid from her trunk. It rained a lot during this season, she said, so she always carried reserves of wiper fluid. "I'd use the spritzer water for the front of your shirt and the wiper fluid for the rest." Then she withdrew to the grassy embankment and appeared to be studying the traffic. Heat waves rose from the asphalt and made wavery squiggles around her thin white form. The good thing about the heat was that my shirt was dry before I even finished cleaning the car. When we were on the road again I apologized for the smell. "All I smell is wiper fluid," she said.

After we crossed the causeway to the island, she stopped by a store with gas pumps in front and we bought some things for supper. The man at the counter told her the day's shrimp catch had just come in, but she said, "My nephew has already had his fill of shrimp for the day."

## 11.

*W*henever I try to crawl back into the skin of that boy Aunt Charlotte suddenly found invading her precious solitude, a boy who was neither a charming child nor a promising young man, I am surprised that after living alone by choice for so long she was able to tolerate my company as well as she did. She spoke like someone who wasn't used to social talk. She said what needed to be conveyed and stopped. ("Are you hungry? Spray yourself with sunblock even if it's overcast. If it's anything *urgent,* Marcus, you can always knock on my studio door.")

Mom had guessed right about the Lee surname: Aunt Charlotte had made it up. ("It was the obvious choice to take the surname of their hallowed Confederate general, Robert E. Lee. In these parts people still refer to the American Civil War as 'the great unpleasantness' or 'the war of northern aggression.' If I was a 'Lee,' I had a better chance of blending in.")

Aunt Charlotte and Mom had grown up in West Virginia, known to Southerners as the "turncoat state" because it separated from Virginia and joined the Union in the Civil War. Neither of them had any accent other than a mid-Atlantic one, if there was such a thing. Aunt Charlotte's voice was dispassionate and flat compared to my mother's emotional range. Mom could please, tease, or appease, whatever the situation called for, whereas Aunt Charlotte, even when she was in one of her rare good moods or making fun of somebody, stuck to a gruff and matter-of-fact monotone.

After we had established a routine for ourselves that consisted mainly of each mapping thoughtful routes around the other's privacy, she had a serious talk with me about money and my "trust." She invited me into her studio for this. She removed some books and papers from a chair and asked me to sit down. There was the smell of turpentine and oil pigment, a smell that connects me even today with the pleasant idea of someone making something alone. Her studio faced the north end of the beach and had a milky, regulated light, less yellow and warm than the other rooms in the cottage. She also slept in the studio behind a curtain.

It took me longer than it should have to realize she had given up her bedroom to me.

"I have always worked," she began. "Ever since I left home at sixteen, I have held a job. When I married, I supported the first of my no-good husbands and I worked twice as hard as the next two slackers. I will never be rich, but this fluke of a talent has made me safe for the time being. People want paintings of the beach. My style is on the primitive side, but that's an asset, too, don't ask me why. For a large part of my life now I have lived alone and supported myself by my painting and it has suited me." She was perched on a high stool in front of a gigantic paint-spattered easel on wheels. Its large canvas was covered with a cloth. She was looking at me, but actually she was looking through me as she carefully picked her words. "When they contacted me back in February about your mother, they said I was the only living relative. I asked about your father's people, but I was the only name listed on the policy. Did you know she had taken out an insurance policy on her life?"

"It was in case anything happened to her." Mom and I had imagined some fatal illness that would take her away and leave me all alone. We didn't foresee that something as ordinary as driving two miles on a winter night to pick up a pizza could accomplish the same ending.

"I met your mother only once. She was a girl, still in high school. Your grandmother brought her to visit me here. I liked her and I felt she liked me. But it was not a successful visit. Did she ever mention it?"

"She talked about your beach house and how nice it was to lie in bed and hear the ocean so close. She said maybe one day we would go back and visit you. I mean, not stay with you, but in a hotel."

"You would have been welcome to stay here. It was my sister Brenda who spoiled that visit. Always putting everyone down. She couldn't stand my lifestyle. I think that was her reason for bringing your mother to see me; I was to be a warning. But I must remember that Brenda was your grandmother, so you probably loved her. Funny how the same person can be an entirely different entity to various people. Where do you think you'd like to go to school? There's the public school across the causeway and a few of those so-called 'academies.' Or you could go to boarding school. There's enough money. You know that, don't you?"

"It was supposed to be enough to get me through college," I said.

"Then it will be, we'll see to it. Meanwhile, it will pay your expenses until you're old enough to live on your own. And as your guardian I get a nice monthly stipend from the trust. You understand about that, don't you? I want everything to be aboveboard between us."

I said I understood. But her insistence on aboveboard-ness, which would turn out to be one of her sterling qualities, had a bitter effect on me that day. *So it was the money,* I thought, she only took me because of the money. Without that nice stipend she would never have forfeited the solitary life that suited her so well. She went on to explain the trust and how it was set up with a law firm in Charleston that specialized in that sort of thing. There would be monthly statements about how the money was invested and how well it was doing. It seemed that if you had a certain amount of money, you should expect it to make more money out of itself. "And you are welcome to examine these statements anytime you want, Marcus."

"Maybe I'll just leave them to you for now," I said.

It was all I could do to sort out the information arising out of this talk we were having. The revelation about her "nice stipend" had deflated any grand illusions of my being wanted simply because I was me. On the other hand I saw advantages to her scanty information about my past. When she had said, "I asked about your father's people, but I was the only name on the policy," I realized she had assumed that my father was the person whose last name I bore—Harshaw—even though Mom and Mr. Harshaw had parted ways two years before I was born. With my background being so vague to Aunt Charlotte there would be less embarrassing information to worry about her finding out. "Look at it this way, Marcus," Mom had said when I almost killed the grandson of her employer and we had to leave her good job at Forster's furniture factory in the flatlands of North Carolina and move to the mountains. "In a new place we can tell people what we want them to know and that will be our past."

To cover the readjustments going on inside me, I asked Aunt Charlotte what she was painting. After apologizing for it being one of her "bread and butter commissions" she removed the cloth from the large canvas on the easel. So far she had only outlined a substantial-sized beach house and some palmetto trees in dark blue. She explained she was working from a color photo provided by the owners. "I don't paint from life anymore. It's too messy. Sand blows into the pigment and nosy people crowd around and make dumb remarks. If you're interested in seeing the actual house, it's down at the south end of the beach, where they're building the new McMansions. So far it's the only one with three stories. And a fake cupola. For my honest paintings I go to the north end of the island. Those are the old houses, when people built behind the dunes. There's one old house I must have painted at least fifty times. But people keep asking for it. Since I took my business online I can't keep up with the orders for that one house. I paint it from photos now, but they are photos I took myself."

"What's a fake cupola?"

"A cupola is a tower where you can look out at the view. But this one is just stuck up there for show, with no way to get to it."

"Why do people want paintings of that other house?"

"It's a very old cottage, what's left of it. It's a ruin and it has a haunting quality. I'm still trying to do justice to its quality. Walk up there and see it for yourself. It's the very last structure at the north end. It's half gone, but it emanates a powerful mood. The locals call it Grief Cottage. The town commissioners have been dying to tear it down, but the historical society's on their back because it was built in 1804. I need to go up there and get some more photos in case they lose the battle."

"Why do they call it Grief Cottage?"

"A family was lost there in Hurricane Hazel. A boy and his parents. The parents were out desperately searching for him, when all the while he may have been in the cottage. Anyway, none of them were ever found. Some of the locals think the boy may have been hiding in the house somewhere smoking. They thought it might have been a cigarette that started the fire that burned down the south end of the cottage, but they never found a body. Others think that when he realized his parents had gone out searching for him he rushed out searching for them and got swept out to sea. But his body never washed up either."

"Maybe it still could."

"I don't think so. It was fifty years ago. I can show you the last *Grief Cottage* I painted—I mean, on my computer screen. As soon as I get this commission out of the way, I'll give you a tour of my online gallery. But now I must earn my bread and butter while the north light is still strong."

# III.

alk up there and see for yourself," Aunt Charlotte had said, and I had the rest of the afternoon ahead to do it in. I sprayed myself with sunscreen, marched down the rickety boardwalk that bridged the dunes between the cottage and the beach, descended the wooden stairs, and before heading north stopped for my usual inspection of "our" roped-off hatching site with its big red diamond-shaped warning sign. LOGGERHEAD TURTLE NESTING AREA. EGGS, HATCHLINGS, ADULTS, AND CARCASSES ARE PROTECTED BY FEDERAL AND STATE LAWS.

The eggs buried in our dune had already survived their first catastrophe. Back in mid-May, just before my arrival, the people renting the cottage to the right of Aunt Charlotte's had been negligent about smoothing out the sand at the end of their badminton games, and that night a mother turtle had mistaken the hilly clump for a dune, laid her eggs, and departed. The Turtle Patrol had to dig them out, a "clutch" of 110 eggs, tenderly transfer them into buckets lined with wet sand, and re-bury them in a suitable spot. The patrol knew Aunt Charlotte's way of life and could depend on her boundaries to stay untrammeled and safe.

I kept my sneakers on because my beach walks had taught me you made better progress on sand with rubber soles. Aunt Charlotte hadn't said how far the north end of the island was but surely she wouldn't have said I could walk there if she had judged it too far.

Before I came to live with her I had never seen the ocean. Mom and I had lived first in the North Carolina piedmont, which was a long way from the coast. After she had to leave her job at the furniture factory, we moved west to the mountains, which was even farther from the coast. Although I was a competent swimmer in a pool, I was still nervous of the ocean. After being knocked down about twenty times, getting water up my nose and sand in my eyes, I postponed trying to master the waves and took to walking on the beach. There were new ocean things for me to discover every day, comparisons to be made, conclusions to be drawn. Everything I encountered seemed to be sending me some kind of message. Some of the messages made me feel good, others not so good. The patterns made in the sand by the outgoing wash redrew themselves again and again, different each time, and would continue to do so after I was dead. The stately pelicans flapped in a single line toward their destination, while the skittish gulls zipped and zapped, shrieking at one another and getting diverted. When the tide went out, as it was starting to do now, it left behind these tiny-shelled creatures frantically trying to dig themselves back into the wet sand before the birds ate them. Some made it, some did not. And on top of that, all the birds I saw, plus all the crabs that came out at night, were already programmed to gulp down the tasty defenseless little loggerhead babies when they hatched in mid-July and raced for the sea.

I knew why the tides rose and fell; it had been part of seventh-grade science. I also knew that we were composed of seventy-eight percent water when we were born, though it went down to sixty percent as we got older. Our brains remained eighty percent water, however, and the ancient part of our brain remembered that when we were formed many millennia ago, we swam before we could crawl or walk. Even now we began our lives immersed in the waters of our mothers' wombs.

Children playing in the shallow waves screamed with exaggerated terror while mothers hovered close by. There was this one mother sitting in a low chair near the surf. She wore a straw hat and oversized sunglasses. Her toddler, about three, was carefully transporting a shovel full of water from the receding ocean to pour on her feet. By the time he reached her, the ocean had all spilled out and he emptied a waterless shovel on her painted toenails. But then I saw her raise her eyebrows at him behind the oversized sunglasses. Her glossed lips gave him a special ironic smile, meant for just the two of them. Better luck next time, the look said. Meanwhile, I'm staying right here. There were little eddies of security going back and forth between them and it wrenched my heart.

Yellow trash barrels were placed at regular intervals along the beach border where the grasses and dunes began. To date, I had walked north as far as the fourth yellow barrel beyond Aunt Charlotte's cottage. The barrels stretched ahead of me, getting smaller and smaller in perspective toward the island's north end until I could no longer count them.

But today, even before I reached the third barrel, something horrible happened. It was like I had been turned upside down. Everything was so terrifying it stopped me in my tracks. My heart was pounding a mile a minute and, worse than that, I found I no longer knew how to walk. Somehow I found myself sitting down in the sand—it must have been abrupt because my bottom was stinging. A couple in bathing suits passed by and the man looked over and acknowledged me with a man-to-man wave. After lifting my hand in return, I quickly unlaced a sneaker, pretending there was a pebble inside it and that was why I needed to sit. I turned the sneaker upside down and made a big deal of shaking out the pebble. I put the shoe back on but when it came to tying the laces in a knot I couldn't remember how. The boy whose stepfather had smashed his face in had lost his memory for weeks. "A whole bunch of my life was just wiped out forever," he went around bragging to anybody at the foster home who would listen. Maybe I was going insane. When Mom was still working at the furniture factory, a woman who worked in the sanding department "lost it" one day and never came back. Two men had to carry her from the floor. She had to go to a mental hospital. This sometimes happened to people, Mom said, either because they couldn't endure their life anymore or because, through no fault of their own, something suddenly went haywire in their brains.

I didn't think it was the first reason, because I could endure life at Aunt Charlotte's much better than the foster home, where nothing was private and you never had a moment alone. At Aunt Charlotte's I had plenty of time to myself and didn't have to listen to platitudes about how everything horrible that happens to us is part of "God's plan." I no longer had to share a room with a boy who made noises under the covers. At Aunt Charlotte's I had my own room and could listen to the ocean at night, just as my mother had done as a girl that time she had visited here.

If it was the other thing, and something in my brain had suddenly gone haywire, what would happen to me? At the very worst, I would be discovered insane on the beach, unable to remember anything or tie my shoe, and sent off in an ambulance to a mental hospital. If the brain somehow righted itself and I made it back to the house, what then? If I told Aunt Charlotte about the panic, she would get on the phone and call in another grief counselor, if I was entitled to any more of them—or did you get to start all over in a new state?—or I'd have to go to a therapist and Aunt Charlotte would resent having to drive me there and we would be diminishing the money in the trust.

It took some rude plops of water on my head to remind me that if I was using my brain well enough to figure out possible outcomes of my madness I probably wasn't mad. The skies had opened and people were fleeing the beach or sheltering under umbrellas. The woman in the big sunglasses and her little boy had vanished. I looked at my feet and saw that both sneakers were tied. Walking home in the pouring rain, I decided not to mention anything to Aunt Charlotte.


"THAT'S THE TROUBLE with afternoon walks," said Aunt Charlotte. "In this season you can depend on it to rain. Sorry it spoiled your adventure, but I'm glad you changed clothes. I had a productive afternoon. I've laid in the sky over my McMansion, and tomorrow I'll tackle the shrubbery. It's not there yet in real life, but I'll duplicate what's in the architect's drawing."

"Maybe I'll go the whole way to the cottage tomorrow morning."

"It's a fair walk, but you're young. I haven't done it for a while. The last time I went up there to take some new photos of Grief Cottage I drove north as far as Seashore Road goes, parked in the turnaround, and then fought my way on foot up through the dune grasses and Spanish bayonets."

"What are they?"

"*Very* prickly plants. They look like succulent bayonets sticking up from the ground. You don't want to sit or fall on one."

Supper was the only meal Aunt Charlotte and I ate together. I did not mind this. I liked making my own breakfast and having a sandwich around midday on the porch. Mom and I had never eaten all our meals together because of her jobs and her different shifts. Aunt Charlotte wasn't a cook and didn't aspire to being one. The foster mom made a big deal about her cooking and baking, but everyone had to sit down together for every meal and we had to take turns praying and then we each had to tell what we had learned that day. As soon as I was old enough, Mom and I had shared the cooking. Spaghetti sauce was her masterpiece (her secret was clove powder), and she made a fabulous thick soup from her own combination of cans. I could fry hamburgers and scramble eggs and do pulled pork in our slow-cooker. For the rest, we got our stuff from delis.

Or went out to pick up a pizza.

No wonder Aunt Charlotte was so skinny. All day she snacked on bananas and crackers and little cartons of yogurt, and at supper she picked around the edges of her meal and kept refilling her wineglass. She ordered her wines and had them delivered in cases. The store on our island had a deli with salads and cold meats and kept a spit going that roasted chickens all day long. So far we had not risked shrimp again and I didn't want to be the first to suggest it.

At our shared meals, she gamely dredged up things to talk about. I could feel her reluctance to probe into my past. After downing several glasses of wine, though, she loosened up a little. What had she done when she ate her suppers alone? There was an old TV in the kitchen, she had probably watched it. Or just sat comfortably, enjoying her solitary life and sipping her wine.

She saw me staring at the TV and asked if I would like to order cable. "I can get old movies and the networks, but maybe you and your mother had other favorite channels. Should I look into it? All the neighbors are already hooked up. I'm the last holdout."

"Mom and I never had cable. They had it at the foster home because the state paid for it. There was this two-year-old boy who sat strapped into his little swing-chair and watched it all day long."

"Is that a yes or a no?"

"Only if you want it." As this sounded rude, I added, "I mean, I can do without it if you can." One less expense to take out of the trust.

"Look, Marcus, we're both new at this. If there's anything missing here, something you'd like to have to make the summer go faster, you need to tell me. I won't know otherwise, I'm not a mind reader. Would you like to have a look at those boxes waiting in the garage, or is it still too soon?"

"Maybe it's still a little too soon."

"Well, you set to work on them when you're ready. School starts at the end of August. You'll be with people your own age. These days won't last forever. No days ever do, though sometimes it's hard to convince oneself of that."

# *iii.*

*A*t night, the tides washed in and out. I did not think I would ever get tired of that sound. It felt like the watery part of the earth taking regular breaths in your ear. Thud-wash, thud-wash, never stopping, doing its job with the same rhythm as millions of years ago when the little loggerhead turtles were waiting to hatch and begin their race for the sea. ("It's their Normandy," an old-timer on the Turtle Patrol told me, "only in reverse.")

My mother had slept in this room before she was my mother. Her young head, like mine, had been divided from the ancient tides by a mere cottage wall and a few dunes. Where had my critical grandmother ("Brenda") slept? Now that I asked that question, it seemed likely she had shared the bed with my mother while Aunt Charlotte slept in her studio. When Mom used to tell me how nice it had been to lie in bed and hear the ocean so close, I had always imagined her alone in the bed. But maybe she had adapted her memory of that night when telling the memory to me. As someone who had slept all his life with his mother, I could identify with that. Whenever I was telling my best friend, Wheezer, about a dream I'd had, I pictured an alternate vision of myself alone in a bed, the way Wheezer, who slept alone in *his* bed, would naturally be picturing me.

That is, until the unlucky day he came to our apartment and found out the truth.

My shoelaces were tied this morning and like the straight-flying pelicans I had a goal: Grief Cottage. In my backpack I had my lunch and a bottle of spring water. Aunt Charlotte reckoned it would take me about forty minutes each way at a normal pace.

"When I first moved here I was in an ecstasy of freedom. I hardly touched the ground, my first year on this island. I was in my early thirties, which may seem decrepit to you, but I had never had so much energy before in my life. Nobody could tell me how to live anymore; nobody could criticize me or lay a hand on me. I spent all my savings on a beach shack. It was even named Rascal Shack. The young scions would gather here when they wanted to get drunk. It didn't even have an indoor bathroom when I bought it."

"What is a *syon*?"

"Offspring. Usually meaning the offspring of privileged families. You put a 'c' after the 's' when you're writing it. S-C-I-O-N. When I first came here I walked to the north end of the island every day. Forty minutes each way. The walk north was exactly the right distance to make me walk out of myself. And then that desolate cottage at the end, falling in on itself and all its secrets. What better spot for sorting through the debris of my own history?"

"If you walked out of yourself going north, what did you do on the return walk?"

"Enjoyed my emptiness. Or sometimes just congratulated myself for escaping."

"Escaping what, if it's not rude to ask?"

"Escaping the kind of life I'd always felt trapped in. But that's another story. Do you know, Marcus, it was Grief Cottage that started my painting. One day there was someone else in my lonely spot. This person had planted an easel in the sand and was painting the cottage. At first I assumed it was a man but when I got closer it turned out to be a woman in a hat and trousers. She was a cheerful tourist, staying for a short time, and I watched her mix her colors. It was fascinating. It was a competent little painting; I could see it hanging on a wall and pleasing someone, though she had missed the mood of the place. I could do that, I thought. I bought some paints and some canvas board and a book called *A Beginner's Guide to Landscape Painting*. It took me a while to figure out how I could capture the mood she had missed. But first I had to teach myself the most basic painting skills. Later I borrowed books from the library to see how the masters had done their skies. Constable would spend hours sketching clouds and skies. He called this practice his 'skying sessions.'"

"Constable?"

"John Constable, English. Late eighteenth, early nineteenth century. Look at his skies up close—he loves approaching storms—and you realize clouds *don't have outlines*. He works them up from within. Clouds are brushstrokes. Constable is the king of clouds."

TODAY THE RISING tide had covered the spot where I had seen the mother and the little boy yesterday afternoon. By afternoon the waters would have receded again and maybe the happy pair would come back. Perhaps they had their own family

routine in one of the beach houses behind the dunes. Was a
father with them, or was he somewhere else, or was he one of
those secret fathers nobody gets to know about?

I was walking up closer to the dunes because of the incoming
tide when a neat white dump truck stopped alongside me. A
sunburned man in shorts jumped out and gracefully upended a
yellow trash barrel into the truck's bin. "Disgusting!" he called
to me over the sound of the waves. "What people will put into
these things!" Without waiting for a response, he asked where I
was headed. When I said I was walking to the north end of the
island he said, "I'd offer you a lift but it's against regulations. I
could lose my job."

"That's okay. I want to walk."

"Well, dude," he said, looking me over, "I'd take it easy if I
were you till you get back in shape." As he raised his sunburnt
arms to swing the empty barrel back onto its concrete platform,
a pungent man-smell issued from the wet underarms of his
T-shirt. "You have a good day," he called over his shoulder,
springing up into the truck and setting off northward to the
next yellow barrel.

Already I was tired and hadn't yet reached the spot where
I had panicked and turned around yesterday. But I had to
keep walking north till the trash-barrel man finished his round
and passed me coming back or he'd see how out of shape I
really was.

After Mom left her job at the furniture factory and we
moved to the mountain town of Jewel, I entered fifth grade.
Then at the end of the year the teacher told Mom I was ready to
do seventh grade work if she had no objection to my skipping a
grade. She didn't—it made her proud because she had helped
me study that first lonely year in Jewel. She asked me my

opinion and I said it suited me. But the seventh grade kids were more developed and must have looked on me as a freak: here was this kid still built like a child and piping up with the right answer every time the teacher called on him in class. At first they called me Baby Wonk. Then when I began to gain weight, they called me Pudge. ("Boy, Pudge sure makes the most of the Reduced Price Lunch Program, doesn't he?")

Back in Forsterville where the furniture factory was, my best friend had had a nickname: everybody lovingly called him Wheezer, because he suffered from bad asthma. But to Wheezer, whose real name was Shelby, I was never anything but Marcus.

*Just the right distance to make me walk out of myself*, Aunt Charlotte had said. I wished I knew what she was trying to walk out of, what kind of debris in her history she needed to sort out. If she came to the island when she was in her thirties, did she have three times as much debris as I had?

One foot and then the other. Remember, each time the water inches closer, you are closer to your goal.

Is it a mirage, that tiny white truck bouncing toward me? No, that's him, heading south. His sunburnt salute. Way to go, dude. Tide swirling closer now. Pride saved.

Oh no, surely *that* couldn't be Aunt Charlotte's famous cottage, rearing up all broken and ugly in front of me. But it had to be because the island ended here. The town commissioners had been right to want to remove such an eyesore from their ocean view. When Aunt Charlotte first came here, it couldn't have looked this bad. After all, some cheery tourist had been painting it. And then Aunt Charlotte taught herself to paint and painted it over and over until it became the kind of picturesque ruin people paid money for.

If a house could be a zombie, this grim husk, guarded by those evil-sharp bayonet cactuses Aunt Charlotte warned about and fenced by sagging wire posted with CONDEMNED and KEEP OUT: DANGER signs, would qualify as one. And more than fifty people had paid money to have Aunt Charlotte paint this zombie house to hang on their walls at home! The porch on the south side had been sheared off and some shingles were nailed up against a replacement wall. Had that been the porch where he left a cigarette while his parents were out desperately searching for him?

When I got closer I could view the rest of the house from the front. The noon sun boiled down on its crumpled roof, mercilessly entering a doorway without a door and the gaping window holes on either side. Maybe at dark this place would pass as a picturesque ruin. But the cottage would have to be almost a silhouette to make you want to hang it on your wall.

I was hot and very thirsty. The zombie house offered the only shade in sight, so I wriggled under the wire fence with the KEEP OUT warnings, snagging my backpack and scratching my arm. I cautiously climbed the rotting steps to the front porch, which slanted downward. At least it was cool under the crumpled roof and I could report to Aunt Charlotte that I had "almost" been inside.

I made a kind of lounge for myself on the slanty porch. As its slope inclined toward the ocean, it was like being teasingly tilted forward, just short of getting tossed overboard. Sweat drying on my shirt, I drank my water, then slowly ate my sandwiches, the high tide crashing around me. I would not be ashamed for the sunburnt man to see me now, though in his official capacity he would probably have to order me off the condemned property. ("Because otherwise, dude, I could lose my job.")

I folded the empty lunch wrappings and stuffed them inside my backpack, which I plumped into a pillow for myself. It was the backpack I had taken to school when Mom was still alive and I sniffed it to see if there were any traces of our old life together in the apartment. There was a faint bread-y smell, but that was probably from today's sandwiches. The porch beneath the backpack had its own smell of salt and old timber and decay. The ocean was so close I could feel the spray and I felt myself sliding into a nap. Which was okay, I had earned my tiredness. I would rest up before heading back to Aunt Charlotte's. She was only in the middle of her day and would expect me to be in the middle of mine.

WHEN I AWOKE, it was out of a dream in which the sunburnt man had been standing in the doorless doorway of the cottage. He leaned lightly against its frame, watching me sleep. I knew not to turn and look toward the door because I would wake completely and I wanted to prolong the way I felt him watching over me. Also, a dialogue was going on between us, though neither of us spoke aloud. We could read each other's minds. I asked him if he had been inside the cottage and he said yes, he sometimes checked things out to see how bad they were getting. I asked how bad were they, and he said bad enough for this place to come down. When I asked if I could have a look inside, he said that is exactly why I am here, to forbid you to go inside. But why? I wanted to know. Because, Marcus, people who go in don't always come out. I asked how he knew my name. Because I needed to know it, he said.

★ ★ ★

NOW THE TIDE was going out, the sound of the waves more distant. How long had I been curled up on the porch, completely awake? It seemed a while ago that the sunburnt man had been watching over me.

But *something still was.* I felt its presence by the electric prickles all down my back and by my serious reluctance to move a muscle. Then the reluctance turned to cold fear. There was no way in the world I could muster the courage to roll over and see what was in that doorway.

Whatever was behind me was not watching over me like the sunburnt man. It was more like I was being *appraised* the way I might appraise some alien creature that had wandered into my scope of vision and curled up with his back to me. I felt no big-brotherly protectiveness coming from this watcher, only an intense, almost affronted, curiosity. Whatever was looking down at me seemed to be waiting to see what I would do next.

I'm not sure how much time I remained sitting there with my back to the watcher. It might have been only a couple of minutes but it felt like the clock had stopped and I was trapped in a timeless state of fright. What I did do next was somehow force myself to sit upright on the slanty porch. My heart was thrashing, louder than the ocean. My back, still feeling the prickles trained on it, stayed rigidly turned to the doorway. My knees were shaking so much it was an effort to stand. Snatching up my backpack, I took a flying leap over the rotting steps.

Even after I had crawled under the fence with the CONDEMNED and KEEP OUT signs and started walking south, my neck felt fused forward on my shoulders. I knew it was beyond my powers to swivel it around and risk seeing whether I was still being kept in sight.

# 2.

Last time you were there, did it have the fence with all those 'condemned' and 'keep off' signs?"

"Those have been up for a while," said Aunt Charlotte. "The fence is in my photographs, but I transformed it into an erosion fence—those picturesque wooden fences you see in so many beach paintings. How did the cottage look?"

"It's in terrible shape. It has to be a lot worse than when you last saw it. It's more of a *zombie house*. Did anybody ever say anything about it being haunted?"

"Not that I've heard. Why?"

"You said they started calling it Grief Cottage. I thought maybe—"

"You mean, the parents coming back to see if the boy ever returned home? Their spirits unable to rest, that sort of thing? No, all I've heard are the stories about how they were all lost."

"Or maybe the *boy*."

"What about the boy?"

"*His* spirit being unable to rest."

"I'll have to check. I have two books about the history of the island. Grief Cottage is mentioned in one of them, but I forget which one. I've never been able to read either of them all the way though. Every time I try, I get angry. Did *you* feel any spirits when you were there?"

"I only went on the porch."

"You shouldn't even have been on the porch. But what boy could resist?"

"Why do you get angry?"

"About those books? Where to start? With the sea turtle eggs, probably. But I need to back up a little. The ladies who wrote these books are from families who have been coming to the island for a zillion years. I don't know which gets my goat more. Their cozy assumption of entitlement, or their cruel ignorance about anything outside themselves and their family histories. The sea turtle eggs are a case in point. You know how sacred the whole egg-laying thing is now. We have to turn off our porch lights after dark so the mothers can come up to the dunes and lay their eggs in peace. And then the whole count-down period—well, you know. We have our very own 'clutch' of eggs with the red fence and warning sign. So I'm paging through this book—I forget which one—and the lady's saying how much fun it was back in the good old days to go out in the morning and find some turtle eggs buried in the dunes and bring them inside and eat them for breakfast. So delicious. The size of ping-pong balls, and even better, the yolks don't get hard even after you boil them, so you can suck the yellow out. A real gourmet treat for the privileged few."

"That was in *a book*?"

"Yes, and more. Of course, both these books were published back in the nineteen-seventies, before the turtle patrols got going. But I'll turn them over to you and you can look up the stories about people lost in hurricanes. As for ghosts, there's this man in gray who appears on the beach before a hurricane. Some say he wears a Confederate uniform, others say just gray clothes. If he looks straight at your house, it won't get washed away. If he avoids looking at it, you'd better evacuate."

"And people have seen him?"

"That you'll have to decide for yourself, Marcus. People see what they want to see. Or imagine they saw. And others *say* they saw something in order to sound psychic or special. I'm not big on ghosts. There are enough horrors in the real world to worry about."

That night Aunt Charlotte gave me the promised art tour of her website. We sat side by side in front of her laptop at the kitchen table and she clicked on the different paintings and then we enlarged them. I was mostly interested in the Grief Cottage painting, which I recognized as the "Abandoned Cottage" post-card Mom and I had received.

It was the place I had seen today but it was also something else. If this painting hung on my wall, it would make me feel sad and spooked every time I walked past it. But I would walk past it again and again just because it made me feel this way. Surprisingly, given its dark mood, Aunt Charlotte's painting wasn't a night scene. Above the derelict cottage was a soft blue sky with innocent clouds. The sand dunes, though heavily populated with sea grasses and Spanish bayonets, were white and pure. The marked contrast made the picture even more unsettling. It was an anterior view of the cottage, though you could figure out it had lost its south side. The front of the cottage, including the slanted porch where I had slept earlier, had sunshine breaking into its shadows. It was the middle of the day in the painting, the light fell much as it had today, but somehow, the way Aunt Charlotte had painted it, the picture reminded you of the impermanence of everything and the treacheries awaiting you even on a nice day.

"You really captured its mood," I said.

"What kind of mood?"

I hunted for a good word. "Well, *forlorn*."

"*Forlorn*, I like that. Too bad you can't really see my brush-work on the computer screen. It intensifies the forlornness." Pleasure softened her gruff voice. "The actual painting is small, only eight by ten. Nestled in a deep frame under the right lighting, the effect is even stronger."

THE DAY AFTER my trip to the cottage, the rain began. "I'm surprised it didn't come sooner," remarked Aunt Charlotte at the end of the second day. "June is always the wettest month. I hope you'll be able to amuse yourself, Marcus."

The first two days of the downpour were a gift. I wasn't ready to repeat that walk to the cottage. And it was a relief to have some indoor time when I wasn't expected to act like a boy pleased to be at the beach. All I had to do was give the appearance of amusing myself. This turned out to be easy. I could lie in the hammock on the covered porch and watch the tides going in and out. I liked the aches all down my legs from the day before. I doubted I had ever walked that far in my life. The aches were a reminder that I had made it. I liked to go back over the moment when the sunburnt man, bouncing south in his little white truck, gave me a thumbs-up. During the rainy days, I was to see the white truck bouncing up and down the beach but couldn't tell if it was him inside. When it rained, there probably wasn't as much trash in the yellow barrels. I wondered whether he thought of me. But then I had to remind myself that he knew nothing about me, except that I had set out to walk north that day, that I was out of shape, and that I was later seen still walking north—probably farther than he had thought me capable of walking. He didn't know I lived here full time: for all he knew I was a one-day visitor with a backpack.

I had Aunt Charlotte's two books by the local ladies. One was called *Chronicles of a Legendary Island* and the other *Our Island Then and Now*. I kept both books with me in the hammock so I could be seen looking into them on Aunt Charlotte's sporadic trips to the bathroom or to the refrigerator to grab a yogurt or uncork a fresh bottle of wine. Though my back was to the house, I was conscious of her checking on me through the window. Just as when I lay turned away on the porch of Grief Cottage and had been conscious of something checking me out from behind. The only difference was: one was an everyday occurrence, the other implausible—maybe just a lonely boy imagining something "in order to sound psychic or special."

First I leafed through the books looking for illustrations. In both there were lots of old maps and reproductions of records and deeds in old-fashioned handwriting, mostly dating from the 1800s. Transfers of property dated as far back as 1791. There were rough line-drawings of the island with the names of owners printed out on little numbered squares representing the lots where the first houses were built. Both ladies' books had this same map, labeled *Courtesy of the South Carolina Historical Society*.

The first numbered square at the north tip of the island had belonged to a family called Hassel. Then, some pages later in the *Then and Now* book, there was a map where the squares bore the names of later owners. #1 Hassel was later sold to Wortham, who later sold to Barbour. But there was a star next to #1, which led to a footnote saying that since Hurricane Hazel, this property was now the site of a ruin "slated for demolition." The *Then and Now,* published in the 1970s, said the demolition was already being announced. Aunt Charlotte had come to the island in the late seventies. Neither book contained a photograph of Grief Cottage, though some other old houses were often included as a backdrop for blurred family pictures: a group of women picking shrimp on the porch of "Sunrise Cottage"; men in hats standing beside a Model-T; women with bathing suits like dresses and men in costumes like long johns setting out for the beach. At frequent intervals there would be a posed snapshot of a black person in apron or overalls looking up from work to grin at the camera.

The only mention of "Grief Cottage" was at the end of the "Fierce Storms" chapter in the *Legendary Island* book. After pages of blow-by-blow descriptions of houses floating out to sea and entire families and their servants dropping one by one from trees into the engulfing waves of the 1822 and 1893 hurricanes, a single paragraph was devoted to Hurricane Hazel ("the most devastating storm since 1893"), which struck with merciless fury in 1954, "the year before the island got telephones." But due to an efficient neighbor warning system, most of the islanders made hurried escapes to safe places on the mainland. The only missing people had been a fourteen-year-old boy and his parents, an out-of-state family staying in the Barbour cottage after the summer season. No one knew their fates for sure because their bodies were never found. It had been a sad tale of out-of-state people underestimating hurricanes, the book said: the parents having gone out in the storm to search for the boy and the boy possibly having gone out in search of the parents.

The house itself, the oldest on the island and tucked safely behind its dunes, withstood the tempest, all except the south porch, which was destroyed by fire before or during the hurricane. Since then the cottage had remained empty and been allowed to fall into ruin. Islanders had taken to calling it "Grief Cottage."

I was glad to be able to report my findings to Aunt Charlotte. "It was an out-of-state family, but it didn't give their names or mention anything about a cigarette."

"I must have heard that part from the locals, then. Did both books mention this out-of-state family?"

"No, just the one. The same one that had that story about the turtle eggs."

"I'll bet the Confederate ghost made both of the books."

"Yeah, they had the same painting of him walking along the beach."

"That painting has become an industry all by itself. You can order it in a variety of sizes, either as a framed print, a metal print, or a canvas print."

"What's a metal print?"

"When the painting is reproduced on a thin sheet of aluminum. It gives a very high gloss effect. Looks good on large walls in offices."

"But they don't get to have originals. The artist doesn't paint it fresh, over and over again, like you."

"He can't. He died in the 1930s, shortly after he painted it. His heirs are still raking in the bucks from that one picture. He was an excellent landscape painter. I saw a local retrospective once. That painting was the only time he ever put in a human figure. What would he think if he knew his one gray guy would make him famous?"

"Do you ever think about being famous?"

"As I said, Marcus, I'm thankful to have this fluke of a talent. It's my livelihood and I enjoy it. When you're painting you don't dwell on old miseries. There's something about the smell of pigment and the way time becomes meaningless when you're painting."

As the rain continued to fall, those boxes from my old life stacked in the garage nagged at me. I didn't want Aunt Charlotte to think I was at loose ends. If she found me hanging about, she might worry she wasn't doing enough for me and start feeling guilty and then the guilt would turn into resentment. I had watched my mom fight this progression in herself after we had moved from Forsterville to the mountains and had been cooped up for too long in our miserable upstairs apartment in Jewel while our life went from bad to worse.

Mom and I had always shared a bedroom and a bed. I had never given this a second thought until the day I brought Wheezer to our apartment back in Forsterville. It was a far better apartment than the one we were to have in Jewel, but there was only the single bedroom. I invited him home with me reluctantly—it was much nicer to go to his house, where he had his own room and his grandmother, who ran the household, made us special treats. His father traveled around the state selling Forster's furniture, and his mother—they had long been "estranged"—lived in Palm Beach, organizing women's golf tournaments. Wheezer had confided to me that he had been "an accident." His mother had been eager for his big brother, Drew, to leave for college, "but then when Drew turned eighteen, she and Daddy messed up and I was the result." Drew, who worked for an accounting firm in Charlotte, was old enough to be Wheezer's father. He came home frequently on weekends, tanning himself in the backyard if it was warm enough and shut up in his bedroom listening to jazz and blues except for mealtimes. He treated Wheezer and me with a grumpy, bemused forbearance.

Wheezer was fascinated by my closeness with my mom. He was also curious—perhaps too curious—about the "socio-economic" differences between us. It would be safer, I thought, for him to go on romanticizing my home life as frugal but noble, like the homes of the poor in Dickens. But he persisted in digging for details about how we lived until Mom said to ask him over one Saturday when she wasn't working at the furniture factory. She would go out and get pizza for our lunch. (This was to be the first time her going out to get pizza would precede a disaster.) She said it was only right that we return his hospitality when I spent so much time at his grandmother's house. How different our life might have been if I had not invited Wheezer over that Saturday!

"Wait a minute," he said when I was showing him our bedroom. "You sleep in the same bed with your mom?" "Where else would I sleep?" I flashed back. "Some poor families sleep four to a bed." That shut him up until I made the fatal mistake of showing him the picture of a man I was never supposed to show anyone. Mom kept this small framed photo in a tin box at the bottom of a drawer, and said she would tell me more about him when the time was right. But after Wheezer's remark about our sleeping arrangements, I was desperate to divert him with a new mystery. Without a word, I walked over to the bureau, opened the bottom drawer, opened the tin box, and took out the photograph. "This is my real dad," I said, "but you can't tell anyone. He's dead now, but when I'm older she's going to explain everything." In his eagerness, he snatched the photograph out of my hand. He examined it, turned it sideways, shook it in its frame, scrutinized it some more, and then handed it back to me. "This is something that's been cut out of a book," he said, giving me a hostile look. "This person could be anybody. You and your mom are both crazy. I need to leave." Those were the last words he ever spoke directly to me. By the time Mom got back to our apartment with the pizza, he was gone. I told her he'd felt an asthma attack coming on and rushed home for his medication.

At recess on Monday he had waited until I was in hearing range and then announced to the other boys. "Guess what? Marcus sleeps with his mom. He's his mother's own little husband."

And then I did go crazy. I grabbed a hunk of his beautiful salon-cut hair and banged his head backward against a rock wall until there was blood on the wall. The asthmatic boy gasped and gagged and then stopped breathing altogether. Everyone including me thought he had died. But I went on punching that neat little face until others pulled me away. He almost lost the sight in one eye. Mom gave up her job, and as soon as my sessions with the psychiatrist came to an end we moved away. I had felt thankful when I heard the eye was out of danger. But deep down, below the level where right and wrong stayed separate, I was awed at myself for being able to summon such wrath.

When the psychiatrist had asked what I had felt when I was attacking Wheezer, I said I had "blanked out." But even as I lied I knew that to bloody Wheezer's head and crush his face and stop his breathing had been my supreme task. And as I saw this being accomplished before my eyes I was filled with elation. I felt that I was driving out the badness from my life through my fists and feet. But I had been wise enough to keep this from the psychiatrist. He would have judged that anyone admitting to such things needed to be in an institution. Yet I had also been able to tell him, in all truth, that I had been sickened and appalled when I heard how badly my friend had been hurt. It was as though Wheezer had been in a terrible accident and I was hearing about it afterward.

Aunt Charlotte had not mentioned the boxes again, but as the rain hadn't let up I got the first one from the garage and carried it to my room. After a quick glance inside, I fetched a black trash bag from the pantry. The slow-cooker could stay; I could impress Aunt Charlotte with my pulled pork. The rest—aspirin, Q-tips, even our old toothbrushes, for God's sake, and two pathetic chipped mugs—into the black bag. Some social worker-in-training had probably packed these boxes. "This boy lost his mother and had to go into foster care," the supervisor would have said. "Pack everything even if it seems worthless. There are always lawsuits to consider."

*vi.*

During the rainy spell I dreamed that the sunburnt man picked me up on a motorcycle. The dump truck was in the shop, he said, so our job was to ride up and down the beach on the motorcycle and *check the levels* of the yellow trash cans. Riding behind him felt wonderful. I was the one who had to hop off and inspect each can. He laughed so hard I could feel his back shaking when I said, leaning against him as we rode straight into the wind: "Yuck, you wouldn't want to know what was in that last can." When we got to the trash can in front of Grief Cottage, I said, "I guess we won't need to check that one."

"Why not?"

"Because. Nobody has been in there since Hurricane Hazel."

"That's what you think," he said. "I'll check this one out myself."

"Just as I expected," he said when he returned. "Remember what I told you, Marcus. Do not go in that house."

"But what was in the can?"

"I could tell you," he said, laughing, "but then I'd have to kill you."

★　★　★

THE RAIN BEATING down on Aunt Charlotte's tin roof shut out
the sound of the ocean. At supper a few evenings back, she had
announced that she was within days of completing the McMansion
painting. I told her I had made a start with the boxes. "Then this
rain has been good for something," she said. In the bathroom I
always rinsed the sink after using it and wiped it dry with my
towel. Mom had taught me this when she had to take a second
job cleaning houses. It was the little touches, she said, that pleased
people. Dry sinks and soap dishes, shiny taps. A single hair in the
tub could ruin the whole effect. And I always made sure the seat
was back down on the toilet. So far, I had erred only once, and
Aunt Charlotte had let it go with a dry comment about sharing a
bathroom with a man.

I brought in a second box only to shrink back as soon
as I had taken a sneak preview. This box contained a different
set of sorrows. Underneath some childhood books (*Goodnight
Moon, Mrs. Ticklefeather, Winnie the Pooh*, and *The House at Pooh
Corner*) were my mother's winter coat, her sweatpants and
tops she wore at home, her shoes, nightgowns, underwear,
elastic stockings (which held in her varicose veins from
standing at work), her laminated badge ("Section Manager")
that she had proudly worn at Forster's furniture factory, her
makeup and moisturizers, a box, half empty, of super-sized
Tampax. Had the social worker-in-training made a phone
call to his or her superior? "Listen, should I go ahead and
throw some of the really personal items out, or what? I mean,
Goodwill would take the winter coat, though it's sort of shabby,
but the other stuff?" And the superior must have repeated the
lawsuit spiel.

The whole of that box, even the coat (let Goodwill find its own shabby coats!) went into the black trash bag. After paging nostalgically through *Goodnight Moon* and feeling sad, I tossed the books. Then remorse overcame me and I rescued the Pooh books. Mom had been so proud of herself for finding them at a library sale. ("They're like new, except a child crayoned over a few pages in *Pooh Corner*.") Best to pace myself with these boxes. What if they were going to get incrementally worse, each one harder to take than the one before?

It was a relief to return to the books by the privileged ladies with their cruel ignorance about anything outside their own history. When I was out on the porch in the hammock, the ocean noises drowned out the softer patter of the rain. I watched the Turtle Patrol, clad in slickers and rain hats, make regular visits to our clutch. And from Aunt Charlotte's porch there was always the chance of spotting the little white truck bouncing north or south.

I went back to the "Fierce Storms" chapter in *Chronicles of a Legendary Island,* remembering how I had aced my research paper at the mountain school where I was Baby Wonk and Pudge who had skipped a grade. Our teacher, who liked me so much she often looked at me while she was addressing the class (which didn't lessen my freak reputation), said that instead of rushing to start writing your paper you should read your material through several times and treat it like *clues in a mystery.* Because each time you read through something, the more things you would realize that you had missed the time before. What clues like in a mystery could I extract from the single paragraph that dealt with Hurricane Hazel at the end of the "Fierce Storms" chapter?

In the early parts of that chapter, which had recounted lost lives in the bad hurricanes of 1822 and 1893, all the drowned family members and their drowned servants were named. Even visitors and strangers had been diligently listed by name, even if only part of a name. ("Also drowned on that fearful night, a century and a half ago, were Mr. Warren Botsford's nephew, Botsford Channing; Captain Wise, a visiting architect; a Dr. Venn from Charlotte, N.C.; a Miss Satterwhite and a Mr. de Vere . . .")

Yet the only missing people after Hurricane Hazel hit on October 15, 1954, were not named. There weren't yet telephones on the island in 1954, but due to an "efficient neighbor warning system," most of the islanders made hurried evacuations to safe places on the mainland.

The only people who could not be accounted for were the fourteen-year-old boy and his parents, the out-of-state family staying in the Barbour cottage after the summer season. It was an unfortunate chain of circumstances, the out-of-state family most likely being unfamiliar with hurricanes, and underestimating the force of this one. One evacuating islander, Mr. Art Honeywell, reported having been stopped in his truck on Seashore Road by the desperate parents searching on foot for their son, but the boy had not been seen by anyone. It was later surmised that he had set off in another direction in search of the parents. As their bodies were never found, it is assumed that all three were washed out to sea. The house itself, the oldest on the island, withstood the tempest, all except the south porch, which had been mysteriously destroyed by fire during the hurricane. Afterward the cottage was sold and the new owners allowed it to remain empty and fall into ruin. Because of its sad fate, islanders took to calling it "Grief Cottage."

★　★　★

WHAT EXACTLY WAS the "efficient neighbor warning system"? Did it mean only your neighbors got warned? What about strangers? Especially out-of-state strangers unfamiliar with hurricanes, who underestimated their force? Why hadn't Mr. Art Honeywell in his truck said to the parents, "Climb in and we'll search for your son together?" Where did the "age fourteen" come from? Had the parents told Mr. Honeywell, "We are out looking for our son, who is fourteen . . ."? Why hadn't the boy been in school? And what kind of family stays in a beach cottage in October, "after the season"? Most likely a family who needed to take advantage of reduced rates. If Mom and I had ever gone to the beach we would have had to wait for after the season.

I was almost sorry this wasn't a school assignment. I knew exactly how I would go about making the most of the material from the privileged lady's storm chapter. Baby Wonk would have aced that assignment and earned more contempt.

I would have called my paper "Who Is My Neighbor?" after the story in the Bible where that "gotcha" lawyer tried to pin Jesus down by asking, "Who is my neighbor?" Jesus had trounced him with the story of the Good Samaritan. ("Luke ten, twenty-nine!" the little kids at the foster home would have shouted wildly.)

Last year Mom had started imagining a future for us. In this future, she would pass the high school equivalency exam and we would "start college at the same time." The more excited she got about this plan, the more conflicted I became. I began counting the years ahead of us: seventh grade through twelfth. I saw myself turning into my mother's "own little husband," as Wheezer had called me at school in front of our friends.

Mom would often say, "I may not be able to afford the best, but I do know what the best is." And where I was concerned she did go for the best: the best dental treatment at a clinic free to children, but not open to adults (while sadly neglecting her own teeth), the best life insurance for $24 a month (a stretch when you're making less than $24,000 a year). I kept hoping I would have an important dream about her. I had seen her in several dreams, but she was not at all like herself or else hurrying away in order to avoid me.

The weird thing was I regularly dreamed of Wheezer, who still lived in Forsterville. In the dreams I called him by his birth name, Shelby, and he was very much like himself. Occasionally he wore a patch over one eye. ("See what you did, you devil?") In the patch dreams he really had lost sight in that eye but he had forgiven me. In the dreams we were closer than ever, learning about the world and growing up together.

# VII.

The Aunt Charlotte I went to live with when I was eleven could have qualified as a hermit. She made use of modern conveniences, but lived the life of a solitary. And even after I came, she maintained most of her solitary ways. She called out on her land phone to order things but never picked up incoming calls. The caller was transferred to voice mail and could leave a message—or not. She often let days go by without checking her messages. She used the laptop computer that lay sleek and closed on the kitchen counter to look up information and weather and "to see if the world still existed," as she put it. Much of her business was conducted online, between her website and potential customers. She also had linkups to local and online art galleries who liaised between her and potential buyers and charged finders' fees. As I didn't pine for it, she continued not to have cable television. So far, I had not seen her turn her old TV on. She usually retired soon after we'd had supper, taking her wineglass and the unfinished bottle to her studio with its sleeping quarters behind a curtain.

She could rise to most household emergencies: change a fuse, replace a washer on a leaky faucet, fix a misbehaving toilet, rewire electrical switches, unstop a gutter, replace rotting boards. Near the ocean, boards were always rotting. After buying her "beach shack," she had required the services of professionals to add rooms (her studio and her bedroom, which was now mine, and an indoor bathroom) but she had done most of the finish work, teaching herself from books the way she had taught herself the basics of landscape painting. She could even do rudimentary carpentry and had built shelves and trestle tables to hold her art supplies.

She had no official religion and didn't call on God or Jesus, either for help or as an oath. I think painting was the closest to any religion she had. For proof that she practiced charity, you had to look no further than myself. Of course there was the "nice stipend" attached to my person that she had been so "aboveboard" about at the start, but I soon dropped any notion that she had taken me only because of the money. If my mom hadn't bought that policy, I believe that Aunt Charlotte, once aware that she was my only kin, would have welcomed me under her tin roof no matter what.

When I first laid eyes on her at the airport, she wore her wiry white hair in a very short brush cut. But in 2004 the shorn look was becoming fashionable for women, because of feminism or because they were cancer patients or because they wanted to announce to the world they were lesbians or because it made them look more dramatic. It made Aunt Charlotte look like a Roman centurion and emphasized her well-shaped skull. She cut it herself.

She had no love interests of either sex. Had the three good-for-nothing husbands in a row soured her on relationships altogether, or had there been intimacies during the earlier island years, when she was always in the company of carpenters and plumbers and electricians? After all, she had been in her early thirties when she moved here. My mother was already twenty-eight when I was born and was asked out by men until she died eleven years (five months and four days) later. Mom never went out with anyone more than a few times, but she would report on what she called her "dates" when she got home. "Never again," she might say. Or, "He's kind. When you get to my age kindness becomes a major attraction." But no one lasted very long because, as she said, she could recognize the best and she had loved the best. The mere memory of my father would always outclass all living suitors. There was a quote she liked: "Better to have loved and lost than never to have loved at all." It was from a long poem Tennyson had written after the death of his beloved friend. It took the poet seventeen years to put down all the thoughts and emotions he felt about the loss of this friend.

After the remodeling of her house was finished, Aunt Charlotte had continued to work with men: first as a receptionist for a veterinarian on the island and then as a receptionist at a foreign car repair shop on the mainland. ("I also changed the oil and did other unladylike repairs when the customers weren't present.") Later she and the foreign-car man, a local old "scion" named Lachicotte Hayes (pronounced "LASH-i-cott") became partners in a taxi service. They took turns picking up people in vintage cars. ("For a while we were driving a 1935 Rolls-Royce, until Lash got an offer for it we couldn't refuse.") Eventually, they sold their taxi business for a profit. ("My half provided me with an income until my paintings started to sell.")

On the first day we had clear skies again, Aunt Charlotte finished her big McMansion painting. "Good timing," she said. "Now I can examine it in natural light. Come into the studio, Marcus, I want your opinion."

"Oh," I said, when I stood in front of it.

"Oh, what?"

"It's different from how I expected it to be."

"And how was that?"

"You said it was a bread and butter commission, not one of your honest paintings. This looks pretty honest to me."

She was standing right behind me, so I couldn't read her face. But I could hear her indrawn breath and sniff the ferment-y smell of the red wine she sipped all through the day. I sensed that she really was anxious to have my opinion. The painting *was* different from what I had expected. It had the qualities of the ones I liked the most on her website. Actually, I thought it was wonderful, but *wonderful* was such a used-up word. "It has your mood," I said.

"My mood?" she coaxed.

"It's in your sky. It's in the house, too. I mean, it's more than just a painting of a McMansion. It's saying something about how life is. I wish I could express myself better."

"You're doing fine. How is life in this painting?"

"You know the way you painted Grief Cottage? When you look at it, you think right away of the overall sadness of life. But your McMansion house's sadness creeps up on you. The way you've painted it, you can feel it thinking. 'I'm new and too big, and if I have a message it's a shallow message. But I can't change what I am.'"

My aunt's hand gripped my shoulder, and then quickly let go. She wasn't a toucher.

"Well," she said, moving into my sight line, "I hope the Steckworths won't see all that in my painting, but I'm obliged to you, Marcus. I especially like the sky in this painting. It came out just right. I agree with you, the McMansion does have its own quality of sadness. A hint of impermanence for those who wish to see it."

"Could they turn it down and not pay you?"

"I've never had that happen, but I suppose it could. On the commissioned ones I always take a deposit. Nonrefundable. And this is a very big canvas. It costs money to buy enough pigment simply to cover a canvas this large. And I have another kind of protection, too. It's called 'hard to get' or 'what if she turns me down?' or 'waiting list.' By now I'm known well enough for people to want a Charlotte Lee and be willing to wait for it. Oh, hang it, I have to clean the house before they come. People expect *some* occupational clutter in an artist's studio, but I've let things go too far."

"I can help. I know how to clean."

"Yes, I've noticed you don't leave the bathroom a mess. Your mother raised you well."

"My mom cleaned houses. I mean, that's one of the things she did to supplement our income. She taught me some tricks people like."

"Well, I hope you will teach me those tricks."


"SHE MUST HAVE been a gutsy woman, your mom," Aunt Charlotte said the next day while we were doing the kitchen together. "It's not easy to be a single mother. I'm sure I would have got on with her. We might have had things in common. I liked her that time your grandmother brought her to visit when she was a teenager. Too bad we never got to know each other better. Though Brenda would probably have ruined it, warned your mom off the hippie aunt. Not that I ever thought of myself as a hippie. I have worked nonstop all my life and will go on working till I drop."

"You had things in common," I said. "You both ran away from home when you were young. Mom ran away before she finished high school."

"Now that I didn't know. Why did she run away from Brenda?"

"It was Brenda's father. He was coming to live with them and Mom said she'd rather die than live under the same roof with him."

"Her grandfather was my father. I ran off at sixteen to get out from under his roof. Isn't it just bloody amazing how defilement can become a family tradition? Why on earth did Brenda ask that monster to come and live with her?"

"She needed him to help her run the lumber mill after my grandfather died. When Mom heard about it, she ran away with an older man who was a foreman at the mill. She talked him into marrying her. The two of them moved to North Carolina and got jobs in a furniture factory. Mom said he was kind and a good worker and she felt safe with him. It broke her heart not to get her high school diploma, but she had to escape a worse situation."

"Damn right." She dropped to her knees on the kitchen floor. "Always escape a worse situation, even if escaping it is going to rob you of an education and ruin your life. Hand me that scrub brush, Marcus."

"But I'm not tired yet."

"Just hand it over. I need to scrub something within an inch of its life. It's either that or kill someone."

She snatched the brush from me and began making angry circles of soap foam on the tiles. "Why don't you go down to the beach?

"But—"

"Just *go*, Marcus! Don't make me ask you again."

# *ω111.*

*I* would have liked to hang out in my room or the hammock until suppertime, but Aunt Charlotte had ordered me from her house, and it wasn't raining anymore, so I went to the beach. What had I done to turn her off? We had been getting along so well; she had even gripped my shoulder when I said something good about her painting. Then I had told her what cleaning products she needed and we had driven to the island store and I found them for her on the shelves. We had been dusting and polishing and scrubbing as a team, saving the tiled kitchen floor for last so it would gleam for the Steckworths the next day.

Had I said something wrong? We had been talking about my mother and how Aunt Charlotte and she might have been friends. It was the first time I had heard my mom described as a gutsy woman and it made me proud to think of her like that. Everything had been going so well.

I stopped to check on the dune that held the protected loggerhead eggs. All was quiet and untrammeled. *Caretta caretta* was their Latin name: the world's largest hard-shelled turtle. Fully grown they ranged from almost a yard to a hundred inches long and weighed anywhere from three hundred to a thousand pounds. They could live until the age of a hundred, but they didn't reach sexual maturity until they were in their thirties. "Which, when you think of it, isn't such a bad idea," said the old guy who had compared the hatchlings' dash for the sea to "Normandy in reverse." His name was Ed Bolton and he said these turtles had been doing their thing for forty million years, whereas modern *Homo sapiens* had appeared on the scene a mere two hundred thousand years ago.

I walked down to the surf and studied the patterns the outgoing tide was sketching in the sand. But the shrieking children all around me only intensified my agitation. It was too late in the day to look for the sunburnt man. The little white truck was gone from the beach by noon. What did he do for the rest of the day? Did he have other trash routes on the island or did he go to a second job?

What would happen if Aunt Charlotte's tolerance for human company were to run out? ("Listen, I've given it a try, but I've been a solitary too long. He's a nice boy, but I'm too set in my ways.") Would she send me somewhere else? ("He was a nice helpful boy and the stipend that came with him was nice, but I have worked nonstop all my life and will go on working till I drop. And I have my painting. I'm known well enough for people to want a Charlotte Lee and be willing to wait for it.")

I would go as far as the fourth yellow barrel and then head back slowly and sit on the steps leading up to her boardwalk. I would keep company with the turtle eggs for a while. Funny, I usually thought of Aunt Charlotte as a self-sufficient older person, but when she had dropped to the floor like that and started that desperate scrubbing, I had glimpsed a scared and angry girl.

It was too late for the white truck, but I could create my own dialogue with the sunburnt man as I walked north.

He would be surprised to see me still on the island.

*"You? Still here at the beach?"*

*"I live here. With my great-aunt."*

*"Whereabouts?"*

*"Back there. It's the gray shingle house with the dark blue trim. It was just a shack when she bought it, but she added on. She's a painter."*

*"A house painter or the artist kind?"*

*"Artist. She's pretty well known. She does paintings of the beach and of people's houses. All the local galleries show them. She has a website, too. There's this one painting people keep asking for. She must have painted it fifty times. You know that old cottage at the north end of the island? That zombie house they call Grief Cottage?"*

*"'Zombie House' is the perfect name for it! That place is waiting for a major accident. Why they haven't torn it down beats me."*

*"It's pretty bad. I ate my lunch on its porch. But I didn't go inside."*

*"Don't even go on that porch again. The whole structure is rotten through and through."*

*"A boy and his family disappeared from that cottage. They were staying there after the season was over, and they didn't know about hurricanes, and Hazel came and washed them all away. But their bodies were never found."*

*"That was a long time ago," says the sunburnt man. "Long before my time and even longer before yours. Look, dude, it's one thing to be interested in history, but you want to stay away from that house. Because people who go in don't always come out."*

# *IX.*

*I* had never met people like the Steckworths. They were half an hour late, which got Aunt Charlotte's bristles up.

"Now we'll wait to hear what their excuse is," she said, pacing up and down the scrubbed and gleaming kitchen floor. "You can tell a lot about people from their excuses."

"How?"

"Nice people simply apologize. Others, the sort who want to impress you, give you a story about how something *really* important came up. To put you in your place."

"What would something 'really important' be?"

"Oh, our good friend the governor dropped by—or my uncle the senator. Or, the plumbers who are installing our ninety-foot hot tub showed up unexpectedly. That sort of thing."

It was hard for Aunt Charlotte and me to keep a straight face when the Steckworths had hardly stepped through the door before announcing that they were late because the tree company putting in the thirty-foot mature palmetto trees around their Olympic swimming pool had dropped by unexpectedly to check measurements.

The Steckworths—Ron and Rita—were suntanned the color of mahogany and both wore heavy gold chains around their necks. They lingered just inside the front door, which opened into the kitchen, and treated us to a blow-by-blow chronicle of the building of their McMansion—though naturally they didn't call it that. The two of them made it into a kind of duet, Ron vocalizing the measurements of rooms and staircases and trees, and Rita chiming in with the frustrations of having to deal with architects and contractors and landscapers. "Not to mention the decorators," wailed Rita.

This was my aunt's cue to say, "Well, let's go into my studio and have a look at your forty-two by fifty-six painting."

I watched from the doorway, nervous. What if they took one look and said in chorus, "Oh, this is not what we wanted at all!" Aunt Charlotte would be stuck with only the non-refundable down payment. Or what if one of them asked a stupid question and earned a caustic retort from my aunt which would humiliate them, make them feel obliged to retaliate in some way—perhaps to quibble over the agreed-on price, or ask for changes in the painting?

"Oh, look, Ronnie!" was Rita Steckworth's first reaction. "All our palmettos are already in!"

"If only life was that simple," said Ron Steckworth, winking at my aunt. "Have you ever painted one this large before, Mrs. Lee?"

"No," said Aunt Charlotte. "Ordinarily I prefer to work on a smaller scale."

"*How* small?" asked Ron.

"Oh, sixteen by eighteen, twelve by sixteen. I have a particular fondness for four by sixes, about the size of my palm." She held up a palm.

"A sixteen by eighteen would be completely swallowed by our mantelpiece," said Ron.

"That's why we agreed on a forty-two by fifty-six," my aunt replied.

"Wait, is that *yellow* paint I'm seeing up there in the sky?" Rita asked, standing so close to the painting that her nose almost touched it.

"Very observant," said my aunt. "It's cadmium yellow. If you'll step back a bit, you'll see it disappearing into the blueness. Someone standing at the proper distance when it's hung in your house will see a richer blue sky than if I had used blue pigments alone."

"Oh, *richer*," Rita Steckworth echoed, obediently stepping back. "Yes, you're right."

"Turner used yellow in his skies a lot," Aunt Charlotte said. "And Sisley. I learned the trick from Sisley."

"Sisley? Now where does he—?"

"We'll Google him when we get home," Ron cut her off. Sauntering around to the rear of the big studio easel mounted on wheels, he examined the reverse side of the canvas. "What will you do back here?" he asked.

"Do *back here*?" inquired Aunt Charlotte.

"I mean, you gonna put something back here? Or do you leave it open like that?"

"Most professionals leave it open. An oil painting never completely dries. If you were to cover the back, it couldn't breathe and condensation would set in . . . followed by mold."

"Euw, mold!" cried Rita.

"Your framer may want to finish off the back with a sheet of porous brown paper so the air can circulate," Aunt Charlotte said. "But the paper is mostly for looks."

"We were thinking gold for the frame," said Rita, "but what would *you* suggest?"

"If it were me, I'd keep it simple. You don't want the frame to distract from the painting. I'd suggest a simple molding. No more than an inch. And I would go for chrome or silver rather than gold."

"Maybe just a *thin* gold molding?" Rita Steckworth entreated.

"Well, if you keep it very thin," said Aunt Charlotte.

# *X.*

*A*fter Ron Steckworth had written his check with a flourish, and Aunt Charlotte had given loading directions to the strapping handyman waiting outside with a van to transfer the forty-two by fifty-six safely to the Steckworths' McMansion ("No, do *not* cover it, let it breathe during its short ride. And please be careful of those impasto areas where the paint is thickest . . ."), my aunt, sighing and looking inconvenienced, said she ought to drive over to the mainland to the bank. "I don't like keeping a check this large in the house. If I should drop dead tonight, Marcus, it would make things difficult for you." She asked if I wanted to accompany her and when I said an enthusiastic yes—I had not left the island since the day I arrived—I thought I saw a flicker of annoyance on her face. Too late I realized that she probably looked forward to going somewhere all by herself again.

However, she had brightened by the time we were rattling over the causeway. It was early afternoon and some black men with fishing rods were leaning over its railings. Aunt Charlotte replayed some choice Steckworthian utterances (Rita's "Look, Ronnie, our palmettos are already in!" and Ronnie's "What will you do *back here*?")

Then she floored me by announcing she was going to buy me a really nice beach bike out of her cash cow. Struck dumb by her offer I let the moment go by during which a proper boy would be voicing his excitement and gratitude. Moreover, I couldn't yet ride in her Mercedes without recalling the shrimp vomit from our first day. Did a whiff still linger?

When we got to the bank she merely said, "I'll be right back," not asking if I wanted to go inside the bank with her. What had she meant about dropping dead when the check was still in the house? Why would that make it difficult for me? Why had she said such a thing in the first place? It seemed insensitive given that the only other person in my life had just died.

Back on the island again we stopped at the store and bought a chicken roasted on the spit, various cold cuts and salads, and more bananas and yogurt for Aunt Charlotte. "I'm going to collapse," she announced as soon as we got home. "If I'm not up by suppertime, go ahead without me and I'll see you tomorrow." Off she went to her studio/bedroom carrying an unopened bottle of red wine and the corkscrew.

I put away the things and ate a banana with a cheese sandwich and drank a glass of milk. The chicken, still warm from the spit, called out to me, but I imagined her getting up late in the afternoon and finding one of its legs hacked away. ("Couldn't the boy have waited for me?")

Soon it would be the longest day. I had hours more daylight to get through. I could leave a note and walk to the north end of the island and back and the sun would still be strong. Checking myself in the bathroom mirror that cut me off at the collarbone, I marveled that my aunt could exist without a full-length mirror. At our poorest, Mom had always had a full-length mirror. A woman had to know how she looked from behind, she said. A hem could be crooked, a heel worn down, or something hanging that wasn't meant to show. But Aunt Charlotte seemed to get along fine without knowing how the rest of her looked. She cut her hair in front of the mirror above the sink and that must have been as far down as her grooming concerned her. As she wore only pants and shirts and sandals, there were no skirts or heels or slips to worry about.

I missed seeing my whole self. It would soon be half a year since I had been able to stand in front of a long mirror and see myself from top to bottom, dressed or undressed. I was aware of changes going on below where Aunt Charlotte's mirror stopped, but I couldn't judge the whole picture for myself.

I was in a sacrificial frame of mind as I headed north on the beach. I was not meant to enjoy the march, not to look forward to seeing little white trucks or discover meaningful patterns in nature. I simply set myself on automatic to march to the north tip of the island and back, where Aunt Charlotte would probably sleep through the night just to have some time all to herself. The march was something I had to do to keep my mood from getting any worse. If only I could walk until I was empty, like Aunt Charlotte used to do.

Since coming here back in May, I had taken it for granted that I would live with my aunt until I went off to college—though she had mentioned boarding school, if I wanted. Now I was wondering if I should take her up on the boarding school before she got really sick of me. Yet I saw myself doing better if I stayed on the island, going to public school with the children of the ordinary working folks who lived here year-round. If I were to go away to a boarding school, there would be snotty questions about family and fathers. I would have a better chance at passing with the local kids.

Passing for *what*?

Here I tried not to think my next thought, because I knew it would make me feel horrible. But have you ever tried not to think your next thought? Which was *that I would be more respected coming from Aunt Charlotte's house*. Artists could get away with living as they pleased. And Aunt Charlotte was a woman solitary by choice who had a website and a waiting list. My mom had been a single mother who worked minimum wage jobs to support herself and her child. How unfair for Mom that there was plenty of money for Aunt Charlotte and me because of the high-quality insurance plan she had chosen while she lived. I had been the spoiler of my mother's life.

And here came a worse thought: though I loved her and felt it was unfair that she hadn't had an easier time, I had been ashamed of her in life as I would never be ashamed of Aunt Charlotte.

My sacrificial march moved me past the yellow trash barrels at a smart clip. I had hardly noticed anything or anybody along the way, although I was aware that the tide was going out. A perverse plan was taking shape: in this punishment mode I would go right up on the porch of Grief Cottage and stand facing the door and confront whatever had scared me there. What was the biggest thing I could lose? Myself. And how bad would it be to empty the world of Marcus? The idea thrilled me. Too bad it wasn't hurricane season so I would have a better chance of being destroyed. ("Marcus knew better than to go out in that storm. He'd read those books about people drowned and washed out to sea. I'll never forgive myself for letting him slip out like that.")

If I got destroyed, what would happen to the insurance money that came with me? Would Aunt Charlotte get it, or did it stop when the beneficiary was dead? If it was nontransferable, she would be sorry, but then she would hate herself for even thinking about money when she should be concentrating on her grief.

Lost in my fantasy I was totally unprepared for the Grief Cottage I saw ahead of me. Last time it had been an eyesore. Today the dazzling afternoon light had transformed it. Before its downfall it must have looked like this to walkers approaching from the south. In the golden haze of five o'clock sun, it shimmered like a mirage.

In school we had learned that light was just a wavelength that made you think you saw colors. It all had to do with the light sensing cells in your retina. They activated a chemical reaction that sent an electrical impulse through your nerves to the brain. And then your brain had to decide what to call the wavelength you were seeing. ("Oh, that's a *yellow* trash barrel; a *golden* light has magically transformed the zombie cottage.") Technically there was no such thing as yellow or golden light. That was just your psychological name for it. First the physiological eye-brain system had to do its job, and then what they called the psychological distinctions kicked in.

Keeping to my forced-march agenda, I wriggled under the wire fence more expertly than last time, and noisily stomped up the unsteady stairs to the sloping porch. I *wanted* to be heard approaching. As soon as I was on the porch, I "announced myself" by grunting and exhaling loudly the way people do to express their relief at arriving.

This afternoon there was no backpack, no lunch to eat, no nap to sink into, no dream of the sunburnt man standing in the doorway to watch over me. Today I sat on the edge of the slanted porch, my feet on the next-to-top step, but still keeping my back to the house. As I had been climbing the stairs I braved a single glance at the gaping doorway, enough to see that the golden haze filled the room inside. I decided that if something was watching from within that haze, it would be a good plan to *sit with my back to it* so its curiosity could feast on me.

I don't know how long I sat with my back to the door before I felt a change in the air that caused me to tense up. The tension was close to fear, but not the usual kind of fear. This was a brand-new sensation. The longer I sat there straining to stay alert, the stronger the sensation became, until it felt like something was coming closer. Then something made me stand up, as though I was being challenged to show more of myself. Still keeping my back to the house, I pulled myself up by the wooden railing and stood on the next-to-top stair where I had been resting my feet. I could hear my heart knocking in my chest. But then whatever was behind me wanted more. It wanted me to step up on the porch *and show my full height*. This I did, my knees shaking, my back still to the house.

At that point I realized that if something actually *did* touch me from behind, I would pass out. Drawing on what little courage I had left, I forced myself to turn around and look straight at the gaping doorway. I could hardly breathe as I stood and offered my full body and full face to be seen.

And was met by the violent realization that someone was also showing himself to me. Pale and gaunt, the boy slouched against the frame of the doorway, wearing a faded red shirt and jeans and boots. Because his back was against the light his face was in shadow. But I could make out its lean contours and the flat unsmiling mouth and the hungry dark pools of his eyes. He seemed *posted* there in a rigid stillness, having perhaps made an effort as strenuous as mine to confront the creature facing him.

Countless times since then I have replayed that scene, trying to imagine what else might have happened if I could have endured the tension between us for a little longer.

But before I even registered what I was doing, I was flying off the porch, scraping knees and elbows in the sand, crawling under the wire fence, and running south, the late sun blinding my vision.

# XI.

*A*unt Charlotte had answered my note that told her I was going for a long walk. ("Got some more wine and went back to bed. I always crash after finishing a painting. Tomorrow we'll find you a bike.")

Now that she had made the first move on the chicken, I ripped off the remaining drumstick, laid it on some squares of paper towel, poured a glass of milk, and headed outside for the hammock. I needed to hear the close sound of the real ocean and feel the ropes of a real hammock against my body and try to find a place in my scheme of things for what had happened at Grief Cottage.

Recalling it now, minus the fear, it seemed as though we had somehow been trapped together in a net of golden light charged with energy. Using what science I knew, I worked out that if technically there was no such thing as "golden light," no colors at all, only *the electrical impulses* that made you give names to wavelengths, then maybe the same theory could apply to ghosts. An electrical impulse caused by some unusual wavelength produced an image in your brain and over the centuries people had given that wavelength the name "ghost."

From the safety of Aunt Charlotte's hammock (I was relieved that she had crashed for the rest of the day!) I pursued my speculations. I knew a lot about how nature worked. But I was also one of those people willing to accept that uncanny things might turn out to be aspects of the natural world.

Before it got dark the moon rose from the northerly direction of Grief Cottage. It was a large, round moon, first the color of butterscotch, then tangerine, as it climbed higher. Its light would be shining directly over his cottage now.

Maybe I would get a pillow and a blanket and spend the night out here in the hammock, close to the ocean, watched over by the moon that watched over him. I was comforted by the ocean's thud and wash, thud and wash. Not everyone would have seen him; perhaps no one else. He appeared because I had prepared for him, because I sensed the presence of him before he showed himself.

Now the moon changed color again. It was Aunt Charlotte's cadmium yellow and it had grown larger, a super-moon advancing southward and ascending higher until it was directly in front of me, lighting Aunt Charlotte's porch and my own face if I could see it. For *him* the main moonlight would now be past.

Even from this distance, I felt that charge between us—his curiosity coming to meet mine, mine going north toward him.

I wished I knew his name—for all I knew it could be Marcus. I wished I knew if he could think about me when I was not there, as I was thinking about him. I didn't know whether ghosts could keep track of what was going on in the living world, imagine what could be happening, or be likely to happen, by comparing it with what had gone before. Or were they like animals in not being able to project or imagine the future?

It struck me that he might need me to keep faith that he was still there. He had been waiting all this time, fifty years Aunt Charlotte had said, for someone to *wonder where he was*—to miss him after he was gone.

★  ★  ★

I DID GO inside after it was completely dark and bring out a pillow and a blanket. I felt safer outside in the darkness; in the house, there were more possibilities of my doing something wrong. I fell asleep in the hammock and had dreams that seemed to be knitting opposing things together—something about embarking on an important mission that was accompanied by almost unbearable fear. But all details were lost when I was awakened by a thud that shook the house, followed by a smashing of glass.

A halting outburst of obscenities followed, like someone experimenting with profanity. After that came a groan, and then "Stupid, stupid, stupid!" Followed by a final, crisp "Shit!"

I found Aunt Charlotte lying on the kitchen floor, her body curled around a table leg, her right hand, in an awkward position, still clutching the neck of a beheaded wine bottle whose dark red contents were spreading across the tiles.

She groaned. "I fell."

"Are you hurt?"

"I don't know."

My mom had fallen in the snow once. But before she'd let me touch her she systematically ran her hands up and down her body. Then she said, making light of it, "Nothing's broken. You can help me up."

"Do you think anything's broken?" I asked Aunt Charlotte.

"My ankle hurts. And my *wrist*, oh hell my wrist! Marcus, can you *very gently* loosen my fingers from around this bottle?"

I knelt beside her, but she screamed when I unclutched her fingers from the jagged bottle top.

"Shouldn't I call 911?"

"Call the Island Rescue Squad, they come faster. The number's at the top of the tide chart on the wall. No, wait. Put that phone down. First we need to clean up this mess."

"But shouldn't I call the number first?"

"*Do what I say, Marcus.*"

It seemed the wrong way to do things, but I got the dustpan and the sponge mop and the bucket and swept up all the glass and mopped the tiles while Aunt Charlotte lay curled around the table leg, alternating her *stupid, stupid, stupid*s with moans of pain.

"Can you smell anything?" she asked when I had rinsed the tiles and put everything away.

When I said all I smelled was Mr. Clean, she allowed me to call the number. While washing the floor I had been planning what to say and when a man picked up I told him my aunt had fallen and hurt herself. He wanted to know if she was conscious and if her breathing passages were clear and if she was an elderly woman. I said yes to all, glad she hadn't heard the questions. He took down the address and told me not to let her move and to keep her calm.

When I sat beside her on the floor she became chatty. "The Rescue Squad pride themselves on efficiency. They like to say they can be anywhere on the island in seven minutes. Of course the island is only three miles long and two-tenths of a mile wide. Which is why I wanted to tidy up first. Everybody knows everybody's business on this island. I don't socialize much, but the locals can tell you when I came here and what I do and then they invent the rest. But I don't intend to give them any new material for their inventions."

While the rescue men were wrapping Aunt Charlotte's left leg and right arm in stabilizing tubes and plying her with questions as they worked, I stood above watching and feeling guilty for looking forward to the ride to the hospital in an ambulance. The two responders reminded me of my sunburnt man; they were around his age and spoke with his kind of drawl.

"You're lucky it wasn't a hip," said one curtly while they were easing her onto the stretcher.

"But I'm right-handed! I make my living painting pictures!"

"Maybe it won't be so bad," the other consoled her. "It might be just a light sprain. How did you manage to twist yourself around like that?"

"My foot caught against the table leg and I put out my hand to break the fall."

"You'd be surprised how often people do that," said the curt one. "Break the fall and break something else. You need to bend your knees and try to roll over on your butt. Keep your hands out of it."

"I'll try to remember that, next time I fall," said Aunt Charlotte.

"Should we lock up the house?" I asked my aunt.

"You'll stay inside and lock up after us."

"But aren't I going with you to the hospital?"

"No, Marcus. You'd be—you'd be bored to death."

"I wouldn't!"

"Please, Marcus. Don't argue. This is the way I want it."

They lifted her up, one in front, the other in back, commenting on how light she was. ("Bet *you* never had to diet, ma'am.")

Aunt Charlotte's undamaged left arm wafted toward me in a conciliatory gesture. "Be a good boy," she said, making it sound like I was about six years old. "And be sure and lock up, front and back. I'll be in touch as soon as I know what's what."

"Don't worry, son, we'll take good care of her," the nice one said.

I locked the front door after them, but rebelled by leaving the back door unlocked.

*This is the way I want it*—as they were carrying her out on a stretcher. She was dying to go somewhere without me—even if it was to the hospital in an ambulance. Just as earlier today she had not invited me to go inside the bank with her. And before that, the annoyance that flickered across her face when she had asked if I wanted to accompany her to the mainland and I'd said yes. And I knew what she'd stopped herself from saying before she changed it to "You'd be bored to death."

*You'd be in the way. For a large part of my life I have lived alone . . . and it has suited me very well.*

Disappointed and angry that I didn't get to ride in the ambulance, I returned to the oceanside porch. The night had moved on. When I lay down in the hammock the moon was no longer in my face. I was in the same darkness as *he* was, up at the north end of the island. I wished he could be here with me, but probably he could only stay where he was. A further idea arose: if a dead person could make himself known to a living person, then why wouldn't the reverse apply? Couldn't it be equally possible that I was haunting him?

Too much had happened today. The Steckworths and the trip to the mainland in the morning, the encounter at Grief Cottage this afternoon, rounded off by Aunt Charlotte being carried away in the night on a stretcher.

Though she was at this moment being safely conveyed by ambulance to receive hospital care for non-life-threatening injuries, the incident dragged me back into the winter night not six months ago when I waited for someone who never returned. *Where was she*, why was she taking so long? Ordinary delays, a road closed, or maybe the place had run out of pizza dough and they had to send out for more. Then on to imagining car break-down (our Honda had 125,000 miles on it)—or a car *accident*—then feeling hungry and eating cereal, then resenting her taking so long to get our pizza and making me ruin my appetite. We had been going to watch that movie we liked on Turner Classics, and I watched it anyway and let her existence slip my mind for chunks of time: *The Ladykillers*—the crooks posing as musicians and renting a room from a clueless old lady, who ends up, still clueless, picking up sixty-thousand pounds for them in a suit-case at the railway station. I laughed and cackled just as I had done with her the last time we watched it together. We loved Alec Guinness. He never knew who his father was, but lived a successful life all the same.

If he couldn't come south to me and share my porch, I would try to send an emanation of myself north to share his. Down the boardwalk to the beach, the tide coming in. All alone, except for the moonlight, and the little turtle eggs maturing as fast as they could in their protected dune. And then the next ordeal of breaking out of their shells and crawling on their little legs as fast as they could, down a vast stretch of beach to the safety of the waves. Some would make it, some would not.

Since I was sending an emanation of myself, I could order time and space as I pleased. I didn't have to wait forty minutes, I could be at the wire fence immediately, crawl under it, climb the rotting steps to the porch—and stand facing the doorway.

Then, heart knocking against ribs, I approached him through the darkness, not running away this time.

*You came back*, a voice says, as if speaking from underwater. Despite its hollow tone, I can hear pleasure. I keep on moving toward him, though it's too dark to see his shape. I know without seeing that he stands in the doorframe, no longer slouching against it, but upright and welcoming. The energy charge between us is still there. Though I can't see him, I feel his outstretched arms. I walk forward into them. There's no going back now.

# XII.

A persistent knocking yanked me out of a sleep so profound that I couldn't recall where I was or who I was. The nearby crash of the waves against the surf brought me back to Aunt Charlotte's island and then I remembered my mom had died, and something else bad had happened more recently. It was morning though I had no memory of going to my room the night before, but obviously I had left the hammock, changed into my pajamas, and crawled into bed.

I was remembering Aunt Charlotte's fall only as I opened the front door to a stranger, an elderly man, built like a bantam-weight wrestler gone to seed, with shaggy white hair and white stubble all over his face. The only things neat about him were his clothes: a freshly ironed short-sleeved shirt with small red and white checks, khakis with the crease still in them, white socks, and docksiders.

"Good morning, Marcus," he said, though what I actually heard was *mawnin, Mah-kus*. "I'm Lachicotte Hayes, a friend of your Aunt Charlotte's. She wanted me to check on you. May I come in?"

I hadn't found my voice yet, but I stood aside to indicate he was welcome.

"First things first," he said. (*Fust things fust.*) "Your aunt is going to be okay, though she's vexed because her arm's in a soft cast and she won't be able to paint for a while—her wrist wasn't broken but she tore a ligament. They're releasing her at noon and I'll be bringing her home."

"What about her ankle?"

"Well, it's broken. Clean break in the fibula. It's in a cast, too, which poses another problem. She can't do crutches with one arm so she has to make her choice between a walker and a wheelchair. I told her I'd opt for the wheelchair, but if I know your aunt she'll prefer to hop around on one leg in order to retain some control. Have you had your breakfast yet?"

"I just woke up."

"And I woke you. May I make amends by cooking your breakfast? I'm a good cook. My third wife said she married me for my cooking."

Both of them had been married three times, I was thinking. Had they ever had sex? It was hard to imagine, when people were so old. As it seemed polite to say something back, I asked if he was still married to his third wife, which made him laugh, exposing a mouthful of small, brownish teeth.

"Oh, she had enough of me a long time ago. These days, I'm taking a page from your Aunt Charlotte's book, though I'm a speck more sociable than she is. How about breakfast?"

As the house opened directly into the kitchen, he was already en route to the refrigerator. "Uh-oh," he said, after examining its contents. "No eggs, no bacon, no butter (*buttah*). What do you all have for your breakfast?"

"We don't eat breakfast together. Usually she has a banana and microwaves some coffee in the middle of the morning."

"I see nothing's changed there, except she used not to have the microwave. What do you eat?"

"I usually have a bowl of cereal and a glass of milk. That's really all I want."

"Well . . . ," scratching the shaggy head. "I guess you better have that, then. I'll join you in a cup of tea." He opened a cabinet above the sink. "There used to be a nice tea caddy in here, from Queen Elizabeth's coronation . . ."

"A red tin box with a lion and a unicorn on it?"

"That's the one."

"It's in her studio. She keeps her brushes in it."

"Oh, my, isn't that just—" He cut himself off midsentence and patted the upper shelves until he seized a plastic container filled with tea bags. "At least she saved my Typhoo."

And so I sat down across the table from Lachicotte, as he asked me to call him. It was the first time since coming to live with Aunt Charlotte that I had faced another person at breakfast. He took milk in his tea and settled for two packets of sweetener after unsuccessfully digging at the rock-hard substance in Aunt Charlotte's sugar bowl.

"I've been commissioned to go shopping with you for a bike," he said. "I know a place."

"You mean now?"

"Sure. It's only half past nine. We can't pick her up until noon, after the doc has checked her out. If you don't absolutely have to have a new one, they've got some prize vintage models at this place. I'm partial to vintage models when it comes to cars, but it's completely up to you."

"But won't it seem thoughtless?"

He looked perplexed. "Come again?"

"I mean to shop for a bike the same day she's coming home in two casts."

"That's very thoughtful, but the sooner we get you some wheels, Marcus, the better for her. She won't be able to drive for some time. You'll be running errands, doing the grocery shopping. We'll get you a roomy basket to go on the back, and you're going to need a helmet. Until she phoned last night from the hospital, I didn't know she had anyone living with her. I offered to come over right away, but she said you were a mature young man and had locked all the doors and would be fine. We haven't been regularly in touch, your aunt and I, though she knows she can always count on me. And I feel the same about her."

I had never set eyes on a car like the one waiting outside Aunt Charlotte's house. A dazzling creamy white with a long swooping back and a majestic hood in front crowned with silver wings. Its upholstery was buff-colored leather, the dashboard a highly polished wood, and the steering wheel was on the wrong side.

"It smells good" was all I could think to say once I settled in the passenger seat.

"It's the leather cleaner I use. They ought to make it into an aftershave. This is a 1954 Bentley Sports Saloon. It was built in England, which is why the steering is on the right. You should have seen it when it came on the lot, it would have made you cry. Restoring these old beauties is my passion, like your aunt's passion is painting. I love this automobile. Pray God nobody makes me an offer I can't refuse. Fasten your seat belt. I was required to install them if I planned to drive in traffic. When I was your age, Marcus, nobody dreamed of seat belts in cars. We expected them on airplanes but that was it." He keyed on the ignition and pulled away from the curb. The engine sound was a discreet, obedient murmur.

As we were driving across the causeway he said, "I'm very sorry about your mother." (*muh-thah*) "Charlotte told me about it. But your aunt's a good person. You can trust her. That doesn't mean she can't be provoking sometimes, but we all have our warts. I used to provoke her on a regular basis."

"How, if it's not rude to ask?"

"She said I tried to repair people like I do cars. And I nagged her about—certain of her habits. Like not ever picking up the phone. And some other things. Are you looking forward to school?"

"Some parts of it."

"Which parts are those?"

"Well, I really like studying and learning things. Making friends is the hard part. I had a best friend at my old school, but then Mom and I had to move away and I never found anybody at my next school."

"What grade will you be in?"

"I'll be in eighth. I skipped a grade."

"You'll like our middle school. My second wife's daughter went there. She loved it. The kids are friendly. It's too bad you had to leave your best friend, but my guess is that a new one is already waiting in the wings for you to show up."

"What happened was, Mom worked in this furniture factory in North Carolina. Then we moved across the state to the mountains and she worked for a small outfit that made custom furniture for people. It was time for us to make a change." That had been Mom's and my story after we moved away and I thought it sounded very credible as I told it to Lachicotte Hayes.

"I've always been partial to the mountains myself," he said.

"After I got older and could be on my own, Mom was planning to take the high school equivalency exam and go on to college. She wanted to make something of herself."

Lachicotte Hayes took some time to mull this over. "I would say she had already made a great deal of herself by bringing you up so well."

# XIII.

*I*t was a subdued Aunt Charlotte that Lachicotte Hayes and I helped into the passenger seat of the Bentley. Gone was her edginess, her gritty independence. It was as though she had hired a stand-in to represent her in the role of the humble invalid who was grateful for any help offered to her by fully-mobile people until she could resume her self-sufficient remoteness.

She had been stoically awaiting us in a chair in her hospital room, dressed in last night's clothes and sheathed in two serious-looking casts. She looked smaller and defeated. In the other bed was a lady watching a game show with the sound turned up much too loud. But for all that, Aunt Charlotte might have been deaf. *I am not actually here,* her face said. When the nurse came with the wheelchair, which was "policy," she allowed herself to be folded into it and wheeled out to Lachicotte's car. I carried the shiny new walker she had been issued, stowing it beside me on the backseat. By the time Lachicotte got her settled into the Bentley, she had mumbled several half-audible thank-yous without appearing particularly glad to see either of us, though she did call me by name once. Lachicotte didn't get even that: she called him "you" and I saw her roll her eyes at him once when he attempted to say something optimistic. He helped her fasten her seat belt and told me to fasten mine, and off we went with a swish of tires. In the backseat it sounded like I was riding inside the wind. Lachicotte told Aunt Charlotte we had found me a bike and it would be delivered to the house, along with its accoutrements, later today. "Repay you" was her barely audible reply. These were her only words on the trip home.

Just before we reached the causeway, Lachicotte announced he was going to take a "teeny *shoaht*-cut" in order to drive by the middle school I would be going to. He cruised slowly around its circular driveway, the Bentley's reserved engine ticking over, and pointed out where the school bus would unload me. "I used to pick up my second wife's little daughter from this school and take her to my shop on the days her mother had classes: she was studying to be a psychologist." The school was a single-story brick building that had been added onto. Its grounds were well kept and there were bright shrubs in bloom. Though Lachicotte had meant well, I felt queasy at the thought of school buses and classrooms and recesses, the whole thing starting over.

"Some days, if I happened to get there a little early," Lachicotte said, "I would go inside and wander the halls. There's a school smell that carries you right back: floor polish, metal lockers, chewing gum. I loved my one year in middle school, only back then they called it junior high."

"Why did you have just the one year?"

"My folks sent me off to boarding school. It was the customary thing. My sister had to go, too, when the time came. She loved her school in Virginia. I about froze to death in New

Hampshire. I ended up going to four boarding schools, but each one was farther south so at least I got warmer."

"Then did you go to college?" I asked.

"I lasted half a year at the College of Charleston. Then I embarked upon my true calling as grease monkey."

Aunt Charlotte uttered a scornful *humpf*.

When we got home, I unfolded the walker and with Lachicotte's assistance she made it up the front stairs and into the kitchen, where she planted herself in a chair and announced she was perfectly all right. "It's not as though I've been permanently damaged," she said, as if we had inferred she was.

"You might want to consider getting someone in," suggested Lachicotte. "I could rustle up some names for you, if you like."

"Marcus and I will manage on our own," she said firmly. "But thank you, Lash." It sounded like she was dismissing him and he must have picked up on it because he left, saying to call him if we needed anything.

When he was gone, she said, "Listen, Marcus. I want us to go on as before. You'll have to put up with the annoyance of my *hopping* around the house, but other than that things won't be all that different—except I can't paint! I may be symmetrically challenged, but I still have a working right leg and left arm. I can dress and undress myself; I can also get myself from one room to another and open and close the refrigerator door."

"But I *want* to help. Are you in pain?"

"The painkillers haven't worn off and I have the rest of the container and a prescription for more if I want them. But I'll probably tear it up."

"No, don't do that."

"I don't want to become an addict or anything. Of course you can help, Marcus, but I don't want you to feel trapped." Then she laughed, which I thought was a promising sign. "But since you're here, could you bring me a bottle of wine and a glass? You'll have to open a new one. I can't manage the corkscrew. And while you're at it, you'd better uncork an extra bottle. I think I'll sleep away the afternoon. Maybe when I wake up, I'll discover all of this has been a bad dream."

How far back did her "all this" cover? As far back as before her fall in the kitchen? Or as far back as before I arrived?

All was silent in her studio/bedroom by the time they delivered the bike, a vintage 1954 beach cruiser, suitable for riding on sand. In addition to the helmet, Lachicotte had purchased a large rear basket, which could be attached to the fender when I went to the island grocery store, and a saddle pack for small items that fitted beneath the seat.

I would have liked to inaugurate my bike on the beach, but high tide was rolling in. So I set off north on Seashore Road, which ran parallel to the beach. This was the road Aunt Charlotte used when she carried too much painting equipment for walking to Grief Cottage, even if she had to climb over the prickly dunes at the end. It was the same road on which Mr. Art Honeywell in his truck, fleeing Hurricane Hazel, met up with the nameless parents "on foot," desperately searching for their nameless boy.

There had been an awful moment on the track behind the bike shop when Lachicotte and the shop owner stood by dotingly to watch me "test drive" the beach cruiser I had chosen. But what if I had somehow forgotten how to ride and fell off? Lachicotte would be so embarrassed. Every boy in the world could ride a bike, though it had taken me a while to learn on Wheezer's older brother's bike. "Your trouble, Marcus, is you're *thinking* about falling off," Wheezer said. "Stop thinking and just ride."

I wished Wheezer could see me on this beauty. How odd that he felt like the dead one, though he was still living in Forsterville, doing his old things—whereas the nameless dead boy in Grief Cottage was so alive.

When Lachicotte and I had been doing some emergency grocery shopping, leaving Aunt Charlotte in the car, he had given me his business card with work and cell phone numbers. "Call me if you need me, doesn't matter what time of day or night," he said. "It may get depressing for her. She won't be able to paint for a while and she hates being beholden to anyone. We've got to try and keep her from *festering*."

When Mom had the flu really bad once, I did everything for her. I made sure there were always liquids beside the bed and that she took her medications when she was supposed to. I changed her sheets and pillowcases sometimes twice a day and made simple things for her to get down (Jell-O, chicken noodle soup from a packet) when she didn't want to eat. I slept on the sofa and cleaned house and did the laundry and still kept up with my homework. Aunt Charlotte wasn't actually sick. She was, as she said, "symmetrically challenged" and couldn't paint for a while, and our job was to keep her from festering, though I wasn't entirely sure what Lachicotte had meant by that.

But one thing I did know: until I turned eighteen, she was all that stood between me and foster care.

My bike tires made an exciting thrum on the paved road. On my left side was what they called "the creek," where people fished and crabbed, but it looked wide enough to be a river. Whatever they called it, it needed a causeway over it between the island and the mainland. On my right side were high dunes, which allowed passing glimpses of the ocean from the driveways cut into the dunes. The driveways led to the beach houses, a few spiffy ones with sprinklers going on lawns and bright shrubs in bloom, others varying from needful maintenance to shabbiness. Most of the houses had names carved on lintels or displayed on boards. Rossignol House, No Saints, Pryor's Folly. Had my aunt chosen not to name her house, or simply not bothered to? The house to the left of Aunt Charlotte's, facing the ocean, belonged to an old lady named Mrs. Upchurch. Its name, Seacastle, was carved deeply into a driftwood signpost. Though it stayed empty most of the year, except when the old lady came with her caregiver from July through October, the house was faithfully maintained by a local service. There was also, Aunt Charlotte said, a middle-aged son who lived in Washington and visited for short periods. The house on Aunt Charlotte's right, facing the ocean, was one of the shabbier rentals with no name, hardly visible behind its dunes and tall grasses, from which we often caught bursts of rock music between the roar of the waves. It was some renters in that house who had forgotten to smooth down the sand after their badminton games and caused the mother turtle to mistake the humps for a dune.

After she told me about old Mrs. Upchurch, I imagined a very old Aunt Charlotte with a caregiver and myself as a middle-aged man coming to visit. But it didn't feel like something that would ever happen. What I could imagine quite well was a very old Aunt Charlotte, wheeled out on the porch and telling someone, "My great-nephew lived with me for a while. He was a thoughtful boy and I liked having him around. He was so helpful that time when I hurt myself and was laid up. I often sit here listening to the waves and wonder what he would have been like as an adult."

The bike's momentum gave me a sense of power. With my own speed I was creating a breeze. A fishy smell rose up from the creek. The sky had wisps of clouds with strokes of purple. Aunt Charlotte and her skies. How was she going to get through the days without her paints? The Steckworths had happened only yesterday! I had seen the boy in the doorway only yesterday. Then later came the moon shining on the hammock and the thud and the smash of the bottle, followed by the ambulance men and then the new bike today and seeing the middle school where it would all start up again.

Was Aunt Charlotte still sleeping? She ordered her wines in cases from a discount store in Myrtle Beach and had them delivered to the island. ("They have a much better selection than locally, and nobody around here needs to know my business.")

"I can show you how to take care of your bike," Lachicotte had offered rather shyly. Wheezer had been right, why not just ride and stop thinking? But that was easier said than done. "You are a deep thinker," Mom would say. "You get it from his side. I'll tell you all about it when you're a little older. All you need to know for now is that we loved each other, and he would have loved you if he had lived. When you're old enough to understand, I'll try and answer all your questions."

*Did he even know you were going to have me before he died?*

I had told Wheezer he was dead and showed him the picture I was not supposed to show, the man she kept in a tin box in the bottom drawer. It was a small posed black-and-white photo, just the frowning face.

"This was before I met him," Mom said. "He was younger then. But it was the only picture he had to give. When that picture was taken he wasn't in a place he wanted to be. When he did choose to smile, he could light up your world."

# *XIV.*

*I* had reached the end of the road, where Aunt Charlotte had to park the car when she brought her heavier painting equipment. Hiding Grief Cottage from sight were the tall dunes that she'd had to climb, negotiating her way around the Spanish bayonets.

What I had been intending to do suddenly seemed completely insane. I had been planning on showing him my new bike. ("This bike frame is from a 1954 design that has become a classic. You might have been riding a bike like this if Hurricane Hazel hadn't happened.") But there were two levels of reality I had completely left out. Why would it please him, even if he were alive, to see another boy with a bike he probably couldn't afford? And beyond that, the more serious level: why would a dead boy, trapped in his rotting cottage for fifty years, unknown and uncared about by everyone in the world, wish to celebrate my new bike?

I needed to keep the different parts of myself in their proper places or I could go insane. Aunt Charlotte would be in her rights to send me to an institution.

Yesterday afternoon, at just about this hour, I had seen him slouching in the doorway. I had seen him with my daytime eyes and though his face had been in shadow, he was gazing straight at me. We were in some kind of electric time warp. In the moonlit hammock last night, I had fantasized sending myself north to be with him at Grief Cottage because he could not come to me. And, although this was in my willed imagination, as I walked into his outstretched arms there had been actual physical rapture, which had left results on my body and on my clothes. These results were nothing new. They had been happening for years in my sleep. Mom said it was perfectly normal for little boys. "What about little girls?" I had asked her. "They have those episodes, too," she said, "only with little girls it happens inside them and there isn't any evidence."

If I hid my new bike in the tall grasses, would it be safe from thieves, or had I better drag it with me up through the dunes? I was still headed for Grief Cottage, though not to show off the bike. I would leave it outside the wire with the CONDEMNED and KEEP OUT signs and go up on the porch and simply show myself to him. It was important, I felt, for me to come every day so he wouldn't think I had forgotten him.

But just as the roof of the cottage showed itself above the dunes, I heard men's voices fading in and out against the sound of the ocean. And sure enough, when I reached the top and looked down, there were two middle-aged men standing outside the wire fence, one in sunglasses and khakis with a polo shirt and docksiders like Lachicotte's, but without socks, and the other looking hot and out of place in a dark suit and tie. Not far away in the sand was parked a strange two-seated vehicle with fat wheels and an open frame. The man in the suit was writing in a small notebook but the other man looked up and spotted me and called out. I called back that I couldn't hear and slid down the dunes dragging my bike.

"I said I hope you weren't planning on breaking into this place."

"Oh, no sir, I—"

"Because it's about to fall in all by itself, and we wouldn't want anyone to be inside when that happens." He spoke with Lachicotte's accent.

*But there is somebody inside.*

"I'm supposed to take photographs of the cottage for my aunt to paint from. She just broke her ankle, so I said I would ride up here and take some new shots of the cottage."

"Well, son, you better get cracking. It's going to have to be leveled pretty soon."

"But it's the oldest house on the island."

"Eighteen-oh-four, to be precise. The Historical Society never loses a chance to drum that date into me."

"Eighteen-oh-four?" inquired the man in the suit, still writing in his notebook. "They might want to put that in the brochure. 'The Old—' Does the house have a name?"

"Grief Cottage," I said, earning a sharp look from the local man.

"You'd want to call it the old Hassel House," he told the other. "That's the family that built it. Rice-planters who came here in summer to avoid the cholera. Back then the cypress was hewn on the mainland. They chiseled numbers on the pieces so the house could be assembled on the island. Then the timber was conveyed by horse-drawn—"

"But why 'Grief Cottage'?" the man in the suit asked.

"Oh, it's just a name that sprang up after Hurricane Hazel hit the island in 1954," the man with no socks replied. "There were some folks staying in the cottage and they were swept out to sea. They weren't even *in* the cottage. No bodies were ever found. If they *had* stayed inside, they'd have probably survived. These tough old houses withstood the storm because they were built so high off the ground on solid brick pilings. Plus the dunes protected them. This house would still be usable today if its successive owners hadn't let it fall to pieces."

"Why doesn't anybody bother to know the name of that family?" I heard myself asking belligerently.

"What family is that, son?"

"The people who *died* in that hurricane. The family that was in the cottage."

"Well, I expect their names are known by somebody. It surely would have been in the papers."

"My aunt has two books about the island's history and neither of them said a name. Just that it was an out-of-state family, the parents and a boy. And yet they were the only ones lost in that hurricane."

"Maybe someone should look into it," said the man in the suit. "It could make interesting copy for the brochure— like that gray ghost you told me about that wanders the beach before storms."

"I'll look into it," said the man with Lachicotte's accent. He had regarded me coldly since my outburst. I was probably considered a threat to his transaction with the other man. "If you want to take pictures, son, you'd best get on with it."

"Oh, today I was only scouting out possible angles," I said. "My camera's back at my aunt's house. To tell the truth, I wanted to try out this new bike."

"It's handsome. Vintage beach cruiser, isn't it. You get it locally?"

I named the bike shop. "Lachicotte Hayes helped me choose it."

The atmosphere warmed. "If *Lash* helped you choose it you can be sure it was the best bike in that shop. My name's Charlie Coggins." He bounded forward and thrust out his hand. "And this is Mr. Sampson from Chicago."

Mr. Sampson nodded me into existence and resumed his note-taking.

"You see that vehicle over there?" Charlie Coggins pointed toward the strange contraption on fat tires. "That's what is called an amphibian. You can drive it through water, up and down dunes—it's ideal for my line of work. I thought I knew everything about assembling things, so I sent for this kit. When it arrived I couldn't make head or tail of the directions, so I had the parts trucked over to Lash and he helped me put it together. Lash could put together a space shuttle if he had all the parts. Well, we better get on with our work, Mr. Sampson has a plane to catch this evening. Nice meeting you. Say hello to Lachicotte for me."

Producing a metal tape measure, he knelt down and shot it across the sand, calling out dimensions. The Chicago man wrote them down. Once he interrupted Charlie Coggins to ask, "Won't that be too long for the property?" "Not at all," said Charlie. "You've got to remember that this property sits on two lots." They appeared to be designing a long terrace, where people could dine out above the sea. Understanding I had been dismissed, I mumbled a goodbye and prepared to drag my bike back up the dunes.

Before I turned to go, I stared hard at the cottage door. It was lit up, like yesterday at this time, but there was no figure in the doorway staring back at me. What had I expected? For him to be lounging there watching the men who had come to destroy his house? Yet in case he was looking out from some unknown spot, I leveled a powerful gaze at the cottage which I hoped would send the message that I knew he was there, and that I would be back, and that I had by no means forsaken him.

But as I was pedaling home I realized he might not have recognized me in the new bike helmet.

## *XV.*

ooking back on that period Aunt Charlotte referred to as
her "house arrest," I am touched by my faith in my young
powers. I felt pretty sure that I could take charge of any problem
that arose. And who is to say that this confidence, even though
founded on the heroism of inexperience, didn't make a difference? Riding my bike home from its first outing to Grief
Cottage, I was already deep into ways of helping Aunt Charlotte
get through her laid-up spell without hating herself for being
*beholden*, to use Lachicotte's word. My job was to keep her
spirits from *festering*—another of Lachicotte's words.

For a start, I knew she was going to be another kind of
patient from my mom. Mom had a completely different temper-
ament. Mom was the kind of person who tried to fit in with the
situation, always ready to admit she was at fault, and grateful—
too grateful, sometimes—for attentions shown to her. You
might say Mom's major tactic for enduring (though Mom was
hardly a tactician) was appeasement. After stowing my bike in
the garage, I was surprised and a little crestfallen to find a very
in-charge-looking Aunt Charlotte presiding at the kitchen table
with a banana and a glass of wine before her. Wearing fresh

clothes, she announced that she had just taken "a bath of sorts" by perching at an angle on the rim of the tub. "I left the floor wet, but other than that it was a success. It will be easier next time."

"I'll run the mop over it."

"Sit down first and tell me about your bike ride."

"I went up to Grief Cottage on the road—the tide was too high to ride on the beach. There were these two men up there talking about tearing it down."

"Who were they?"

"One was a real estate man named Charlie Coggins. He knows Lachicotte."

"Yes, Coggins sold me my shack. Not him, but his father. Back then it was the only real estate firm. Who was the other?"

"He was from Chicago, a Mr. Sampson. I think he was a representative for some buyer. They're planning on building something bigger because the property has two lots."

"Ah, I wanted to take more photos, and here I am grounded."

"I'll take them for you. I already told them I was going to. All I need is your camera and for you to show me how to use it."

"You're very thoughtful, Marcus. Unlike most boys your age. Not that I know any boys your age except you."

"Mom had to work, so I did the things at home."

The swervy way she guided the wineglass to her lips showed how new she was at using her left hand. "Did you like the look of your new school?"

"It looked okay. I think Lachicotte is very nice."

"Well of course he's nice. Tiresome sometimes."

"How is he tiresome?"

"He nags too much. He means well, it's just his way. He wants to fix things. Rehabilitate them, smooth out their kinks, polish them up. But people aren't cars. And it does wear a little thin, his aw-shucks-grease-monkey routine. His family is older than God, at least in these parts, and he has tossed away more advantages than most people ever dream of having. Marcus, since you're here, would you mind peeling this banana for me?"

For the first few days of Aunt Charlotte's house arrest, things went smoothly. We had established our routine. She slept later into the morning because she wasn't painting. She hated hopping along behind her walker and soon dispensed with it, preferring to hop on her own steam, steadying herself against walls and furniture with her left hand. I got used to hearing her hop down our hall and shut herself into the bathroom, which was next to my room. She would mutter to herself while taking her "bath of sorts." I kept the bathroom super-clean, leaving supplies of fresh towels and washcloths and extra rolls of toilet paper in easy reach. Whenever I finished in there, I made sure the floor was dry, the sink had no hairs in it, and the toilet seat was down. Now she asked me to open four bottles of red wine at a time. I was to put two of them, lightly re-corked, in her studio, and the other two on a kitchen shelf in easy reach. She stayed in her studio all day, with the door closed. I heard her hopping about intermittently, muttering and moving things around, and then long periods of silence. Our one meal together continued to be supper.

She was still in her quarters when I set out on my early morning bike rides. From six to eight the beach was wonderful. Dogs were allowed to run without leashes during those hours, and there was an entirely different kind of beachgoer. There were the dog owners, of course, and the very old, with hats and sleeves, who needed to avoid the stronger sun. The bird life was louder and bolder down at the surf before the children cluttered it up with their shrieks and toys. There were also the runners and the exercisers and a few bike riders like me. This one old man had his black poodle tied to the back of his bike, which distressed me until I saw that the poodle seemed proud to be trotting along and showing off his obedience. I couldn't believe how much faster biking was than walking. I could bike from Aunt Charlotte's to Grief Cottage in less than fifteen minutes.

I hadn't seen the ghost-boy again, but, like with Aunt Charlotte and me, he and I had a routine of sorts. I would sit on the top stair with my back to the open door and talk to him. I kept it safe and casual, the way you might turn away and pretend to be talking to yourself to put a nervous animal at ease. I had thought about warning him they were planning to demolish the cottage, but then decided it would be cruel. Besides, what alternative dwelling could *I* offer him? Also, he might connect the bad news with the person who brought it. Of course, it was possible that he knew already, that he had seen and heard the men—or absorbed it in some ghostly manner unknown to me.

There was so much I didn't know about relationships between the dead and the living. Whenever we had indulged in one of our ghost story binges, my former best friend, Wheezer, friend would grumble, "There ought to be a *rule book* on how to behave with ghosts!" He improvised a few rules for us to follow if we ever met a ghost, but so far none of his rules fit the situation with my ghost.

At first I limited my talk to nature, the ocean, and the surroundings we shared. I remarked on the sunrises and the tides and I worried aloud about the fate of the baby turtles, which had been much on my mind. ("They need to get out to those ocean currents fast because the coastal waters are thick with predators and the babies are defenseless and very tasty." And when I felt a knot of sadness behind me, like the gathering of someone's woe, I quickly reassured him: "Don't worry, they are born knowing what they have to do. They have been doing it for forty million years.")

It was hard work courting a ghost, requiring constant exertions of empathy. Some subjects left him cold. For instance, I had thought I would initiate personal topics by filling him in on what the islanders thought had happened to him and his family during Hurricane Hazel. But I'd barely begun when I felt his withdrawal. I was a crazy boy talking aloud to an empty porch.

I recalled how stealthily I had courted Wheezer back in first grade. At the beginning I observed him from a cautious remove. He was a delight to watch—a complete little man, everything about him defined and sharp: his precise and finicky modes of movement and speech; his lovely floppy roan-colored hair, cut often at a salon in the style of an old-fashioned boy, like Christopher Robin dragging Pooh down the stairs. He had a soft, reedy, hoarse voice and employed his own phrases for keeping aloof from the mob. "Come on, people," he would say, or "behave yourself, people." When his friends displeased him, he called them "people," which crushed them. But when someone impressed or surprised him he would reward you with an "Outstanding!" in his hoarse little voice that was a side effect of his asthma.

For the whole first half of first grade, I watched and listened and kept my distance. Besides being a natural leader, he was a keen placer of people. Aware that I would be seen by him as an outsider, I decided to play up my outsider-ness. I had studied him long enough to guess that the way to his heart was to be as unlike his friends as possible. I could see that they bored him with their lack of imagination, their likeness to one another. The phrase "single mom" was just coming into popular usage and I told him that's what my mom was. His grandfather owned the furniture factory where Mom worked as section manager in the polishing and packing department.

Wheezer was fascinated by anything to do with the paranormal and was always devising tests to see how extrasensory we were. (I was more developed than he was, he concluded.) He did a brisk business on eBay, acquiring old issues of *Weird Tales* dating back to the thirties. He introduced me to the stories of Roald Dahl, Harlan Ellison, and Ray Bradbury.

He loved gossip and hearsay, the more shocking the better, stories about the extreme things people had done, true things that made one lower one's voice in the telling. ("Tell me a *true*, Marcus," he would command.) I was always on the lookout for the kind of trues that would appeal to him. ("Did you know that Van Gogh the artist cut off his ear after a fight with his friend Gauguin? He wrapped it in a handkerchief and on the way to the hospital he handed the ear to a prostitute and she fainted.")

Wheezer also had trues to offer, including a dramatic one from his own family. His father's older brother, the brilliant Uncle Henry, who could read Greek and Latin, dropped out of Harvard to return home and become a heroin addict. ("His IQ was off the charts, it almost killed Granny to watch her favorite son disintegrate in front of her eyes. When Grandpa finally kicked him out, he moved into a rusty trailer with rats and died in bed shooting up.")

As long as it wasn't about himself, my Grief Cottage friend also quickened at the lure of a true. As soon as I began, "I'm eleven, and I'm an orphan," I could feel the air behind me snap to attention. "My mom was killed in a car accident last winter and my dad died before I was born. She never told me who he was but when I'm older I'm going to try to find out."

But if I got too digressive or laid on too many details, the frequency between us faded. Like Wheezer, the listener in the space behind me was a sensationalist. He liked me to head straight for the extremes.

Commuting between Aunt Charlotte and the boy in Grief Cottage, I felt torn. I had specific duties at each place and I told myself my mental health wasn't in danger as long as I remembered the *differences* between those duties. It was a matter of keeping separate realities separate and steadying myself inside an awareness that seemed to be expanding too fast. Some days my balancing act felt wobbly or downright precarious and I feared I was on the slippery slope to insanity. If only I had somebody I could ask! But what exactly would I ask them? ("Do you think if your consciousness starts growing too fast it could be just as frightening as the beginnings of insanity? Maybe you could even confuse it with insanity.")

One morning as I was returning to Aunt Charlotte's after my hour with my back to the inhabitant of Grief Cottage, I passed the sunburnt man in his white dump truck heading north. I waved enthusiastically, and he waved back. But I could see that he didn't recognize me. How could he? I was wearing my helmet and riding a bike. In a flash of insight I understood how it felt to be the ghost-boy, who knew others could not ordinarily see him. For a moment I looked forward to sharing this parallel experience with him until I remembered that references to him had so far earned me a cold withdrawal.

# XVI.

*A*unt Charlotte's mood was deteriorating. And at supper one evening I made it deteriorate further with a stupid question meant to cheer her up.

She had confided to me that she had been attempting to paint with her left hand. ("I thought why not try for mood expressed through color? Just those two things: mood and color. Well, maybe a few shapes.") That morning she had squeezed out her colors and chosen a big flat brush and started to work. ("I was going to do a minimalist version of Grief Cottage. After all, I know the proportions, having painted them so many times. What could be so hard about laying in some sky color and some brushy Constable-like clouds and then roughing in a dark broken shape at the bottom? Who knows, I thought, these restrictions might lead to something exciting.")

But her left hand had refused to go where she wanted it. When she tried to hold it steady it started shaking. She got more and more frustrated, then depressed, then gave up in disgust. She drank a bottle of red wine and slept the rest of the day.

After Aunt Charlotte finished telling me this, I got my dumb inspiration. I asked her what she had done with her days on the island *before* she started painting. Thinking this would give her ideas on how to while away the time until her wrist healed.

She stared at me incredulously, as though I had switched to an alien language. "Well," she said bitterly, "let me see. For one thing I could *walk*. I walked a lot. Up and down the beach. I walked until I got tired. And I went over and over my rotten past and gave myself credit for finally breaking free. I walked until I walked out of myself. Then, as I told you, I had jobs. I worked for the vet and then with Lachicotte. And, as you know from your mother, a job fills up your days. And then I saw that woman painting Grief Cottage and I thought, 'I can do that.' And I could.

"Now, however, I can't walk and I can't paint, and there's— well, I have other responsibilities. And I'm twenty-five years older. This mishap is like a preview of old age. It's a foretaste. I can see myself like Mrs. Upchurch in her wheelchair next door. And what's the point in living on for that?"

By "other responsibilities" she had meant me. Her ominous follow-up question was even worse. How could I get us onto safer ground?

"But even if you were old and in a wheelchair," I reminded her, "you'd still be able to paint."

"One Grandma Moses is enough for this world."

"Who is Grandma Moses?"

"An old woman who started painting in her seventies because her arthritis was too bad for her to embroider anymore. She lived to be a hundred and one and there's a postage stamp in her honor."

"What kind of paintings?"

"Oh, nostalgic country scenes that made people feel *safe*."

She pronounced "safe" in such a sneering way that I thought it wise to drop my safer-ground plan. I could have simply shut up, or cleared the table, but something egged me on. Since I had already done the opposite of cheering her up, since her future in the wheelchair was getting us nowhere, why not go for her rotten past?

"Why was it rotten?" I asked.

"What?"

"You're always mentioning your rotten past."

"I wasn't aware I was always mentioning it. I'll try to curb myself."

"But I'm *interested*. We're from the same family and I don't know anything about anyone in it! Mom kept things to herself, and the few times my grandma visited us she didn't want to talk about the family, either."

"Ha. I can well imagine. So what did my sister—your grandmother—talk about?"

"What Mom and I were doing wrong and how we could improve ourselves. And how well she had done for herself. After she left, Mom always cried for a few days. She never said why, but I don't think it was because she was sorry to see Grandma leave."

"I don't think so, either. How is it that some people can make us feel worthless even when we know we're seeing ourselves through their eyes? Certain humans are poison. If I had to sum up my past in a few words, I would say: 'Beginning at age five I was poisoned.' End of story. But I can see from your face that's not enough. Well, here's a shrink-wrapped follow-up. There are very few family stories in this world. My family story consists of a useless cowardly mother, a poison fiend of a father, and an older sister who chose to pretend there was no poison in the house. Take your pick of the variations, down through the ages, of the good old family horror story. Try the Greeks, try the Bible, try Shakespeare, or choose from the abundant pity-memoirs on your local bookstore racks. When you are able to shrink-wrap your family story down to a few words, Marcus, maybe we will exchange further notes."

Aunt Charlotte's screed appeared to have converted her despair into an angry energy. I was congratulating myself for the turnaround, but then she asked me to uncork more bottles of red wine because she had run through all the open ones. I must have displayed some qualm because she harshly added, "This is a bad patch, Marcus. Just do it."

A day or so later, more cases arrived from the Myrtle Beach wine shop. She must have made the phone call while I was out on my bike. The delivery man carried the cases in and I later unpacked and stored them, continuing to uncork them as stipulated. But the number of bottles for me to leave in her studio had now increased to three. It was then that I started wondering if it was time to make a phone call to Lachicotte. But Aunt Charlotte would hear me if I made it on the house phone, and this was in the first years of the new millennium, before everyone carried a cell phone. I would have to wait until my next bike trip to the island grocery store, which had a pay phone.

But would a phone call to Lachicotte qualify as disloyalty—going behind her back—joining forces with "the nag"? I was starting to have an idea about what Lachicotte's nagging had addressed. I had unpacked some more boxes from my former life and looked up *fester* in my dictionary. "To form pus to fight off a foreign body." For there to be pus there had to be some foreign body that needed to be fought off. Mentally, that foreign body was her depression. Physically it was alcohol. Though I wasn't exactly sure how that worked. Alcohol was supposed to numb your pain. Wheezer had told me how in the Civil War they poured whisky into a soldier before amputating his leg. But though alcohol-numbed pain, could it cause another kind of festering underneath the pain?

I tried to find a disloyalty comparison from my life with Mom. If a phone call to Lachicotte to snitch on my aunt's drinking was a disloyalty, what were the ways my loyalty had been challenged when I was living with Mom? Well, Mom wasn't a drinker for a start. She could hardly move when she got home. Her feet and lower back hurt. I gave her massages. (The thought of giving Aunt Charlotte a massage seemed not only improper but bizarre. I didn't want to imagine what she would say if I were to offer such a thing.)

The weak spots in my loyalty to Mom concerned anything in our life that would reinforce Wheezer's taunt that I was my mother's little husband. In those last years with her, I was always torn between wanting to give her what comforts I was capable of giving (my last Christmas present to her had been a drugstore kit of massage oils) and feeling shame when the comforts recalled Wheezer's unforgiveable assessment of my home life. Whereas with Aunt Charlotte the loyalty conflict was between what would be best for her and how much I would sink in her estimation if I went behind her back and reported on her to Lachicotte Hayes.

While I continued to fret over these options, Lachicotte dropped by one afternoon bearing an oyster pie.

"These are farm oysters, the season's over (*ovah*), but they work perfectly (*pufectly*) well in a pie."

He'd had a haircut since I last saw him and seemed altogether more spiffed up. He smelled like someone just out of the shower, and I could smell the pie as well.

"If I could make crust like you, Lash," said Aunt Charlotte, who had taken an urgent hopping trip to the bathroom following his arrival, "maybe I would start baking pies." Now Aunt Charlotte smelled of mouthwash. "I'm sure Marcus must miss his mother's pies."

I let this go by rather than say our pies were from the frozen section of the supermarket.

"It just came out of the oven," said Lachicotte, setting down the pie dish on the kitchen counter. "I'd advise you all to have it for supper. It tastes better before it's refrigerated. I hope you like oysters, Marcus."

"Oh, yes," Though I'd only had cans of oyster stew.

"There's nothing to making crust," he said to Aunt Charlotte. "All you need to remember is that bowl of ice water for keeping your fingers cold."

"Maybe I'll try it when I have ten fingers again," she said.

"Marcus, I bring you a message from Charlie Coggins. He stopped by my shop yesterday. You made quite an impression on him. He wanted to know how old you were and when I said eleven he wouldn't believe it."

"Will you sit down, Lash?" Aunt Charlotte had remembered her manners.

"What was the message?" I asked when we three were seated at the kitchen table. Lachicotte had turned down my offer of a cup of tea because he was meeting a potential buyer for his 1962 Rolls-Royce Silver Cloud at five.

"It was about that family who got swept away during Hurricane Hazel. Charlie said to tell you he checked the firm's listings for 1954 and it wasn't a Coggins rental. It must have been a private transaction by the owners. In fifty-four that cottage still belonged to the Barbours, but they sold it soon after

Hurricane Hazel. What was it you were interested in knowing, Marcus?"

"I just think it's strange that nobody remembers their *names*. In those two ladies' books about the island, the man in the truck who talked to them when they were out looking for their son—*he* gets named, but not the only people on the island who were lost. It's like they didn't *count*."

"Marcus feels the pain of others," said Aunt Charlotte, "even when they're dead and gone."

"Well, we can surely find out," said Lachicotte. "We can track them through microfilms of local newspapers at the library (*li-bry*). I'll take you there tomorrow if you like, Marcus. Then you'll be able to bike over there whenever you want."

"Speaking of which," said Aunt Charlotte. "I need to reimburse you for his bike and all those extras. Marcus, would you bring my checkbook from my purse? I've been practicing my left-handed signature. I called the bank to alert them to expect the scribble of a five-year-old child and they said no problem. But you'll have to fill in the rest."

Lachicotte insisted there was no hurry and Aunt Charlotte insisted there was, and they almost had a fight before the check finally got written. Then we all played at writing left-handed signatures on Aunt Charlotte's note pad. Lachicotte's clumsy attempts got a snort out of Aunt Charlotte. My efforts recalled to me how shaky my early right-handed attempts had been when I was a child. How quickly you forgot how hard it had been to control your fingers when you first started! Aunt Charlotte's left-handed signature was far better than either of ours, which lifted her mood. "Though of course I've had all day to practice," she said, almost gaily for her.

"Well, your neighbor Coral Upchurch will be arriving right after the fourth," said Lachicotte.

"How is it you always remember such things, Lash?"

"It's just this little thing that I do." He laughed. "My first wife used to call me her walking anniversary book."

After Lachicotte left, I asked Aunt Charlotte if she knew why he'd had three wives. "Did he leave them, or did they leave him?"

"They left him. Lash is the kind of man who lets women walk all over him. I was just the opposite: I always sought out the kind of men I could depend on to hurt me. Then I left them when I'd had enough."

"I wonder how many times I'll get married."

"Oh, Marcus, you make me want to laugh and cry at the same time."

# XVII.

When Aunt Charlotte told Lachicotte I felt the pain of others even when they were dead, I worried that I had been talking in my sleep. But thinking it over I decided she was simply referring to the interest I had expressed about the nameless boy and his parents and to my sensitivity on their behalf.

Though he was the most compelling presence in my life, I knew better than to tell anyone about our connection, and certainly not that I had *seen* him. I was drawing from the same fund of wisdom I had called on when the social services psychiatrist kept asking what I had felt while beating up Wheezer and I kept replying that I had "blanked out."

Funny enough, of all the people in my life, past or present, it was Wheezer alone I would have loved to tell about the dead boy. How he would hang on to my every word. His favorite thing was the occult. He would insist on going over every detail.

"Now Marcus, tell me again, what *exactly* did you see?"

"He was there in the door frame, facing me."

"What door frame?"

"It was the front door leading out to the porch. I mean there's no door, but he was slouching against the frame."

"You're sure the whole thing wasn't a trick of the light or something?"

"I'm sure. He was thin and had a sharp jaw and . . ."

"Was he tall or short?"

"More like tall. But very skinny. And he wore a faded red shirt and jeans and boots. He was somebody specific. And I not only saw him, I felt him."

"How do you mean you felt him?"

"The way you feel people when they're standing right in front of you. I felt I was being looked *back* at. I felt his curiosity. He was as interested in me as I was in him. The whole thing was as real as you and me facing each other right now."

"What kind of faded red shirt? Polo?"

"No, it buttoned down the front and it looked a little small for him. It had short sleeves—or maybe they had been cut off."

"What were the boots like? Why would someone be wearing boots at the beach?"

"I'm not sure. The whole thing was pretty intense while it was happening."

"Oh, God," he would have cried out with envy. "Why couldn't this have happened to *me*?"


I LIKED TO keep to my schedule of the early morning bike ride to the north end of the island, but Lachicotte was picking me up from Aunt Charlotte's at nine-thirty to go to the library, and I didn't want to seem rushed while I was at Grief Cottage. When you visited someone they could sense if you were in a hurry or had to be somewhere else after you left them. I would go in the late afternoon. After all, it was the late afternoon when I had seen him that one time.

Lachicotte brought Aunt Charlotte a lettuce and two cucumbers from his garden and some rolls, still warm, that he had baked. I had peeled two bananas for her and sealed them into plastic quart bags. The requisite uncorked bottles were ready in her studio, the ones in the kitchen discreetly out of sight. As she did not come out to say hello, I told Lachicotte I thought she was still sleeping.

"How's she doing, in your opinion?" He asked this before the Bentley had pulled away from the curb.

"Okay, I think."

He appeared to be pondering my stingy reply as we drove down Seashore Road. He was still pondering as he drove us across the causeway. He was expecting more, but what could I loyally add?

"She tried to paint with her left hand," I said. "It didn't work too well. She couldn't control the brush and she gave up."

"What did she do after that?"

"She slept for the rest of the day."

He pondered some more. Though I tried not to I could hear his thoughts.

I kept quiet until we were on the causeway, passing the people fishing over the railings. "What kind of fish are they fishing for?" I asked.

"Catfish mostly. It's also an opportunity to socialize." A resignation in his voice indicated that he was not going to pry any further. I had let him down.

"Look, I'm not sure I can—" I had to stop; I was choking up. I looked out my window so he wouldn't see. "I'm not sure I can keep her from fermenting."

As soon as it came out I realized my stupid mistake. In terms of loyalty to Aunt Charlotte, it was probably the most ill-chosen word I could have hit on. "I meant to say festering," I corrected myself. "I don't know why I said the other."

"They both have a certain applicability," he remarked and left it at that.

"Did you sell the 1965 Rolls-Royce yesterday?"

"Ah, no. The minute he laid eyes on my beauty here, he fell out of love with poor Silver Cloud."

"But you can't sell the Bentley. You said you loved it."

"He made me a handsome offer, but I haven't decided. It doesn't do to get too attached to things. But as I say, I haven't decided yet."

Like the middle school, the mainland library was a well-kept one-story building with extensions added on, surrounded by bright bushes in bloom. In one of the extensions there were a lot of glass windows and they were open and you could hear the commotion of children and a woman's voice telling them to settle down.

"That's my niece Althea in there," Lachicotte said. "I recognize her voice. She runs the summer pre-K for the little kids. You're going to be surprised, Marcus, at how up to date we are in our gadget room. We have the very latest in microfiche."

The computer and microfilm room was in one of the new extensions. On the wall to the right as you entered was a large bronze plaque that read THE MARGERY LACHICOTTE HAYES WING. 1994.

"Is that one of your relatives?" I asked.

"My mother. Our family has always been passionate about libraries. I'm glad she lived to see this wing finished."

A smiling lady in a crisp pantsuit hurried forward to meet us. "This is Mrs. Daniels, our librarian," said Lachicotte. "Lucy, this is Marcus Harshaw, who's interested in Hurricane Hazel."

"I'm very happy to meet you, Marcus. We are all so proud of your aunt. We have one of her wonderful paintings above our front desk. Lash, I have all the envelopes ready. I got them out after you phoned yesterday."

"We're much obliged, Lucy."

"No trouble at all, they were close at hand. Being as this summer is Hazel's fiftieth anniversary, we've had a right many calls on those old newspapers. And I've got a new magazine for Marcus as well. This month's *State Magazine* is featuring stories by people who lived through Hazel. Marcus, I expect you'll want some help setting up the scanner and printer?"

"No, thank you. I used one like this when I was writing my research paper at school. I just need a user's card to stick in that slot."

The librarian was impressed and I think Lachicotte was, too. They hovered over me until I had taken the first fiche out of its envelope—being careful not to leave fingerprints on the film—and slid it into the tray, and started reading the screen. Then Lachicotte said that since I seemed to know what I was about, he and Mrs. Daniels would go and print me out a library card. "Would you like your middle name on it or a middle initial?" he asked. I said Marcus Harshaw would be enough. I didn't have a middle name.

Left alone with my research, I became impatient then indignant at the skimpy information found on the screen. Here were the microfiches from *three* state papers of fifty years ago reporting on the aftereffects of Hurricane Hazel, and not one of them rendered up anything as useful as the *one* state paper I had pored over from *a hundred and fifty* years ago while researching my seventh-grade school project back in Jewel about a nearby North Carolina mountain town that had been split in half by the Civil War. One side was Confederate and the other Union and the two sides slaughtered each other.

The South Carolina state papers of fifty years ago offered plenty of nonhuman information about Hazel. The hurricane had hit on the day of October's full moon high tide, the highest lunar tide of the year, which meant the most water damage. Hazel left Haiti as only a Category 2, but kept gathering strength as it headed up the Atlantic coast. When it hit north of Myrtle Beach on the morning of the fifteenth, it was a Category 4. The newspapers reported wind velocities and estimated the millions of dollars of property damage it left in its wake. There were some eyewitness evacuation stories, but they all ended safely. All told, Hazel left nineteen fatalities along the coast of North Carolina and one fatality in South Carolina—but there were *no names*. Where were the names? I scanned the film until my head began to hurt and I still never found a single name. If even the accounted-for fatalities didn't rate getting their names in the papers, what hope for you if your body was never found?

I gave up on the fiches and paged through the "old-timer" stories in the fiftieth anniversary state magazine the librarian had left for me. Their Hazel recollections were the kind that began "Mamma and I were driving to the island to see her sister, who was a year-round resident. But when we got to the causeway, we were stopped by a highway patrolman who told us we had to turn around, everyone was evacuating . . ." Or "A week after the storm, when J. W. McLauren of Charleston finally crossed to the island, he found his family's hundred-year-old island cottage with all its tongue-and-groove joints miraculously intact, only the waters had moved the house a hundred yards down the beach."

There were a few vivid descriptions—winds snapping trees like chicken bones and a family hunkered down in a truck bed with salt water filling their noses, but the eyewitnesses of those scenes had lived into safe old age and gotten interviewed by this shiny magazine fifty years later.

I left everything in a neat pile for Mrs. Daniels. She was not around, so I returned the user's key for the fiche machine to the woman behind the front desk. Involved in her own work, she barely looked up from her computer to acknowledge me, so I was able to study the painting that hung over her desk in peace. I recognized it from one of those postcard reproductions Aunt Charlotte had sent to Mom. It was a long, wide painting of the island's shoreline at dusk, just the sand patterns and shallows at low tide, not a single breaking wave, not a living thing in sight, not even a single shore bird, everything glowing and peaceful in a soft orange end-of-day light. It made you feel glad you lived close to such beauty. I made a mental note to tell Aunt Charlotte how well I thought the painting graced the library wall, setting the tone for the whole place.

Then I went to find Lachicotte, who was in the pre-K room, sitting at a table beside a gray-haired lady, their backs to the open door. Below them on the floor, the children were finger-painting on sheets of paper. I had never seen children wearing kid-size latex gloves to finger-paint, but it seemed like a very practical idea. Moving closer I saw that Lachicotte and the gray-haired lady, who must be his niece, were making small finger-paintings of their own at their table. They, too, wore latex gloves, and were so wrapped up in what they were doing that I hung back in the doorway, not wanting to disturb the scene. The gray-haired niece was painting a still life of the jar of yellow roses placed in front of her on the table. Aunt Charlotte would have judged it "a competent little painting." Lachicotte, hunched forward raptly, swirled vigorous circles of dark blue paint behind what looked like either a lopsided mountain or a crouching white beast. I would have stood there longer if a watchful little girl hadn't broken the spell. "Why is that man over there *spying* on us?" she cried.

# XLIII.

*L*achicotte's painting of the lopsided mountain or crouching white beast turned out to be his "farewell portrait" of his 1954 Bentley R-Type Continental. "Even while I was painting her—or trying to, I'm no artist—I knew our time together was over" (*togethah, ovah*). He told me this as we ambled around downtown Charleston while Aunt Charlotte underwent her wrist surgery at the medical center.

Her "sprain" had been a misdiagnosis. The first x-ray taken weeks ago at the local hospital had missed the lesion and now everything had to be done all over again, with a projected twelve more weeks in a new cast. What she had was an "occult fracture of the scaphoid bone"—I tried not to read any messages into the *occult* word beyond its medical meaning of a hidden injury. The break was found in her follow-up x-ray, which also revealed a loose piece of bone fragment that had to be excised. So now the ligament and the scaphoid bone were being properly reconnected and "fixated" with a metal screw. The surgery was being done under general anesthesia, after which she would spend a further hour in the recovery room before we could take her back to the island. Lachicotte was driving her car now, the old Mercedes sedan, while the mandatory seat belts were being installed in the Silver Cloud Rolls-Royce, which the buyer hadn't wanted after he laid eyes on Lachicotte's beloved Bentley.

"Were you sad when you saw your Bentley driving away?"

"You might say I felt an elegiac pang. But then I turned my mind to all I could do with the proceeds."

"Was it a lot of money, or is that rude to ask?"

"It was a fair amount because it's a rarity and he had to have it. I can buy my niece a waterfront condo and donate a much-needed new roof to my church."

"You must really like your niece."

"Althea has gone through some rough passages, but she's kept her humanity intact. Which is admirable in itself."

"What kind of rough passages?"

"Well, she was fifteen when she lost both parents. Her mother was my sister. They were flying up to see Althea at her school and my brother-in-law's Cessna crashed in a fog."

"That was your sister who loved her boarding school in Virginia?"

"You remembered that. Yes, I had only the one sibling. When Althea was in her late teens she hit some turbulence. She blamed herself for her parents' death because they had been coming to see *her*—but we got her through that, Mother and I. But then as soon as she turned twenty-one, she eloped with a deep-dyed scoundrel who had been waiting in the wings. After he'd run through her money, he decamped and left her with all his debts and a broken heart."

"Did she have any children?" I wondered whether Althea's story would meet Aunt Charlotte's standards for a shrink-wrapped tale of family woe.

"One daughter. Unfortunately their temperaments clash. But Althea adores her little granddaughter, who I'm afraid was that child at the library who accused you of being a spy."

We went to the art supply store because Lachicotte wanted to buy Althea a paint set. "When we were finger-painting with the kids while you were busy at the fiche machine, my niece said to me, 'You know, Uncle Buddy, I haven't had so much fun in years. Isn't it a shame that grown-ups forget how to play?'"

While Lachicotte consulted with the saleslady about what kind of paint set to buy for his niece, I wandered around inspecting the lavish displays of paints and crafts. This was the temple of Aunt Charlotte's vocation, and not only was she not here with us to inhale the smells of her art and be tempted by new brushes and pigments, but she was lying anesthetized on a table while an orthopedic surgeon cut and clamped and probed and "fixated" her painting hand. He would do his best, he told Lachicotte, but he couldn't guarantee total return of flexibility. We would just have to wait and see. There would be months of physical therapy to help, of course. The new x-rays had shown some arthritis, and we had to remember Mrs. Lee wasn't a ten-year-old skateboarder with miraculously supple bones. No, Lachicotte had told him, she's only a gifted and successful painter at the peak of her talent and her earning ability, and you are the head of wrists and hands over here, so we're counting on you to do your utmost. They knew each other, of course. Lachicotte seemed to know everybody.

There was something I needed to consult with Lachicotte about. I had been preparing how to ask it in the art store and as we were walking back to the medical center I took the plunge.

"Don't you think it would be a good idea if I went off to boarding school?"

Lachicotte came to a full stop on the sidewalk, clasping his gift-parcel to his breast. "What has given you this idea?"

"I'd be out of the way. Aunt Charlotte could have her solitude back, except for when I came home for holidays."

"Wait a minute. Help me think this through, Marcus. What would be the advantages for her?"

"She wouldn't have the burden of being my guardian nonstop."

"What makes you think it's a burden?" He commenced walking again.

"Because I'm always *there*. When people are cooped up together too long they get—"

This wasn't going so well. What was it about Lachicotte that made me choke up when I was trying to say something important? "I mean, even back with Mom, we sometimes got on each other's nerves. And Mom was out at work most of the time. But Aunt Charlotte's always in the house with me. And now she's going to be in the house more than ever."

"So you're saying if you weren't there she'd have her solitude back. How else would it be an advantage to her, not having you around?"

"I don't mean *right now*. I know I can be useful right now while she's in her casts and has a hard time, well, you know, filling her days without being able to paint. But I think . . ." Here came the choking-up danger again. "I think if I went away to school for most of the year it would be better in the long run."

"What do you mean by the long run?"

"Until I'm eighteen and don't need to have a guardian anymore. When I'm eighteen she'll be free of me. I mean, I know she gets a stipend for being my guardian and all, but I really think she'd prefer going back to her old lifestyle."

"Has it occurred to you there are ways you might be *her* guardian?"

I said it hadn't.

"Well, you might want to take a little time to consider it. However, let's look at this proposition from another angle. What would be the advantages for *you* if you went away to boarding school?"

"The main advantage is I wouldn't wear out my welcome with Aunt Charlotte. The disadvantage would be that at a boarding school they might be more curious about genealogy and that kind of thing. Whereas at the local school, they'd know who I was *now*. The thing is, I don't know much about my father's side. What I mean is, I don't know *anything*, not even who he was. Mom was going to tell me when I was old enough to understand."

We walked on in silence. Lachicotte appeared to have sunk into one of his pondering states and I had time to wonder whether my disclosure had been more than Lachicotte wanted to hear.

"You know, Marcus, I was delighted when your Aunt Charlotte discovered she could paint. It was just what was needed. Nothing better in the world could have showed up in her life at that time. And now I'll tell you something else. The day you and I met, when I came to the house that morning (*maw'nin*)—it took me only a few hours in your company to feel the same delight again. Nothing better in the world could have showed up in her life. You were just what was needed."

# XIX.

*A*unt Charlotte's mood underwent a further change as she began her extended convalescence. Strangely enough, she had been more annoyed and despondent when she had believed she was facing only a matter of weeks with her arm in a soft cast and then a return to painting. Now she seemed to have entered a state of passive indifference, spending hours in a chair on the screened porch gazing out to sea, her right arm in a more serious cast resting on the chair arm, her left foot in its cast propped on a stool. I had felt more at home with her old combative self.

In this new phase she spent less time shut away in her studio/bedroom. For a while I was required to uncork fewer bottles of red wine. She was in pain after the surgery and condescended to take the Percocet the doctor had prescribed. That may have decreased her desire to drink, or maybe she was simply taking seriously the dire warnings on the bottle about mixing opioids with alcohol. She had expressed a horror of "turning into a dope fiend" and made me keep the bottle hidden in my room and dole out the pills as needed.

Lachicotte's suggestion that I was also her guardian had sunk in, and I swung between pride in this responsibility and resentment at some of the restraints it imposed.

The worst restraint was the sacrifice of my late afternoon bike ride to the north end of the island. Aunt Charlotte seemed to appreciate my company particularly in the late afternoon. Of course, I continued to go faithfully to Grief Cottage every morning, via the road or the beach, depending on the tides, while she was still asleep, but those morning visits had become sterile. There was no longer the sense that he was somewhere just behind me. He might be inside the cottage but he was no longer available to me, even as an unseen listener. I felt I was being punished for dividing my attentions. Now whenever I spoke aloud with my back to the door, I was more than ever the crazy boy talking to himself on the top step of a ruined cottage.

After I got my own card, I had biked over to the library a few times. In my saddlebags I brought home promising books that either fulfilled my hopes or didn't. I tried *The Count of Monte Cristo,* which I had started back in Jewel, but then had to return to the school library because someone else was waiting. Now even opening the book made me sad and a little queasy and I returned it on my next trip. I took out Ray Bradbury's *Fahrenheit 451* and read it straight through. Bradbury always reminded me of Wheezer, who had introduced me to him. I had hopes for a horror writer's thick omnibus of his "favorite scary stories," but found I had read many of them already.

On one trip I hauled home three art books for Aunt Charlotte. I picked a heavy book of English landscape paintings, making sure Constable was included. Mrs. Daniels, the librarian, had recommended my other choice: a slip-cased two-volume collection of Paul Klee's drawings and paintings. "Your aunt Charlotte might find him an inspiration while she's recovering. He can be playful and quite philosophical. And it has his notes about what he's doing. These volumes aren't really supposed to go out of the library, but since it's your aunt . . ." Aunt Charlotte was touched when I showed her the books. She made me lug them off to her studio. What she did with them after that, I didn't ask. It would be like asking someone if they were enjoying your gift. When it was time to return the books, she remarked how thoughtful I always was; she said Klee could be a hoot and it was nice to see all her English friends together in one book.

She was at her most sociable on our porch around the time the pelicans were flying home in their straight line from their day's fishing. She seemed to enjoy whatever I had to say.

"Well, Marcus, what do you have to report?" She would ask this while gazing at the ocean, not turning her head to look at me. This freed me to talk more easily. I remembered how, in my old life, after Mom and I had moved to the mountains and we didn't know anybody, I had wished for someone to "report to." Mom mostly came home too exhausted to make more than a dutiful inquiry into my day. Aunt Charlotte, facing out to sea as if she could accept whatever arose in my mind, was the ideal listener. Like the ghost-boy, and like Wheezer before him, she harkened to a good "true." As with them, I could feel her interest quicken when I was on the right track. She liked hearing about my first trip to the library with Lachicotte.

"I'm sorry you didn't have better luck," she said when I complained about the slim pickings on the microfiche and in the fiftieth anniversary magazine. "I know you were hoping to find something about that family, the boy in particular. I can see why he would capture your imagination."

That's when I came close to telling her about the ghost-boy. Not dangerously close, but closer than I had ever come to telling Mom about showing Wheezer the forbidden photograph and about why I beat him up the next day. I had learned during my sessions with the psychiatrist that certain experiences must be kept to myself—perhaps forever. So all I finally said to Aunt Charlotte was that it made me mad that a whole family could be wiped out of human memory as though they'd never existed. Her reply was that billions of people had suffered that fate and billions more were destined to be forgotten as though they never existed. ("That is, if we don't all destroy this planet first.") She sounded satisfied with the prospect.

The finger-painting part of the library story made her snort with laughter. She wanted to hear again how I had first thought Lachicotte had been painting a white mountain and then a white beast, and didn't know till he told me later that it had been a farewell portrait of his Bentley. Then she wanted my assessment of the niece's painting of the yellow roses. I told her she would have judged it a competent little painting, "like you said about that woman's painting of Grief Cottage that started you painting."

"Really?"

"Well, I never saw that woman's painting, but the niece's roses were something you might want to frame, or at least tape up on a wall, especially if you knew the artist. The roses in a jar had a nice—I don't know the art word for it, but the way the paint sticks up from the paper sort of imitates the way the artist painted it."

"I think you mean impasto, if it was thick. Was it thick?"

"Yeah, it stuck up in little whorls. Of course, she was pinching it up with her fingers."

"Or you could say 'brushwork.' 'Fingerwork' in this case. You describe paintings very well, Marcus."

"She told Lachicotte she hadn't enjoyed herself so much in years. She said adults forgot how to play. That's why he bought her that paint set while you were having your surgery."

"What kind of paints did he get?"

"I think he said water-based. But they weren't just kids' finger paints."

"'Water-based' covers a large choice. And they all wore gloves?"

"Those thin latex gloves. The kids had little kid-size gloves."

"I can see the advantage of gloves when you've got a roomful of pre-kindergarteners, but I would think gloves would deaden your tactile advantages. I don't know. I've never finger-painted."


DURING OUR AFTERNOON porch talks, Aunt Charlotte extracted more of my history. Some information I volunteered; other disclosures escaped as a sort of overflow. Since I had already spilled the beans to Lachicotte about my secret father, I figured I might as well admit to my only living relative that I had no idea who he was. I had been unpacking more boxes from the old apartment life. It made me increasingly sad that so many of the contents, things Mom and I had formerly liked or needed—or were even proud of—went straight into the black bags. I showed Aunt Charlotte the small photo in the silver frame that had ended my friendship with Wheezer. Like Wheezer, she turned the picture sideways and shook it.

"Could we open this frame?" she asked, making me wonder why I had never thought of this myself. She handed it over to me and as I was folding back the four metal clips that held it in place, I let myself imagine there would be a name of somebody on the back of the picture. But it turned out to be a glossy photo cut out of a book, most likely a yearbook Aunt Charlotte said, because there was a photo of another man, posed the same way, on the back.

"Well, that's that," I said angrily.

"What do you mean, 'that's that'?"

"I'll never know who my father was because there's nobody left to tell me."

"Well, he's a nice-looking man," she said. "He has your wide-apart eyes and quizzical eyebrows, and I definitely see a likeness in the set of the mouth when something annoys you."

"You know the actor Alec Guinness?"

"Not personally, but I know who he is," said Aunt Charlotte with a welcome return to her old dryness.

"His mother never told him who his father was, either. She died without telling him and he never found out. He wrote about it in his autobiography. Mom said this photo was taken before she knew my father, when he was a lot younger."

"So you did talk about him."

"Not much. She said he would have been proud of me if he had lived to know me and that I would be proud of him. But she wanted to wait until I was a little older before she said any more. The reason I have Mr. Harshaw's name is because people at the factory remembered him, though he had moved away by then. So Mom could get away with saying that they had tried for a reconciliation and it hadn't worked and I was the result. Mr. Forster, the factory owner, was one of those—what's the word for someone who owns the business but wants it to seem like everybody's just one big family?"

"Feudal? Paternalistic? I know what you mean."

"Somebody once told Mom Mr. Forster was a patriarch in socialist's clothing. I think the person meant it as a joke, but I'm not sure."

"It's a provocative remark, however it was meant."

"But Mom liked the way Forster's factory took care of its workers. They even had a free nursery so the workers could visit their babies at lunchtime. She said long before I was thought of she used to pass the nursery and think how nice it would be to have a little somebody she could pop in and see."

"Did she and Mr. Harshaw ever think of having children? They were married for a long time, weren't they?"

"She ran away with him at sixteen and they split up when she was twenty-six. So that's ten years. He was a lot older than her and had been married before. He didn't have kids in that marriage either, so maybe he couldn't. The reason he and Mom decided to separate was because he was sick of doing what he called 'fancy side work.' He wanted to go back to logs and own a sawmill. The sad thing is he did get his sawmill and was crushed by a log falling off one of his trucks. But Mom loved Forster's. When they made her supervisor of finish work there wasn't much of a raise, but she said she felt appreciated. And even when we had to leave, Mr. Forster wrote her a recommendation to a custom furniture maker he knew in the mountains and that's why we went there. But Mom only worked at that place for a short time because he went out of business and she had to start looking for other jobs."

"Did you ever tell me why you and your mother had to leave Forster's?"

"It was my fault. I beat up a boy so bad he stopped breathing and almost lost an eye. He was my best friend. He was also

Mr. Forster's grandson. His family had settled the town and pretty much ran everything. The name of the town itself was Forsterville."

"It doesn't sound like you, Marcus. Did he do something?"

"He said something really horrible and they say I went crazy."

"My word," Aunt Charlotte said, pressing her left hand flat against her heart.

"After that I had to go to a psychiatrist for some mandatory sessions and when those were over we packed up our things and drove to the mountains to start a new life."

"Well, Marcus, if you ever want to tell me more about it, I'm here. And if you don't want to, that's fine, too." She repositioned her left leg in its cast on the stool in front of her. "I'm sorry you didn't get to know who your father was before your mother died. But from the little you've told me, he sounds like someone who would have loved you and been proud of you. I did know who my father was, for all the good it did me. It turned out he was the devil incarnate."

"How would a person know that their father is the devil incarnate?"

"You wouldn't at the time. It would be later, when you were safe enough to look back. At the time all you would feel at first would be a misgiving, that something wasn't as it should be. Later on, it may grow into a full-blown sense of wrong. But it's a wrong you're part of. You can't do anything about it because you're a child and you have no way to compare your life to other people's lives. Your foremost need is to stay safe within the only life you know."

The only specific past history she had offered in our porch talks were some caustic anecdotes about her no-good husbands and more information about her former jobs. She and my mom would have had so much to talk about. Aunt Charlotte had stocked shelves at a Home Depot ("I loved riding around on the forklift cart"), mixed drinks in a bar, seated people at a Howard Johnson's restaurant, been secretary to a funeral home director ("I also did the makeup on the stiffs, undercover, of course") and a "Jill of all trades"—house cleaning, yard work, care-taking, and pet sitting—her third husband serving as the titular and mostly useless "Jack" of their short-lived enterprise. ("We lived from hand to mouth, most of the time.")

"Where did you get the money to buy this house, if it isn't rude to ask?"

"I won a lottery. No, I did, really. Actually I won two lotteries. Every week I bought one of those cheap scratch-off tickets. Without fail, every week, tongue in cheek. The first time I won thirty-five dollars. The second time I won ten thousand. Just enough to get out of West Virginia and buy a beach shack in South Carolina."

"What about your husband? Didn't he want his share?"

"Luckily, we were divorced by then, or he would have wanted it all. At the time of my lottery windfall I was bartending at night and I was still in a state of ecstasy to be free at last. You have no idea."

"So that was the beginning of your solitary life?"

"Yes, I guess it was. You're good company, Marcus. You listen and put things together."

# *XX.*

While being good company for my aunt, I was also thinking about the ghost-boy who waited for me at Grief Cottage. Did he feel slighted that I had cut down my daily visits to the single morning ones? Did he wonder what he had done wrong, or was I pushing my human tendencies onto him? In my afternoon talks with Aunt Charlotte, I felt disloyal about neglecting him. Or maybe I should start thinking of him as the ghost-*man*. After all, Lachicotte's niece's little grand-daughter had mistaken me for a man. ("Who is that man *spying* on us?")

But stop, I would warn myself: What sane person would be equating one's loyalty to a great-aunt with one's loyalty to a ghost? What, after all, was the figure I had seen once in a dazzle of afternoon light? How could I consider it a relationship when the person I thought I saw had been dead fifty years? The truth was, I felt love for him the way someone feels love for another living person.

I went back and tried to track the whole thing from the beginning, as you would trace on a map a route taken. When had it started, our strange relationship? Well, with Aunt

Charlotte's story about Grief Cottage—the history of the place itself—and, following that, the story about what that derelict cottage meant to her, what it stood for, when she walked up there in her first days of freedom on the island. It had reminded her of the debris in her past, but then also it had started her painting.

Having heard her say it had a haunting quality and a powerful mood, my first view of the actual thing had been a letdown: what an eyesore, the sooner it's leveled the better. And then I had crawled under the wire fence and eaten my lunch on the porch and fallen asleep and dreamed that the sunburnt man was standing in the broken doorway behind me, watching over me while I slept. And then I woke up and was scared to turn around and face the doorway. I sensed something watching me from behind and I felt its motives were not as friendly or protective as the sunburnt man's had been. But then, *what were they*? And I had caved and fled.

And then the rains had come and I'd read the two ladies' books and felt anger on the part of the boy. He and I had things in common, except that he was dead and couldn't stand up for his rights, or even how truly or falsely people remembered him. And then Aunt Charlotte finished her big McMansion painting for the Steckworths, and later that afternoon I had walked to Grief Cottage and actually seen him. And that same night, I lay in the hammock and watched the moon rise and concentrated on sending my spirit north. And then, without my ever leaving the hammock, there was the embrace and the rapture. From that point on, I couldn't account for it in literal or sane terms. We were connected: he was always with me.

I used to cringe with embarrassment when the foster mother talked about how Jesus followed her around the house, always a few steps behind her, just out of her line of sight. He is always with me, even in my most private places, she told us. I had imagined what private places she meant and cringed some more. But how was my connection with the ghost-boy any less embarrassing than hers with Jesus?

Sometimes I resurrected the psychiatrist back in Forsterville who had grilled me so patiently and professionally about what my feelings were while beating up my friend. I imagined sitting down in his office once again and explaining to him, this time without holding anything back, my relationship with the ghost-boy. What questions would the psychiatrist have asked? What diagnosis would he have given? So far this exercise had not been very fruitful. I could hear the psychiatrist asking the first thing Wheezer would have asked: was I absolutely sure what I saw wasn't just a trick of the light? Then he might ask me to describe the onset of the fascination, what had triggered it, how long had it been going on? He would end up prescribing medication, "just for a while, to see how it goes."

At the end of our final session, the psychiatrist in Forsterville had given Mom a prescription for me—"If needed"—but after we left his office she said, "I don't think we need to cash this in, do you, Marcus?" and she had torn it up and thrown the pieces into a trash can on the sidewalk. "Let's make a completely fresh start in this place where we're going," she had added, with forced courage in her voice.

Unlike Aunt Charlotte, Mom never said it was "up to me" whether or not I wanted to reveal what Wheezer had said to make me fly at him. I had told Mom that Wheezer had said something about the way we lived. And I told her this only after we left Forsterville. I never told the psychiatrist even that much, because I knew he would pass it on to her.

Naturally I never explained to Mom why Wheezer left our apartment. That would have meant admitting I had gone into the tin box and showed the secret photo to someone else. After she came back with the pizza for our lunch, when I told her he had felt an asthma attack coming on and had bicycled home, she had said, "Oh dear, I hope it wasn't something in our apartment that set it off."

But right up until the night she died, she would wait for moments when we were close and then tilt her head wistfully and spring it on me afresh: "I wish you'd *tell* me what he said about how we lived, Marcus. After all, I am your mother. Whatever it was, it might not be as bad as you think."

*Oh yes it was.*

★   ★   ★

THE FOURTH OF July came and went, much to the relief of the island's Turtle Patrol, whose members had set up NO FIREWORKS! zones up and down the entire length of the beach and had taken turns, in twos and threes, guarding the nest sites of the logger-head babies, due to hatch soon and make their live-or-die dash for the sea. I had made friends with the retiree on the Turtle Patrol. After he became aware of how often I checked the site below Aunt Charlotte's boardwalk, he gave me his beeper number on a laminated card so I could call him from our cottage, whatever the hour, if I spotted any threat or change in the protected dune. ("I always carry my beeper, when I'm out on the beach or working on my jeep in the garage.") This was his beloved wartime 1944 Wilys Jeep, with its original camou-flage paint, which he drove up and down the beach to check on the nests. He also lent me one of the patrol's infrared flashlights.

Soon we would be in countdown mode, he said, and proceeded to explain ways we would be able to tell when the hatchlings were going to crawl up through the sand and "boil out" of their nest, usually a few hours after sunset. ("Last year we rigged up a microphone and amplifier and installed it next to the site. We'll do it again this year when we get close to hatching time. You can actually hear the hatchlings as they crawl up through the sand. It's a rattling sound, like pebbles being thrown against a metal roof. The first time I heard the amplified sound of those little fellows I had to wipe away tears, it was so affecting.") His name was Ed Bolton, a retired high school science teacher from Columbia. He'd lost his son, a helicopter medic, in the Viet Nam war. After he retired, he and his wife moved full-time to their beach cottage. "It's one of the real oldies, with the brick footing columns and the tongue-in-groove joints. But we've modernized it a lot, of course."

He knew the story of Grief Cottage, though Hurricane Hazel was long past before he and his family started coming here. He belonged to the faction of locals who wished it had been leveled decades ago. ("It's one more disaster waiting to happen.")

I had not gone to Grief Cottage on the Fourth, which fell on a Sunday that year. All day long the beach had been thick with tourists, and I knew from Mr. Bolton that the north tip of the island was a traditional spot for serious firework displays, with preparations starting early in the day. With so many people milling around, I would surely be seen defying the CONDEMNED and KEEP OUT signs as I crawled under the wire fence. I might become the agent of immediate demolition. ("If that boy is crawling under that fence with us watching, isn't it time we get moving on the safety measures and level that thing to the ground?") I tried to imagine how the ghost-boy marked such occasions. Did he enjoy watching the spectacle, or did he hide out from the noise in some safe corner?

But here I was crossing a line again. Hadn't I reached the limits of imagining what he could do without me? By now I had more or less accepted that we worked in tandem: to a great extent he was dependent on my awareness of him. Since ghosts didn't have living brains, the work must be done by the living person. The living person had to offer his brain as the dwelling place for the ghost. Once again I reminded myself how imperative it was to my mental health to keep the different levels of reality separate.

I did not go to Grief Cottage on Monday because it rained in the morning and in the afternoon Aunt Charlotte decided to rearrange her studio and asked for my help. She wanted to take down the items pinned on her wall-high cork board and then completely clear her two trestle tables and move them to the middle of the room. "I'm going to try some experiments while sitting down." When I asked her about the experiments, she said she didn't want to talk about it. ("In case I fail. So you'll just have to contain your overdeveloped curiosity, Marcus.") She allowed me to dust and vacuum and change her sheets, as I had been doing since her fall. She also talked me through changing a washer on the big laundry sink in her studio, which she used for cleaning up after a day's painting. But after praising my work, she announced in a cordial but no-nonsense voice that I was to stay out of her studio until she invited me in again.

"Maybe I'll finish off my boxes from the garage," I said, anxious to remain in her good graces. The "overdeveloped curiosity" remark was not exactly a compliment. "I need to rearrange my room, as well."

"That's a good plan," she said.

The next box I tackled contained our "linens" on the top, towels and sheets so worn that they went straight into the black trash bag. Underneath those I found Mom's old GED Practice Test Manuals. I started leafing through them, testing myself on various questions, until I became sucked down into not-so-happy memories of our last years together, things I hadn't thought of since coming to live with Aunt Charlotte. I heard conversations between me and Mom that made me wince with shame, and I recalled humiliating instances of our "downsizing," as Mom jokingly referred to it, with forced courage in her voice.

After she lost her job when the joinery in Jewel went out of business, she returned with a vengeance to her GED hopes. ("It's now or never, Marcus. You must support me in this, *make* me do it even when I'm tired.") Many were the nights I quizzed her out of these practice manuals while she lay on the floor, her legs up against the wall to reduce the swelling in her ankles. First the test-taker had to read a passage "for comprehension" and then pick the right answer from the multiple choice questions below. ("Who were in attendance at Oliver Twist's birth? A. grandmothers, B. doctors, C. nurses, D. a slightly drunk woman and a parish surgeon.") "That was too easy," Mom had said from the floor, "almost insulting." And I had agreed with her: Any moron who had read the passage would know it was D. The way we did it, she would first read the passages to herself silently in a particular area of testing—literacy, math, social studies, science—hiding the questions and answers with a piece of paper. And then she'd lie on the floor with her legs up while I quizzed her. ("Unemployment now has less severe effects than it did in the 1930s. Why?") When she got an answer wrong she would ask me to put a checkmark by the right answer so she could come back and review it. ("I should have known that! 'No countervailing social programs!' With the many social programs that keep you and me afloat, how could I have missed that one?")

From her preoccupied air at supper I sensed that Aunt Charlotte had begun the experiment that was to keep me out of her studio. But now, having discovered the GED practice manuals, I was caught up in my own private quest. The manuals had been given to Mom by the teacher of her first night course back in Forsterville. They were used, but he knew she couldn't afford to buy new ones. ("He was a wonderful teacher, devoted to us. He had been teaching Latin and Greek at a nearby private school until he got fed up and quit. He said his heart would always be with the strugglers rather than the already-haves. But then he got sick and died."

"What of?"

"He didn't take care of himself. He fell into destructive habits and there was no one to guide him out of them. It was such a sad waste. Later the class was moved to another location, to suit the convenience of the next teacher—otherwise she wouldn't come. I kept going for a while, though it was a forty-five-minute commute each way. But the new teacher, you could tell *her* heart wasn't in it. She did it for the extra income. She despised us. She was one of those people who fight their way up the ladder and then have contempt for others trying to follow her. Finally I lost faith and decided to leave well enough alone. I had my good job with full benefits at Forster's. And then you came along. What more did I need?")

# *XXI.*

*I* stayed up late into Monday night, obsessed with Mom's GED practice tests. I would close my eyes, stab at one of the four manuals, open it to a random page, and test myself on the first question that swam up. In a free market what are some of the ways in which prices can be fixed? What distinguishes the skeleton of a pterosaur from that of a bird? What conflicting impulses can be seen in the democratic ethic? (Correct answer: duty to self vs. duty to society.) When I got one wrong, I would pencil my initials beside the right one. As the night wore on, I entered a manic state. It seemed totally possible that I could pass these tests *now*. Though I always got A's in math at school, the math part of the GED tests would bring down my total score because I hadn't studied geometry or advanced algebra yet. But if I aced the other parts I could balance out the low math score. If I put my mind to it, I might attain high school equivalency without ever going to high school! I could head straight off to college and Aunt Charlotte would have her privacy back and look forward to seeing me on the holidays. She would be proud of me and might even miss me.

When I woke up next morning, it was much later than usual: I could tell from the position of the sun hitting the front of the house. Long gone were the hours of the capering unleashed dogs and the stalwart seniors with their sleeves and sunhats. I lay hating myself for missing my favorite part of the morning, but also struggling to remember the dream I had waked out of. I heard Aunt Charlotte in the kitchen, foraging in the refrigerator, then hopping back to her studio and firmly closing the door (*Keep out until further notice. This means you, Marcus*). I made my bed as soon as I got out of it, a habit begun long ago to save Mom the trouble and to keep our small space looking neat. Now I did it so Aunt Charlotte wouldn't think I was a slob if she decided to take a peek into my—her former—room. Dressing quickly, I wolfed a handful of cereal in the kitchen, swigging it down with milk.

Riding north past the third or fourth yellow trash barrel, I remembered my dream. The whole thing came back in a single whump, like a fist to the stomach. Finally I had dreamed about my mother. It was the first dream in which she was facing me. This was Mom at her best, smiling and opening the door to me. Inside was an apartment better than the ones we'd lived in. It was spacious and filled with light and everything in it was clean and new. My mom looked clean and new, too. She looked refreshed and young, freed of burdens.

"Marcus, I never told you this," she said excitedly, "but I have another son. He's your half brother."

"Was Mr. Harshaw his father?"

"I don't think that's important, do you?"

"Is he older or younger?"

"Older. Oh, Marcus, he's the most wonderful man. He's going to take care of me now. I wish you could meet him, but he's sleeping. He works so hard."

"Is he—in your room?"

"Goodness, no, why should he be in there? He's got his own room."

HOW DENSE PEOPLE are when they reassure you it was "only" a dream. Never in my waking life had I felt such wretchedness as when my refreshed, excited mother, surrounded by the security provided by another, informed me she had a better son sleeping in his own room. In the dream I experienced the castoff's full horror of realizing he has been supplanted and is no longer the main object of someone's love. And then the frantic disbelief ("It's not true, it's not final, I can still win her back!") followed by an agony of hopelessness and the wish to die.

That night last September in Jewel when Mom arrived home triumphant over the life insurance policy she had just bought in honor of my eleventh birthday ("It's twenty-four dollars a month, but now I know you'll be okay whatever happens"), what was my unsporting reply? "Too bad kids can't take out life insurance. If I died first, you could stop cleaning bathrooms."

And then in the winter—which was to be our last together— when she was working day shift at the new Waffle House near the interstate and cleaning the County Housing Authority offices at night, she had prophesied with her forced cheer: "Things are going to get better from now on, Marcus, I feel it." And what was my smartass comeback? "That must mean we've finally hit bottom and there's nowhere to go but up."

Our first year in Jewel while Mom still had her nice job oiling and lacquering furniture at Mountaintop Joinery before it closed, she came home one night in a kind of ecstasy. "Oh,

Marcus, I wish you could have heard the song they just played on the radio. I was so moved I had to stay in the car till it was over. Do you remember Captain Kirk?" (How could I *not* remember Captain Kirk? Wheezer had made me a present of the entire set of the original *Star Trek*. He had got it on eBay for VCRs because that was all Mom and I had.) "Well, he's made a new album under his own name, William Shatner. It's called *Has Been*, and there's this heart-stopping song called 'It Hasn't Happened Yet.' I got chills all over, because he was expressing exactly what I was feeling. *It Hasn't Happened Yet!* He *speaks* the song in his rumbly Captain Kirk voice against this background of haunting music." Deepening her own voice, she chanted snatches from the song: *dreaming of success . . . I would be the best . . . what I might have done . . . falling, falling . . . I'm scared again.*

"Isn't it wonderful what art can do, Marcus? It was so sad, I saw my life in every line, but at the same time it made me feel part of the human family—it made me feel so *alive*."

Later, as things got progressively worse in Jewel, I would resort to those phrases as a teasing form of recrimination. Every time Mom came home and broke the news of another "downsizing" in our lives I would deepen my voice to a Captain Kirk rumble and chant: *falling, falling . . . I'm scared again.* Or: *It hasn't happened yet.* She always laughed, but I could tell it hurt her.

PEDALING FASTER TO get ahead of the rising midmorning tide, I was already talking to the ghost-boy, filling him in on everything that had happened since the last time I was there. ("No wonder she had to go and find herself a better son. Here's what worries me, though. What if—however bad a son I was—I loved her *as much as I am ever capable of loving anyone*? Did you ever feel like this? Did you love any special person when you were alive? Did you ever worry that you weren't capable of loving enough? But it's all over for you. Your life is a complete thing. I envy that. Is it worth it to go on living, knowing I let my mom down and dreading the new school and worrying how long it will be until Aunt Charlotte tires of my company and gets rid of me? Why not save her the guilt she'd feel after she kicked me out? And, I mean, what's the point of 'climbing the ladder' when you know you'll never fit in with the already-haves at the top? Did you think things like this when you were alive?")

A temptation presented itself. Then it morphed into a dare and then into a compulsion, something I knew I had no choice about doing. Today would be the perfect day for me to go up on the porch of Grief Cottage and sit down *facing the door.*

If you have reached the point of wishing your life was completed but knowing you haven't got the guts to complete it yourself, wouldn't the next-best thing be to seek out something that might do the job for you? Today I would face the door of the cottage and stay facing it, inviting annihilation. Surely I wouldn't be the first person to die from fright.

But my plan was aborted when I rounded the last curve of beach and saw the group gathered around Grief Cottage. Charlie Coggins, the realtor, was with two men wearing some kind of summery uniform with shorts. Coggins's weird-looking amphibious vehicle that Lachicotte had helped him assemble was parked next to a white truck bearing an insignia. The men in shorts were looking through instruments on top of tripods, while Mr. Coggins hovered near them. I could either conceal myself behind some dunes and wait them out, or go home before high tide forced me to return by the road. The mood was all wrong now. It would be better to come back tomorrow at my early hour and have the place to myself.

ED BOLTON'S JEEP with its wartime camouflage was parked in front of our dunes when I got back to Aunt Charlotte's house, and there he was in his squashed sun hat crouched reverentially beside our loggerhead site.

"Just checking," he said, knees cracking as he rose to greet me. "All that rain we had yesterday could make a difference to our countdown. Where are you coming from?"

I told him I liked to ride to the north end of the island every morning to sort out my thoughts. "But I got a late start today, and people were already poking around Grief Cottage. There was this realtor I know, Mr. Coggins, and two other men with tripods, measuring things. They were wearing some kind of uniform with shorts and they had instruments on tripods."

"Dark shorts, gray shirts, and blue caps?"

"How did you know?"

"Army Corps of Engineers. Coggins knows he's never going to get rid of that real estate until the erosion experts have weighed in."

"But there was a man from Chicago who seemed interested."

"He pulled out. Nobody wants to start building a beachside inn and have it falling into the ocean before it's finished."

"How do you know all these things?"

"Everybody knows everybody's business here. Our cottage is only four doors south of Grief Cottage, so naturally we keep our antennae on the alert. What's probably going to happen, the Army Corps will do their deformation survey and recommend we invest in geotube bladders. They're expensive as hell, so all us owners at the north end will have to vote on it in a referendum. Coggins will be stuck with those lots unless someone's foolish enough to buy with no guarantee of future shoreline protection."

"What are geotube bladders?"

"They're like great big culverts made of special textiles and buried beneath the high tide line. They're filled with a sand-and-water mixture and can usually block immense waves caused by hurricanes. Note I said *usually*, not always."

"How will the rain change our countdown?"

"It will have cooled the sand. The embryos prefer warmth at this stage of the game. That's why we always detect a rapid rise in temperature with our little thermocouple gizmos when hatching time is imminent. Yesterday's rain may set it back a few days. What's the matter? You look troubled."

"I just wish I knew more about how things worked in the world. The way you do."

"Give yourself a break, son. If you keep on asking questions at your present rate, you'll be a downright sage before you reach thirty."

# *XXII.*

Cleanup was in full force at the house next door. A team of guys shaped hedges, whacked weeds, mowed and raked the sparse patches of grass on the sandy lawn, hosed down stairs and walkways. One was down on his knees, hand-clipping the overgrown path that led to the beach. Another was planting a last-minute border of hardy annuals. From inside the house came the high-pitched whine of several vacuums going at once.

"That's the life, isn't it, Marcus? You're ninety-five in a wheelchair and won't be going anywhere near the beach but you maintain a full retinue to prink up your paths and grounds and boardwalk so everything will look the same as it did seventy-five years ago."

"Seventy-five years ago?"

"She came to her husband's ancestral beach cottage as a bride of twenty. Ninety-five minus twenty is seventy-five. Lachicotte can furnish you with all the specifics, they're buddies. Could you phone him and tell him she's on her way? He'll want to bake her a pie."

"An oyster pie?"

"No, she hates oysters. Steak and kidney, probably, without the kidneys."

"Will she be coming today?"

"Tomorrow. Her retinue precedes her. As soon as she arrives, she sends her caregiver over with a calling card to let us know she's receiving visitors. The card used to be on a silver salver but now it arrives on a sweet-grass tray made by Roberta Dumas, the current caregiver."

"Will you visit her?"

"She knows my ways. She understands. She respects artists. Roberta herself comes from a dynasty of basket weavers who have examples of their work in the Smithsonian. Where have you been? Let me guess."

"Mr. Coggins was up there with the Army Corps of Engineers."

"What were they doing?"

"I didn't talk to them. But Mr. Bolton from the Turtle Patrol says they're measuring erosion around the cottage. I met him down by the egg clutch."

"How are our little friends?"

"He says yesterday's rain may delay their hatching."

"I've been on this island for twenty-five years and never seen a hatching. What's the term they use? 'Boil up'?"

"Want me to knock on your door?"

"Well . . . why not?"

"Even if it's late?"

"Sure. If I'm feeling up to it, maybe I'll hop down and see it for myself. After all, they have incubated under *our* boardwalk."

I called Lachicotte, who sounded glad to hear from us. "I'd call more often, but I don't want to be a bother (*bah-thah*)." We

made plans to go over to Mrs. Upchurch's early the next afternoon. "You'll appreciate her. She's quite the raconteur. Will
you tell your aunt I have taken the liberty of tuning up her
Mercedes and replacing the tires? It's my little thank-you for
the extended loan."

AFTER SUPPER WITH Aunt Charlotte, I walked down to the
surf and stood on the shiny wet surface mirroring the same
orange light of her big *Sunset Calm* painting that now hung in
the library—and had once been taped as a postcard on Mom's
refrigerator. I was thinking how awful it must be to have
painting taken away from you. It could happen in all sorts of
ways. You could hurt your painting arm, or some fascist regime
could come in and forbid you to paint. At supper Aunt Charlotte
had been telling me about this German painter, Emil Nolde,
who was forbidden by the Nazis to paint anymore when he was
seventy years old and at his peak. For the duration of World
War II, he painted small secret watercolors on Japan paper,
which he hid in his house.

"What is Japan paper?"

"Well, it's not necessarily made in Japan anymore, but it's a
high quality paper made from bark fibers rather than wood
pulp. It's tougher. If you have to paint with water like poor
Nolde, you can build up layers, like in oil. He wrote notes to
the secret paintings."

"What kind of notes?"

"Things like 'Only to you, my little sheets.' That's the one I
like best."

He couldn't paint in oils because he couldn't be seen buying
any, and also if they raided his house they would detect the

smell. During this period of artistic oppression, he abandoned the landscapes that had made him famous and made little water-colors of dreamlike figures and faces on his Japan paper. He called them his "unpainted pictures," and Aunt Charlotte turned on her laptop while we were still eating and showed me the vividly-colored little paintings of surreal or grotesque people, some in lewd and threatening poses, that seemed to have come straight out of his dark regions. I told Aunt Charlotte they made me think of the fiends and fantasies a person had inside of him that maybe he didn't even know he had. "That's very astute, Marcus," she said, sipping her wine. Her face bunched up as it tended to do when she was trying to figure something out. Having impressed her by saying this, I was about to ask how her secret project was coming, but decided to stop while I was ahead. Soon after, she asked me to uncork another bottle and hopped off with it to her studio.

Making patterns in the wet sand with my sneaker, I recalled my extravagant despair of this morning when I had hoped to be scared to death by the ghost-boy. How could a person's moods change so many times in a day? Was it my age, or was it going to be like this from now on? What if a person decided to kill himself in the morning and then woke up dead and realized he had made a huge mistake? Now here I was, the same person in the same body, the same clothes, even, standing in the placid orange light of Aunt Charlotte's *Sunset Calm* and feeling excited about those little turtle embryos under the sand who, if they survived all the intermittent dangers, had eighty to a hundred or more years to go before they could die an old turtle's death and become part of loggerhead ancestral history. Soon they would be bursting out of their shells, flat-tening out into proper turtle shapes, clambering on top of one another to "boil up" for their dash to the sea—which we would be part of.

For some reason this led to thoughts of William, my ad litem friend, and of our final Vulcan salute to each other at the airport. I wondered what kind of minors he was guarding now and if he ever missed me.

How lucky I was to be assigned to a person who would understand that I needed to see my mother's body *before* it was embalmed so I could truly accept that she was dead. We drove to the hospital in his truck. He had arranged everything with the head of ER, who took us down in the elevator to the hospital morgue. The ER person unzipped the black body bag on the gurney. There she was. It was her and not her. I had been told what to expect. The bone and cartilage of her nose was exposed where it had hit the steering wheel—our Honda was from the pre-air-bag era. Her eyes were open, but the life had drained out of them. The blue irises were now a lusterless yellow-green. Her mouth was ajar, exposing the tooth gaps she was so self-conscious about. She had hennaed her hair recently; it was at its glossiest mahogany-brown. ("At least I didn't die with my roots showing." I heard her exact living voice with its equal mix of self-put-down and resolute humor.)

William and I had gone over burial plans during our drive to the hospital. As an adolescent Mom had read a novel by a famous occultist who had warned against cremation, the reason being that you had to stay in one piece so you could be brought up whole out of your grave. "You might need your bones," Mom said. "It may be superstition, but you find it all the way back in the Book of Ezekiel, so I'd rather not take chances." When we still lived in Forsterville, Mom and I often talked about death and where we would like to be buried. We took walks in a beautiful little cemetery a short way out of town. "If we're still here when I die," Mom said, "I'd like to be buried in this place." But after we moved to Jewel, we stopped romanticizing about graves and cemeteries because we weren't sure how long we'd be staying in Jewel, especially after Mountaintop Joinery closed down and Mom lost her good job.

William took me to the little country cemetery where most of his family had their graves. It was on a hill overlooking mountain ranges stretching as far into the distance as you could see. When the life insurance trust was set up, he said, you'll be able to buy a nice stone with her name and dates. "So wherever you go, Marcus, you'll know you can always come back and find her in the same place."

# XXIII.

With the approach of bedtime came the start of a bad feeling. Usually I looked forward to shutting the door to my room, Aunt Charlotte's former room, knowing that nothing more would be required of me until the next day. For at least eight hours I didn't have to be astute or useful or empathetic. I could just fall back on my pillows with childish irresponsibility until I fell asleep.

But this was a new fear that kept me from wanting to fall asleep. It was stronger than my top supernatural fear (could I survive an extended face-off with the ghost-boy without going crazy?) and it was stronger than my top realistic fear (could I survive being sent away by Aunt Charlotte and starting over in another foster home?)

The new fear was that tonight, as soon as I fell asleep, I would dream a continuation of last night's dream. I would be standing in the open doorway of my mom's beautiful apartment and she would have just told me about my wonderful half brother in his own room, and then I would look beyond her and see a door in the rear of the apartment slowly opening. I did not believe I could endure seeing him face-to-face.

To put off going to bed, I made two after-dark trips to the beach. On the first trip, I paced around the dune protecting our egg clutch. I got down on all fours and sniffed. No fresh earthy smell. I shone my infra-red flashlight on the thermocouple stuck in the sand: no rise in temperature. On the second trip, I sat down cross-legged on the dune and talked to them in the same spirit that Mom would talk to me at night when she was not too tired. She told stories about when I was an infant. ("We used to look into each other's faces. I never tired of looking at you and seeing you look back. You were so new, you didn't have words yet, but I could see your thoughts and moods play across your face.") Or she made up stories about our future prospects, how we were going to prevail.

So I spoke to the turtle embryos about their present secure state of egginess and about their future great voyage. ("It's been programmed into you, so don't worry, your ancestors have been doing it for over a hundred million years. You'll just get out of your egg—rip the shell with your 'egg tooth,' which is that hard little projection on top of your snout—and take care not to get exhausted as you're climbing up because you'll need all your energies for later. It will only be about a twenty-inch climb, and you'll have all your brothers and sisters to step on, as they will step on you in turn, and the whole pile of you will rise like a slow elevator, an elevator made out of yourselves, and then you'll pop your heads through the sand, and we will have scooped out a path through the sand to the ocean. Just follow the path and don't get diverted and crawl up the sides—but if you do, a human hand will be right there to gently guide you back into the groove. It will take you about fifteen minutes to crawl from nest to water, moving at about ten feet a minute. We will escort you the whole way to the water to guard you from the ghost crabs. The reason we can't pick you up and carry you is because you need to do the walk yourselves so you can smell the sand and remember your way back to this beach when you're grown up.")

I did eventually sleep, but woke early into the weird no-light that precedes morning. My first thought was: *I escaped the continuation of the brother-dream.* Then I lay very still to grab onto another dream that was fading away—not a nightmare, not even what you'd call a bad dream, because there were some parts of it I wanted to keep. I salvaged as much as I could, and then quickly made my bed, dressed, snatched some stand-up breakfast, and headed north on my bike. The sky had not yet separated itself from the flat gray of the ocean. I had never been out this early. The empty beach contained not a single living creature.

"It's like a video game," Wheezer had explained to me in the dream I'd tried to hold on to. "But what you need to remember, Marcus, is we're *inside* the screen. Someone else is at the controls." What we had to do, he said, was avoid the "powder-colors." When the game was switched on, whoever was playing on the outside would try to shoot colored powders at us through little holes. Already we could see those powder-colors amassing and waiting to be sent forth from their chamber: thick crusty reds and blues and yellows, like those primitive colors in the un-paintings by the German artist my aunt had showed me on her laptop. If we wanted to stay alive, Wheezer said, we had to keep alert. When the powders hit us, we needed to wipe them off fast. "What happens if some powder gets stuck on us?" I asked. "If *too much* gets stuck on you," he warned in his hoarse little asthma voice, "the colors will *paste you over* and you'll be trapped inside the screen forever." Even though the dream had its scary aspects, it had been nice to be with Wheezer again.

The wind hissed past my ears as I sped north without my helmet, which I kept fastened to the back of my seat. The old people never bothered with helmets on their early morning bike rides. I was anxious to stay within this eerie zone, no longer night but not yet day, until I reached the cottage. It was like the beach was under a spell. The tenuous light through which I rode seemed to wrap itself around me and push me forward to meet whatever I had to meet.

Looking back on that morning, as I have so many times, I calculate that the ten or twelve minutes it would have taken me, pedaling at top speed, to reach Grief Cottage would have given an ordinary summer dawn more than enough time to break through. But as I felt it then, the penumbra stuck to me all the way to the cottage like a faithful cloud cover. It lasted through my dismounting and hiding my bike between two dunes, and it hung above me as I crawled through the sand beneath the wire fence with its warning signs. It was as if time and light and sound had conspired to hold themselves back so that I could receive the full impact of what I saw.

He stood there in the doorway on his own terms, not mine. I reeled with the vividness of him. He was stronger and sharper in substance, and, unlike our last encounter, he didn't slouch or seem to wait passively to see what I might do next. The tense way he braced himself against the door frame, pushing himself outward with both hands (I saw the prominent knuckle ridges between the spread fingers), was that of a figure ready to spring after having been kept trapped for too long.

I saw the long narrow face with indented cheeks, the small raisin-dark eyes lodged deep in their sockets, the pale stalk-like neck, an off-kilter nose that looked as though it had been broken and not properly reset; I saw the wide mouth and the thin lips, and the gangly, slightly bowed legs in jeans, and the black ankle boots. The faded red shirt I had seen before, but this time buttons were left open, exposing the articulated chest of a man.

It felt like turning a corner in a corridor at school and suddenly coming face-to-face with an older boy. He's just there, this totally other being; you're right smack in the center of his attention, and you have no idea where this is going.

Whether daylight had by this time edged out the gloom I don't know, but I remember being thankful for a couple of observations that presented themselves like solid posts of realism for me to clutch onto, as he looked ready to burst out of his door frame. The first thought came in the form of a calculation: If you measured by *an unbroken stretch of time,* he had been in this place longer than all the previous dwellers put together since 1804. The second observation, seeing those knuckly hands braced against the door frame, was a practical question, the kind Charlie Coggins might ask: Why had nobody bothered to replace the door or at least board over the space to slow down the decay? Maybe it was these infusions of practicality that kept me standing there for as long as I did. Was it long enough for me to gauge that I had reached the toleration point of what I could sanely handle? Or had my primal brain propelled me into flight without giving me the luxury of thought?

On this occasion I hadn't even gotten as far as climbing the rotting stairs to the porch. All I knew was that one moment I stood below him in the sand, transfixed by our mutual gaze, and the next thing I knew I was standing far from the cottage, my face turned toward the ocean. The first sound to come back to me was the thud of my heart racing inside my chest. Then the sound of surf and birds followed, and daytime was definitely in control. I knew that if I turned around now all I would see would be a falling-down cottage and a gaping doorway.

At some point I realized I wasn't by myself at the ocean's edge. Not far away there was a woman holding a golden retriever on a short leash. Both of them stood still as statues facing the breaking waves, as though they were competing to see which could outlast the other in utter stillness. The dog wore a dark green vest with a number and an insignia. The woman was about my mom's age and had her small upright build and coloring. Only this woman had the means to take care of herself. Mom would often comment on the ways you could spot this when she saw a certain kind of woman in a store. "That's a very expensive look," she would remark about the woman's hair. "It looks like casual sun streaks, but it's actually a three-color process."

Suddenly the retriever lunged at an incoming wave and the woman tightened the leash and murmured something. The dog sat down and was perfectly still again. This happened several times. It seemed cruel to bring a dog to the edge of the ocean and then not let him play in the surf. The longer I watched this tug of wills between them, the more indignant I became.

Both woman and dog watched me approach. The woman's look was questioning but not unfriendly. It was as though she already knew what I was going to ask.

"Why can't he go in?"

"It wouldn't be a good idea. He's in training to be a service dog. Normally, Barrett is the calmest dog you can imagine, but when we brought him here, he got excited as soon as he heard the sound of the ocean, and when he saw the surf he went wild." She had a Lachicotte-type accent, though not as pronounced.

"Is he for a blind person?"

"No, he'll go to a disabled vet. It's a new program. Prisoners at the Navy brig in Charleston train the dogs. My husband and I are volunteers. We take one dog at a time during weekends and holidays and get him accustomed to new experiences. Distractions and unexpected sounds. This afternoon, my husband is taking Barrett to a firing range, and after that to a children's playground."

"Who named him Barrett?"

"They name them at the brig. Each dog is given the last name of a fallen person in uniform. That's a nice idea, don't you think?"

"Do you know who Barrett will go to?"

"Not yet. That gets decided in his final weeks of training. There's a long waiting list and it gets longer and longer. It's such a strange, awful war over there in Iraq. I never knew there were so many ways a person could get wounded and still be alive."

"Maybe the wounded vet who gets him will live by the ocean and they can go on walks and Barrett can splash a little in the waves."

"That's a sweet thought. Well, Barrett, that's enough beach time for us. It's been nice talking with you. You take care, now."

I PUT ON my helmet for the ride home. The seniors and early exercisers were trickling down to the beach, some unleashed dogs racing back and forth between surf and owner, then bolting off to chase and smell other dogs, activities that would never be part of Barrett's life. And yet he would be loved and needed. He would have a fabulous dog bed in a permanent home. He would feel, in whatever manner dogs felt things, indispensable to his veteran.

My cowardly bolt from the boy disappointed me. I'd had my chance and blown it. This was the fullest he'd ever shown himself, and I hadn't been able to endure it.

What I was sure of was *that I had seen.* I was also sure that I couldn't tell anyone. What I was *not* sure of was whether I was different from others my age. Could another person of eleven have had the same experience? But I didn't believe another person *would* have had this experience. Why not? Here I strained to reason it out. Because the whole series of episodes that had led up to this morning was inseparable from myself, from my history, from my personality. The ghost-boy was related to my life, yet he was also an entity on his own terms. Yet how could that be? How could he be both? Didn't something have to be one thing or the other, either real or imagined? Or could it be that the two things weren't mutually exclusive?

There was no one to ask. What I needed was someone wise and experienced, a mature personality who could take all of my information and give me back a definition, a diagnosis, a concept large enough to contain it all. There were surely such people in the world—only, so far, not in my world. Maybe later there would be a special teacher, like Mom's esteemed night-school teacher who had been so generous with his knowledge until he died, someone I could consult and look up to, who knew things I needed to know and if he didn't know them could show me how to look for them.

# XXIV.

*I* had never met a person as old as Coral Upchurch. I had never met a person of any age remotely like her. Lachicotte had promised I would appreciate her, that she was quite the raconteur, but I certainly never expected to hear the story she told that first afternoon.

Lachicotte came to get me at two o'clock, leaving behind a steak-and-mushroom pie identical to the one he was taking to Coral Upchurch next door. "Preheat your oven to three-fifty and put this in for thirty minutes," he said. "Do not use the microwave or your (*yoah*) crust will be soggy." He had been to the barber and smelled and looked like an older gent who had taken extra pains with his appearance.

During the seven hours since returning from Grief Cottage, I had been pretty busy myself. After a shopping trip to the island store, I had spent some quality time with the turtle eggs and done two loads of laundry. I had been neatening the kitchen shelves when Aunt Charlotte had burst out of her off-limits studio and asked if I had time to wash her hair before Lachicotte arrived. "I wonder if we should cut it first," she said, frowning at herself in the mirror over the sink.

"You want *me* to cut your hair?"

"I don't see why not. Unlike me, you'll have the advantage of seeing the back of my head. All it needs is an inch off."

"Should we do it after we wash it, or before?"

"Before. Just grab a clump and take an inch off. Then grab another clump and do the same thing all the way around."

"What if I mess up?"

"I'd make a bigger mess if I tried to do it with my left hand. Start at the back. You'll improve by the time you get to the front."

I felt uneasy laying hold of my aunt's wiry mop. It was barely long enough to get a grip on. I had cut Mom's hair and she had cut mine, but that was another world from this. Seated below me, humbly baring her neck to the scissors, Aunt Charlotte looked defenseless. I could snip-snip carelessly and brutally and make her look terrible. I could go crazy and stab her in the back. All kinds of worrisome associations ran through my mind. The last time I had *grabbed a clump* of someone's hair, it had been Wheezer's silky roan locks, when I was holding him close so I could better hit his face. Aunt Charlotte's neck was dead white and on the stalky side, like the ghost-boy's. What if I should suddenly blurt, "Listen, Aunt Charlotte, I know how you feel on the subject of ghosts, but I had a sort of hallucination this morning and I need to tell someone." Even imagining such a confession made me cringe. I could hear her alarmed thoughts: *Oh no, when things were working out so well. Hallucinations are not something I'm equipped to deal with. He'd be better off going somewhere else.*

On the other hand, the service I was performing for my aunt was one more way I could be of use to her: cutting her hair and keeping my hallucinations to myself. And after I had washed and dried it, Aunt Charlotte raised her eyebrows at herself in the bathroom mirror and told me I had made her look "formidably sleek."

Coral Upchurch's cottage was in another class from Aunt Charlotte's "renovated shack," as she liked to call it. The Upchurch cottage was one of the old ones, not as old as Grief Cottage, but built in the mid-nineteenth century by a family with money who took it for granted that their descendants would be enjoying it long after they themselves were dust. The kitchen was on the ground floor across from the garage; the main body of the house was above, resting on the sturdy bricked footing columns that supported all the old houses, only these columns were screened by a painted white trellis. Lachicotte imparted all this to me as we walked from Aunt Charlotte's to Mrs. Upchurch's. Her caregiver, Roberta Dumas, sat outside in the shade of the breezeway between kitchen and garage. Her fingers flew, weaving a very large basket. When she saw us coming, she rose from her stool, brushed bits of grass from her smock, and picked her way around a barrier of buckets filled with different shades of tall grasses. She was one of those heavy people who carry their weight lightly. Her skin was truly black, with highlights of blue and purple when she moved out of the shade into the sunlight. She wore a white pantsuit uniform beneath a colorful, flowing artist's smock.

"Mr. Hayes, you always come bearing gifts."

Lachicotte introduced me and handed over the steak pie with the same warm-up directions he had given Aunt Charlotte and me.

"I'll take it up and show her," she said, "so she'll know we're gonna eat well tonight."

"How was your all's winter, Roberta?"

"Well, you know Mr. Billy passed away in January."

"No! How come she didn't tell me when I phoned yesterday?"

"It knocked the wind out of her. She says it's not natural, the parents are supposed to go first. Mr. Billy was just turned sixty-five. He went to get his pacemaker batteries replaced and had a heart attack right there on the table."

"And her not saying a thing!"

"She's still taking it in. When they called her from Washington, she hung up on them. When it commenced to ring again, she told me, 'Don't you dare pick up that phone, Roberta. Some nasty person is trying to frighten me.'"

"But she sounded just like herself yesterday."

"Oh, she's herself all right. It's made her mad, more than anything. Just go up and talk about it normally. She likes to talk about him. She knows he's buried in the family plot in Columbia, but we're almost back to the place where we're expecting his annual visit. The mind is a wondrous thing, isn't it, Mr. Hayes? It hasn't got to stay in just one place at a time."

"What is that imposing object you're weaving?" Lachicotte asked.

"That's my monster. My grandson calls it my Boogie Basket." Laughing, she lifted it from the breezeway floor and set it on her stool, which it overlapped. "They wanted it this size, but the proportions are all wrong. The handles, if I get to them, are going to look like elephant ears. I've a mind to stop while I'm ahead and send word that I passed on."

"A commission, is it?"

She nodded. "They saw it in the Smithsonian book and wanted one just like it, only triple the size. It's one of Granny's models. She'd turn over in her grave if she saw this. Mrs. Upchurch said if I decided not to send it, she'll pay the commission price and we'll use it as our laundry basket."

This struck me as hilarious, because that's exactly what it looked like. I got the giggles and then Lachicotte laughed, and Roberta joined in.

"My aunt just finished a huge painting of these rich people's beach house," I said. "It was forty-two by fifty-six and they wrote her a check too large for her to keep in the house overnight. She said the next thing she painted for herself was going to be six by ten, or maybe even four by six. Unfortunately, she broke her right wrist that same night and can't paint anything for a while."

"Now that's a shame," said Roberta. "I slammed some fingers in a car door once and couldn't work with my hands for six weeks. I about went crazy."

Roberta led us up a flight of outdoor stairs, next to which had been built a ramp for a wheelchair. Inside a screened-in porch a tiny lady sat in the wheelchair awaiting us. As we rose into her sightline, she was taking a last greedy puff of her cigarette before extinguishing it in an ashtray on the glass-topped table next to her.

"What were you all laughing at down there? I thought you were never coming up."

"It was my monster basket. Look, Mr. Hayes has brought us a steak pie."

"Bless you, Lachicotte. Roberta won't have to drive to the store and interrupt her art. And this is Marcus. Welcome, Marcus. This pie smells heavenly, Lachicotte. Come kiss me and we'll dispense with condolences over Billy. I'm still cross with him for breaking ahead of me in line like that. Marcus, why don't you sit in that chair across from me?"

For the second time that day, I imagined how Mom would see a woman who'd had better breaks in life than she'd had. ("Now that simple summer outfit, Marcus, was really costly in its day. And look how well-preserved it is. It's gone back and forth to a quality cleaner for the last forty years. And notice her pampered complexion and the teeth! She's had them capped or veneered, otherwise they'd be yellow from age and smoking. And she's still got all of them! This old girl is a prime example of high maintenance over the long term.")

"I'll leave you all to socialize," said Roberta. "What do we want to have with Mr. Hayes's steak pie?" she asked Mrs. Upchurch.

"Oh, ice cream will be fine," replied the indulged little child-queen of ninety-five, ensconced on her wheelchair throne. Close by her on the glass table, besides the ashtray, were binoculars, a bird book, a carton of cigarettes with a silver lighter on top, a carafe of ice water covered by a drinking glass, and one of those pill containers with slots for a week's supply of morning and evening doses. On our side of the table were two tall glasses, a pitcher of iced tea, two folded cloth napkins, and a plate of unusually flat cookies.

Coral Upchurch's lively old eyes engaged with me. "So you are Charlotte Lee's great-nephew."

"Yes ma'am."

"Oh, please call me Coral. I'm trying to strip down to essentials. If I live much longer, I'm hoping even the 'Coral' will become superfluous. When you reach my age, you want to perform archaeology on yourself, get beyond family names and given names and polite forms of address." Her accent had a Lachicotte base with what sounded like overlays of voice training from somewhere in her past.

"What would be beyond Coral, archaeologically?" I asked.

"That's what I'm trying to figure out! Maybe you'll help me. What would 'beyond Marcus' be like?"

This was a really interesting question. I had to close my eyes in order to think harder. "Maybe not *any* given name," I said. "I mean, for instance, say you had a turtle and you named him Luke. Before he was Luke he was just a turtle. Or, if you wanted to be specific, a loggerhead turtle. And before that—I'm going to have to think about this some more."

"I wish you would. I've never known a Marcus. Plenty of *Marks* but no Marcuses. The only Marcus I can think of offhand is Marcus Aurelius."

"That's who my mom named me after! She loved his *Meditations*. She had two copies of it. One of them was in Greek on the left side of the page. He wrote it in Greek, you know."

"Was your mother a scholar?"

"She loved studying and learning things. She was planning to go to college and become a teacher." I was about to add how determined she was to make something of herself, then remembered I had been through this before with Lachicotte, who had generously suggested that she'd already made something of herself by bringing me up so well.

"Lachicotte told me what a great help you are to your aunt," said Coral Upchurch, "but when you're not being a great help, what do you do to amuse yourself? Have you made any friends?"

*Well, I've been spending a lot of time with this boy. He's a little older than me, fourteen, and he's been dead for fifty years.*

"I ride my bike a lot. And I've made friends with this man on the Turtle Patrol, Mr. Bolton. This year there's a clutch of loggerhead eggs buried below my aunt's boardwalk steps."

"Marcus has taken quite an interest in our local history," Lachicotte said. "Particularly the old Barbour cottage up at the north end. We went to the library to look up that poor family that was lost during Hazel, but he couldn't find a single mention of them in the microfiche."

"Well, I expect I can tell you more about them than anyone else still living," said Coral Upchurch. "I don't mean the Barbours, who still reside in Columbia as far as I know. And I don't know much about the unfortunate parents, except that the father's cousin sued the Barbours. But Billy knew the son. They were the same age. The boy was kind of a dark customer. Archie, my husband, made us leave the first weekend in October because he thought the boy was corrupting Billy. We usually stayed for the entire month of October. It was my favorite time. I would be by myself during the week, then Archie and Billy would drive down from Columbia on weekends. Archie had his law practice and of course Billy had school during the week. I was quite put out, having to pack up and leave—like we were being evicted or something!—and lose my favorite month just because of that boy."

"Do you remember his name?" I asked.

"It was something simple, like Billy, only of course it wasn't Billy. The family name wasn't one you hear every day, but it was an Anglo-Saxon name. When I remember I will write it down for you. These days, Marcus, I have to put in requests to my brain, as one does at the library, and then a little worker takes my slip and disappears into the stacks. It may take him a while, but he always comes back with the goods."

"How was he corrupting your son? If it's not too rude to ask."

"Billy came back with smoke and liquor on his breath. Archie said it wasn't just any smoke, it was marijuana. You have to understand. Back in that era marijuana was considered the 'stepping stone to heroin.' It was way before the time when doctors started prescribing it to sick people. In the early 1950s the states were enacting severe penalties for narcotic offenses. And the boy was . . . peculiar . . . in other ways. He never went into the ocean. Billy said he never even took off his clothes or shoes. He just walked up and down the length of the island, fully dressed—that's how Billy met him, as he was walking past our house, scowling. That would appeal to Billy's open nature. Billy loved to reach out to scowlers. There'd been some hardship or setback with that family, as I recall, something to do with their house, and there was a problem with the boy as well. The father was employed by a coal company in Kentucky, some low-level management job, not a miner. Some friends of the Barbours knew of their misfortunes and felt sorry for them, and since the Barbours weren't using it in October they offered their beach cottage. I don't know if it was charity, or whether there was payment involved. But the Barbours certainly paid for it later. After the family got washed away in the storm—*Dace!* That was their name, Dace. My little worker just came back from the stacks! The boy's name was Johnny Dace. Now where was I?"

"After the family got washed away," I said.

"Oh, yes, even though no bodies were found, a cousin on the father's side sued the Barbours. The cousin said the father was all she had left, and she only wanted her due. Money changed hands—the cousin even asked that the family's old car and their personal belongings be returned to her!—and soon after that the Barbours sold the cottage. In Archie's opinion, the proper defendant in the cousin's lawsuit would have been Hurricane Hazel. It wasn't the *cottage's* fault. It's too bad, really, that the Daces didn't stay inside it during the storm. That house was built to last. They'd probably be here today. The only part that didn't last was the south porch they say the boy burned down with his cigarettes."

I felt like Barrett the dog on his tight leash, straining toward the beguiling waves. There my beguiler sat, approximately the same distance from me as the waves had been from Barrett this morning, and I wanted to plunge in and immerse myself in whatever she could remember about the boy. My list of questions piled up, but I was on my "company" leash: Lachicotte and I were paying a social call on an ancient neighbor and we each had to take turns telling our news. We had to drink our iced tea and eat the unusual cookies, so thin they demanded you eat more of them. Aunt Charlotte's injuries were described and assessed, her recovery time speculated upon and wished for. Lachicotte brought Coral Upchurch up to date with island news, which at least touched upon the latest developments pertaining to the fate of Grief Cottage.

"The people who bought it from the Barbours should have either restored it or torn it down," said Coral Upchurch. "But they ended up selling to someone else and then Mr. Coggins the realtor, the late father not the son, snapped it up and couldn't sell it again. But I never understood why it was allowed to fall into ruin like that. Most townships would have forced the issue, was Archie's opinion. Every year until Archie died he'd walk up to see the cottage and come back appalled. He said it was a disgrace to the island and made us all look bad. It was Archie who frightened old Mr. Coggins and the commissioners into putting up the wire fence and those warning signs. Otherwise, he told them, you are just shopping for injuries and lawsuits. And even then it took twenty years to force the issue. By that time it had become a genuine ruin. Everyone had long since been calling it Grief Cottage when that fence finally went up."

"It was up when my aunt moved here." A perfectly natural next question would be for me to ask if Billy had visited Johnny Dace at the cottage. "It was Grief Cottage that started my aunt's painting career."

"Yes, she told me that. Please, Marcus, take that last Benne Wafer. It won't make you an old maid. That's an expression left over from my generation, but it only applies to girls. It's a sesame wafer. The slaves brought the spice with them from Africa. Benne is the Bantu word for sesame. Roberta can give you the recipe. She makes trays and trays of those cookies every year after Christmas when her family celebrates Kwanzaa. Do you know what Kwanzaa is?"

I had to admit I didn't know, and thus Barrett and I were reluctantly parted from our beguiling waves while Coral Upchurch filled me in on the first African-American holiday, established back in the sixties, when black people were starting to take pride in their roots.

"YOU COULD SEE her beginning to flag," said Lachicotte, as we walked back to Aunt Charlotte's. "And she kept eyeing those cigarettes."

"I wouldn't care if she smoked."

"Neither would I. I was raised inside a fog of parental smoke. But smokers nowadays have their individual rules of honor. Obviously hers are outdoors only and not in the presence of others."

"Why not in the presence of others?"

"The hazards of secondhand smoke."

"Oh, I knew that."

"It was kind of you to offer to shop for them every day."

"No problem. They eat mostly deli, like Aunt Charlotte and me, and this way Roberta won't have to take the van out of the garage and interrupt her art."

Lachicotte laughed. "That basket sure was a fright."

"Just because people are rich doesn't mean they have taste." A direct quote from my mom.

Lachicotte paused beside Aunt Charlotte's Mercedes, which he'd been driving since he sold the Bentley. "How is she doing?"

"She has some kind of project going in her studio."

"Oh? What kind?"

"It's secret. I'm not allowed to go in there. I think it involves paint but I can't be sure because I can't smell anything through the door. I always used to be able to smell the oils. She spends hours and hours in there every day."

"How is the—?"

"Festering?"

"You read my mind."

"Pretty much the same. It's a bad time for her, she says."

"Well, when we go back to the surgeon in Charleston, I'm hoping we'll hear encouraging news that will make her feel better. Is she having pain?"

"Not that I know of. She made me hide her painkillers and there's still a fair number in the container."

"Well, we may just make it through the summer. If we do, it will be largely thanks to you, Marcus."

"Won't you come in?"

"Thank you, no. I've got things to do, and we've already said hello. One hello is usually enough for your aunt."

*   *   *

"TELL ME ALL," Aunt Charlotte said at supper. "I hope it wasn't too boring for you."

"Oh no, I enjoyed it. I liked Roberta, too. She was making an ugly misshapen basket for some people who wanted it extra large. She wishes she could send word that she died so she won't have to finish it."

This amused Aunt Charlotte. She was enjoying Lachicotte's steak pie—heated according to his directions—and putting away her usual amounts of wine. She was in a mellow, receptive mood.

"So, what did '*you all*' talk about?"

"Her son Billy died last winter."

"Really? What of?"

"He had a heart attack at the hospital. He was having his pacemaker batteries replaced."

"Is she devastated?"

"Roberta said it was more like she was angry. She was supposed to go first. She told Lachicotte that her son had broken ahead of her in line. She was in a pretty good mood. Though toward the end Lachicotte noticed she was dying to have a cigarette."

"Depend on Lachicotte to notice something like that."

"She said she'd never known a Marcus before. She asked what I did to amuse myself on the island."

"And what did you tell her?"

"About the Turtle Patrol. And riding my bike."

"That doesn't sound like much. I wonder how you'll look back on this period of your life, Marcus, how you'll describe it to someone in the future. 'When I was eleven, my mother died and I went to live with my peculiar great-aunt on an island.'"

"I don't think of you as peculiar."

"Naturally you have to say that. I've tried to isolate my peculiarities. Being solitary has been a great advantage. At least I don't force my peculiarities on others. I hope I don't."

There was no good reply to this. If I said "You don't," that would be admitting she had peculiarities. So I just said I liked living here on the island. I stopped myself from adding that I hoped I didn't intrude on her solitude too much. That would sound like I was fishing for her to say I didn't, and then to repeat her usual praise about how helpful and thoughtful and astute I was.

As I was tinkering with these moral mathematics, I realized that I was not going to tell her what Coral Upchurch had said about the boy. He had a name now and some character traits (mostly negative ones, except for the walking on the beach). I wanted to keep him to myself until I had time to think about him some more. Ever since I could remember, I had kept a little private zone where I could work out important things for myself.

I had certainly not told Mom everything—a lot of it would have hurt her. In my mandated sessions with the psychiatrist I stuck to safe answers. With Wheezer, up until our rupture, I had left out significant "trues" in my history, allowing him to create his own pictures of how I lived in idealized poverty with my courageous single mom.

But I did tell Aunt Charlotte that I had offered to shop for Coral Upchurch and Roberta every day. "That way Roberta won't have to get the car out of the garage and interrupt her work. They eat mostly deli, like us."

"Sometimes I think you are too good to be true, Marcus."

"I'm not all that good."

I had known as I made my shopping offer that it would link me to their lives on an everyday basis. Coral Upchurch wasn't ready to receive company until early afternoon, but she said she wished I would be her daily visitor. I looked forward to sitting across from her and asking casual questions. And she would send her mental librarian off to the stacks and he would come back with more just-remembered facts about Johnny Dace.

"Actually, I selfishly hope you *will* turn out to be good from the bottom up," said Aunt Charlotte. "It might restore some of my faith in human beings."

# XXV.

The dune beside Aunt Charlotte's boardwalk steps had become my meditation post and checkpoint for sanity. Here I could sit in the evenings above the clutch buried below the sand where 110 turtle embryos squirmed in their shells and know that, despite whatever weirdnesses I had undergone through the day, I was also part of the real day that was now ending. And this day linked me to the real days of the ancient world, when the turtles were already old news, and to a future world when I would be dead, when the whole human race might be dead, but these turtles might still be doing exactly what they had always done without any help from my extinguished species.

I felt like the turtles' guest. I wanted to be unobtrusive so as not to upset their progress. As they approached their hatching time, I talked to them in a wise and soothing murmur. I told them stories of what to expect, from the moment each used the little egg tooth on top of its snout to rip through its leathery shell and then stretch its body out straight ("Remember, you've been curled into a ball for two months, so you'll need to do this. And while you're wriggling around getting straightened out, your body will knock against the shells of your unhatched brothers and sisters and stimulate *their* breakthroughs . . .")

This July was a "two-moon month," Ed Bolton had informed me. Approximately every three years there would be two full moons in a calendar month. We'd had a full moon last Friday and we would have the second one on the last day of July. The second full moon was called a blue moon, which referred to a rare blue coloring, which usually wasn't seen, caused by high altitude dust particles. Tonight's moon was a waning gibbous—*gibbosus* was hunchback in Latin. The curve inside the gibbous moon did look like something hunched. But when the moon shrank to its last quarter the hunch would straighten up. Ed Bolton had given me the turtles and the moon. I would have liked to have been in his high school science classes. He made everything in the natural world sound like it mattered to him—as it would to you, if you saw it right.

How sickening that I had missed Billy Upchurch by one year! He could have answered the really crucial questions. I would have asked him, in gradual increments, what they talked about. Johnny may have told Billy about the Dace family hardship Coral Upchurch had referred to. And she said there had been a problem with Johnny Dace, too. If he wasn't in school in October, maybe he had been kicked out of school. He would have told Billy why he never took off his clothes at the beach, or made up an excuse. And I would love to know why Billy had picked him out when he was walking the entire length of the beach and back, something I had yet to do myself. I would have asked who spoke first. My guess was Billy, who was attracted to scowlers. And did Johnny invite him to the cottage or did Billy invite himself? And when they got there, what did they do together?

If the ghost-boy had lived he would be sixty-five, like Billy, unless he had died before Billy.

I still hadn't become used to the beauty of the island. You are one lucky boy, the foster mother had said, when it was firm that I was going to live with my aunt at the beach. I did feel lucky, though the feeling wasn't free of remorse and guilt. If Mom hadn't died, we would probably still be living in that awful upstairs apartment on Smoke Vine Road with the downstairs landlady from hell. Though Jewel was set in the midst of beautiful mountains, for me its very name would always evoke shame and poverty. Mom had to die so I could get out of Jewel and live at the beach. How sad that we hadn't shared beauty in any of our surroundings. Forsterville (pop. 10,000+) was a piedmont town with a furniture factory and railroad tracks, a few adulterated rivers and streams, and a manmade lake, where prominent citizens had summer cottages, fifteen miles away. The closest to a beautiful setting Mom and I had shared was the quiet cemetery on the outskirts of town with its cypresses and well-tended grass, where we could walk and she could inhale air that didn't smell of sawdust and chemicals and shellac. We strolled among the headstones—many of which bore the name of Forster, the founding family—and played our funeral and burial game. The clothes we would wear in our coffins, the hymns and psalms we wanted. ("We should probably attend church more often," Mom would say. "Then there would be more of a crowd at our funerals. But I don't think God grudges me my Sunday morning sleep-in.") Mom was cheerful and serene when we walked in the Forsterville cemetery.

Things would now be different between the ghost-boy and me. I knew that. Everything in his presence and posture said: *You summoned me. Here I am. Now what are we going to do?* But I had failed the test. I was certain he would not appear to me again. If only I had remembered the rules that were spread all over the ghost stories Wheezer and I used to devour. The living person was either up to the challenge or he was not. If you wished to keep the connection going with the ghost, you had to measure up to the moment of testing. Wheezer and I had often discussed it: if we were ever fortunate enough to meet a ghost, like in one of the stories we loved where the living person measured up, what would we do and say? We were always adding to our rules for ghosts.

"That is, for the ones you feel *deserve* your help," Wheezer once stipulated, "not the other kind." For the worthy ghosts, you had to stand your ground even if your legs were shaking and ask: What do you need? What can I do for you in the land of the living that you can no longer do for yourself? Is there a message you want conveyed to a living person? Is there a wrong that needs to be righted before you can rest in peace? If so, I'll be your errand boy.

"But how would you know the difference between a ghost worthy of your help and *the other kind*?" I asked Wheezer. He thought it over. "Maybe you wouldn't, at first," he said, "until your intuition kicked in. Then you'd feel either sought out or creeped out. If it's creeped out, you'd better cut and run."

But facing my ghost this morning I had felt sought out *and* creeped out. If only I had stood my ground and asked him, What do you want of me? What can I do for you in the land of the living that you can no longer do for yourself? Maybe if I hadn't cut and run I would have experienced an advanced stage of human consciousness.

I needed to ask Ed Bolton to explain more about the problem of time. In school we had been prepped with just enough rudimentary Einstein to unsettle us. Yes, boys and girls, after your brains develop some more you'll have to deal with concepts of time beyond the clock and calendar.

I had been zipping through too many kinds of time to keep track of: waking and dreaming time, outer and inner, since yesterday's dreaming of my mom opening the door of her beautiful apartment and telling me I had an older brother to this afternoon's meeting of a very old lady who was able to tell me the first and last names of the ghost I had seen that very morning.

# *XXII.*

*A*rchie and I were married ten years before we had Billy. We concluded we were going to be a childless couple, and to be honest we had a good old time. We went places we wouldn't have gone if we'd had small children, and we developed an intimacy that might not have flourished otherwise. I was just twenty when I married and quite ignorant and provincial in lots of ways. Archie was eighteen years older and he said it was like having a daughter and a lover all in one package. I'm not shocking you, am I, Marcus?"

"Oh, no. My mom was married a long time before I was born. Her husband was a lot older than her, too. He died before I was born." Not a single lie in those three bare statements. As long as I kept them bare.

"Are you hungry? Roberta has stocked my little minibar over there with nice things."

"I'm not really hungry. Could I get you something?"

"I'm not a great eater, but thank you." Her downward glance at the cigarette carton was barely a flicker.

"I wish you would go ahead and smoke."

"I'd much rather enjoy your company."

"You can enjoy us both. I've been around plenty of smokers." Wheezer's granny could count for at least twenty smokers. Because of his asthma, she did go outside to smoke, or into the bathroom with the exhaust fan turned on. Wheezer and I used to count how long she could get by without lighting up and she maxed out at forty-two minutes.

"Well, I'll keep it in mind. As soon as he walked in the door every summer, Billy would start lecturing me about quitting. And now look, he's jumped the gun on me. I told Roberta I needed to get myself another bad habit so I won't stick around forever. Enough is enough. Besides, I'm fascinated by death. I don't know whether there's an afterlife or not—I'm not a believer in a conventional heaven and hell—but I'm prepared to be surprised. How about you?"

"My mom said the only heaven and hell she believed in were right here on earth. I'm fascinated with death, too."

"At your age? Oh, forgive me. You lost your mother so recently."

"Do you ever wonder if, well, the dead have ways to get in contact with the living?"

"Archie has been gone forty-three years and he speaks to me every day. 'Let me do that,' he'll say, though of course he isn't there to do it anymore. Things I always did wrong, like folding up a grocery bag properly so it would lie flat. And I'll make the extra effort and do it his way. After Billy bailed out on me last winter, I tried to scold him into appearing. I wanted to see him again. Even though the last few years he'd gotten red from high blood pressure, just like Archie. But Billy was drop-dead gorgeous in his younger years. You know what, Marcus, with your permission I will have a cigarette."

I watched the tiny woman transform herself into a forties film star as she attended to the glamorous ritual of lighting up.

"The boy you were telling us about—did you ever see him?"

"The boy?"

"The one your husband thought was a bad influence on Billy. Johnny Dace?"

"Oh, I saw him only once, when Archie and I were looking for Billy on the beach. Archie decided they must have gone up to the Barbour cottage to do bad things, and we were debating whether we wanted to walk all the way to the north end or go back and get the car. Then we saw them walking back toward us and when they got closer Archie said, 'Please don't tell me that sorry-looking lout is Billy's wonderful new friend.'"

"How was he sorry-looking?"

"Oh, ruffianly and sort of . . . paltry. After Billy's great buildup."

"How did he look?"

"We never saw him close up. When Billy spotted us, he leaned over and said something to him and the boy spun around and headed back north. He was taller than Billy—Billy hadn't got his full growth yet—but that might have been because Billy was barefoot and the other boy was wearing shoes."

"What kind of shoes?"

"I couldn't say."

"Could they have been boots?"

"They could have been, I suppose. Billy told us his friend always wore his clothes on the beach, and never went in the water. Billy thought maybe he couldn't swim. Or he might not have owned a bathing suit, was Archie's opinion."

"Did he have on a shirt?"

"I think so, but Marcus, this was half a century ago." She turned away from me to responsibly exhale her smoke toward the ocean. "Lachicotte said you were intrigued by that unfortunate family. I wish I had more to tell you."

"It just seems wrong they were the only ones lost in that hurricane and they're never mentioned."

"Oh, but it was talked about at the time. Billy was quite distressed when we got the news from the Barbours. He kept saying, 'But he'd promised to come and visit me!' Archie said he'd never been glad of anyone's death except Hitler's but he confessed to being relieved we were spared the boy's visit."

The next time I rode my bike to Grief Cottage, I pictured the two friends walking south toward me. Billy Upchurch saying to his friend Johnny Dace when he spotted his parents walking toward them, "Oh, shit, here come my parents." Or did he say, "There's my mom and dad! Now I can introduce you!" And Johnny Dace would have said, "Count me out." Or something more ruffianly. And then spun around on his (shoe? boot?) heel and decamped. It was easier to do it from Johnny Dace's side. Of course he didn't want to meet Billy's parents. He wanted to escape being judged. How did he know they would judge him? Well, ever since he and his own parents had arrived to be charity occupants of the Barbour cottage, they must have felt some of the ways people like the Upchurches conveyed their judgments on people like them. I myself was more of a Dace set down in the midst of Upchurches than otherwise. I simply had more camouflage: my great-aunt was a respected local artist and had given herself the surname of the general of the Confederate army, and I had entered this island community with Lachicotte's seal of approval.

Recent events concerning the figure in the cottage had changed my perceptions. He was now two beings. There was the ghost-boy, the presence that I had sensed behind me on my first visit to Grief Cottage and that I had seen twice since, standing full-length in the doorway. And there was Johnny Dace, short-lived friend (and bad influence?) to Billy Upchurch. And the Johnny Dace who came to the beach with his parents and without a bathing suit.

After my last encounter with him, I altered my routine at Grief Cottage. I still crawled beneath the wire fence with all the warning signs and climbed the rickety stairs to the slanting porch. But I now sat *facing the door*, my back against one of the upright beams that propped up the roof. My old way of sitting with my back to the door had been so he could observe me without feeling threatened. But now I was the one who felt threatened. Better to face the door than to suddenly feel the grip of an unseen hand from behind.

Since I had flunked the test of standing my ground when he appeared to me, he may have, in his ghostly manner, established new rules for my appearances. Rule one: No more "showings" to the visitor. *I* had become the "nervous animal." We had reversed roles. Now he needed to ration his presence so as not to scare me off.

I continued to talk to him, however. I believed it still offered the best chance of maintaining the frequencies between us—if any remained. As before, I opened with the "safe" natural subjects: the ocean and the surroundings we shared, the current phase of the moon, the progress of the loggerhead embryos ("Ed Bolton, the retired science teacher, predicts they'll hatch the middle of next week . . ."). Then I filled him in on my recent routines ("My aunt had to go back and have a metal pin put in her wrist . . . Now she's started some secret project. I'm not allowed to enter her studio . . ."). Then I thought it worth a try to suddenly drop in my visits to Coral Upchurch. ("You never met her, but she's the mother of Billy Upchurch, the boy you made friends with when your family was staying in the beach cottage before the hurricane? Do you remember Billy Upchurch? Now I have to tell you something sad. Billy died this past winter. He was sixty-five. He was having the batteries changed on his pacemaker, that's a device invented after your time, they plant it in your chest and it regulates your heartbeat . . .")

I did feel some kind of agitation in the air between me and the empty doorway. What had set the agitation going? Was it sympathy for Billy or revolt at the mention of Billy's name, or was it exasperation with the tiresome boy on the rotting porch cluttering up the silence with "trues"?

# XXIII.

Aunt Charlotte and I were having our one meal of the day together. "His mother told me Billy Upchurch was drop-dead gorgeous. Did you ever see him?"

"Of course I saw him. That first summer when I was fixing up this place he was over here every day of his visit. He was enthralled by all the construction going on. He couldn't stop gabbing with the hunky young men doing the work. He was certainly good-looking. He was very attentive to me, too, though I knew he didn't swing that way and he knew I knew."

"Did his mother know, do you think?"

"I would guess like a good Southern lady she saw only the parts of him she wished to see."

"She wasn't in a wheelchair then, was she?"

"Oh, no. She was all over the place. Then about ten years ago she was going to fly up to D.C. to visit Billy and when she got to the airport she just crumpled and had to be carried out. Her spine had disintegrated. Lachicotte says she can still put herself to bed and doesn't need to be helped onto the toilet. You really are a good egg, Marcus, not only shopping for them but sitting with her every afternoon."

"She's one of the most fascinating people I've ever met."

"Have you known many old people?"

"I forget she's old. We talk about interesting things—she's doing archaeology on herself to get beyond her name and the way people see her. She won't let you call her Mrs. Upchurch and now she's working on getting beyond the 'Coral.'"

"You're making me feel I've missed something."

"I haven't known many old people. Before I met Coral, my image of an old person was our landlady's mother. Her name was Mrs. Harm. That really was her name. And her daughter, who was our landlady from hell, her name was Mrs. Wicket. Mom and I called them Wicked and Harm."

"Why was she a landlady from hell?"

"You really want to hear?"

"Wicked and Harm—who could resist?"

"Well, when we moved into this upstairs apartment on Smoke Vine Road—this was in Jewel, the place we lived before I came here—Mrs. Wicket made this deal with Mom. She would take fifty dollars off our rent every month if I would stay downstairs with her mother on weekday afternoons after school. This gave Mrs. Wicket some time to herself and saved her from having to pay for someone to be with Mrs. Harm until six-thirty, when the next home help came. Old Mrs. Harm wasn't much trouble. She just lay in her bedroom with her oxygen tank and her TV. And she had on a diaper in case—you know. I got used to doing my homework to the sound of TV. It was one of those channels that played the same watered-down music, on and on. I had to go in regularly and check to see that she hadn't yanked her oxygen tubes out of her nose, and I had these numbers to call if there was an emergency. I'm not sure she knew I was a different person from Mrs. Wicket. Lots of times, the home help evening shift was late and I was supposed to stay until she came. So sometimes Mom and I didn't eat supper until eight or even later."

"That is taking advantage."

"Well, there's more. Mrs. Wicket's niece came to visit and Mrs. Wicket told Mom I had earned a little holiday and that her niece would sit with Mrs. Harm in the afternoons. But when we got our next rent bill, it was thirty dollars more. The niece had only stayed four days, but Mom said there was no use wasting time doing the math. It was ungenerous of Mrs. Wicket, Mom said, but she was our landlady and we didn't have a lease. But even when I was back on the job next month's bill was still thirty dollars more. Mom went down to speak to Mrs. Wicket and when she came back she was really upset. The landlady told her the cost of living had gone up and she couldn't spare that thirty dollars anymore. Mom said then maybe she didn't need me anymore, but Mrs. Wicket said, 'If Marcus stops coming I'm afraid I'll have to raise the rent.'"

"This makes me so mad I want to explode."

"It all worked out eventually."

"*How?*"

"Mrs. Harm died and I lost my job, and then we only had to pay the increased rent until Mom was killed. You might say fate worked it out for us. Mrs. Wicket came out of it well because she had some kind of limited income insurance which reimbursed her for the month we hadn't paid and until she found new tenants. My guardian ad litem told me she tried to get the state to reimburse her as well."

"Marcus, it grieves me to think how many more unhappy stories you are sitting on." And Aunt Charlotte did look grieved. She spoke like someone who was hurting because she cared for me. Heartened by this, I was able to recall something else.

"Believe it or not there was a good part to that night. When Mom came upstairs and told me about Mrs. Wicket's meanness, we both flew into a rage—well, a mixture of rage and despair. I really lost it and called our landlady every disgusting name I could think of, and then I started calling down curses, all the horrible things I wished on her, and after a while Mom came over and hugged me and told me that was enough. Then she said, 'Because we are poor, shall we be vicious?' and went to make us some cocoa. At first I thought it was a question she had addressed to me, but when she came back with the cocoa she said it was out of some violent play written even before Shakespeare's time. She hadn't read the play, but this night school teacher she admired so much was always giving them famous quotes that might help them on future tests. And Mom said the quote stayed with her because it gave her a morale boost when she was beating up on herself for being poor. She said maybe it had been selfish to bring me into the world when she had so little to offer, but nevertheless she had wanted me more than anything in her whole life. She said I was her great prize."

AUNT CHARLOTTE AND I had moved outside to the porch. A balmy evening breeze was blowing across the dunes and the tide was on its way out. The sunbathers and families had packed up their things and departed, leaving only strollers and owners walking their dogs. There was no leash-free "dog hour" in the evening, which I thought was a shame. Barrett was probably back at the Navy brig where his prisoner-trainer would be putting the final touches on his skills. I had been down to check on the turtles: the thermocouple stuck in the sand had registered no rise in temperature. Aunt Charlotte had said to leave the dishes for later and hopped on ahead to the porch, calling over her shoulder for me to bring out another bottle of wine. Ordinarily, since she had begun her secret project, she hopped straight back to her studio immediately after supper, but tonight she was being sociable. Maybe she felt sorry for me after my sad story.

"Oh, I forgot," she said when I joined her with the fresh bottle. She had arranged herself to accommodate her casts: the little table that held her bottle and glass on the left where she could reach them, her left leg propped straight ahead on a stool. "Lachicotte phoned while you were next door. He said to tell you he's booked you for the school bus. School starts the third Monday in August. Do you realize, Marcus, you'll be in school before my casts are off."

"We'll have a celebration."

"Let's wait until we're sure I have something to celebrate."

My heart clenched at the mention of school. So far I had stayed on top of the first summer of my new life. Though recent days had been demanding, I had so far been able to handle everything on the schedule: turtle check, followed by early morning bike ride to Grief Cottage, where I worked at building back my credibility with the ghost-boy, then home to do general housework, get the shopping list from Roberta, bike to the store, deliver order to Roberta in the kitchen, a solitary lunch, sometimes eaten on the beach beside the turtles, then laundry—if any. (I did worry about the state of Aunt Charlotte's sheets inside the off-limit studio, but refrained from inquiring.) Next came my afternoon visit with Coral Upchurch, if she was feeling up to it, then supper with Aunt Charlotte, washing up and putting away, evening meditation beside the turtle clutch, unpacking more boxes (if in the mood), then bed, thoughts, dreams, sleeping, and waking to the tides. I was managing everything on the list, and so far keeping enough of a wary balance between inner and outer happenings to stay in the realm people called sanity.

School would be another thing. School would mean judgment again. It was one thing to try to please a great-aunt who was more or less stuck with me, and visit an old lady who fascinated me, and pursue a precarious relationship with a dead boy, but being reminded that soon I would be thrown back into that cauldron of merciless peers made my spirit shrink.

"You know," Aunt Charlotte mused, "the Internet has its upside and its downside. The upside is I can sit in front of my laptop and go room by room through the great museums of the world. I can loiter in front of a picture as long as I please without someone blocking my view or saying something stupid or hurrying me on. I can replenish my wine and art supplies without leaving the house. The downside is that all I have to do to spoil a day is to type 'wrist sprain, stage 3' into that little rectangle on the screen and have instant access to all the less than ideal ways the rest of my life can turn out."

# XXVIII.

When I had been going through airport security before my flight to Aunt Charlotte's—the first airplane ride of my life—the lady in front of me got into an argument with the official who wanted her to open her suitcase. Something inside it had looked suspicious when it passed through the x-ray machine. The suitcase was now open on the counter, and the official asked her to take everything out. "You mean I am to lay out my personal items in front of everybody?" "Yes, ma'am, it will be neater if you do it." "This is highly irregular," she said, "I have never been asked to do this before in my life. I can assure you there is nothing dangerous in this bag. Do I look like a terrorist?" "Please, ma'am, just remove the items and we'll locate the problem." "What if I refuse?" she asked. "Then I can't let you into the boarding area for your flight." He had tuned his patience down a notch. "Very well," she conceded, and in exaggerated slow motion began to lay out the contents of the bag. Faded pink nightgown and worn terrycloth slippers, a yellowing white bra, underpants also in yellowing white, a scruffy stuffed animal that looked like a rat in a red vest, a magnifying glass, a hairbrush with hairs in it, a toiletry bag—"Wait," he stopped her, "Can we have a look in that bag?" "You're running this show," she said with a scornful smile, handing it over for him to ferret out the culprit. "I'm afraid we'll have to confiscate these, ma'am." "Be my guest," she said, repacking her suitcase as slowly as she could. "They are harmless embroidery scissors. Maybe your wife will enjoy them."

I often thought of that lady's things when I was unpacking yet another box from my former life. Laid out "in front of everybody," many of the contents would look embarrassing or mystifying to others. For me, an occasional item in a box would restore a memory; another would shed light into some obscure corner of my past. But on the whole I would be glad when the final box, packed by a social worker back in Jewel, was emptied and stomped flat and put outside for the island's trash collection.

Weeks ago I had concluded there had been no system in the packing of these boxes. If I had been the social worker I would have gone room by room. I would have packed all the books together, all the woman's clothes, the boy's things, the kitchen stuff, the bathroom stuff. After all, it was only three rooms, counting the bathroom. But having grown used to finding toothbrushes and kitchen items packed together, children's books on top of elastic stockings and a shabby coat, I expected to find discrepant bedfellows in each new box.

In tonight's box was Mom's heavily underlined paperback of Marcus Aurelius's *Meditations*, which she always kept rubber-banded with the "serious" hardback that was in Greek on the left side with a stranger's interlinear translation. And underneath those was an eight-by-ten framed photograph of my coiffed and stylish grandmother, who I now also thought of as

Brenda, the older sister, who had referred to my great-aunt as "Crazy Charlotte." And beneath those was a furry black bear in a gray hoodie—which had reminded me of the lady's rat in the red coat. At the bottom of the box, its sides buttressed by crumpled newspaper, was a toy lumber truck my mom had loved as a child. Once it had carried six-inch logs of real wood, but all but one of them had disappeared by the time it became mine. I had loaded its truck bed with toy cars, or twigs piled like logs, and once, briefly, a live frog who jumped off in a huff and vanished into the shrubbery. Later, the black bear in his hoodie rode in it, sitting sideways against the one remaining log. GASTON & SONS LUMBER was emblazoned on both sides of the truck in gold letters against a background of forest green.

Gaston & Sons Lumber had been founded by Samuel Gaston, my great-great-grandfather, in Cass, West Virginia, and after that I hadn't paid attention whenever Mom tried to take me through her side of my forebears. She must have figured I needed her forebears all the more since for all intents and purposes I was a bastard. For the summer of my twelfth year, which would have been next summer, she had been planning a trip for us to ride the Cass Railroad up to Back Allegheny Mountain, so I could get a feel for the land I came out of. And at a later date, when I had reached a "responsible age," she had promised to tell me about the other side, the side of the man in the photo in her drawer. Regarding the responsible-age thing she had been right. I certainly had failed to be responsible at age nine, when I showed Wheezer the photo in the drawer. Now I was left to guess what age she'd had in mind for the responsible me—not that it mattered now because it was never going to happen.

Marcus Aurelius, who I was named after, had been three when his father died. Later Marcus was to write that he had learned "manliness without ostentation" from what he had heard and remembered about that father. In those days, a father acknowledged a child as his own by lifting the infant up from the hearth in a special ceremony, which I thought was a wonderful idea. Marcus's father had lived long enough to do that. Marcus's mother stayed faithful to her husband's memory. She had always been rich, and died young without remarrying. Marcus remembered her in his meditations as his model for "piety, generosity, refraining from wrongdoing, simplicity in life, and distancing herself from the ways of the rich." I liked that phrase: *distancing herself from the ways of the rich.*

After his father died, Marcus was adopted, raised, and educated by his grandfather, from whom, Marcus writes, "I learned courtesy and serenity of temper." At seventeen, Marcus was adopted by the emperor, whose wife was Marcus's aunt. The emperor had no sons of his own and named Marcus as his successor. Marcus later wrote of his adoptive father that "all men recognized in him a mature and finished personality that was impervious to flattery and entirely capable of ruling both himself and others." I also liked the idea of a mature and finished personality, and wondered if I would have one someday.

When Marcus was forty he became emperor and ruled wisely until he died of the pestilence at fifty-nine.

Alec Guinness's mother refused to tell him who his father was. Later, when he was an old man, he confided to a friend that she probably hadn't known. A snob, she gave him the surname of a famous brewery family on whose yacht she had once been a guest. However, it was a banker who had been sixty-four when Alec was born who paid for his schooling and visited him often in the guise of an uncle. Alec was ashamed of his mother and stayed angry with her all his life. She sent him away to boarding school when he was five, paid for by the banker. Alec loved his school. When he got his first acting job at seventeen, his mother showed up intoxicated at the stage door and asked him for money.

When Aunt Charlotte gave over her bedroom to me she left it so hospitably bare that, as I've mentioned, it took me longer than it should have to realize it had been her room. When I entered it for the first time back in May, I faced a double bed with two views of the ocean, front and side, a table with a lamp on it and a straight-backed chair tucked under it, an empty bookcase, and a bureau with four drawers. Nothing hung on the walls, which had been freshly painted an off-white color that I would discover took on the yellow of clear mornings, a pearly gray on overcast days, and changed into a lavender-blue as it grew dark outside.

On the table that served as my desk were Mom's GED test books, which I had been studying, and the island histories authored by two local ladies who remembered the days when turtle eggs were gathered for fun breakfasts. The bookshelf, which Aunt Charlotte proudly admitted she had carpentered herself, along with the ones in her studio, was too long without a middle support and sagged in the middle. So far I had refrained from displaying any of my possessions above the top shelf, but the Gaston & Sons Lumber truck was the first thing I judged worthy. It was part of my heritage and also it diverted attention from the sag.

I felt conflicted about the black bear in the hoodie; my first impulse was to toss it. Eleven was too old to be holding on to a toy bear, though it wasn't so long ago when I insisted on having him. I was not at my best that day and it hurt to remember it now. Mom and I had been in the new Walmart in Jewel, buying my school supplies. When you were on a budget like ours, you calculated the difference between a $1.99 and a $2.39 box of pencils, and decided that it would be foolish to pay forty cents more just because Batman was on that box. I was accustomed to reading my mother's face and I knew how almost every shopping trip turned into an ordeal for her because she was one of those accursed "crossovers" in society who knew what the best was but couldn't afford it herself. Sometimes she would let resentment get the upper hand and point out to me someone "trash-shopping" in the stores we shopped in by necessity. ("Look at her, she just snatches up something without looking at the price and drops it in her basket.") On that day when I was not at my best, we were already in line at a checkout counter when I noticed a bin full of black bears in hoodies. They had probably been placed there strategically for people like me who were following a parent through the checkout line. I plucked one off the top of the pile and fell in love. He was so soft. He smelled so new. "Isn't he adorable?" I demanded. Mom looked at me rubbing him against my cheek. After scarcely a beat she asked: "Would . . . you like it?"

For now, in honor of my mother, the bear got to ride in the truck. Grandma *alias* fault-finding sister Brenda went facedown into a lower bureau drawer, not the upper drawer that held Mom's tin box with the only photo of my real dad and other cherished items: snapshots we had taken of each other with those throwaway cameras, Mom's supervisor's badge from Forster's Furniture, old Mr. Forster's *To Whom It May Concern* letter, which got Mom her nice first job in Jewel. It was a letter of high praise and must have cost the old man some moments of soul-searching, considering that he wrote it while his grandson was still in recovery from her son's brutal beating.

The two Marcus Aurelius volumes joined the other books on my desk. In the scholarly bilingual hardback, whoever had handwritten their own translation between the lines stopped halfway through the book. Midway down a page of Greek, the penciled interlinear translation broke off at the end of a paragraph.

The same paragraph on the English side of the page completely balked you with its antiquarian twists and turns:

> What then there can be amid such murk and nastiness,
> and in so ceaseless an ebbing of substance and of time,
> of movement and things moved, that deserves to be
> greatly valued or to excite our ambition in the least, I
> cannot even conceive.

The unknown person's penciled translation was simple and clear.

> In all this murk and mire, then, in all this ceaseless
> flow of being and time, of changes imposed and
> changes endured, I can think of nothing that is worth
> prizing highly or pursuing seriously.

# XXIX.

*B*efore Aunt Charlotte's accident, I told her I would learn to use her digital camera and take new pictures of Grief Cottage. The plan had been to bring her up to date on its dereliction so she could incorporate it into her future paintings—if she chose to. How my new photos would affect her new paintings I hadn't been sure. Either she would be inspired by more ruination ("How sad! Do you think I can capture this added sadness in pigment?"), or she would be turned off by it ("No, this has gone too far, Marcus. If I painted it like this it would be a Halloween cartoon").

After she came home with her casts, I decided to put off even the mention of it. It would be cruel to hand over a bunch of new photos—assuming they turned out well—to send her rushing off to her studio to see if inspiration struck when she was no longer able to control a brush.

The other reason I had decided against taking the photos concerned the ghost-boy. It might set back our relationship. I had to base my behavior on how I would follow my instincts with living people, and I thought he might feel threatened if he saw me outside, clicking away at the cottage that had sheltered him for fifty years. Was I trying to take something from him? I had heard of those tribes who wouldn't let you take pictures of them because you would steal their souls.

Anyway, that was how I had reasoned up until now. Since I had failed to measure up to our last confrontation, my old precautions no longer applied. His spirit still remained inside the cottage, but he had turned away. Maybe he heard me, maybe not. Perhaps he had removed himself to the collapsing upper floor, where the roof had caved in to make him skylights. He could see and hear the birds without hearing me. The worst had happened to him a long time ago and some part of him had endured. This part had managed to exist without friends and without hope. And then I had weaseled into his space and offered false hope. All the ghost-boy desired now was to get outside the range of any more overtures from the coward-boy and be at peace with what he'd had before.

After making room for the things I had chosen to keep out of the latest box, I revisited my mom's memorials in the tin box. The tin box had been with me since she died—except while I was in the foster home. During that interim, I entrusted it to William, my ad litem. I didn't want the curious foster mom or some nosy child to be rifling through its contents—or stealing something—while I was at school.

First I studied for the umpteenth time the photo of the man Mom said was my dad. I took it into the bathroom to compare my face with his in Aunt Charlotte's only mirror. Did the picture, which Aunt Charlotte said had been cut from a school yearbook, reveal any more secrets since I had last studied it? It did appear we shared the same arched ("quizzical") eyebrows and wide-apart eyes, but that might just seem so because Aunt Charlotte had suggested it. The man's face looked too mature for a high school yearbook, so it must have been college. Compared to his, my face looked undeveloped and embarrassingly open. His face above the coat and tie was still the face of a young man but it had shut down in some way. Aunt Charlotte had said my mouth was like his when I was annoyed, but it was hard to "look annoyed" on demand in the mirror. My mouth was fuller than his and slightly puckered, like someone expecting a kiss. His lips were set in a thin derisive curl as if serving notice to the photographer that this was a crappy waste of time.

Then I reread for the umpteenth time old Mr. Forster's *To Whom It May Concern* accolade to Mom. (". . . this young widow . . . exemplary work habits . . . bringing up a son on her own . . . uncompromising values . . .")

For the first time cynicism raised its ugly head. If I had been the grandfather of a boy who had almost lost an eye, who had stopped breathing, wouldn't I praise to the skies a factory worker whose son had done the deed in order to get her out of town?

Next I looked through the photos Mom had chosen to save from those we had taken over the years. Until now her small collection hadn't excited me much, because she was still in the world and we expected to be taking many more pictures. As it turned out, our bleak time in Jewel had offered nothing we thought worth memorializing on film. The photos she had saved had all been taken back in Forsterville. Most of them were of me: "graduating" from kindergarten in my white cap and gown; standing on a stone wall looking down at her like I owned her; caught studying unaware in my pajamas under lamplight (her favorite). We had become expert with our Kodak throwaway cameras. Learned when to use the flash, when to move someone out of direct sun, when they were overshadowed. The sunshine was never too harsh at the Forsterville Cemetery because we walked there after my school day or in summer evenings after Mom's shift. I particularly liked the one I had taken from the top of the hill looking down on all the graves. It had just rained and there was a glowing mist over the landscape—it looked almost like a painting. There were several shots I had taken of Mom, sitting in front of some upright gravestones at the top of the hill, hugging her skirt close to her knees, her head tilted, smiling shyly to herself.

"Why don't you move over to that weeping angel and stand next to it?" I asked.

"I like it here," she said, patting the ground in front of her. "The view is nicest from up here."

"But *I'm* the one who's supposed to be picking the views!"

To oblige me, she stood by the weeping angel for a couple of shots. But either her eyes were closed or the body language was wrong: she had not kept those pictures. She did look best on top of the hill, though that whole upper section was filled exclusively with Forster headstones.

"Well, of course," she said, when I pointed this out. "They were the first people to get here, so naturally they picked the choicest spot."

THE ISLAND MARKET where I shopped every day stocked those throwaway cameras. If you turned in your camera by five P.M. you could have your photos back by noon the next day. It was popular with islanders and tourists who couldn't be bothered to drive to the mainland for the one-hour service.

I bought two cameras with twenty-four exposures each and set out the next morning with them tucked in my saddlebag. It was too chancy to wait until Aunt Charlotte got her cast off and I had mastered the complexities of her digital camera. The cottage was falling apart atom by atom, minute by minute. I would kick myself if I showed up one morning to find it razed to the ground or cordoned off by a sizzling electric fence. OUT! THIS MEANS YOU, MARCUS. YOU HAD YOUR CHANCE.

For a start I took distance shots of the cottage. Sky above and behind, dunes on either side, roofs of other cottages receding to the south, a wide expanse of empty beach in the foreground. If I angled the lens craftily I could make the wire fence all but invisible. From this distance my subject could pass for a tumbledown cottage rather than a hazardous wreck. I stood at the water's edge, near the spot where I had met Barrett. For a last panoramic shot, I removed my shoes and stepped back into the water up to the line of my biking shorts until I could include the mirrory surf.

As I was wheeling my bike toward the cottage to hide it in its usual spot behind a dune, a figure appeared atop this dune and began a cautious descent. Waving his arms for balance, he partly stumbled, partly slid down the steep incline until he pitched sideways into the waiting spikes of a Spanish bayonet. His sun hat flew off and rolled downhill ahead of him. I was close enough to hear the outraged string of expletives though not the specific swear words. Now he was scrambling to his feet and patting his behind for damage. It was Charlie Coggins, the realtor. He looked around furtively to see if anyone had witnessed his disgrace. I jumped on my bike and pedaled in the other direction so he wouldn't know I had seen. Shit. I should have come an hour earlier.

By the time I approached him openly, walking alongside my bike, he had brushed off his pants, shaken the sand out of his docksiders, and restored his sun hat to his head. He had his back to me, surveying his real estate, so I called out a good morning in order not to startle him.

"It's Lachicotte's young friend, isn't it? You've gotten so brown. Did you ever tell me your name?"

"Marcus."

I indicated the empty spot in the sand where his strange land-and-water vehicle had been parked last time. "Where's your amphibian today?"

"At home in its custom-built hangar. I use it mainly to impress out-of-town clients. I drove up by the road in the company car. Took a right smart spill getting down that blasted dune. You want to avoid those evil Spanish bayonets at all costs."

"My aunt already warned me about those."

"The artist. Broke her arm, right? Last time we met, you were going to come back with a camera and take some pictures for her."

"It was her wrist, but it's still in a cast." No use complicating matters with the ankle as well. "Today I brought some cameras. The cottage is getting worse by the day."

"Tell me about it! When I hear a siren at night, you know what I pray for? That some firebug will have burned it to the ground before the trucks get there. Every time I come here I run through my litany of 'why didn't I's: Why didn't I sell it to the highest bidder before the roof caved in? Why didn't I keep the empty lot next to it and donate the cottage to the Historical Society, claim my gift deduction, and let *them* deal with property taxes and hazardous structure policies and erosion engineers' fees until they got fed up and torched it themselves and had the state put up a nice historical marker? Why didn't Pop sell it back in the sixties after he bought it from the people who made a mess of the renovation and then ran out of cash? What were we at Coggins Realty thinking? That it was going to magically reconstruct itself one night while we were sleeping, and we'd wake up to find the pristine new cottage as it looked in 1804, with the *shoreline* of 1804, and assessed at twentieth-century value?"

"I thought I'd better get some pictures while it's still standing—so Aunt Charlotte will have something to go by when she can paint again."

"What kind of camera do you use?"

I took my throwaways out of the saddlebag and showed him.

"These do everything you need if you know how to use them. You can get the prints back from the island market over-night. I brought two cameras so I'd be sure to have enough exposures."

"And what pictures were you planning to take?"

"I thought some close-ups from inside the fence—maybe a few from up on the porch."

"I'm guessing this won't be the first time you've crawled under that fence."

"It will be more official now you're here."

"I suppose you expect me to accompany you in your trespassing."

I didn't, but I saw the advantages. If Charlie Coggins trespassed with me under the fence and up on the porch, he would serve both as my buffer and my cover. If the ghost-boy was watching from some new vantage point, he would know not to "count" this visit even if we had still been on good terms. He would know to remain invisible because I came in the company of the realtor who must have inspected this cottage on many occasions over the years. And the bonus was that with Charlie Coggins in tow I could brave the inside of the cottage with no fear of being surprised by more ghost than I could handle.

# XXX.

*I* need not have feared. The ghost-boy was so not there. Charlie Coggins held my cameras while I crawled under the fence, then I held his hat and sunglasses while he shimmied under with some grunts and groans.

I went first up the rickety steps. "I always hold on to this part of the railing. And watch the porch slant, it comes as a surprise."

"I see you've become a pro at this."

On the porch I snapped the front of the cottage with its gaping windows and door. I used the flash since the east side was still in shadow. "I've never gone inside," I said. "But with you here I think it would be a shame not to."

"I haven't been inside for a good long while . . . but for Pete's sake, test every board before you put any weight on it. Lachicotte would have my . . . well, on a platter if you were to get hurt."

I paused to snap some close-ups of the doorless doorway. These were for me in the future more than for anybody else. In my future, when I came across these photos, they would bring it all back: *When I was eleven I saw a boy standing in that space—his hands were braced against the sides—I saw the ridges of his knuckles and his eyes like dark raisins—he looked straight at me—this really did happen.*

As I wound the film forward, I asked Charlie Coggins why they hadn't replaced the door. "Wouldn't it help keep people out?"

"Not when everybody's already been in and removed everything of value. The last door we put in was, let's see, ten years ago . . . fifteen? I'd have to check. Time gets cagey as you proceed in life. The other day my doc asked me could I recall offhand when my last colonoscopy was and I said five years ago. When he looked it up in my file it was eleven."

"What did they remove of value?"

"Faucet fixtures, copper pipes, all the old cypress wood paneling, the wooden latches and the original iron hardware, a toilet . . ."

*"A toilet?"*

"Not everyone can afford a new toilet. They took the sink, too. Mind you, this wasn't all done in one trip. Just covert truckloads on moonless nights over the years."

"Couldn't you have locked the house?"

"We did. They stole the locks. Before we gave up on doors we must have installed at least half a dozen. Pop was still alive when we put in the last one—whoa, that makes it over *twenty* years ago. Like I said, time can get cagey. Pop said, 'Might as well let in the clean ocean breeze. See what it can accomplish. The whole thing might fall down sooner, quicker, and cleaner.' Of course the Historical Society was still making big noises about fund drives and restoration. But the money just wasn't there. So Pop said put the high wire fence around it with threatening legal signs and let nature have its way. With beachfront values rising we were sure someone would come along and snap up those prime lots and take care of the demolition themselves. Only they didn't and then it was the nineties and then the millennium—and here we are."

We were actually inside. At last I had crossed the threshold. But if I had expected any thrill from Grief Cottage, it didn't come. The room was about as unhaunted as any room could get. It was as though by entering with another person I had canceled its ghost-aura. Sand intermixed with debris had piled high into the room's corners, and cobwebs swagged from its timbers and walls. Droppings from animals speckled the bare floor. A spotlight of sun penetrated a broken place in the roof and revealed the almost transparent skin of a snake. The only other snakeskin I had ever seen had been hooked on a bush in Wheezer's grandmother's backyard. "Look, you can even see where its jaw was!" he cried. "It probably rubbed against that bush to start the process and finally crawled out of its own mouth!"

I rotated in a slow circle, snapping flash exposures. In the middle of the room was a boarded-up fireplace whose mantelpiece had been ripped out. "Yeah," said Charlie Coggins, "that was a lovely mantel, a local carpenter's pride. Wonder where it's living now? Oh, see the blue paint on the facing of the doorway we just came through? I'll tell you a little story about that blue paint. Has anyone told you about Ole Plat-eye? No? Ole Plat-eye is a spirit the Gullahs are absolutely terrified of. Some of them still paint the inside of their doors with this sky-blue color to keep him out. Only it's not always a him, it can be part dog or cow or woman with extra limbs and a big eye hanging down from the center of its forehead. It's one of those completely malevolent and unredeemable spirits."

"Why is it unredeemable?"

"To be honest I don't know. Maybe it's got some unfinished business of the kind that can never be finished. You'd have to ask a Gullah."

"I don't know what a Gullah is."

"Gullahs are the descendants of the slaves who worked in the rice fields down here. They still keep up the old African traditions."

"Did any of them ever live in this cottage?"

"No, they had their own cabins near the owners' cottages. When Pop was selling off the last of those slave cabins in the seventies, I used to see these same blue door facings when we went inside. I painted that blue for the best Halloween party that ever got thrown on this island. Right here in this cottage. Nineteen sixty-eight. Sundown to sunup. The mantel was still here and the toilet and most of the fixtures. We had a band, I was on drums. The girls made a wicked punch. One showoff actually came as Old Plat-eye, with three legs and a disgusting eyeball on a string Scotch-taped to his forehead but we made him take off his costume before he was allowed to pass through the door. Honoring the spirit of the night, my blue paint and all. After the paint had dried, I rubbed it down with steel wool to make it look old, like in the slave cabins. A lot of people still remember that party."

"Can we go up those stairs?"

"I'd rather you didn't. Well, if you're super careful. Last time I went up it was already hazardous, but you're a light fellow. But test *every* stair before you put any weight on it and hold on to the wall. You be the canary in the mine and I'll creep along in your footsteps. You'll find a mess up there. When they were boarding up the south wall after that porch fire, a lot of junk got stashed upstairs and nobody ever took it to the dump."

"You mean the porch fire during Hurricane Hazel?"

"Oh right, you're interested in that family that got swept away. But after the hurricane and the fire, the Barbours sold the cottage and the new owners were going to rebuild it and use it as a vacation home, but then they decided not to and put it back on the market. The next buyers didn't even pretend they wanted to live in it. They were looking for a quick flip. You know, strip it down, clean it out, and resell at a profit. They got as far as bulldozing and leveling the ground where the burnt porch had been and boarding up the south wall. Then they ran out of money and Pop bought it back as an investment. I had to get all this information from Pop's files, seeing as I was only two years old when Hazel hit."

"But didn't they think it was a cigarette that started the fire?"

"Maybe it was a cigarette, maybe not. Folks can't tolerate loose ends—they've got to tie up a story. Pop said the fire could just as well have started *after* the hurricane had passed, because who was paying attention? Everybody was busy picking up the pieces of their own properties."

"It's too bad those flipping people didn't do a better job closing off the south side. Those shingles without any windows in them make it look so blind and sad."

"They ran out of money, like I said. The shingles you see now were a cosmetic afterthought, courtesy of Coggins Realty. I put them up myself. The flipping people, as you call them, had just tacked up sheets of tar paper any old how on the south side of the house before they went belly up. We couldn't leave it like that, it'd put off any buyer, so I found some weathered cypress shingles that would fit in with the rest of the old houses and nailed them up tastefully. I was still in high school, just learning the business—Hey, hey, *hey*! Watch that step!"

He had gripped my arm so hard it hurt. "Look at that! The riser has cracked down the middle. A heavier person could have fallen right through. Son, I'm not sure this is a good idea."

"I'm fine. We'll just be extra careful." We were halfway up now. I was determined to see the upstairs.

He was right. It was a mess. There was nothing you wanted to waste a photo on. It revived unhappy memories of some of the places Mom and I had looked at when we were apartment-hunting in Jewel. "They haven't even cleaned up after the last tenant," Mom would say. "It amazes me how inconsiderate people can be." Nevertheless, I snapped a few pictures so I could finish off the roll and start on the second camera.

"None of these rooms have doors," I said.

"Well, they did when the last people slept in them. Doors are very easy to make off with, all you need is a flat-blade screwdriver. There are places that sell old doors and windows exclusively for fancy prices. The whole layout of this cottage has been compromised. It's more noticeable up here where things went truly awry. Of course I wouldn't point this out to a potential buyer."

"How has it been compromised?"

"For a start, the stairs would have made way more sense on the north side."

"Why didn't the builders think of that?"

"The original builders had a simple, pure plan. Four rooms on one floor with an oceanside porch. H-shaped chimney in the center of the house. It had to warm all four rooms because the rice planters' families stayed into November. Kitchen was to the back, separated from the house by a breezeway. The kitchen had its own chimney. Then came the makeovers of the successive owners. 'Let's build another porch and add a bedroom. Let's add two bedrooms. Let's incorporate the kitchen into the main house. Let's convert the outhouse with its breezeway into an indoor bathroom at the end of a hall. Let's put in an upper floor. Oh, dear, the previous owners have used up the north side with those added-on ground floor bedrooms, so we'll have to break through the roof on the *south* side and put the staircase there.' This may be the earliest cottage still standing on the island, but its vernacular lines have been completely compromised."

He had recounted the compromises so vividly that you could see them piling up, mistake upon mistake, until all that was left was the present ruin we were standing in.

"Are there any cottages left that haven't been compromised?"

"Oh, yes. One's even got a National Register marker—it's been kept up beautifully and added to responsibly. It still serves as a rental house, though the owners are very particular. We are honored to have it on our books. And there's your neighbor's house, which has stayed in the same family since it was built. But the late Mr. Upchurch committed an atrocity, hiding those indigenous brick footing columns behind a painted trellis. And then the old lady had that unsightly ramp built—not that it's her fault she's in a wheelchair. But it can be ripped out easily enough when the time comes. She's a real piece of work. You met her yet?"

"We're friends."

"Ah. Well, then, give her my best regards."

He undoubtedly would have said more about Coral Upchurch if I had said less.

"You can take a picture of the oceanfront room, but you're not going in there. Before the fire, was there a nice dormer window on the south wall, but it was so damaged they sheared it off when they were taking off the burnt porch. Okay, take a photo, but do *not* step into that room. I want to get you out of here without falling through any floors. As you can see, the other upstairs rooms are so piled with trash they're not worth a photo. I hadn't realized how far gone these floors are. Let's see if we can make it downstairs without any broken limbs and we'll finish our cottage crawl with a look at the kitchen. Happily, none of the owners covered over its lovely brick floors, from the days when people still cooked in their fireplaces, and so far no thief has come up with the right tools to dig out those bricks. You won't find any more bricks like those unless you visit the brick collection at the Charleston Museum."

# XXXI.

"What's a colonoscopy?"

"Something you won't need for a while. Who's having one?" Balanced on her right foot, Aunt Charlotte was extracting a container of yogurt from the refrigerator with her left hand, which already had a banana in it.

"Charlie Coggins, the realtor, was using it to explain how time plays tricks on you when you get older. He thought he'd had one five years ago but it turned out it was eleven."

"Where did you run into him?"

"I went up to Grief Cottage to take some photos for you. He was there, and we went on a tour inside the house. He called it our cottage crawl."

"You went *inside*?"

"Yeah, the upstairs is pretty bad. I pretty near fell through a stair when we were going up."

"*Marcus!*"

"No, it was fine. He was right there to grab me. I took two rolls for you on those disposable cameras. I can pick up the prints tomorrow. You'll have them when you go back to painting your best sellers."

"If I ever regain my full range of motion."

She must have been on the laptop again, trawling for dire wrist stories.

"You will."

She met my optimism with a sour look. "But here you are, just in time to peel my banana and uncork a bottle of wine. Oh, my bed linens are already in the washing machine—they can wait until there's a full load. I've already put fresh sheets on."

"You managed alone?"

"One-armed people have to learn to make their beds."

"How is your . . . private project coming?"

"I'm either onto something or deluding myself because I can't do real work. A colonoscopy is when they insert a tiny camera into your rectum and send it up through your intestines to look for polyps—or worse things. I've had one. If you want, you can watch the procedure on a TV screen while they're doing it."

"Did you watch?"

"Naturally. I'm the visual type. It looked like the inside of a soft, pink tunnel, going up and up, with little craters and bumps along the way. No alarming bumps in my case. If you'll uncork that bottle of wine for me, Marcus, I'll be off to my obsession or delusion—or whatever it is."

WALKING NEXT DOOR to the "compromised" Upchurch house to get Roberta's list for my ride to the island store, I debated whether those old brick footing columns would look better "uncompromised," without the white latticework in front of them. But I decided the latticework made the house look more solid and neat.

"No list today, Marcus. We're going to Myrtle Beach this afternoon to get her hair and nails done, so I'll do my shopping at the Piggly Wiggly," Roberta said.

"Is there some special occasion?"

"Tomorrow is around the time Mr. Billy arrives."

"But—how—?"

"How we going to handle it? Like the inchworm does." Roberta made a spritely humping movement with the back of her hand. "One inch at a time. She's no fool, she's just taking it slow. She knows he's not coming, but she wants to reverence the occasion in her own way. She hopes you'll be visiting tomorrow at the usual time."

"But, how should I act?"

"The way you always act. She'll do the rest."

BIKING TO THE island market, I racked my brain for tempting meals I might make for Aunt Charlotte. As I considered the options within my range, I was aware that the real problem hovered above me like a sneering gremlin, biding his time for a pounce.

Aunt Charlotte didn't care about eating. Since I had come to live with her, neither did I. We had more interesting matters to attend to. That weird unlit morning when the ghost-boy had showed himself to me in the doorway of Grief Cottage, I had breakfasted on a fistful of dry cereal before I hurried north on the spellbound beach.

Mom and I had enjoyed our meals. Supper was usually our only one together, and though she was worn out from work, that was our time for conversation: *conversation* meaning the kind of talk when people tell their day, complain, and make plans for the future. Aunt Charlotte and I didn't really have conversations. Our exchanges were more like brief Q & A's ("Where did you run into him?" "How's your project coming?"), or requests for things (mostly her requests since her accident—like haircuts and peeling bananas and opening bottles . . .).

"At last!" shrieked the gremlin, nose-diving through space to sink his claws into my back. "You finally said *bottle!*"

Eight cases were delivered to our door at intervals. I carried them in, made a stack in the pantry, and unpacked each case as the necessity arose. Ninety-six bottles allows you three a day for thirty-two days. If you ran out before then, you ordered the next eight cases. There were never more than eight cases, but since I had arrived in mid-May, the deliveries had become more frequent. She ordered mostly Bordeauxs and Burgundies and always chatted, more than usual for Aunt Charlotte, with whoever was on the other end of the line at the Myrtle Beach wine store. She could make it sound like she was having regular guests, who knew the difference between Bordeauxs and Burgundies and why, if you did order Beaujolais, it had to be from a good year.

I had been telling myself that when she got her casts removed she'd taper off. But, now that I thought about it further, she'd always had an open bottle in reach. She always drank when she was painting, which was almost all the days I had lived with her. The only time she had stopped cold had been for a few days after the second surgery when she was afraid to mix painkillers with alcohol. So, what was the problem? She had been doing this for years and turning out paintings and enjoying her solitary life. Why should she stop now?

Maybe it was just my problem. It was all about me. I was afraid if she started drinking more bottles a day, stumbling and falling on a regular basis, maybe really damaging herself, she would be declared an unfit guardian and back I would go into the system.

Yet I shrank from the thought of confronting her: "Aunt Charlotte, do you think maybe you ought to slow down a little with the wine?" I knew her sour look, which I had received as recently as today. "Marcus, just open it," she would say. And I would open it. She could also kick me out of her house for being a pain. ("He was a nice boy, but he became judgmental. Like Lachicotte. My life was no longer my own.")

The "monthly stipend" would of course be taken from her, but she had lived without it all these years, and there would be family court and lawyers and maybe the court would appoint a trustee to manage the funds—I didn't know all the legal details, and also I was in another state now where they had their own rules. I would be sent to another house, not a relative's since there were no more relatives—or, if there weren't any vacancies, an institution.

I stopped here. I would have to trust the fates that she would avoid another disaster between now and getting her casts off. Maybe she'd finish her secret project and go back to taking orders for her paintings. What power did I have to change an old and comfortable habit? I wondered what Lachicotte had said in former days when he "nagged" her . . .

"Congratulations," mocked the gremlin straddling my back. "You're not the brightest bulb in the drawer, but you finally saw the light."

I had carried Lachicotte's card in my saddlebag ever since the day he gave it to me. Once I came close to using it, but then decided it would be disloyal to call him from the pay phone outside the market to tattle about Aunt Charlotte's "fermenting."

I called his work number first and a pleasant woman answered. "Vintage Motors, how can I help you?"

"Is Mr. Hayes there?"

"He's out at the moment. Would you like his mobile number?"

"I have it on his card. Thank you."

"Would you like to leave any message?"

"No, thank you. I'll try the mobile."

"Hello," said Lachicotte's recorded voice. "You've reached my voice mail. Please leave your (*yoah*) number (*numbah*) and I'll get back to you as soon as I can."

I was still trying out phrases that could convey my message discreetly when I was cut off.

What would I have said? "This is Marcus. I need some advice. Aunt Charlotte is—Aunt Charlotte is—"

"You're off the hook for now, but I'm still here," conceded the gremlin. He was behind me but, unlike with the ghost-boy, I knew how he looked. The reptilian skin, the pitcher ears, the grinning saw-teeth. Wheezer and I had spent hours expanding gremlin traits beyond the simpleminded possibilities offered by movies. "Don't you feel," Wheezer said, "that there must be an advanced model of *mogwai* more imaginative and intelligent than Gizmo and, to balance things out, a much scarier and evil model than Stripe?" "Why does there always have to be a *balance* between good and evil?" I asked. "Because those are the rules," said Wheezer. "I didn't make them. There always has to be a baddie to balance out the goodie. And if you have a more complex and interesting goodie, you need to make an equally complex and interesting baddie."

As I approached the market entrance, I saw a fit, sun-browned boy about my age loping toward the door. He wore a helmet like mine. With a jolt I realized he was my reflection in the glass door. When had this happened? When Charlie Coggins said it was probably safe for me to precede him up Grief Cottage's hazardous staircase, I had wondered how he could call me "a light fellow." But he had been right. Someone called Pudge had been nowhere near that staircase.

"Do you want duplicates?" asked the man when I handed over the disposable cameras.

"Will it cost more?"

"A dollar more a roll."

"I'll just have the singles then."


I SHOULD HAVE asked for the duplicates, I thought, biking home. Then I could have mailed any good ones to Charlie Coggins as a thank-you. But I was still living in two worlds and perhaps always would be. The world in which you forfeited having Batman on your pencil case to save forty cents, and the world in which you could afford to pay two dollars for extra copies of pictures because of a dead mother's trust.

# *XXXII.*

ut don't go trying to use the same route twice. Indeed, don't try to get there at all. It'll happen when you're not looking for it. And don't talk too much about it, even among yourselves. And don't mention it to anyone else unless you find that they've had adventures of the same sort themselves . . ."

HOW COULD I have forgotten the Professor? There he had been, lying at the bottom of one of my boxes all this time, with his sage advice about commuting between reality and the supernatural and *the importance of keeping it to yourself.*

I had unpacked the final box from my old life this afternoon after putting away the groceries, checking the turtles' thermocouple (no change), doing the laundry, including my aunt's sheets and pillowcases, and tidying the bathroom. Inside the last box were the usual candidates for the black trash bag: first aid stuff, including our eye cup, some outdated medications, Mom's Ace bandages she sometimes wore at night for her varicose veins, and the little bottle of arnica the dentist had given her to rub into her gums after a tooth extraction. Clothes I was already outgrowing last summer had been folded and stacked carefully, as though the boy who unpacked this box would be the exact same size as last year. And there on the bottom, wedged beside a pair of sneakers (also getting tight last summer) was my boxed Narnia set, which cheered and saddened me at the same time. We had devoured these books, my mom and I, reading them over and over again, aloud to each other and by ourselves, discussing the characters, and figuring out the meanings.

I was sprawled in the hammock with all the books in my lap, thumbing through them at random, letting the illustrations recall the stories, when footsteps approached up the rarely-used outdoor stairs to our porch. It was Lachicotte Hayes, carrying a paper sack in the crook of his arm. "I brought y'all some tomatoes. I used the rear entrance so I wouldn't have to knock and disturb anybody."

"She's in her studio. I haven't seen her since I got back from the market."

"It was you I was hoping to find. Oh, *The Lion, the Witch, and the Wardrobe*. I read that to my niece when she was young. I don't know which of us enjoyed it the most."

"The niece I met at the library."

"Yes, Althea. We were out condo-shopping for her when you called."

"You knew it was me?"

"My receptionist said a young man phoned but didn't need the mobile number because he had it on my card. Then when I checked my voice mail, there was a silence until the cutoff."

"I couldn't think of an appropriate message to leave."

Lachicotte transferred the sack of tomatoes to the stool Aunt Charlotte used to prop up her broken ankle. "Do you fancy a walk on the beach? My father used to say if you went a whole summer without getting your toes in the ocean you were either too busy for your own good or getting too old for your own good. And here is July half over."

LACHICOTTE SAT DOWN on the lowest step of the boardwalk, rolled up his pants cuffs, removed his shoes and socks, tucking a sock into each shoe, and placed them neatly beneath the step. I did likewise: I hadn't been barefoot on the beach since I'd got my bike. It occurred to me as I placed my sneakers next to his docksiders that a passing stranger observing these side-by-side shoes might assume that some father and son were taking a walk on the beach.

The tide was ebbing, leaving a generous expanse of glassy surf where you could walk and still make contact with the incoming wavelets that broke over your feet.

"Are you liking it here, Marcus?"

I was glad he kept walking straight ahead and not looking at me.

"I like it, but it still feels weird to realize my mom is dead. I'm not sure I can explain it, but often it seems like she's more alive than ever. I think about her more than ever and I keep seeing new sides of her."

"You explain it perfectly (*puh-fectly*) well. After all the human noise and conflicts have stopped, the absent person has more room in your heart to spread out and be herself. My mother's been gone ten years and I know her much better now than when we saw each other every day."

I felt it was probably time to say something about being grateful to Aunt Charlotte for taking me in. "But I like living here at the beach. Before I came here I had never even seen the ocean. And I love my bike. And Aunt Charlotte is very good to me. She doesn't preach or pry or interfere. She lets me do pretty much as I like and goes her own way."

"That she does. The first time I met your aunt was at the hardware store. I was putting back some items on the shelf that I had decided not to buy and she came up and asked could I help her. 'I'll try my best,' I said. She said she was laying ceramic tiles in her bathroom and was tempted to buy the more expensive brand of sand grout, but was it worth it? What did it have that the others didn't? I read the information on the can aloud to her. It was mildew and mold resistant, but for best results you needed to finish it off with a water resistant sealer. 'Is the sealer really necessary,' she asked, 'or are you just trying to sell me the extra product?' At that point the owner, who is a friend, came over and made some jokey remarks about my fancy foreign cars. Then he turned to her and asked if he could be of service, and she realized I was not a salesman."

"What did she do then?"

"She looked mortified. Like she'd been forced into violating some taboo. She apologized to me very formally and went her way. But I was left with the sense that she held me responsible for letting her make the mistake."

I had no trouble imagining my prickly aunt reacting like that. "Did she buy the grout?"

"I don't remember. I felt like an oaf. Soon after, I learned she was new to the island and was renovating an old place known as the Rascal Shack. Young bucks had used it as their drinking club for as long as anyone could remember."

"What was she like then?"

"Much like she is now. Straightforward, laconic, a loyal friend—once she decided you were worth it. Lean as a string bean and handsome in an imperious sort of way—she still is. Her hair was dark then and she may have worn a little lipstick in those days."

"I'm not sure I know what *laconic* means."

"Sparing of words. She wasn't like any woman I'd ever known. To a Southern boy like me, her straightforwardness was exotic. No guile, no gush. The next time we met she was working as a receptionist for the local vet and I had brought in my dog to check out a limp she had developed. All the signs indicated bone cancer, and the options were heart-sickening. I came out of the examining room shattered. When I got to the desk to settle the bill, your aunt glanced down at what the vet had written while I was digging out my credit card and hoping I could make it out of there before I broke down. 'Mr. Hayes,' she said, 'why don't you and Dinah go on home?' She did not look at me once. 'We have your address, we'll send the bill.' Then she turned her back on me real fast and looked very busy with some filing."

"What kind of dog was Dinah?"

"Oh, she was a wonderful mix. Shorthair, the color of butterscotch, long, long legs. The vet said he thought she was part golden retriever, part German shepherd, and possibly some greyhound. When she ran on the beach, she scarcely touched the ground. She used to ride everywhere with me, sitting up straight in the passenger seat. She rode like that on our final trip to the vet, although I could tell it hurt her to sit."

"Was my aunt there?"

"There was someone else on the desk that day. But she came by my shop soon after. She said she was sorry about

Dinah and I showed her some of the automobiles in their various stages of rebuilding. She said she wished she could take a class in auto mechanics, she was sick and tired of being clueless about what went on inside her car. Did I know of any class? I said I could teach her better than any class. She wanted to know how much I would charge, and I told her it would be my pleasure. And then she offered to work for me part-time as payment."

"But what about the vet?"

"That was a part-time job, too, but it wasn't long until she came to me full-time. For a while we went into the taxi business as partners. She ever tell you about that?"

"It was a success. She was able to paint full-time after she got her share of the proceeds."

"Painting was the best thing that ever happened to her. You are the next best thing."

"But I'm not really—" To distract from the break in my voice, I veered away from him and stamped and splashed in the shallow waves until I got control of myself. "I'm not doing such a good job taking care of her. Like you said, being her guardian. That's why I called you, but then I couldn't think of a suitable message just to leave on someone's voice mail."

"Well here I am. You don't have to leave any message."

"She spends all day shut up in her studio. She's working on that secret project I told you about. She said it will either amount to something or she's just deluding herself because she can't do real work. I'm not allowed to go in there even to change the sheets, which I've been doing since the accident. The thing is, I'm still in charge of uncorking her wine and the number of bottles keeps increasing. I thought about saying something to her about cutting back, but I knew she wouldn't appreciate it. I was wondering if you ever said anything like that to her and how it went over."

"It didn't, other than shrinking my welcome mat to the size of a lady's handkerchief. Usually people with harmful habits don't want to be told about it. They have to come around to it themselves."

"But what if they don't come around to it until it's too late?"

"I'm working toward that, Marcus. I'm thinking this out as I go."

"Oh, sorry."

"The project, as far as you know, involves painting?"

"I saw some traces of paint under her fingernails when I was cutting them the other day. Not a lot. She has this separate laundry sink in her studio where she always washes up."

"Well, look here, next week we're going back to the surgeon in Charleston. She'll have new x-rays and we'll have more information. Knowing him, he'll say he can't tell for sure until the cast comes off. And then there has to be rehab: squeezing tennis balls and so on, slowly building back the use of that wrist. She's not the only one who's been scouring the Internet for scaphoid stories, only I'm on the lookout for the positive outcomes. After we've been to the surgeon, we'll see how her spirits are. If they're tolerably hopeful, let's let her complete her secret project. It's possible, you know, things will take a turn for the better. Have you known any folks with addictions, Marcus?"

"Well, Mom didn't drink. She wasn't against it or anything, but she was too tired after work, and also wine and beer cost money. My best friend's grandmother was a smoke addict. The longest she could go without lighting up was forty-two minutes. We timed it once. And our landlord in Forsterville had to attend an AA meeting every morning before he went to work so he wouldn't fall off the wagon. And the man in Jewel who had hired Mom for his mountaintop joinery business just before it went bankrupt—he became a meth addict and the next time Mom saw him his teeth were all rotted and he kept picking at sores on his face. Oh, and Mom had this night school teacher in Forsterville she admired, he really cared about his students, but then he overdosed on something and died. She said if he had gotten the proper help in time he might still be alive. I never met him, this was before I was born. So I guess you could say that I've never been close to anyone who had an addiction. But what if Aunt Charlotte doesn't get the proper help in time?"

"That's not going to happen, now we're on the case. There are places to go for treatment."

"But she'd have to go away, wouldn't she?"

"For a while, yes."

"Then I'd have to go somewhere else, too. I'm a minor and I'm not allowed to live alone."

"We can find someone to live with you, like Roberta Dumas lives with Coral Upchurch. But let's wait to hear the surgeon's opinion next week. My first wife liked to say that the only thing in life you could absolutely depend on was change. And sometimes these changes can be for the better."

"But not always."

"No, not always. I'm not denying that."

# XXXIII.

"Mystery solved," Ed Bolton said, cheerfully hovering above Lachicotte and me as we sat on the boardwalk step, putting on our socks and shoes. He had dropped by in his World War II jeep for a routine check on our turtle clutch. "I recognized your sneakers, Marcus, but I couldn't for the life of me figure out who belonged to the docksiders. Good to see you, Lachicotte."

"Ed. How's my favorite jeep?"

"A–OK thanks to you."

"Still not sorry we replaced that tub?"

"Only thing I regret is that I didn't capitulate a whole lot sooner. I was under some notion that the old rusty tub was what kept it authentic. Marcus, their temperature's way up. Tonight may be their night."

"But when I checked it earlier there was no change."

"You remember how much earlier?"

It was before I did the laundry and unpacked the final box from Jewel. "Maybe three hours ago?"

"Even more auspicious. That means it's risen fast. Listen, Marcus, would you be able to babysit this clutch, say, for the next hour until I can get some other volunteers here? If there's any change in the sand just phone my beeper."

"What kind of change?"

"The sand collapsing inward would be the first."

"Does that mean they're coming out?"

"No, they usually boil up within an hour or so after sunset, when the sand's cooler. But it could mean they're getting ready. Tonight would be favorable. Early crescent moonrise, tide coming in so they won't have to race so far. You ever seen a boil, Lachicotte?"

"I never have. If I didn't have to drive up to Sumter to let a customer test-drive an automobile, I'd love to stick around. As it is, I should have been on the road an hour ago. Marcus, we'll be in touch." Fixing me with a "you-know-what-I-mean" look, he hurried off, brushing his trousers as he went. It was because of our walk, I realized, that he was an hour late.

I told Ed Bolton that I would have to go back to the cottage and leave my aunt a note.

"You go on, Marcus. I'll stay here till you come back and make calls to volunteers on my mobile. We should probably go ahead and set up the sound system and shovel the path. If I'm right, there's a backup of hatchlings under there right now, waiting for the sand to cool. It's exciting, isn't it?"

"What's a tub?"

"What? Oh, the jeep you mean. See the bottom frame that rides above the wheels? When it's sitting by itself on the ground it looks like a tub. Lachicotte was after me for fifteen years to put in a new one. But I was afraid if I replaced it I'd lose my direct connection with the past. As it turns out, all I lost was a lot of rust."

★   ★   ★

*Dear Aunt Charlotte,*

*I will be down at the turtle clutch. Tonight may be the night! They usually come up after sunset as soon as the sand cools down. Chicken salad and cucumber salad in fridge, also a tomato from L's garden that I cut up in wedges for you. Uncorked bottle in the usual place.*

*Marcus*

I WONDERED IF some subtle change in my behavior would give me away as having "told on" Aunt Charlotte the next time she laid eyes on me.

I left the note on the table. I had considered shoving it under her door in case she decided not to come out to eat. After all, I had said I would let her know if the turtles showed any sign of boiling up. But what if she were to see it as soon as I slipped it under? ("You can always knock, Marcus. You don't have to go creeping around sliding notes under doors. What's the guilty look for?")

I had anticipated having the next hour all by myself with the turtles. Just me and the peaceful fading light and the wash of the ocean and a more or less empty beach. I was going to be the herald of the long-awaited event, the lone witness to that first little hole in the sand. I might even see a little head pop up, decide it was still too early, and disappear. And then the other volunteers would eventually gather in the cooling dusk, one or two at a time. In my scenario Ed Bolton would be the first to return. He would announce to each new arrival: "Marcus here's been watching this nest like a hawk. As soon as he spotted that hatchling scout, he phoned my beeper and I was on my way. Marcus actually *saw* the little fellow poke his head up, look around, and go back to tell the others it wasn't time yet!"

But during the short time I had been up at the house, Ed Bolton must have been working his mobile nonstop. Because very soon after he had headed away in the jeep to collect digging tools for the hatchlings' path to the sea, other volunteers started appearing over the dunes. They must have parked their vehicles near our house. Yet it was still daylight, no sand had collapsed inward, nothing out of the ordinary had sent me rushing off to the house to telephone Ed's beeper. Some of the volunteers said Hello, or Hello, you must be Marcus, but most of them went straight to their tasks, which must have been prearranged. They were mixed in age: retirees like Ed Bolton; middle-aged ladies in knee-length shorts; younger men, some still in work clothes; and a sprinkling of teenagers.

Two ladies carefully pulled out the wooden stakes and rolled up the orange plastic fence surrounding the clutch. A man knelt near the nest and inserted something down in the sand while another man set up an amplifier on a pole. The teenagers were marking out a path for the hatchlings' crawl to the water.

"But what if it doesn't happen tonight?" I asked the friendlier of the two ladies, one of those volunteers who had greeted me by name. "Then you'll just have to put the fence back up again."

"Oh, Ed has a second sense about these little guys. He said the temperature was way up within the last three hours and there's likely a backup of them under there right now. Here comes Ed now, you can ask him."

The sun had just set and a pinkish haze was forming to the north out of which the jeep was bouncing toward us. At first, I took the waving straw sticking up on the passenger side as some kind of broom, a tool Ed was bringing to scoop out the turtles' path to the sea. But as the jeep came closer, I saw it was the straw-colored hair of a person. Not till I saw him slide out of the jeep did I see it was a boy, taller than I was, light hair cut short on the sides with a fringe swept over the forehead. He wore an orange T-shirt with a large white paw print on the chest, khaki cargo shorts, supersonic-looking gray-and-orange sneakers, and a huge black watch on his wrist. His face was sunburned; the rest of him, not so much.

"Marcus, this is Pickett, he's staying with his grandparents, our neighbors, until his school starts. Pickett, this is Marcus, who lives in that cottage behind the dunes. Marcus, I've told Pickett to stick close to you and you'll fill him in on our drill."

Pickett did not strike me as the kind of boy who would stick close to anyone, or pay much attention to a peer "filling him in" on anything. So far he hadn't looked at me once, but when I said "Hi" he echoed it, looking me over with a languid glance.

"You two could help shovel out the path," suggested Ed, "if you're so inclined. Pickett, go and get that rake and scoop shovel we brought."

"WHAT GRADE YOU going to be in?" I asked as we set to work. I had offered to take the shovel and let Pickett follow along with the rake.

"My school doesn't have grades. I'll be in second form. That's eighth grade."

"Oh, so will I!"

"Funny, you look younger."

"Well, I skipped a year."

This earned no comment. "How wide am I supposed to rake this path?"

"Maybe a little wider? But leave a little mound on each side so they won't be wandering off."

"Such a big deal for a few turtles!"

"It's hardly a *few*. There are a hundred and ten eggs in this one nest. Loggerheads just happen to be the world's largest hard-shelled turtle and they're threatened with extinction. They've been doing this race to the sea for forty million years. *We've* only been around for the last two hundred thousand."

He heard me out, grinding the toe of a sneaker into the sand. "So what did they do for all those million years before we were on the scene to rake their paths for them?"

"They were on the way to *extinction* before this conservation thing got going. People were eating their eggs for breakfast and making jewelry out of them, and . . ."

"Just kidding," he said, like you would to a child who had gotten overemotional about something. "You live here all year round?"

"I live with my great-aunt. My mother died last winter."

"Oh, sorry."

"Why did you want to come, if I'm not being rude."

"Excuse me?"

"I mean, you don't seem very interested in seeing them hatch."

"Oh, the turtles. Ed said I might enjoy it. And I might. The grandparents don't exactly rock. He's glued to the presidential race, she's in the kitchen dreaming up another spicy dish, and by midafternoon they're both in the bag."

We dug and raked in silence for a bit, each thinking our own thoughts. I could not imagine what his were, and didn't want to try. At my new school there would certainly be a Pickett or two: shifty, withholding, sizing you up, putting you down. The whole ordeal of assessment starting all over again.

It may have been my disappointment, but all the other volunteers seemed wrapped in a congenial bubble, calling to one another, all working toward the same purpose, while Pickett and I were outside the bubble, deadlocked in a contest for—what? Supremacy? Survival? Why had Pickett been foisted on me? Ed Bolton had been my friend and mentor: through him I had grown to love the turtles. And now, because he thought the grandson of some neighbors might "enjoy it," he had separated us from the turtle community. Was his ache for his dead pilot son so enduring that he went around collecting boys to be nice to?

The light faded from the sky, except for the new crescent moon on the rise. The volunteers became vaguely distinguishable figures moving about in the gloaming. The lingering quality of the not-quite-darkness reminded me of that morning when daylight held itself back until I could reach Grief Cottage and see the ghost-boy braced in the doorway, waiting for me to make the next move.

Then the tempo of activities increased; voices rose, calling back and forth. Volunteers gathered around the base pole where the amplifier was set up. A woman snuggled belly-down beside the nest and stuck her face in the sand.

"Listen," said Pickett, "I need to use your bathroom."

"Why don't you just go behind the dunes?"

"I need to take a dump."

"Can't you wait? I think the boil is about to start."

"No, I can't." He was holding his gut. "Just tell me where your bathroom is in your house and I'll make a run for it."

His going alone was out of the question. What if Aunt Charlotte was in the kitchen and this strange boy barged in, demanding her bathroom?

"No, come on, I'll show you. Let's hurry."

As we were running up the boardwalk steps, Ed Bolton cried after us: "Boys! Where are you going? It's about to happen!"

"He needs to—we'll be right back!"

"Oh, freaking Christ, I'm not gonna make it," moaned Pickett.

"Go straight through the kitchen and turn left. The bathroom's at the end of the hall." I pushed him ahead, and he wobbled as fast as he could with his ass tucked in. The back of his orange T-shirt said Clemson Tigers. If he hurried, how much could we miss? Wait, little turtles, hold on till we get back.

My note to Aunt Charlotte was still on the kitchen table. The bottle of wine was gone.

"Go!" I said. Immediately following the slam of the bathroom door a violent explosion resounded. I could envision its far-flying brown discharge hitting every nook and cranny inside the toilet bowl. In my mind I was already cleaning up: toilet brush, Mr. Clean for the splatters, followed up by Pine-Sol to cover the odor.

The toilet flushed, and then reflushed. Water ran. Pickett emerged, having taken the time to wet-comb his bangs. "Sorry about the stink in there."

"It's okay. Go on back to the beach."

"Aren't you coming?"

"There's something I need to do. Go on ahead."

"You're sure?"

"Yeah, I'll be out in a minute."

The cleaning scene followed. It was like having a nightmare turn into an exact replica of the way you had imagined it ahead of time.

MY EYES HAD to readjust to the dark of the beach after staring at the white toilet bowl under bright light. The volunteers, most of them squatting, had spread out on either side of the path Pickett and I had helped to make. By the time I reached the group, my night-vision had kicked in and I could see a swarm of dark little creatures scrambling over one another and racing toward the ocean as fast as their flippers could carry them.

A hand gripped my shoulder. "Ah, Marcus, you missed the boil," Ed Bolton said sadly.

"I know. But I had to." A tear slid down my cheek but it was too dark for Ed to see.

"Well, don't worry. There'll be another one next year."

"How many came out of the nest?"

"We've counted ninety out of a hundred and ten. That's a good crop. Some don't make it. They get out of the egg before they've absorbed all the albumen and then they're too weak to survive. Why don't you go join Pickett—he's over there helping to guide the strayers. Just the gentlest touch with the back of your fingers to get them back on track. Like this." Ed Bolton demonstrated, lightly pressing his fingers against my cheek.

The last person in the world I felt like joining was Pickett, who was absorbed in preventing would-be delinquents from scuttling up the sandbanks on either side of the path. The titanium dials on his wristwatch glowed in the dark as he knelt in the sand, conscientiously rerouting the scuttling little newborns back onto the path.

"Aren't they awesome?" he exclaimed as I sank to my knees beside him. "Look at them haul ass! A minute ago they were crawling out of their hole. I actually *saw* the first one come out—the scout. Its little flipper broke through the sand first, then its little head, then the other flipper, and I swear it looked like it was scoping things out—and then it scooted off for the ocean. Then all of them just started *pouring* out, this living mass of prehistoric creatures. It was totally awesome!"

# XXXIV.

"Marcus, are you okay?" It was morning and Aunt Charlotte was outside my bedroom door.

"Uh-huh."

"May I come in?"

"Yes."

She hopped in and leaned against the door frame. "Were you sick last night?"

"You mean the smell in the bathroom?"

"No big deal. It happens to all of us." The whites of her eyes were netted with little red veins and she looked haggard.

"It wasn't me. It was this boy. We were down on the beach with the Turtle Patrol waiting for the boil and he said he couldn't hold it any longer."

"I saw your note. Did the boil happen?"

"Yeah, but I missed it."

"You missed the whole thing?"

"No, but I missed the boil, when they're bursting through the sand. Pickett said it was awesome. When I got back, I helped escort some of them down to the water."

"Pickett, I take it, is the boy."

"Ed Bolton brought him. He's staying with his grand-parents."

"Wait a minute. How is it that Pickett saw the boil and you didn't?"

"Because—" I turned away from her to hide my distress. "I needed to stay behind and clean the bathroom. It was pretty awful."

"Oh, Marcus, I am so sorry. Look, would it be all right if I sat on your bed?"

"It's your bed, but sure."

She hopped the necessary steps and I felt the mattress sink with her slight weight. "Damn it, Marcus, I am just so sorry."

Tears trickled unseen into my pillow.

"You were looking forward to it, I was so excited on your behalf that you were going to witness this amazing thing in nature. You waited for it, you tended their nest so faithfully, I would look out my window and there you would be, sitting down there on the sand, hugging your knees, like you were encouraging them to grow—and then *because you cleaned up after a stranger* you missed the boil. No good deed goes unpunished, does it?"

I couldn't answer because I wasn't in control of my voice.

"Oh, Marcus." Her uninjured left hand fastened on my turned-away shoulder. "What are we going to do with you? You are too thoughtful for your own good. How am I going to protect you?"

I held my breath and bit down on my lower lip to keep from losing it completely.

Then she withdrew her hand and expelled the dry Aunt Charlotte-y rasp that served as her laugh. "They must have been beyond malodorous," she said.

"What?"

"Pickett's awful leavings."

"They were pretty bad." I giggled and she went into another rasp. "What time is it?"

"After ten. Which is late for you. I was starting to worry. I've got a nasty headache. I overdid it last night."

"On your project?"

"No, on the Cabernet Sauvignon. When you go to the store will you pick up another bottle of Extra Strength Tylenol? I seem to have run through the last one."

★  ★  ★

SHE HAD MENTIONED the wine herself. Would Lachicotte count that as a "change for the better"?

I felt really bad as I rode my bike to the market. It was over, the thing I had looked forward to all summer—and I had missed it. "You waited for it, you tended their nest so faithfully . . . and then *because you cleaned up after a stranger* you missed the boil." "You'll never believe what I saw," Pickett would tell the "second form" kids back at his school. "These awesome little turtles . . . they've been doing this race to the sea for forty million years, while we've only been here for the last two hundred thousand." Aunt Charlotte had looked out her window and watched me sitting in the sand. Somehow I had never imagined her stopping her work to look out the window at me, but she had: "And there you would be, sitting down there on the sand . . ."

"How am I going to protect you?" She had sounded like someone aching on my behalf. In all the time I had lived with her, she had laid a hand on my shoulder exactly twice. But now I considered the possibility that we would maybe end up protecting each other.

My photos were ready. Before I did the shopping I went back outside to the bench and looked through them. The ones taken from the beach were okay. Aunt Charlotte would see the cottage at a distance in its early morning light, and then in gradual stages approach its present day wreckage. She could pick and choose her level of disintegration: picturesque abandonment or hazardous finale, or somewhere in the middle. The ones I had taken on the porch were poorly lit but distinct enough to remind me if I came across these photos in my future that I really had seen the ghost-boy braced in that doorless doorway.

The interior shots were a huge disappointment. Every picture I had taken inside the house was murky. You couldn't even make out the original fireplace whose mantel had been stolen, and Charlie Coggins's sky-blue paint to ward off Ole Plat-eye showed up gray. The picture I took of the upstairs room he wouldn't let me go into seemed to have suffered a double exposure. It was also on the murky side, except for a slash of light cutting right through the center of the boarded-up south wall. I was glad I hadn't ordered duplicates: the realtor wouldn't show these to anybody.

I looked for a little present to take to Coral Upchurch later today. There was a souvenir section in the market, but the only thing that caught my eye was a plastic ashtray with a picture of a pelican sitting on a pier. But who wanted to extinguish their cigarette in the middle of a pelican?

★   ★   ★

"YOU LOOK VERY nice," I told Coral. She really did. She wore a white dress with a white lace shawl that matched her freshly-styled white feathery hair. Her nail polish matched her coral necklace. A fragrance that I guessed was her perfume floated subtly in the air.

"Thank you, Marcus. It's a special day."

"Yes, ma'am, Roberta told me. What time did he usually get here?" I had thought this up in advance.

"If he was flying, he arrived in the late afternoon, because that was the best flight from D.C. He landed at the Myrtle Beach airport and had a rental car waiting. If he was driving down, it all depended on where he stopped the night before and whether he took the direct or the scenic route. One time he arrived before daylight and waked me with a breakfast tray."

"That was nice of him."

"It was, though I prefer to be groomed when he first sees me. But he was so pleased with himself that morning he probably overlooked what a fright I was."

"What did you two do while he was here?" In the deep pocket of my cargo shorts the Grief Cottage photos awaited the right moment to nudge us onto the Johnny Dace subject, but it was way too early in the visit to bring them out. Today a lace cloth covered the porch table and our china and silver were more elaborate. Even the ashtray had undergone an upgrade to a light-green cut-glass crystal, one that matched the crystal pitcher holding our iced tea. The pelican ashtray would have been out of place. In the center of the table was a porcelain cake stand painted with little cupids playing their flutes to branches full of birds. The cake, Billy's favorite prune-and-bourbon cake, was still in the oven below.

"Well, when I was still on foot, we always went to Brookgreen Gardens. Billy never could get enough of Brookgreen Gardens, even as an adult. You must get someone to take you, Marcus. There are gorgeous flowers and sculptures and boat cruises and a zoo and walkways through woods with rare birds and two-hundred-year-old trees and even alligators. They issue passes that last a week because there is too much to do in one day. As a child, Billy had to be dragged away, and even when he was in his fifties we had to go back and refresh his memories of it. And let's see. We ate out a lot, even after my wheelchair confinement. Billy liked the local cuisine. And when I took my afternoon nap, he would drive across the bridge to Charleston and shop for antique furniture for his place in Washington."

"What was it like, his place?"

"Oh, Marcus, I never got to see it! We had been planning my visit year after year and something always interfered. And then finally we got everything right. Billy made all the arrangements, I had a first class ticket, and I was waiting in line at the airport to check my bag when I collapsed on the floor. From then on I was in a wheelchair. My spine had given out. I won't bore you with details. It's the great disappointment of my life. For years and years, Billy had been saying, 'Mama, when are you going to come up here and see how I live and meet my friends? I want you to get to know the *Washington me*.' Now I will never know the Washington Billy."

"What did he do in Washington?"

"He had a highly responsible job with an insurance company that takes care of armed service personnel and their families. He loved his job. This isn't always true of artistic people like Billy. They feel somehow *thwarted* if they're not directly connected to the arts. But he never did. He went right on taking voice lessons and collecting old furniture and going on his little jaunts to France and Italy. He had a beautiful rich tenor voice. People were always asking him to sing at their weddings."

"Lachicotte's mother has been gone ten years and he said he knows her better now than when he saw her every day. He said when all the human noise and stuff are out of the way the absent one can spread out and be themselves in your heart. Maybe that will happen with Billy and you."

"Oh, Marcus, I can't think of anything I'd like more. How I would love for Billy to spread out and be his whole self in my heart! We know so very little about the people we are closest to. We know so little about *ourselves.*"

"How is your archaeology on yourself coming along?"

"Oh, you remembered that. What was I saying when we last discussed it?"

"You wanted to get rid of family names and social stuff and strip down to what was below Coral. Or no, you said *beyond.*"

"I think I like your *below* better. Well, I've hit one or two cul-de-sacs since then and now I am coming to terms with my findings."

"What are *cul-de-sacs*?"

"Just a fancy French way of saying dead ends. What am I when I get past being a particular daughter, wife, mother, neighbor, friend? What would be left of the essential me without any of my roles? That was the first dead end I reached. Maybe nothing will be left, I thought; I *am* my roles. Even when I'm dead I'll be in the role of 'Mrs. Upchurch's remains' to my undertaker. When people remember me, it will always be in one of my roles. I must say, that took the wind out of my sails."

"Why?"

"Well, you've gone on your archaeology dig and you've found some nice coins and jewelry and pottery and you think, oh, if I've dug up all this already, the best of all is going to be at the bottom! But then when you get to bottom there's nothing there but dirt."

"But you said that was the first dead end, so there must have been a second one."

"Well, here's what came next. I just couldn't accept that there was nothing more to me than who I am in relation to others. What about this consciousness that inhabits my body and nobody else's, the unrepeatable part of me who experiences everything in the world from its one-of-a-kind viewpoint? After all, every tree in the forest has its one-of-a-kind experience of its own tree-ness. And then I thought about Billy, how he said 'I want you to know the *Washington* me,' and that's when I came to my second dead end, which was not exactly a dead end but a cause for sorrow. I realized that below all our *mes* that become known to others is a self that nobody else can ever fully know. No self can ever share its entire being with another self, no matter how much love there is between them. And that made me cry. I had a really good long cry. And after I dried my eyes, I thought, well, what have I got left? And all I had left at the bottom of my digging was love."

I was debating whether or not to tell her that love wasn't such a bad thing to find at the bottom, which might have evoked the same bitterness Aunt Charlotte had shown when I had assured her that her wrist would regain its full range of motion. Roberta's solid footsteps ascending the outdoor stairs beside the "unsightly ramp" deplored by Charlie Coggins saved me from making the choice.

"Here it is." Roberta slid the fragrant cake from its plate onto the waiting stand. "Four generations of prune cake. That's right, isn't it, four?"

"Four indeed. The recipe came down from Archie's great-grandmother. At first it was baked in ordinary cake pans, then Archie's mother received a Bundt mold as a wedding gift and ever since it's been baked as a Bundt cake. The icing was always made with rum until one day they didn't have any rum in the house so she substituted bourbon, and so this is the cake Archie and Billy grew up on. Roberta, did the tea roses arrive?"

"They're in the kitchen. I just have to cut the stems and shake in those little packets and we're good to go."

"Marcus, I'm going to show you Billy's room before you leave. You'll remember, won't you, Roberta, it's the apple-green vase."

"I'll remember, Miss Coral."

"SHE DOES THAT 'Miss Coral' thing to punish me," the old lady said once we were alone again. "I shouldn't have reminded her about the green vase. Of course she remembered. Marcus, help us both to that cake. Don't be shy. Just pick up that cake server and take the plunge. Make mine a thin slice, make yours a double."

"Why is it a punishment?"

"I was being lady of the manor, so she backtracked into the bad old days of disparity. We Southerners have a different history, Marcus. It will take a while for us to blend in with the rest of the country. I won't see it in my lifetime, but Roberta Dumas and I have made our little start."

She had said "I am going to show you Billy's room *before you leave*," and with that deadline impressed on my mind I brought out the pictures as soon as she lit up her first cigarette in my company, explaining about Charlie Coggins showing me the inside of Grief Cottage.

"The distance shots are best," I said. "They're for Aunt Charlotte when she starts to paint again. They show its up-to-date damage and she can choose how much of it to put in her pictures."

"I see what you mean. The shots with the other houses in them are nice. Oh, poor Archie, I can't see these pictures without thinking how upset he got when he walked up there every summer and saw that thing still standing. He finally shamed them into putting the fence around it—or did I already tell you that?"

"You may have."

"At my age the short-term memory betrays you more than the long-term one does."

"The indoor shots are terrible," I said, spreading them out. "Too dark, and the colors don't show."

"I'm surprised Charlie Coggins allowed you to go inside. It can't be safe at all."

"Did you—were *you* ever inside?" My preplanned takeoff question.

"No, Archie and I were not great socializers. His island time in *this house* was too precious to him. The Barbours were more the rental type of owner than those who kept their houses strictly for their own families. They rented out right through the season, sometimes through October. Those unfortunate Daces were the exception, which of course the Barbours came to regret."

*Bingo!*

"I think I told you already," she went on, "the Barbours got sued by some cousin who said Mr. Dace was the only kin she had left, and they paid up."

"Did Billy ever go inside the house with . . . his friend?"

"I expect he must have. Because he reported things the parents said and did. It may have been while he and Johnny were spying from their hiding place."

"Was it in the house?"

"As I recall, you got there from the outside, but the people inside didn't know you were so close. Mind you, Billy told me some things he didn't tell Archie, and that was probably one of them. The parents were out of their element at the beach. The family was from Kentucky, and they'd had some bad luck, which I think I told you before. They were afraid of the ocean and huddled together in one of the Creekside rooms. The father went fishing every morning with the folks who fish from the creek, and the family ate fish and cornbread and some rice and beans they'd brought with them. Billy said Johnny hated his parents. They were too old and wouldn't let him do anything. He got so hard to manage they put him in this delinquent home several times. Then they would all cry and reunite and try again. Before they came to the beach, Johnny had been suspended from school. Billy told me—this was later, after the hurricane, when everyone had heard about the family's disappearance—that he had been going to send Johnny the bus fare so he could run away to Columbia. They had it all planned. Johnny would go to public high school with Billy. Lord knows where they thought Johnny was going to live! Funny, I had forgotten about those plans till you stirred up my memories with all your questions."

CORAL UPCHURCH SHOT her wondrous machine into action for our excursion to Billy's room. What a great ride it would offer if you were sure of getting out of it again. Its *sissing* sound rose in pitch the faster it went, and it took sharp corners better than we did.

Billy's room was everything someone like Billy—or what I had come to know of him—would feel entitled to. The ocean was right outside the sliding doors, which were open to let in the breeze. The bed was made and turned down with crisp linens. There was a chintz-covered armchair with matching hassock and the prettiest writing table I had ever seen. I would have said more if I hadn't used up too many superlatives on the cake. On the desk was a framed studio picture of a young man with flowing hair and perfect features. Everything in his countenance testified to expecting nothing in life other than unqualified admiration. "Billy's about twenty in that picture," said Coral. "Isn't he handsome? That's an antique Provençal desk, Billy had it shipped here direct from France." On the desk was the apple-green cut-glass vase full of pale orange roses in bud.

"I'll leave y'all to yourselves," said Roberta Dumas.

"Before you go, tell Marcus what we did with your Boogie Basket," Coral said.

"Thanks to her I sent back my commission money to those folks, and now we have ourselves a great big sweet-grass laundry basket," said Roberta, laughing softly as she went.

# XXXV.

The period of time following my afternoon with Billy and Coral Upchurch and leading up to Aunt Charlotte's return date with the surgeon had a mournful feel. Some things were drawing to an end, other anticipated things had not happened. For me it was a time of flat days and anxious thoughts. The sun rose later and set earlier. It was as if the summer knew that its best days were gone and was giving in without a fight. I continued my morning rides to Grief Cottage, wearing my helmet and ducking my head as I hurried past the final few cottages in case Pickett happened to be looking out. There was nothing going on with the ghost-boy, no sense of my being seen or heard. My visits to the cottage were so blank that I began questioning the relationship I'd had with him before going inside with the realtor. It was as if Charlie Coggins's sky-blue paint to ward off Ole Plat-eye had driven away my ghost. I still talked to him, updated him with alluring trues ("Billy Upchurch's mother said he invited you to run away from home and go to school with him in Columbia . . . she said you two had a hiding place where you could spy on the people inside . . . I missed the turtles' boil because I had to clean up after this boy who left a mess in our bathroom, but I did get to see them racing for the ocean . . .")

Not a flurry in the air between us, no vibrations of either interest or disgust, just a boy by himself on a rotting porch disturbing the peace with his human noise.

Ed Bolton had apologized. ("The boy was at loose ends and I thought it would be exciting for him. But you got the short end of the stick.") Ed had returned to Aunt Charlotte's dune to clean out the nest and count the little corpses and unopened eggs and carry them away to the sea turtle conservators for research. ("I'm sorry, Marcus. And Pickett was mortified, for what it's worth.")

I missed talking to the turtle eggs and sorting out my day. Their presence had been an aid to my meditations.

Coral Upchurch had overtired herself with Billy's "welcome home" celebration and had taken to her bed. I still went over daily to get their list, but there wasn't much on it. I asked Roberta had I done anything to tire her. "No, she's getting down to her real grieving. Lord knows it's about time." Roberta was weaving an elegant bread basket of modest size.

Aunt Charlotte and I still had our evening meal together, though she ate less and less and I opened more bottles of wine. Sometimes when she asked me to open another one, she gave me this measuring look like she was seeing how close she was to goading me into "nagging" so she could counterattack with her "Just *do it*, Marcus."

I told her about Coral's "welcome home" for Billy. And about her collapse at the airport, which kept her from ever seeing how her son lived in Washington and meeting his friends.

"Did it ever occur to you that she might not have wanted to see how her son lived in Washington and meet his friends?"

I said no, it hadn't.

"People have so many ways of shooting themselves in the foot to avoid facing something."

These days her supper talk bristled with this kind of caustic observation. After that one, I asked myself if her kitchen mishap had been a means of not facing up to something. And if so, was she aware of it?

Lachicotte took me to his barber for a haircut—I had asked for this after meeting Pickett. The barber wanted to know how I would like it, as it was too long for him to make out the "line" of my last haircut (which the foster mother had given me). I said short on the sides and in back but leave a little fringe brushed sideways at the front. You could dislike someone and still admire their hairstyle. Then we went shopping for school clothes, which I knew how to do, so Lachicotte sat on a bench outside the store while I let Mom's taste guide me through the Boys section. Trendy is soonest out-of-date. Wear your clothes, don't let them wear you. They should fit your body, not be tight or baggy or out to make a statement. Go for the well-made things—as far as your budget allows. When I summoned Lachicotte so he could pay with his credit card, to be reimbursed by Aunt Charlotte, he said he'd expected me to spend more. I felt sad Mom wasn't around to see how well I'd done.

While trying on clothes in the dressing room, I had scrutinized myself in the full-length mirror and pretended to be others at school watching me come down the hall. The beach and the bike riding had definitely improved the basic shape. Stripped down to my underwear I examined myself front and back from haircut to feet. I was not the boy that my mother had last looked upon. I was definitely on the road to manhood. Was this something to look forward to?

What had I looked forward to this time last year when Mom and I had been shopping for back-to-school things? If the patch of black ice had been somewhere else instead of under of her tires what would we be doing right now? We would probably still be in our upstairs apartment in Mrs. Wicked's house on Smoke Vine Road. I would be *pudge-wonk* going into eighth grade, looking forward to my new books and lessons and building up my defenses against peer assaults. Mom would have two or more jobs to offset our loss of income from the death of Mrs. Harm and still be gamely assuring me that our life was going to get better. If all went as planned, we could be going to college together in five more years.

Aunt Charlotte received parcels from the art store in Charleston. She asked me to slit them open with the serrated kitchen knife. I had made the mistake of pulling out the contents of an early parcel, some packs of paper labeled with oriental writing. "Ah, my Japan paper," she had said breezily, snatching it from my hands. After that she stood guard as I opened the parcels so I couldn't peek inside, then hopped off to her studio clasping them to her chest. She gave me the task of answering the messages on her website. "Just the ones that seem serious. When in doubt, ask me." I was relieved to find some promising inquiries, mostly for paintings of Grief Cottage. One lady asked if the artist would be willing to paint a boy into the foreground if she were to provide photographs of her grandson.

"Send a brief reply that the artist doesn't paint people," said Aunt Charlotte.

"How should I sign it?"

"'Marcus Harshaw, Assistant to Charlotte Lee.' Next someone will be asking for me to paint that Confederate ghost into the foreground."

The art store deliveries, the inquiries on her website, the fact that she spent all day, except for speedy bathroom hops, shut away in her studio with the Japan paper and whatever else had arrived in the parcels: these I took as very positive signs she was getting on with her secret project *and* preparing for resumption of business as usual with her right hand.

Two days before the trip to the surgeon in Charleston, Aunt Charlotte asked me to trim her hair and then wash it. I was halfway around her head, "grabbing small clumps" and snipping, when she said, not for the first time, how handsome I looked with the new haircut. She went on to relate how I had impressed Lachicotte on my back-to-school shopping trip. "He expected you to spend twice that amount."

"Mom and I had to make every dollar count, so I guess I was trained well."

"So much needless want and suffering. All to escape a monster. If she had stayed at home and finished high school and kept inside the lines of Brenda's bourgeois groove . . . but I should be careful about wishing in retrospect. If she hadn't run away, you wouldn't exist."

I followed her line of thinking, though I shied away from contemplating my nonexistence. The line led back to her devil incarnate father who was my mom's grandfather, who had caused them both to run away. I longed to know more, but how much more would be more than I needed to know? It was like in my dream when I asked the sunburned man what was in the trash barrel in front of Grief Cottage and he laughed and said, "I could tell you but then I'd have to kill you."

"Well, Marcus, you've made me svelte for our trip to Charleston," she said after I had cut, shampooed, and blow-dried her hair. Coasting on the good feeling between us and remembering her anguish on my behalf about missing the turtle boil, I said I was really looking forward to it.

"You're not going, Marcus. It's just for a meeting with the surgeon. There won't be time for fun and shopping with Lachicotte."

"But I thought—"

"You thought what?"

"You've always said *our* trip to Charleston. Even Lachicotte—"

"Well, 'our' in this case meant Lachicotte and me. It's not a family outing."

Did I pick up a disparaging twist on the word "family"?

"All you'd be doing would be sitting in the waiting room with Lachicotte."

"Yeah, I'd probably be in the way."

"I'll level with you. If it's unpleasant news I don't want to have to put on a cheerful face. I'd rather be driven home in silence and feel as bad as I like."

"But *I* wouldn't—"

"Enough, Marcus. This is the way I want it."


MY DAILY LIST was no longer full. No more turtle eggs to watch over and keep me company while I ran my reality check at the end of the day and concluded I was still sane. No more boxes to unpack. No afternoon visits with Coral Upchurch, who was getting down to her real grieving. Someone had taken over the sunburned man's route. Had he gone back to college (if he went to college), or had he done something to cost him his job? I still had my housework and grocery shopping. I biked faithfully to an empty Grief Cottage every morning and some afternoons. I was like those characters in movies who are determined to keep faith with the old schedule while the loved one is away or off fighting in a war.

After Aunt Charlotte had set me straight on who was going to Charleston, I looked for things that needed doing so she wouldn't think I was "moping." I cut the tags off my school clothes and ran them through the wash several times so they wouldn't shout "I'm new!" when I was coming down the halls. I missed having the boxes to unpack, but at least I could clean the garage where they had been stacked. Then I worried that Aunt Charlotte might interpret this as a ploy to make her change her mind about the trip. But she was pleased when she saw it and said it had never looked that neat. Then she repeated that thing about me being too good to be true and that I was restoring her faith in humans. It occurred to me that it would take some pressure off if she could accept that I was not as good or as strong as all that.

Since she hadn't asked to see my Grief Cottage photos, I hid them away in the same place where (at her request) I had hidden her container of painkillers. Either she had more important things on her mind or she was superstitious about seeing the photos before she was certain she would be painting from them again soon.

# XXXVI.

"*M*arcus, where did we store that walker I brought home from the hospital?"

"It's in my closet."

"Would you get it? I don't want to lean on Lachicotte more than I have to."

The day of the surgeon had arrived. I helped Lachicotte guide Aunt Charlotte and her walker down the front steps and get her settled in the passenger seat of her own car. "Why does it smell so good?" she asked.

"I had it detailed for you," Lachicotte said.

"*Detailed?*"

"A place just opened, it's their specialty. You leave it all day and they recondition it inside and out. Steam-clean the carpeting, wax the leather, the whole enchilada."

"How nice to be reconditioned inside and out. How much do I owe you?"

"It's a thank-you for letting me drive it."

"You already thanked me with four new tires."

"Then think of it as another thank-you," said Lachicotte.

"Be good, Marcus. Not that I need to tell you that. We should be back by late afternoon."

It smelled so good because she had remembered her car smelling of vomited-up shrimp. They would probably have an early lunch in some nice restaurant. Maybe there would be a shrimp dish on the menu and Aunt Charlotte would say it reminded her of the day I arrived and reveal some specifics, charitably adding "But poor boy, he was mortified." Then she would say, "I'm not hungry, I'll just have a salad and a glass of red wine. But Lash, why don't you have one of the specials?" It would be her first outing this summer without me tagging along as "family."

The rest of the day stretched ahead like an endurance test. It was too early to go next door and see if Roberta had a list for me. I had missed my early morning bike ride to Grief Cottage in order to be around when they left for Charleston, and now it was late morning, the beach filled with shrieking children, the light wrong. I prowled around inside the house, imagining a less honorable version of myself crossing the threshold of my aunt's forbidden studio. Having washed the few breakfast dishes by hand, I was elated when I looked down at the floor and saw scuff marks and sand on the kitchen tiles: overlooked remnants of Pickett's ass-tucked scramble for the toilet? A really good floor scrubbing was needed. Kneeling and applying the hard-bristle brush in serious circles recalled the day we had been cleaning house for the Steckworths' visit, when Aunt Charlotte had dropped to her knees and scrubbed with a fury. ("It's either that or kill someone.") Then she had ordered me from the house. ("Just *go*, Marcus. Don't make me ask again.") This was after she'd learned from me that Mom, like herself, had run away at sixteen to escape a worse situation.

After I finished the kitchen floor, I mopped the hall, cleaned the bathroom, and tidied my own already-tidy room. Following that, I took the trash out.

As I was closing the lid to our bin in front of the house, a silent ambulance with its red revolving light turned into our street and stopped in front of the Upchurch house.

Roberta was beside the ambulance before the two men had finished unloading the stretcher from the bay. She led them quickly up the outside stairs. She hadn't looked my way. Soon they returned, this time bearing the stretcher down the ramp, probably for a less bumpy ride for the tiny figure covered with a blanket. All you could see above the blanket was the breathing apparatus clamped to her face. They loaded her into the bay and, after a short consultation with Roberta, slammed it shut and drove off as noiselessly as they had come, red light revolving. Roberta still hadn't looked my way, so I ran after her as she headed to the house.

"Roberta! What *happened*?"

"They're thinking pneumonia. Her breathing was all wrong when I went in this morning."

"Pneumonia in the *summer*?"

"You can get it any time. Healthy people carry the bacteria without it hurting them. My guess is the beauty salon. The hairdresser could have coughed on her, or the lady under the next dryer. But it's no joke at her age. She was running a fever and I wasn't taking chances."

"Will she be all right?"

"Pray God, Marcus. We've been together since she got in that wheelchair. It's—it's a *friendship*." Tears rolled down her cheeks.

"Do you need anything at the market?"

"No, I'm going to pack her some necessities and drive them over to the hospital and wait until we know something."

"Tell her I said please get better."

"I surely will. She has enjoyed you so much."

I CROSSED THE immaculate kitchen floor and stepped out on the porch. The shady hammock was not inviting before afternoon. Out of habit I went down to the dunes and sat in my old meditation spot. The absence of the turtles' nest made the spot as forlorn as the unhaunted doorway of Grief Cottage. Why had Roberta said, "She has enjoyed you"? Why not "She has *been* enjoying you"? Before the sun went down today, it could easily become "She *enjoyed* you."

It had been like watching some tiny extraterrestrial creature carried respectfully out to the ambulance by some large humans. Just some helpless little bumps under a blanket with an oxygen mask perched on top. I had not seen a single human part of her, not even a wisp of white hair. Now she wouldn't get to finish her archaeology on herself. No, she said she had finished it and down at the bottom found only love. But now I would never be able to tell her, "It's not such a bad thing to find love at the bottom."

I was losing the casing that held me together. I could feel it coming loose, like that boy's cheek melting down the side of his face back at the foster home. I drew up my knees to make a smaller, denser package of myself, and buried my face in my hands. When Mom was alive she would say, "Marcus, when you sit like that with your knees drawn up and your face covered, I want to die."

Well, you did die. I waited for you to come back and you didn't. Whereas I'm still here, coming loose from my moorings, getting ready to fly apart.

The corpses of the hatchlings and the eggs that never opened had been taken away to be studied. It might have been better to be one of those eggs that never opened. No pain, no fight, no terror. Just a kind and curious person in a lab, gently cracking your egg, looking inside to see how your remains might benefit future hatchlings.

When you start feeling sorry for yourself, the foster mother told us, make a list of all the good things you're grateful for. What were the good things of this summer? My bike, my room by myself, the ghost-boy until he shut down. Lachicotte, Coral Upchurch, Aunt Charlotte.

For Wheezer, a "true" was a story that had really happened to someone, the more shocking and sensational the better: Van Gogh slicing off his ear and handing it to a prostitute; Wheezer's brilliant uncle who read Latin and Greek and died shooting up inside a trailer full of rats.

Wheezer also had a term for a person you could always count on to be thinking of you and missing you, no matter where you were. Wheezer called this person a "sure." Like rare marbles, we displayed and discussed our sures. Each of us had only one. ("But, Marcus, lots of people don't have *any*.") The cigarette-smoking grandmother in whose house Wheezer lived was his sure. His mother and father, even his big brother, all of whom lived in other places, were not. ("Weeks can go by without any of them giving me a thought.")

My mom was my sure. "And who knows?" Wheezer had said. "Maybe one day we'll end up being each other's sures."

Fool that I was, I had been on my way to considering Aunt Charlotte and Lachicotte as my potential sures. And maybe even Coral Upchurch, since she no longer had Billy in this world.

If that patch of black ice had been a little to the left a little to the right of Mom's tires, we would still be sleeping in the same bed; there was only room for one bed in the apartment on Smoke Vine Road. I wondered what age I would have had to reach before she said, "Marcus, you're getting to be a big boy, let's go see if we can find a sofa-bed and squeeze it into a corner and pay for it on the installment plan. I may not be able to afford an extra room, but it's time you had your own bed."

*What if the time never comes?* I sometimes caught myself thinking as I lay beside her. And then I would try not to think the next thought: *How will I ever get away from her?*

"I'M NOT STAYING around to think any more 'next thoughts' with you," my gremlin from the causeway suddenly piped up. "I am an evolving gremlin, trying to improve myself. *You* are going in the opposite direction. You'd be more suitable company to the others."

"What others?"

"The evil baddies that balance us out. I've called in a cutting-edge baddie, fresh off the assembly line. Here he comes now. I'm out of here!"

MAYBE I'D HAD my meltdown, after all. Here I was, running from the beach at midday, fleeing a *gremlin*. I didn't want to meet Cutting Edge or even glimpse him out of the corner of an eye. I slammed the kitchen door behind me and wished it had Charlie Coggins's Gullah-blue paint sloshed all around its frame. To put an extra door between us, I shut myself in my room.

What help was in here? I picked up the black bear in the hoodie and rubbed him against my face. I looked out my window at the line where the ocean met the sky. Out there I had felt I was melting away; now my skin felt like it was growing too tight to hold me. The tension was unbearable. I was sweating and heaving but nothing came up. The awful things I didn't want inside me kept expanding.

I opened Mom's tin box with its sacred contents and plucked out Aunt Charlotte's container of painkillers from its hiding place. I had never taken anything but aspirin. Maybe one pill would kill enough physical feeling to tide me over until they got back. Now to wash it down. In the kitchen, on an impulse, I grabbed an opened bottle of wine in its usual hiding place and swigged down the pill, drinking from the bottle. The wine tasted murky and sour. How could she put away glass after glass of this? If I were to become a serious drinker I would choose something light and clear that worked really, really fast. I walked a circle around the kitchen, then another and another. How long did a painkiller take to kick in? It wasn't that my thoughts were "racing," but that every time I started to think any thought my mind recoiled from it. Every subject I approached had some kind of pain or horror attached to it.

I turned on Aunt Charlotte's laptop and checked for new e-mails on her site. No promising inquiries, no inquiries at all. I deleted the junk mail.

"Did you think," said a voice I can only describe as *crumbly,* "did you *really* think you could keep me on the other side of a measly door? I'll tell you something you won't want to hear. You can't keep me out because I'm one of the cutting-edge models. We work from inside. And I don't mean inside the house. I mean inside of you. The upside to this, the only upside, is that you don't have to see me or imagine what I look like. I am beyond looks. I am inside you so I can camouflage myself in your looks."

# XXXVII.

"What's behind that door?"

"I'm not supposed to go in there."

"Who says *I* can't? And since I'm inside of you, you'll have to come with me."

The painkiller must have reached my bloodstream because everything felt . . . not *better*, but a remoteness now muffled the unbearable anguish. Soon they would be having their early lunch in Charleston; they might be at the table already. ("This shrimp dish on the menu reminds me of the day Marcus arrived . . .") They would take care of each other. He would get her to a recovery place in time. They would be each other's family without the commitments. They would become each other's sures. But now this didn't hurt as much as it would have a short while ago.

"Go on, turn the knob. Good boy. Or I should say bad boy. So this is the forbidden temple. What have we here?"

A neat and organized studio. Giant easel pushed out of the way to the same spot where she had ordered me to move it. Laundry sink (where she had talked me through changing the washer) clean, but with paint rags hung to dry on its sides.

The wall-high cork board from which she had told me to take down samples of famous landscape paintings she admired, rough drawings of clouds, postcards of her own paintings, and some write-ups about her in local papers, was filled with tacked-up little paintings, all the same size. ("I have a particular fondness for four by sixes, about the size of my palm," she had told Ron Steckworth the day they carried away their forty-two by fifty-six. She had held up a palm to demonstrate.) I measured my palm against the paintings on the corkboard. My hand was already the size of hers.

"What is it?" asked Cutting Edge. "Some kind of comic strip?"

"Why would you think that?"

"Because, dumbass, the story goes from left to right, then drops down and goes left to right again."

"What makes you think it's a story?"

"Because I'm a speed reader and I've already scanned it. Wow, your aunt is one obscene lady. And so clumsy and crude for someone who passes herself off as an artist."

"She injured her right hand. These are painted with her left hand. Also I think she painted them with her fingers. Except for those first drawings."

"Filthy Auntie!"

"I wish you'd shut up."

"Mum's the word until slowpoke has stumbled through the story."

The few ink drawings before the paintings started were so badly done they were embarrassing. It was like someone with a shaky hand had been struggling to keep control of the pen; like Aunt Charlotte's left-handed signature that day she wrote Lachicotte that left-handed check for my bike. And even for that, she said she had been practicing all day.

But despite their clumsiness it was obvious what she had set out to draw: a figure of a little girl standing before a man seated on a bed. The strange thing was that the trembliness of the lines made the figures appear to be slightly moving. The little girl was standing close to his outspread legs. Drawn on a bigger scale, he bulked over her like a sitting giant. Her outer hand loosely held a doll by its arm and her other arm reached out to the man. In the first picture, this arm stopped at the wrist, but in the ensuing drawings there was a hand that moved nearer and nearer to the man's crotch. Then splotches of color began to be painted over the ink lines until the lines disappeared. The rest of the board was tacked up with progressive paintings of the two figures. A suitcase materialized beside the bed and the doll had been dropped on the floor with floppy legs outspread. The man sprouted a green penis that curved upward. At first you could see its green tip like a small mushroom until gradually it was obscured by the girl's bowed head being held in place by the seated man's large hand.

She had used lots of pink and green, the girl being pink and the man green, though there were other colors, too. She had piled paint on top of paint and the man and girl mutated into less human images, grotesque figures in a bad dream, the man's head becoming anvil-shaped and sprouting stubby green horns, the girl's face widening into a sinister grimace. Where had I seen this crusted-over paint style, these grimaces before?

You could see the little paintings getting sharper as she gained control of those left-hand fingers. On a paper halfway down the board she had finger-painted some blue words, edged in yellow: ONLY TO YOU, MY LITTLE SHEETS.

That's why the pictures looked familiar. It was what the old German artist resorted to after the Nazis had forbidden him to paint: watercolors piled on top of each other on heavy pieces of "Japan paper": his "Unpainted Pictures" small enough to be hidden if necessary.

"I need to get out of here," I heard my voice saying from a hollow place inside my ears. As I was uttering the words, my floaty mind reached out and brought back Wheezer's voice saying the exact same thing that day in our apartment when he was handing back the forbidden photograph.

"Such lengths you humans go to color up the evil inside of you," crowed Cutting Edge. "How many green penises did *you* count?"

"Shut up!"

"I kept my trap shut till you spoke first."

"I'm out of here!"

"Oops, watch it! Oh, too late. Oh, dear, dear, dear. *Now* what are you going to do?"

I had knocked against the trestle table where Aunt Charlotte had left a small work in progress, which I had overlooked when we came in. One of the plastic glasses still filled with colored water slopped over onto the painting, which started to bleed. I ran for the paper towels and he followed right behind. Or from deep within.

"You're done here, you know," Cutting Edge observed, as we re-entered the violated studio.

"What do you mean?"

"I have to spell it out for you? You've trespassed, you've overstayed. You're not 'too good to be true' anymore, you're too bad to be wanted, even by Filthy Auntie. *Especially* by Filthy Auntie. When she sees you've discovered her filthy pictures she'll never want to see you again. We need to hot-foot it out of here. You need to be somewhere else before she sees what you've done. What's ruined is ruined. Oh, ruination, we crown you king."

The little painting-in-progress I had ruined was the girl sitting alone on the bed where the man had sat. From out of a black background, a giant green mask was starting to emerge. The glass I had tipped over was unfortunately the one that held black water.

"You're just making it worse with all that dabbing, stupid. Besides, what could you possibly tell her when she gets home? 'Oh, Filthy Auntie, a weird wind blew up out of nowhere and I heard noises in your studio and I went in to see if anything was damaged and I saw the knocked-over glass. I did my best with paper towels and I didn't look at anything else in the room, I swear.'"

"Do you ever shut up?"

"I'm programmed to keep my mouth running till yours stops."

"But if mine stops it means I am dead."

"I was waiting for you to catch up. So here's the plan. Leave Filthy Auntie a nice note. Don't go on too long and don't get theatrical. Thank her for taking you in. Say you *aren't* too good to be true—you are harboring a cutting-edge baddie— no, dumbass, don't write that second part, just stop at you aren't good anymore. Then close with 'I've decided to go somewhere else.'

"Now I'm going to tell you something you won't want to hear. She'll be alarmed at first. But she'll be relieved to have you gone."

"You're probably right."

"I know I'm right. Give up and let me run things. Now you're going to pocket the rest of Filthy Auntie's painkillers and take along a bottle of water. Then get your bike—that's right, put on that helmet. Don't want shit-boy to spot you riding past his grandparents' house and saying 'freaking little loser, he's gone and copied my haircut!'

"Tell me, Marcus, now we're out on the beach, pedaling north on your usual route, don't you feel you're headed in the right direction? Isn't it a relief to finally face your awfuls? You aren't wanted, you weren't wanted, and you're not going to be missed. You weren't wanted back when Mom kept checking her panties and it didn't come. Then when you were about the size of a bean, she panicked: 'I can't do this, not by myself, scraping it out would be kinder than bringing it up poor without a father.' But when you had swelled to the size of one of those little hatchlings she realized she'd left it too late and submitted to her penance.

"And do you really think when Filthy Auntie received word she was your only kin she ran down to the beach and danced for joy at the prospect of sacrificing her solitary life, not to mention her only bedroom?

"Wait, there's worse to come. We haven't got to the thought you were trying not to think, the thought that was too much for poor Evolving Gremlin and sent him wailing back into the ether. Pedal a little faster. No use trying to arm yourself against it because it's already written on the fleshy, bumpy insides of your pink soul. However, I'll keep up my cutting-edge standards and tell it aloud in my crumbly voice."

"Not yet, please!"

"*Please* isn't programmed into my vocabulary."

# *XXXVIII.*

*I*'ll hang out with you on this squalid porch while you swallow your medicine. We'll think *the next thought* together while you're swigging down the pills. How many did Filthy Auntie leave you? There are seven in the bottle and you swallowed one back at the house. That should cover it. No, no, no, don't cram them in your mouth, swallow each individually and wash it down with water. You don't want to ruin everything by choking up and vomiting. You're such an easy little vomiter. Now, are you ready for that contemptible next thought? The one that takes all the prizes?"

I buried my face in my hands as Cutting Edge spewed out the contemptible thought. I did feel like vomiting, but kept it down.

"So now you know the worst about yourself. And you know what you have to do now."

"No one would want to go on living after hearing that."

"You get the idea. I've done my job. Off to the next client!"

"Aren't you going inside the cottage with me?"

"I'll level with you. Do you know what DNA is?"

"Of course I know what it is."

"The thing is, I share some DNA with Ole Plat-eye. I might self-destruct if I passed through those blue-painted portals. You're on your own when you go through that door."

At first the dead silence inside Grief Cottage felt worse than Cutting Edge's voice. At least he had been company.

I prowled around the cobwebby front room waiting for the pills to take effect. A surge of dark clarity washed over me. I understood what I was going to do now and why it had to be done. I also understood that if I had anything to say to Johnny Dace I'd better get going because my time was ebbing.

"I don't expect you to appear. I don't expect you to respond in any way. But I have to tell you that you got me through the summer. I sought you out and you were there for me as I was for you. You were my *sure*. You were my lifeline, if that doesn't sound too weird.

"Just in case you are listening and wanting to hear the rest of the story in whatever way ghosts want to hear the rest of the story, I'll bring you up to date. This morning my aunt went off to Charleston to find out if her wrist is healing. Strange to think I'll never see her again. Then you know I told you about Billy Upchurch's mother? Well, an ambulance came and took her away. They think it's pneumonia, which is no joke for a person her age, and she'll probably be gone by nightfall. Now I'm like you, I don't have anybody. It's really lonely without the turtle eggs. The hatchlings are well on their journey now, though some of them have already been eaten or caught in the shrimping nets, others didn't have enough energy left over for their ten-mile swim to reach the open ocean, and others never made it out of their egg yolks.

"There are so many things I wish I knew about you. About you and Billy. Where was that hiding place you showed him?

"You will have to be my eighth grade friend. You'll be the boy I suddenly come face-to-face with when I turn a corner in a corridor at school. I have seen you, the long narrow face, the raisin eyes deep in the sockets, the stalk-like neck, the nose that looked broken and not reset right, the bowed legs in jeans and the black boots. You were braced in the door frame, pushing yourself outward with your hands. I was close enough to count the knuckle ridges on your spread fingers. You had unusually large hands.

"Have you ever had a thought as contemptible as this? It's a wonder how I managed to forget it until now. When my mom went out to get our pizza and didn't come back, I got hungry. The smells of our landlady's supper wafted up through the heat register and I got hungrier and hungrier and finally wolfed down some cereal and hated myself—and Mom—for spoiling my appetite. I watched the movie. I watched the whole movie. A lot of it I didn't pay attention to because of this separate track running in my head. The separate track had already killed her. I was at the point in the track where I was fantasizing what would happen to me after she was gone. And I could see possibilities spread out in front of me. I didn't think of Aunt Charlotte that night, my scenarios were more on the line of myself, Marcus, alone, with Mom gone. Independent and alone. People would walk softly around me and ask me what I wanted to do.

"Then I yanked myself off that track and felt despicable for letting the scenario progress as far as it had. By this time in the movie, the old lady had helped them steal the gold with no one the wiser, including herself. At that point I got scared. I worried that I might have already killed her by thinking these thoughts. I got a blanket and a pillow and lay down in front of the TV with the sound turned off. When she got back she would find me on the floor still in my clothes and feel terrible for taking so long.

"And then I really did fall asleep, and was waked by the state troopers knocking on our door.

"I think I can go to sleep now, here in Grief Cottage. But not in this cobwebby room. I want to be where you are. Please show me. Put your hand on my shoulder and when I stand up just push me from behind. I want to sleep where you sleep."

I almost left it too late. I was half asleep when I felt the pressure on my shoulder. How could I ever have dreaded his touch? I wobbled and almost fell when I stood up, and I tripped going up the stairs. ("Hey, hey, *hey*! Watch it!" Charlie Coggins had cried.)

How peaceful it was going to be when all this chatter stopped.

I felt the palm of his large hand guiding me up the remaining stairs, then steering me to the right and to the right again, over the threshold of the oceanfront room Charlie Coggins wouldn't let me enter.

I was somewhere in the middle of saying, "I have seen you and felt you and that's enough. I'm glad your voice never joined the rest of the human noise—"

I may have reached the "I am glad"—then there was a splintering and a falling followed by a crack that brought horrible pain and my weak shout from the bottom of darkness.

# XXXIX.

*B*efore I ever walked through the doors of my new school, I was known as "the bones boy." And all through the school year I was called "Bones." ("Hey, Bones . . .") The nickname trailed me into high school, then faded as more and more people came along who knew nothing about how it had originated. I sort of missed being Bones because the name had evoked awe and respect and some notoriety. But it had certainly done its job, airlifting me out of the realm of merciless peers before any of us had a chance to lay eyes on one another.

I said "walked" through the doors of my new school, but I should have said "swung through on crutches." (Spiral break of the tibia, requiring a plate and eleven screws.)

"Do you know what a realtor's worst nightmare is?" Charlie Coggins went around saying to the news media. "When they find human bones under one of his properties."

"You were still under your self-administered anesthesia," Lachicotte said, "when the paramedics were putting your leg into alignment. But the firemen had to come and knock out a wall so the paramedics could get to you. And there you were, doubled up in that cramped enclosure. They had to stabilize your breathing first (*fust*) before they moved you. The next problem, at the hospital, was what kind of anesthesia to give you for the surgery when the Percocet you swallowed was still meandering through your bloodstream in dribs and drabs. So they opted for the spinal block."

Concerning the subjects of Aunt Charlotte's painkillers and Aunt Charlotte's breached studio, silence reigned. Maybe each of us was waiting for the other to go first, but it felt more like an unwritten restraining order that the three of us had tacitly agreed upon.

I was still on crutches and into regular sessions with a psychiatrist in Myrtle Beach when the painkiller subject got brought up. Lachicotte's former second wife who had become a therapist had recommended this psychiatrist as being excellent with children and adolescents. Lachicotte drove me to these sessions as Aunt Charlotte had not yet resumed driving. Both ankle and wrist were healing, though she would later insist she never did recover full range of motion in her right hand. On one of our drives to Myrtle Beach, Lachicotte suddenly spoke up. "I had to report the container in your pocket, Marcus. For a scintilla of a moment I considered keeping it quiet. But that wouldn't have been in anybody's best interests. You understand, don't you?"

"What's a *scintilla*?"

"A touch, a dash, next to nothing."

"I think you probably did right."

I was more resentful of what I considered "the worst" betrayal Lachicotte had been guilty of while I was still in the hospital. Yet I knew that eventually I'd have to forgive him for that one, too.

★  ★  ★

IN MY SESSIONS with the psychiatrist, I had made up my mind that everything was going to be on the table, even my true feelings when I was beating up Wheezer—everything except for my sightings of the ghost-boy. Since Johnny Dace's remains had been discovered, I had a second reason for keeping the secret. Formerly, it was because I didn't want to be thought crazy and sent away. But if I were to tell about our relationship *after* his bones became public property, I would be seen as a boy who was making up things to get more attention for himself. As Aunt Charlotte had put it, back when we had been discussing the "man in gray" who was said to walk the beach before a hurricane: "People see what they want to see. Or imagine they saw. And others *say* they saw something in order to sound psychic or special."

Predictably, the psychiatrist encouraged me to talk about my mother. In order to get the awful part out of the way, I described the scenario I had been creating on the night of her accident, and how when I finally remembered it as "the thought I didn't want to think," I hadn't wanted to live anymore. The psychiatrist was a lady of about Aunt Charlotte's age, whose disposition was a lovely mix of alertness, humor, and respect. Her filigree earrings swung along with her shoulder-length gray hair when you made her laugh. She wore nice clothes and shoes and spoke with a sanded-down version of Lachicotte's accent. As I completed the story about my awful scenario, I noted, as good students do when they have pleased their teacher, that she was excited by the start we had gotten off to. *This is exactly the right material for us to be facing together,* I could see her thinking.

This is not meant to be condescending to the woman who helped me so much. Having chosen her profession myself, I know all too well how cautiously we must treat our young patients, how we are taught to follow diagnostic guidelines until we can glimpse the individual beneath the presenting material. We start all over again with every new patient—or we should.

The "pleased teacher" being "played" by the student was the perception of a boy whose sessions with an earlier psychiatrist had taught him a few strategies for protecting his secrets. Because he still lives in me I am perfectly aware how cunning an eleven-year-old boy can be when it comes to withholding information. Being super-cunning requires handing over *another* secret in place of the one you want to keep buried.

She was just what was needed and she was in the right place when I needed her. Her most lasting gift has been the little notebooks. She told me to go out and buy a small notebook, small enough to fit in my pocket, and to write things in it that were important to me.

"Anything that strikes a chord. A line a day, or nothing, or as much as you want. Anything that strikes you as worth saving for yourself. A passage from something you read, something someone said—write it down when it's fresh and don't censor yourself. No one's going to see this little book but you. And when you have filled up all its pages, go out and buy another one. Store them in a secret place."

"Can it be just thoughts I have?"

"Absolutely. And also," she smiled, "the thoughts you *don't want to have*." By then she had glimpsed the individual beneath the presenting material.

★   ★   ★

"YOU KNOW THE words a realtor never wants to hear?" Charlie Coggins loved explaining to reporters: "*Secure the site.* That's right, those three little words: *secure the site.*

"But in this case I gave the order myself. I was early on the scene, thanks to Lachicotte Hayes phoning me on his mobile from the spot of the accident. 'Right now the fire squad's knocking down a wall to get to him,' Lachicotte said, 'so you'd better come.' By the time I arrived the medics were getting the boy's breathing stabilized before they set about moving him. I knew just what had happened. He had gone and done exactly what I'd told him not to. He went into that upstairs south room and fell right through the floor. The 'wall' the firemen had been knocking down, on the south side of the house, wasn't a true wall, just a boarded-up makeshift with some shingles nailed on top, so they had an easier time than they expected. The boy fell through the upper floor and landed in a small enclosure beneath the staircase and beneath part of the south upstairs room. Nobody knew this enclosure existed; even I didn't, until our helpful Historical Society kindly obtained the old plans for me. Originally it was a wood storage closet built into the south wall, so you could load in firewood from an outside opening and then fetch it from a door inside the house so you didn't have to brave the elements. Rice planter families stayed though November and it was cold by then.

"Then, when later owners decided to build the south stairs and the upstairs room, they nailed up a partition to close off the wood closet from inside. They removed its lift latch because it stuck out and then whitewashed over the door.

"Then, when Hurricane Hazel hit us in 1954, the south porch burned down for reasons still unknown. The rest of the house stood up just fine. New owners, interested in a quick flip, sheared off the burnt porch and boarded up the south wall. That's the quote-unquote 'wall' the firemen knocked down. After my dad bought the cottage from the flippers, who had run out of money, he sent me over to nail some vintage cypress shingles over that unsightly makeshift wall.

"Like I said, when I got there the medics were still stabilizing the boy's breathing, they hadn't moved him yet, and when they did that's when we all saw what he'd been lying on top of. I say *lying*, but the skeleton was in a cramped sitting position and the boy had fallen right on top. It looked like he was sitting in the skeleton's lap.

"Then everybody began speculating. Folks can't tolerate loose ends—they've got to tie up a story. So it was, Are these the remains of a *murder victim*? How long have they been buried in there? Is the perpetrator still alive? My first thought was, Oh, _____, now I'll be stuck with this property until the victim is identified, and maybe even until the murderer is apprehended! But then I recalled going through the house with this very boy not long ago and him talking so much about the boy that got lost during Hazel. That's when I was almost positive I knew who these bones belonged to. In that case, the sooner I got it confirmed the better, and that's when I said, 'Nobody touch or move any of those remains till we get the forensics people here.' So in this case it was the realtor who gave the order to secure the site. By the way, the inside door to that old wood closet is preserved in fine shape. It's got its original eighteenth-century lift latch and strap hinge, and even the old wrought nails. I'm going to make a gift of it to the Charleston Museum."

★ ★ ★

"SHE MUST BE really mad at me," I said to Lachicotte when I was emerging from my semi-conscious fugue in the hospital.

"Why do you think that?"

"Because, why isn't she here?"

"She wasn't sure you would want to see her."

"Why not?"

I really could not think why. It would be weeks before all the events (both inner and outer ones) of that day were reclaimed. The first memories to swim up were the bike ride with Cutting Edge hectoring me all the way to Grief Cottage . . . then a blank . . . then pain cracking inside me . . . and another blank . . . then being carried across sand in daylight with voices calling back and forth against the sound of the ocean, and me thinking as they carried me, *Please don't drop me on one of those Spanish bayonets.*

"Well, that note you left her," Lachicotte said.

"What was in it?" I didn't remember writing a note.

"You thanked her for taking you in but said you were no longer a good person and you were going somewhere else."

The words sounded familiar, but why had I written them?

Then I remembered they had gone to the surgeon that day. "How is her wrist?" I asked Lachicotte.

"The news was guarded but good. This surgeon never gets overenthusiastic. Most surgeons don't. Your aunt is deeply concerned about you, Marcus. She cares about you, more than she shows. The last thing she wants is for you to feel you have to stay with her when you'd rather go somewhere else."

I was puzzled. "Why should I want to go anywhere else?"

★   ★   ★

AUNT CHARLOTTE'S SECRET project, dubbed *Filthy Auntie's Pictures* by Cutting Edge, and the events leading up to my invading her studio, would be one of the later memory sequences to return. When I did remember and apologized for disobeying her, she simply nodded and then formally invited me into her studio, much as she had that first time when she wanted "everything to be aboveboard" about my trust and about the "nice monthly stipend" she would receive.

In the same matter-of-fact monotone she presented me with a "shrink-wrapped" version of her demon-father's violation of her childhood, beginning when he took her and her doll on business trips when she was five and ending when she ran away at sixteen. ("That's enough now. With your super-active imagination, Marcus, you can fill in the rest." She didn't add, "Besides, you have the memory of the little paintings to help you picture the scenes.")

The paintings were never mentioned. They truly did become her "Unpainted Pictures." I have no idea what she did with them. The corkboard once again bore its former items, tacked up in their former spots: details from landscape paintings she admired, sketches of clouds, of the ocean, the postcards of her own paintings, and gallery announcements and local press cuttings. She asked Lachicotte to move the big easel back to its old spot and would I mind, until her casts were off, changing her linens again and giving the studio a good sweep and dusting in preparation for her return to work.

THE OPENING ENTRY in my first pocket-sized notebook (those Moleskine ones with the elastic band and sewn spine had just come on the American market) was the old professor's advice:

Don't mention it to anyone else unless you find they've
had adventures of the same sort themselves . . .
    —*The Lion, the Witch, and the Wardrobe*, C.S. Lewis

And many notebooks later, when I was in medical school, I
recorded this treasure:

It could be said of all human beings that at times when
instinctual frustrations lead to a feeling of hopelessness
or futility the fixing of the psyche in the body
becomes loosened and a period of psyche and soma
unrelatedness has to be endured. [. . .] The idea of a
ghost, a disembodied spirit, derives from this lack of
essential anchoring of the psyche in the soma, and the
value of the ghost story lies in its drawing attention to
the precariousness of psyche-soma existence.
    —"Dwelling of Psyche in Body," *Human Nature*,
                                    D. W. Winnicott

"Yes, the anchoring of the psyche in the body is very precarious," I wrote on the following page. "What I was sure of at the
time was *that I had seen*. What I was *not* sure of was whether I
was different from others my age. If so, was I super-sensitive to
the uncanny or was I going insane? Could another person of
eleven have this experience? Or was this my experience alone
because the ghost-boy was inseparable from my history, my
personality, my needs? I knew he was related to my life, but he
also appeared to be an entity on his own terms. How could he
be both? What I needed was a mature personality who could
earn my trust, comprehend my contradictions, and help me
form a concept large enough to contain them."

★ ★ ★

"I CAN'T BELIEVE you didn't tell me!" My leg was in its cast. I felt perfectly fine. Why was this my fourth day in the hospital?

"Well, I am telling you now," said Lachicotte patiently.

"But it's too late! They've moved everything. I found him—I was the one who fell on *top* of him, for God's sake. And you're just telling me all this *now*?"

"You were unconscious when we found you, Marcus. We didn't know if you were going to make it."

"But I didn't get to see him."

"You can still do that. The remains are at Johnson's funeral home. I'll take you over when we get you discharged."

"But I'll never see the way he was when—"

"They took lots of *in situ* photographs before anything got touched or moved. Charlie Coggins had the presence of mind to secure the site. You can look at the photographs. And the bones will be laid out in their anatomical order."

"Why is he at the funeral home?"

"The forensic team finished their work on him there. It was relatively quick. Dates and times matched. They concluded he was hiding in that enclosure, probably from the hurricane, and then the fire started, perhaps from his cigarette dropped on the porch, and he died from asphyxiation while waiting out the hurricane. When the cousin arrives, she will be the one to decide where the remains go."

"What cousin?" I couldn't believe the unfairness of it all. I was the one who found him and then they went ahead and did everything without telling me!

"Well, she's that cousin of Mr. Dace, very old now, the one who settled out of court with the Barbours fifty years ago. The

Barbour family was able to provide her old address and it turned out she was still living there. Her DNA matched up with the remains and now Charlie Coggins is flying her in from Louisville at his expense."

"Why is he doing that?"

"She says she won't be at peace till she sees the boy. Or what is left of him."

"Lachicotte, I *need* to see him. This is *important*. Can't you get that surgeon to discharge me?"

"It's not the surgeon who's keeping you here, Marcus. They need to make sure you're not a danger to yourself before they sign you out. If you had swallowed a few more of those tablets, we would be making arrangements for *your* burial, too."

So again I was trapped in my old situation. The wheels of the law had to turn first. Nevertheless, I felt robbed, betrayed. This was far worse than missing out on the hatchlings' boil. Unfairly, I measured Lachicotte against William, my ad litem, who had immediately understood I needed to see my mom's body before it went to the undertaker.

"Can you at least tell me *how we looked* when you found us?"

"How you looked?"

"How *we* looked. After the firemen had knocked down the wall, and you first saw me and him. What did you see?"

"I saw only *you*, Marcus."

"But what about him?"

"You were as much as I could take in. We didn't know if you were going to make it."

"I can't *believe* nobody bothered to tell me."

"Well, I do have some good news. Your friend Coral Upchurch, who's on the floor below you, is recovering. She's going home tomorrow, weak but on the mend."

*   *   *

IT WAS THE kind of human interest story everybody loves. Long ago mystery solved—and on the fiftieth anniversary of Hurricane Hazel, when the mystery had begun. A local boy falling on top of a skeleton boy who had been sitting cramped in a forgotten closet in an abandoned cottage built two hundred years ago. It had all the elements. It had "legs," as the news-people say. It had staying power. Today I can tap in "Johnny Dace" and see those *in situ* images photographed by the foren-sics team. There are his bones huddled upright in a corner of a forgotten closet, waiting to be found. I was identified as the boy who discovered him. Marcus Harshaw, age eleven, a resident of the island.

We buried him in the cemetery of Lachicotte's church. Coral Upchurch was present in her wheelchair, attended by Roberta Dumas. The DNA cousin, in her eighties, took the spotlight—for a while. Her life had clearly been lived at the other end of the spectrum from Coral Upchurch's and she had not held up as well. But she could still walk and talk and had some faded Polaroid snapshots of Johnny Dace in her purse. She blossomed under the attention of the newspeople until the discrepancies in her narrative piled too high and toppled. The Polaroids were of a much younger Johnny, a frowning child who was too much for his parents to handle; they had sent him off several times to a facility for wayward youth, but kept bringing him home to try again. In a later version of the cous-in's, he was a smart, sweet boy if you knew how to handle him and had been like a son to her. Finally, in her toppling version, Elvis himself had passed through Louisville and told Johnny Dace, "You could pass as my double." But the problem was that

Elvis had only begun his career the year Johnny Dace went missing in the hurricane.

That was when Charlie Coggins murmured to her that there was just enough time before her departing flight for him to show her the cottage where her only remaining kin had spent the last fifty years. Refusing the realtor's offer to pay for transferring the remains back to Kentucky, she signed papers releasing him to be buried on the island on the condition that she would not be liable for any of the funeral and burial expenses.

Before Johnny's burial, Lachicotte took me to the funeral home to see his remains. He was five-feet-eight-and-a-half, had bow legs, and large hands. I had hoped to check out the broken and badly repaired nose, but the nose was gone. They allowed me to run my hand along the long tibia bones.

WE ORDERED HIS stone from the monument place Lachicotte's family always used. It was down the coast, near Georgetown, and we drove there in a 1936 Bentley Derby touring car Lachicotte had just taken on. We had the top down, or rather Lachicotte was having a new top made, and my hair whipped in the coastal wind the way Pickett's did when he was arriving in Ed's Jeep to destroy my evening. The steering was on the right side of the Bentley and we'd moved the passenger seat back all the way to accommodate my straight-leg cast.

At the monument place, a very tan young woman in shorts and a T-shirt was at work outdoors chiseling a stone for a monk who had died in 1904. After Hurricane Floyd had flooded the monastery in 1999, she explained, all the monks' remains had to be dug up and relocated to a new cemetery built on higher ground. New stones were needed because marble crumbled when you tried to move it. "This is the longest order we've ever taken on. Eighty-one stones! We've been working on them for almost five years. We have to do it between other jobs, but the abbot said that was fine, because monks were taught to live in a different kind of time anyway."

Lachicotte was fascinated, and so she took us around to the back where some finished stones were stacked on wooden trays, waiting for delivery to the monastery. All the stones were the same modest rectangular size and carved exactly alike. IHS at the top, then underneath the monk's name, below that, his dates of birth, profession, and death.

"What's IHS?" I asked.

"The first three letters of Jesus's name in Greek," she said, and Lachicotte obligingly spelled out the name for me: I-h-s-u-s.

We had gone back and forth about choosing the appropriate stone to lie on top of Johnny Dace's grave. Aunt Charlotte and Lachicotte and I were dividing the cost among us.

"But if we just put his birth and death dates, it'll look like any old boy who was born in 1940 and died fourteen years later," I reasoned.

"Yes, but when in doubt, less is usually more," said Aunt Charlotte. "We want to stay away from the maudlin."

"What's *maudlin*?" I asked.

"Smarmy, sentimental, melodramatic, like for instance, 'Lost in Hurricane Hazel, 1954, Miraculously Found, 2004.' That still doesn't tell enough and it uses far too many letters."

"Let's think what he would want," Lachicotte finally suggested, "if he were here (*he-ah*) to give the order himself."

By the time Lachicotte and I headed south in the Bentley Derby to the monument place, we had settled on the simplest information.

"That's probably enough," I said. "When Mom and I used to discuss our funerals and burials, she said all she wanted on her stone was ALICE HARSHAW, and her dates. She didn't even want her family name on her stone. I still haven't decided."

"Decided what?" Lachicotte asked. "What you want on yours?"

"No, I haven't ordered Mom's stone yet. My ad litem back in North Carolina is going to take care of it when I decide. The money's all set up to pay for it. All I have to do is say what I want on her stone."

The young woman at the monument place sat down with us and made some sketches. JOHNNY DACE with birth and death dates. She showed us the possible fonts on a chart. We both liked the name in square capital letters. "It looks like a Latin inscription," said Lachicotte.

"I wish we had something more," I said.

"Like what?"

"Well, like those monks have. Something above themselves to watch over them."

"There's always the good old STTL the Romans put on their gravestones," said Lachicotte. "*Sit Tibi Terra Levis.* It means 'May the earth lie lightly upon thee.'"

"I love that! It's perfect—especially for him."

"Latin was the one thing I loved at my boarding schools," Lachicotte said.

"But maybe we should just have it in English, so people around here will know what it means."

"We can do that," said Lachicotte.

"And you know what? I think it would be the right thing for my mom's stone. Only maybe both the Latin and then the

English underneath. My mother had a special thing about Latin."

"You can do that, too," said Lachicotte.

★ ★ ★

AUNT CHARLOTTE WAS to become what she called "an intermittent recoverer." At first she tried to limit herself to a bottle and a half a day. She did her hand exercises religiously and began to paint again, though according to her not ever with the same range of motion. The publicity surrounding the Johnny Dace remains brought her a flurry of new commissions for paintings of Grief Cottage. She worked from my photos, and from her memory of her earlier paintings. The cottage was demolished soon after the publicity died down, and Charlie Coggins quickly relieved himself of the two lots to an eager buyer. Then the new owner's neighbors, which included Ed Bolton, advised the man to call in erosion experts before he started building. The experts found that the north tip of the island was dissolving at such a rate that any structure he built would probably be washed away by 2025.

Aunt Charlotte tired herself fulfilling the new commissions and when she was back up to three bottles a day, she let Lachicotte and me talk her into going on a month's retreat at a very nice recovery villa in Savannah. Lachicotte moved in with me, making my breakfast, driving me to school, and leaving the toilet seat up. After that she made it through a two-year dry spell, during which she built an addition onto her cottage: a bedroom and bath and a north-facing deck where she could paint outside without people spying over her shoulder and making stupid remarks. After she had her "deck-studio," her painting underwent a significant change. Small canvases, though not as small as four by sixes. You looked at them and thought, "Oh, she's become an abstract impressionist." But if you kept looking long enough you thought, "No, wait, that square of grays and lavenders is a close-up of a cloud after sunset, the way it looks when the artist has penetrated the mass and shape of its vapor. No, wait, that's the surf at high tide, the way it looks when the artist has gone beyond the outline of the waves and is among the droplets."

We lost a third of my trust in the crash of 2008. Aunt Charlotte continued to draw her "nice stipend," which she deposited straight over into my college fund. "Look at it this way, Marcus. When we were in clover, I was able to draw on my old savings to build my addition, and you got four years with your expensive psychiatrist. We're going to be okay. Whatever happens, you've proved yourself smart enough to walk away with a hundred scholarships, and my 'droplet and vapor' paintings, as you call them, aren't doing half bad. People can live with them. I like them myself. They're both soothing and strange, and they enlarge beautifully on aluminum prints. A lawyer in Columbia bought six of them for her office."

Lachicotte's sudden death in 2013 sent her back for an extended stay at the villa in Savannah. In exchange for reduced rates to cover her stay, she gave art lessons to other guests, demonstrating the therapeutic values of painting with the non-dominant hand. ("You will uncover all sorts of things about yourself," she promised her fellow recoverers. "Your unpracticed hand will waver and wobble into places your controlling hand would never let you near.") It turned out she hadn't needed to barter, as Lachicotte had divided his worldly goods between "My dear niece, Althea," and "My good friend, Charlotte Lee."

"Just like Lash . . . typical, typical," Aunt Charlotte would rage or lament on my visits to the villa—by this time, I was in pre-med at the state university. "I mean, he was old but not that old. If it weren't for his foolish need to please everything that crossed his path, he had some vital years left in him. He had no business switching cars with that boy, just because the boy wanted to drive the Jaguar."

The "boy," a young man in his twenties, was supposed to follow Lachicotte to Hilton Head in his own car and take him home after they had delivered the Jaguar. "I'll never forgive myself," the boy anguished. "I just wanted to drive that beauty for the final stretch, and at the rest stop before the bridge, Lachicotte handed over the keys and said, 'Remember. You're still driving on the right side of the road, but now the steering wheel's on your right, as well.' And then he jams on the brakes of my car to keep from running over a dog and crashes against an abutment. I saw the whole thing through the Jaguar's rear-view mirror. I'll never be able to look through a rearview mirror again without reliving the whole thing: that brown dog streaking across the road and Mr. Hayes's wild, crazy turn straight into the abutment."

"That boy reminds me of those witnesses being interviewed after a disaster," Aunt Charlotte would say. "It's all about *the witness* who saw the tragedy." And she would then mimic a witness's plaintive voice: "'I was sitting in the outdoor café having my cappuccino and planning my sightseeing for the afternoon when suddenly this building right across the road from me explodes! It was close enough to make my table shake and little pieces of ash fall into my cappuccino . . .'"

I could hear Lachicotte as he handed over the keys: *"Remem-bah, you're still driving on the right side of the road but the steering wheel's now on yo-ah right as well."*

In fact, I could hear Lachicotte a dozen times in a day, saying things I knew he would probably say if we were sitting next to each other in the car or walking on the beach or eating supper together. I will go on hearing him for the rest of my life. He makes fresh observations, suitable to the occasion, and my ear-memory still registers his pitch of voice, his speech rhythms, his modest-warm mode of delivery. He is one of the permanent figures of my dream life.

Coral Upchurch lived another eight months after surviving pneumonia and is buried next to Billy in Columbia. She left me the antique Provençal writing desk, which is my nicest piece of furniture. Roberta inherited the Upchurch house in Columbia, which she sold to pay for her grandson's college. The Upchurch family beach house, compromised by Archie's trellis hiding the old brick footing columns and Coral's unsightly wheelchair ramp, was bequeathed by Mrs. Upchurch to the island's Historical Society, which soon restored its vernacular integrity. The William Upchurch Community Center is rented out for special functions, the proceeds going into the Society's coffers. To celebrate my graduation from college, Aunt Charlotte gave me a party on Coral's smoking porch.

When I came home to Aunt Charlotte's during college and medical school breaks, we would make our pilgrimage to where Lachicotte was buried next to his mother.

"Damn it, Lash," Aunt Charlotte would scold his grave. "Why did you think you had to look out for everything on legs and wheels?"

Though another time she said to me: "Isn't it strange, Marcus, that after someone dies you like to recall the very traits that used to drive you crazy."

"I miss him a lot," I would say.

When we visited the cemetery, Aunt Charlotte usually remained on a shady bench near Lachicotte's grave while I walked over to the newer part of the cemetery to visit "your friend," as she called him.

I followed new rules for these visits to Johnny Dace. I wouldn't have dreamed of plunking myself down beside his stone and choking his eternal stillness with my living chatter. He was no longer the missing dead boy crammed into a forgotten closet. His bones were at rest, laid out flat in their anatomical order until they crumbled in their own time and became part of the island's soil. And I was no longer the boy who needed the lifeline of a silent listener who had showed himself, on two occasions, as an entity on his own terms.


"IT'S SO SAD," Aunt Charlotte was to brood at a later date. This was after I had started my residency and was seeing patients, some of them the same age I had been when Aunt Charlotte met me at the airport and shook my hand and said, *Well, Marcus, here we are.*

"What's so sad?" I asked.

"When we don't realize how remarkable someone is while they're still with us. Then after they're gone we wish we had told them, but when they were around *we didn't know yet.* Does that make any sense?"

That was when I told her about the day I had met Lachicotte. "You were still in the hospital after your accident and he was taking me to buy a bike before we picked you up. We were driving across the causeway and I was telling him about my mom and I said that Mom had planned to take the high school equivalency exam and go on to college. I said, 'She wanted to make something of herself.' And he was quiet for a minute and then he said, 'I would say she had already made a great deal of herself by bringing you up so well.'"

"That sounds exactly like something Lachicotte would say."

"Yes, well, it went right over me that day, but later when I thought about it, I felt such sorrow that I had never understood this when she was alive and how it would have pleased her if I had said something like, 'Mom, you are a real warrior, I'm so proud of you.'"

Aunt Charlotte looked at me. "Then you do know what I'm talking about."

FORSTERVILLE: AN EPILOGUE

*The island in late May, fourteen years later, supper hour.*

"WELL, MARCUS, HERE we are."

"That was the first thing you ever said to me."

"Was it?"

"When you met me at the airport, you said, 'Well, Marcus, here we are,' and shook my hand."

"What a memory. I remember nothing, other than being scared."

"Of what you were taking on?"

"I was scared you were thinking, 'Oh, no! I have to live with *her*?' Even now I'm not sure I'd want to know your first impression of me."

"'A thin serious lady all in white, with beaky features and a Roman centurion haircut. When you shook my hand it was such a relief not to be hysterically hugged. Your turn, now. What did you think of me?"

"Marcus, you're the one studying to be a shrink. Don't you know when any two people meet both are thinking, 'What does X think of *me*?'"

"You must have had some impression. What kind of boy did you see when that airline attendant was leading me to you?"

"I'm not sure. Well, let's see. Maybe that you weren't as much of *a little boy* as I'd been expecting. I had no experience of little boys. Though I'm not sure I even thought that much. It may be something I'm adding in hindsight. I guess I was mostly worrying what you thought of me. Sorry to disappoint you."

"You haven't. When people think they're making something up about the past, they're often remembering."

*The island, early next morning.*

"WELL, IT'S TIME to be on my way."

"It's hardly daylight, Aunt Charlotte. Savannah is only a two-hour drive."

"I know, but I get antsy before a trip. I feel neither here or there."

"You're sure you don't want to take along a sandwich and a banana?"

"No, I've got my bottled water and a package of that boring trail mix. I want to make it inside the gates of the recovery villa without falling off the wagon."

"Maybe I'll replace those damaged shingles on the ocean side."

"Marcus, the shingles can wait. You've been slogging nonstop as long as I've known you. Middle school, high school, college, medical school. Now you have ten free days before your residency starts. Why not relax and see what it feels like to do nothing at all?"

"I'm not sure I could handle it. You sure you have all the materials you need for your painting classes at the villa?"

"You loaded them into the car yourself. Now let's exchange a hysterical hug and I'll hit the road. A person my age drives better earlier in the day."

She stuck her hand out of the driver's window, fluttering her fingers in a playful farewell as she turned left onto Seashore Drive. I stood at the curb, watching her little silver car out of sight. When her vintage Mercedes gave up the ghost after Lachicotte's death, she went out and purchased a new Japanese compact along with an additional 75,000-mile warranty that included pickup when it needed service or misbehaved and a rental car delivered to your door. ("This ought to see me through to the end. I never go anywhere except for shopping and my periodical recovery jaunts to Savannah. Lachicotte couldn't stand new cars, but he doesn't have to know.")

I feel neither here or there, she said as her excuse for leaving so early. After she was gone, I kept rerunning that fluttery farewell out her window. It reminded me of the dismissive finger-wave from her stretcher as the medics were carrying her out the door. ("Be a good boy, and be sure to lock up front and back.")

"You can tell when a person has already left you behind," explained a young patient I had been treating under supervision. "Even if that person is right in front of you, you know they're only pretending to be with you and that makes it worse." At fifteen, she had attempted suicide three times.

"Why not relax and see what it feels like to do nothing at all?" Aunt Charlotte had suggested. Still rooted to the curb, I contemplated how I was going to get through the rest of the day and felt the onset of a terror I thought I had outgrown.

I hated it when these *clusters* started to form. One unwelcome subject sought out its counterparts—farewells, people leaving and never coming back, ambulances—like the silent ambulance with the revolving red light turning into our street and taking away Coral Upchurch. And then *those* counterparts attracted similar old hurts and horrors until you were trapped in the nucleus of the cluster. This cluster, I knew, was labeled LOSS in big black letters. I knew this much, thanks to therapy and training, but simply *knowing* it didn't protect you from reacting to it over and over again. Until one day you resolved to sit down in the middle of the nucleus, fold your arms, and invite the cluster to do its worst. And if you survived that, you could look around and see what was left in its absence.

I followed my feet back to the cottage. What they wanted next, it seemed, was to perform a house check. Kitchen in order, bathroom left neat; Aunt Charlotte must have wiped the sink and floor dry with her used towels and dropped them in the laundry basket.

My room was so full of my boyhood self that I felt the urge to report back to him and keep him apprised of our progress. ("Well, medical school is over, now comes four years of residency in a new place, and after that, if we prove ourselves worthy, a fellowship in child and adolescent psychiatry. That gets us into our thirties, but thanks to your skipping that grade back in the bleak Jewel era, we're still a year ahead of ourselves.")

My aunt had left the door to her studio open. It was arranged and tidied as if expecting an imminent tour: "The Painter's Empty Studio." The big easel had been wheeled away from the center, the trestle tables with their tubes of pigment and containers full of brushes moved flush against the walls. (Lachicotte's Coronation tea caddy was still home to the precious sables.) Pinned along the top of the wall-high cork board were Aunt Charlotte's blown-up photos of tidal pools recorded on low-tide evenings over the period of a month. Below were her pastel sketches on Japan paper of the shapes and colors left in the sand. ("I want to see how far I can get toward *pure design* while still remaining faithful to what nature left behind.")

In the "new wing," as we still called it twelve years after it was built, she had made her bed. I had been half-hoping she hadn't, so I could justify running a small load of laundry, just the sheets and towels.

("Marcus, the sheets and towels can *wait*.")

My feet having completed their house check, I was at liberty to go back to bed and start catching up on four years of lost sleep as a medical student, or to walk down to the beach, which, sad to say, no longer offered the unrestricted pleasures of my boyhood.

Our beach had not held up as well as Aunt Charlotte's cottage. Nevertheless, the ocean remained its old self, calming you with its predictable rhythms, taking its ancient watery breaths as it did millions of years ago when the little loggerhead hatchlings made their mad dash for its deep waters.

"The ocean is going to be just fine and the beaches are going to be just fine," explained an unwelcome scientist at a contentious meeting when the island residents were at their most divided. "They will go on together perfectly well. There will always be beaches, but the ocean will move the beaches *to new locations*. The only losers will be the property owners fighting a hopeless battle to make nature stand still." He was booed down and the twenty-three timber groins went up, jutting out perpendicular to the shoreline from the north to the south end of the island. Gone was the wide swath of unencumbered beach as far as you could see, where walkers could walk without going around the regularly spaced four-foot-high beams. Except at very low tide, bicycle tires sank in the sand. Eleven-year-old Marcus would have had to rely on Seashore Road for his daily visits to the ghost-boy.

I sat down on "our" groin, placed a few feet beyond Aunt Charlotte's boardwalk steps in approximately the same place the

Turtle Patrol had relocated the loggerhead eggs the first summer I was here.

The tide had started to go out, but the waves still covered most of the beach. Aunt Charlotte had left so early that there was a good hour left for unleashed dogs to chase one another into the surf, get good and wet, then streak up to shake water and sand on their owners hugging the dry space up by the dunes. Dogs on the beach brought back Barrett, the service dog I had met on the same morning I had seen the ghost-boy poised to leap out from the doorway. Barrett would be an old dog now, his wounded warrior preparing sorrowfully for the loss of him. The warrior himself, approaching middle age, had years more to live with his handicap and his war memories. Would he be given a new dog? Or maybe both Barrett and his warrior were already dead.

The phone in my back pocket buzzed once. Who at this hour was sending me a message?

It was Charlie Coggins:

*Fellow wants you to call him, said it's important. He found my name in all those Grief Cottage news stories and phoned our office to ask if I knew where you were. Here is his contact info. Said you'd remember him as Shelby's older brother. I hear good things about you when I run into your aunt, which is not often.*

Below were the home phone, cell phone, and street address of Andrew Forster. It took me a minute to realize Andrew was Drew and Shelby was Wheezer.

A man picked up the home phone.

"Is this Andrew?"

"He's still asleep. Can I take a message?"

"Oh sorry, I didn't realize it's so early. I'm all turned around today. This is Marcus Harshaw, I'm calling from—"

"Wait, Marcus, give me your number in case we get cut off. I'll go wake him. We've been trying to locate you."

"Marcus? This is Andrew, Shelby's older brother. Thank you for calling back. Do you remember me at all?"

"Yes. Wheezer always called you Drew."

"Hey, I forgot his little friends called him that! We've been trying to find your whereabouts, Marcus. First we found an article you wrote in a psychiatry journal, and Shelby said he would gamble on that being you. Then we found those old news stories—about you discovering the buried boy on the South Carolina island—and we decided to contact the realtor who was quoted. Listen Marcus; Shelby—Wheezer—isn't doing so well. Lymphoblastic lymphoma, Stage Four, if that means anything to you. He had a high response with the initial chemo and we had high hopes he was going to make it, but he had an early relapse and—well, now it doesn't look so good. It's too late for a bone marrow transplant and we've made him comfortable at home. He's been talking about you a lot. Where are you right now?"

"I'm on that same island in those news stories. Where are you?"

"Same old town, Granny's old house. You know it. Granny's gone, but we're all living in her house."

"There are a few things I need to take care of here, but then I could come."

"That's what we were hoping for. But, look, Marcus, don't leave it too long."

"I could get away from here by noon."

"You mean you would come *today*?"

"If I left at noon I think I could be there in late afternoon. What's the street address, I don't think I ever knew it."

"We're Number One Maple Avenue. It's at the top of the street. You'll stay with us. There's plenty of room. Oh, and when you get as far as Asheboro? Why don't you call to let us know you're close. That'll give us a good half hour to get him up to speed for your arrival."

"Will you tell him I'm coming?"

"I surely will, as soon as his nurse gets him bathed and set up for the day. Then he'll have something to look forward to."

Getting a sick person "up to speed" for a visitor could mean anything from disconnecting a catheter or an IV so the person could move around without dragging a pole, or taking injections or pills to block pain, or to keep you sharp and awake for short portions of time. It was useless to try to guess. I would know soon enough.

The route from the island to Forsterville was largely interstate, cutting northwest through salt marshes, coastal plain, up into the piedmont, and right into the foothills of the Appalachian mountains, but what I saw was mostly the asphalt in front of me and signs naming the towns that I was not going to see. "It is still possible to go the back roads and get an idea of how people lived," Mom had said when we had been planning our trip to West Virginia so I could see my roots, at least on her side. "The backroads take longer, but we'll take all the time we need." I had traveled this interstate route before, when I had gone back to see to the stone for her grave.

THE BIG WHITE Forster house at the top of the tree-lined street looked down at a nondescript car packed to the gills with belongings laboring upward in second gear. ("We're Number One Maple Avenue," Drew had said.) Wheezer and I had always taken the back route to the house to avoid the uphill pedaling. Why this surge of anger and worthlessness at the sight of the house on top of its green hill? I was expected, I was wanted; wasn't I an equal player now?

"They got here first," Mom had explained when we had taken our afternoon walks in the Forsterville Cemetery. "So naturally they would choose the highest lots to be buried in." Her favorite spot was at the top of the hill. My best photo of her, which I carried tucked in my wallet along with the head-shot of my unknown father, was of her sitting beside one of their family gravestones, leaning a little sideways, so her cheek grazed the edge of the upright stone. I had wanted her to pose next to a weeping marble angel farther down the hill, and she obliged me, but the body language between them was terrible. Then she had returned to her usual gravestone. "The view is better up here," she called to me.

MY OVERLOADED CAR crackled around the circular white gravel driveway of the front entrance. Waiting in the open doorway was a gaunt, elongated person still recognizable to me as the complete little man in first grade. Wearing jeans and a polo shirt to match the Carolina blue baseball cap tipped low over his forehead, he leaned into the door frame, his unsupported side steadied by a cane. In eager silence he watched me unfold myself from the car and make my way toward him. Before I had reached the steps, I could feel myself entering his realm. Whenever we had been separated as boys, even if for only a few hours, he would beam that "I-own-you" gaze at me when I came back. He was now sending me this gaze from under the baseball cap. I was close enough now to take in the skeletal cheeks, the bony shelf of his clavicle, the stick-thin upper arms;

I also saw the effort it was taking him to stand upright, even with the help of door frame and cane.

"I knew you'd come, Marcus. All we had to do was find where you were. Now you can hug me if you like."

I embraced the emaciated frame, taking care not to upset his balance. My tears wet the front of his shirt, which smelled fresh from the dryer. "Whoa," he said in his new adult voice, "go easy on my bones. I've lost forty pounds. Now step back and let me look at you, Marcus. Funny, I always assumed *you'd* be the tall one, but even in my sorry state you only come to my shoulders. Listen, before we go inside, I've made some house rules. You are *my* company. When I'm awake, we'll catch up on important things. Any *medical* information will be left for the others to relate while I'm asleep. I have it all planned, and it will be perfect if everyone will do what I say."

SUPPORTING HIMSELF AGAINST me on his cane-free side, he led me through the shadowy formal living room, which had been off-bounds to children, and onto the screened porch, where his grandmother had escaped for her smokes. There, seated in chairs, were three people who clearly wanted to give the impression they had simply been relaxing together and not waiting on tenterhooks to see if he could accomplish his solo welcome of me.

The two white men with pleasant faces and balding heads came forward and greeted me, Andrew clasping my hand warmly in both of his and introducing "my partner, Bryson, and this is Tobias, Shelby's resident nurse." The muscular black man in green scrubs bounded forward to shake my hand and in a passing, fluid motion slid his arm effortlessly around his patient, relieving me of the weight.

"Not so fast, Tobias," Wheezer said. "I'm not done yet. Marcus, how long can you stay?"

"I have ten days before I start my new job. No, nine. I used up one of them today. And it's an eight-hour drive to get where I'm going. Then I'll need a few days to unpack and get organized. I could stay here three days."

"Is that counting today?"

"Counting today."

"And you'd leave on the morning of the fourth day? Then here's the plan. Tobias will carry me off for my injection after which I'll snooze, and Drew and Bryson will get you settled into your room and feed you, and then you and I will meet up later in the evening, when I'm usually at my best."

I was to sleep in Drew's former upstairs bedroom, which I had never been inside. When we were boys he had kept it locked when he was away and when at home he shut himself inside and turned up his stereo, except for meals. The bed had been temptingly readied, the counterpane turned down, and a gentle breeze brought the scent of an unknown flower through the open windows.

"We used to hear your jazz and blues coming from this room," I told Drew.

"You probably remember me as Gloomy Gus."

"No, I figured we must annoy you, two loud little boys. You were so much older than us—"

"It's hard to realize I was once that unhappy wretch. This room was always given to the oldest son, or just the son if there was only one in the family. It was Granddad Forster's room, then it passed on to my father's older brother, our ill-fated uncle who threw away his life—I expect Shelby told you about him."

"The brilliant uncle who died of an overdose?"

"That's the one. Shelby was born too late to meet Uncle Henry, who was the most lovable and fascinating human being in the world when he wasn't drinking—or later when he was on the hard stuff. I remember when I was about six, Uncle Henry was reading a book, oblivious to everybody else in the room, and I wormed my way into his lap and asked him to read it to me. 'But you wouldn't understand it, Drewie,' he said. 'No, I will, I will!' I insisted, so he wriggled me into a more comfortable position and started to read aloud in this beautiful, mysterious language. After a while, he said, 'Do you want me to go on?' and I said I did. 'You understanding it okay?' 'Not every word,' I told him, 'but I love it.' This made him laugh and he went on reading until I got interested in something else and climbed down from his lap. Turns out he was reading something in classical Greek, which he often did for pleasure, the way you and I might curl up and read a detective novel."

WHEEZER AND I did not "meet up again" that first evening. "He overestimated himself," Tobias told me. "When he heard you were coming, he got all excited and wanted so many things done. He would have done it all himself if he'd had the strength. He's a perfectionist and he likes to be in charge."

"He was like that when he was six."

"This is one of those forms of lymphoma there hasn't been a lot of research on."

"It's a relatively rare form, which usually strikes the young. I met several children with it during my oncology rotation."

"You're a doctor?"

"As of one week tomorrow. I just graduated from med school and I'm on my way to my residency in Nashville."

"Way to go. Congratulations. I've made up my mind to go on for further training myself. After Shelby doesn't need me anymore. I'm still deciding between physician's assistant and nurse practitioner. What do you think?"

"The pay scale for PA is higher—well, depending what doctor you go to work for. But if you want to be your own boss and have more contact with patients, nurse practitioner would be the choice. I know 'Physician's assistant' sounds more important because it has 'physician' in the title, but . . ."

"Isn't it the truth. What something's *called* can sway you before you rightly know what it is."

DURING THE LONG evening that Wheezer slept through, Andrew and Bryson updated me on Forsterville and on themselves. Forster's Fine Furniture had gone out of business back when Mom and I were still enduring the indignities of Wicked and Harm on Smoke Vine Street in Jewel.

"Forster's downfall can be summed up in three words," Andrew said. "'China is cheaper.' We held on longer than most, but it was swift and merciless when it hit. It killed Grandpop. His factory was his family, his preferred family, actually. His employees were his children, his preferred children. He handed out the severance checks himself, crying the entire time, and then came home and collapsed. We buried him five months later. There were occasional renters, who ended up doing more damage than good, until finally someone left a coffee machine on and burned down an entire wing. By then, Granny was gone, having got Shelby through his disaster—this was before the cancer, but since it's not strictly a medical subject, he'll probably want to tell you himself—and Bryson and I had taken the marriage vows twice, first a civil service in North Carolina, and then the following year, when it became the law of the land, we had a ceremony here at the house. Shortly after that, we were walking around the empty factory, inspecting the abandoned machinery, debating whether we should sell to someone who wanted to gut it and turn it into condos, when Bryson had his idea. We could make it into a museum. Today's public doesn't want too much reality, Bryson said, they're happier with simulations and reenactments. They like their reality broken into manageable pieces and then stylishly arranged for them as an entertainment. So that's what we're doing. Bryson even got us a state grant, and the building was already on the historical register, which helped. We're both accountants, that's how we met, but Bryson has all the creative savvy. It's going to be a Furniture Factory Museum, with rental spaces for custom-furniture makers if they're willing to ply their craft while people watch. And woodworking courses, with credits from the community college. And we've sent out a call that we're buying fine old pieces made at Forster's, and we've already got some in hand: the idea being that we'll hold contests for woodworkers to duplicate these pieces, the way painters sit in front of old masterpieces and copy them. And we're having an old film digitalized—it's the factory workers doing their various jobs and talking about it. Grandpop had it shot back in the early nineties, and the museum-goers will watch that first in a comfortable screening room."

"My mom was at Forster's in the nineties. I wonder if she's in it."

"We'll send you a copy, let's make a note. Wouldn't that be something?"

The second day, the first full day I was to be there, Wheezer stayed in bed without his baseball cap. They had made the downstairs sunroom into his bedroom and Tobias had the guest room next door. A hardly visible stand of fine hair was making a comeback on Wheezer's scalp.

"Come here, Marcus, I want you to feel it."

I sat down on the edge of his bed and ran my palm respectfully across the new growth. Naturally I thought of the last time I had touched his hair, gathering it into a silky clump so I could hit his face better.

"Bryson says it feels like petting a baby rabbit. How does it feel to you?"

"I've never petted a rabbit. Maybe putting your hand down on new grass?"

"Let me guess. Drew and Bryson have got as far as touching on 'Shelby's disaster,' then one of them said, 'No, no, that's outside of our medical guidelines, he'll want to tell you about that himself.'"

"How did you know?"

"I lie here and read people's minds. Drew is so at one with himself he goes whole stretches forgetting he exists as an individual. He plans the meals, pays the bills, and thinks up more things for them to do at the Furniture Factory Museum. Bryson goes around plotting happy little surprises for Drew. Tobias wonders if he'll be able to register in time for courses in the fall, then feels guilty for having the thought, and rushes in to bring me a fresh glass of shaved ice or a smoothie and ask if I want a backrub."

"Are you sure you're not just imagining what they might be thinking because you know them so well?"

"Oh, either way, Marcus. My point is, the mind doesn't use one-thousandth of its powers. It can be all over the place simultaneously and go down roads you didn't even know existed.

I've learned that through being sick and all the drugs that go with it and from my coke and heroin era and even when I tried and failed to kill myself."

"Oh, Wheezer."

"Yes, that was my 'disaster.' However, I hate to say it, Marcus, but when you're high you get glimpses of other ways your wonderful mind can operate. That's one reason people keep doing drugs. Do you remember how we'd tell each other 'trues'?"

"I certainly do."

"You used to *do research* in order to dig up stories to shock me. Van Gogh handing his sliced-off ear to a prostitute. That's what I was leading up to, telling you a true about the awful year I spent with my mother. I'd flunked out of college here, so in a rare moment of motherliness she invited me to live with her in Boca Raton and try the local community college. Well, to keep it nice and short, I dropped out after a couple of months and went to work for a contractor. Basic grunt jobs, like climbing on a roof and removing old tiles, doing coffee runs, picking up supplies, but I loved the outdoor work and I loved the paycheck. The contractor had a sixteen-year-old daughter named Cricket, who brought him lunch every day on her bicycle; she was too young to drive. She was a user and a dealer, still in high school, very small and smart and irresistible, she was an awesome little creature, and we fell in love and she introduced me to her wares. Then one night when we were together she didn't wake up from an overdose and when I woke up I was devastated. It was clear she was dead, and I tried to join her. But I cut the wrong way. If you ever get serious about cutting your wrists, do it lengthwise, not crosswise. But you'd know things like that, being a doctor. Anyway, Mother said she'd raised one queer and one junkie and she was packing it in. Actually, she *hadn't* raised me, but I was too despondent to contradict her. Granny came and got me and brought me back to life in this house and then died. Drew had paired up with Bryson by then and they'd started work on their Factory Museum. I went to work for the contractor they hired to do the renovations. As I said, outdoor work suits me and I would still be at it if I hadn't come down with this children's cancer."

"The cutoff age for it is usually around thirty, though I met one man in his sixties who had it."

"Did he survive?"

"To be honest, I don't know. It was at the end of my oncology rotation."

"How much longer do you have to go to school before you can hang out your shingle?"

"Four years of residency, which includes two of general psychiatry and two of child- and adolescent-specialty training. After that a two-year fellowship. It seems long, but at least I know what I want to do and am on track to do my chosen work."

"I wanted to read your article we found in that psychiatry journal—I forget its title, it had *supernatural* in it, but in order to read it I had to join something first and time was running short. We still had to find you."

"It was called 'Psyche and Soma in the Human Child: the Supernatural Episode.' Actually I co-authored it with my supervisor, otherwise it probably wouldn't have been accepted. I'll send you an offprint as soon as I unpack my boxes."

"You always were so smart, Marcus."

"You were the best friend I ever had. I spent part of first grade watching you so I could learn how to please you. And I never stopped dreaming about you. I still do. You are a permanent member of my dream theater—there are only about ten people in the entire repertory."

"I don't know whether to ask this or not."

"Go ahead."

"You may be sorry."

"No, please. Ask it."

Wheezer raised himself to an upright position, wincing a little from the effort, and took a dramatic deep breath. "Okay, here goes. What did I do, or say, that day I came to have lunch at your apartment, that made you try to kill me the next day?"

"It was something you said at school."

"What? I know I must have done something, but I can't remember."

"It was about my mom. About us sleeping in one bed. Next day you told your other friends, 'Marcus is his mother's little husband.'"

"I said that? And this was at school the next day?"

"Yes."

"Funny, all the times I've tried to remember, I was *sure* that whatever I did took place at your apartment. Didn't I come for lunch?"

"Yes, but you didn't stay. You left in a huff before my mom returned with the pizza."

"I don't remember *any* of this! Why did I leave in a huff?"

"I had shown you this picture of a man Mom kept in her drawer. I said it was my father and she was going to tell me his name when I was old enough to be responsible."

"Why don't I remember any of this?"

"We all have these blank spots. Sometimes it's because we repressed it, other times it's because another memory shoved it aside. You took the picture and shook it in its frame and said, 'Someone cut this out of a book.' And then you said, 'You two are crazy. I need to get out of here.'"

"I didn't stay for lunch?"

"No, when Mom came back with our lunch, I told her you'd felt an asthma attack coming on and had rushed home to get your medication."

"You know what's funny? I never had another attack after *your* attack. You're probably the last person in the world who calls me Wheezer. So did she tell you later who your father was?"

"No. As I told you, she died in that accident when I was eleven, so I never knew. But not knowing doesn't torture me as much as it once did. I was lucky enough to make friends with a man when I went to live with my great-aunt, and he became a sort of fatherly stand-in. He's dead now, but he stayed around long enough for me to get an idea what having a father would have been like."

"Well, you'll have to tell me about it because I've never had the experience. I don't know if Drew told you, but all those years my father was traveling for Forster's Furniture he had a second family in Roanoke, Virginia. Married and children and all and this was before Mother divorced him, so he was a full-fledged bigamist for a while. I didn't learn about this until I was in my teens. I used to fantasize driving up to Roanoke and introducing myself to my half-siblings, but I never got around to it. What would have been the point? I haven't even told my mother about my present state. She'd feel obliged to rush up from Florida and make a bedside appearance and Drew and Bryson would have to feed her and she'd say something mean to hurt their feelings. But look, you were born in Forsterville, your mom worked at Forster's Furniture. I mean, we all assumed your father was Mr. Harshaw because that's what your mom said, but it must have been someone around Forsterville."

"Whoever it was died before I was born, that much she told me."

"Do you still have that picture?"

"It's in my wallet upstairs."

"No, don't get it right now. We need to make the most of my waking time. But maybe Drew being so much older, he might recognize the face. Shit, my mouth feels like a sewer and I have so much more to ask! Would you go and find Tobias—he's probably doing laundry—and tell him I could use a lemon swab?"

"I can do it. Where are the swabs?"

"No, Marcus, the inside of my mouth is not pretty. I can't let you see it."

"I'm sure I've seen a lot worse. Besides, I'd like to do it for you. I promise I'll do a good job."

"They're in the top drawer of that bureau. They come in individual packages. Will you also promise you'll be here when I wake up—in case I fall asleep?"

ANDREW AND BRYSON were off to the Furniture Museum and asked me to go along.

"He usually sleeps for hours," Andrew said.

"Well, but I promised I'd be here when he woke up."

"Understood," they said.

"MARCUS, I WANTED to say about Cricket—it was the total thing and we both knew it. Just because she happened to be sixteen—I mean, I was only six years older. That's not a lot. Have you ever loved someone totally like that?"

"When I was fourteen, I fell in love with my therapist. She was fifty-one."

"What did you do?"

"I brooded and anguished and dreamed up scenarios where I saved her from danger or her husband died, or left her. I finally broke down and told her. And she said it had a name, *transference*, it happened a lot in therapy and if handled correctly it could sometimes turn corners. She said, 'We can do one of two things, Marcus. I can refer you to someone else, or we can work through this ourselves—within the bounds of therapy.' And we did that. I still loved her afterward and probably would still love her if I were to meet her today."

"And that's all? Your therapist when you were fourteen? Was there anyone after that?"

"I shared a house with another med student for a semester. It started off—well, it started off in a passionate . . . *collision* . . . that's the best way to describe it. So I asked her to move in with me and after the passion dried up we were nothing but roommates who shared the rent but didn't like each other very much."

"So you've never known the total real thing?"

"There's still time. The loggerhead turtle doesn't reach sexual maturity until he's in his thirties."

*Forsterville, the last full day.*

"MARCUS, I'M GOOD for the whole day. Tobias has given me a shot."

"A steroid? You'll probably pay for it later."

"I don't mind. You said last night you had saved up a true for me that you'd never told anyone."

"I couldn't have. They would have thought I was mentally unbalanced and sent me away for treatment, or they'd think I made it up to seem clairvoyant and 'special.' It's about that boy—well, that skeleton I fell on top of. The one in the news stories that led you to me."

"Were you more grossed out or freaked out when you felt him under you?"

"I was out cold. I didn't learn about him until I was in the hospital. But I need to start back at the beginning of that summer. I was eleven, my mother was dead, and I was sent to live with my great-aunt on a small island in South Carolina . . ."

I WAS SURPRISED, and frankly let down, to realize that the entire story of Grief Cottage had taken less than twenty minutes to relate to Wheezer. How could that be? I had gone chronologically through those summer weeks fourteen years earlier, bringing in the necessary side-stories, the lost family in the hurricane, Coral Upchurch's memory of seeing Johnny Dace on the beach that one time fifty years before. I had been careful not to exaggerate the ghost-boy's manifestations to me: that first time on the porch when I felt invisibly watched from behind; then the two visual showings in the doorway; and the final time when I had taken the Percocet pills and felt his large hand on my back guiding me up the stairs of Grief Cottage.

"Wait, let's go over this again," said Wheezer. "That first time, when you fell asleep on the porch and then woke up and felt someone watching you from behind, was that before or after your aunt had told you about the missing family?"

"It was after."

"Okay, now, I'm going to play devil's advocate. The first time you saw him was in what you say was dazzling afternoon sunshine. Are you sure the dazzling light wasn't playing tricks on you?"

"No, he looked like a real person standing in the doorway. His face was in shadow because the dazzling light was behind him, but he was looking at me and he had on a red shirt."

"Okay. Now what about the big showing? The morning you got there before sunrise and everything was crepuscular and spooky, and he was braced in the doorway ready to spring out at you. You saw his red shirt again, unbuttoned this time, and his broken nose and the expression of his mouth, and his bow legs and jeans and boots. Right? And then later Mrs. Upchurch told you he never undressed at the beach and he was wearing some sort of footwear that might have been boots. Am I accurate so far?"

"An accurate devil's advocate."

"But then! Then everything changes. You go to the mortuary and see the bowed leg-bones. The nose was gone and the clothes were gone, but it turns out this *was* the remains of Johnny Dace, the boy lost in the hurricane, and now there's the DNA to prove it. It seems to me, Marcus, that somehow you were able to make contact with his spirit. It's like he needed you and you needed him and there was some kind of collapse in time and you were able to save each other. He got out of that cramped little closet and is laid peacefully to rest, and you are still here instead of being laid out underground yourself. It's got something to do with how time interacts with spirit, only you're going to have to figure it out for both of us. I think you do have special powers, Marcus. I give you permission to try them out on me."

"What do you mean?"

"Look. If you could reach a boy you never knew, a boy *who'd been dead fifty years*, why, reaching *me*, as close as we have been, will be a piece of cake."

TOBIAS ENTERED, BEARING a tray with a protein smoothie and a glass of shaved ice. He suggested his patient take a rest to conserve his energy for my farewell dinner that evening. Wheezer had asked for the dinner, and was planning to show up for it fully dressed and on his feet. Making ready to assist Wheezer to the bathroom, Tobias suggested I take a little walk outside in the sunshine, "and maybe you could use a little rest yourself."

I hadn't been outside the house since the first night, when I reparked my car and carried in my overnight bag. As I embarked on my assigned walk, I realized suddenly how drained I was. It was like coming off duty after a twenty-four-hour stint at the hospital. Seeing patients face-to-face, concentrating on their needs, you put yourself on hold, only to be confronted at the end of your rounds, cradling your pent-up umbrage like an ailing pet. *Now. What about me?*

Circling the backyard once, twice, a third time, I tried to recall how this patch of land had looked and felt when I was a visiting child. I passed the row of boxwoods where Wheezer had seen a snakeskin floating from a branch. ("Look, Marcus, you can even see where its jaw was! It probably rubbed against that bush to start the process and finally crawled out of its own mouth!") Or were these the same boxwoods? Shouldn't they have been more mature by now? In acute self-consciousness I performed this memory ritual in Wheezer's backyard: Now I am looking at the same boxwood or a replacement of the boxwood where the snakeskin floated; now I am remembering how Wheezer's grandmother stood under that tree, her back to the house, puffing her cigarette; now I am approaching the path where Wheezer taught me to ride Drew's old bicycle: ("If you'd just stop *thinking*, Marcus, and ride!")

Eventually it dawned on me that I didn't have to continue this forced-march down memory lane. Before a trip she felt neither here nor there, Aunt Charlotte had said, and I, too, was in that sort of antechamber between what was ending and what had not yet begun. I sank down on an outdoor chaise whose canvas pillows bore a faint scent of mildew and fell into a sort of half-sleep in which I was floating above a MapQuest aerial view of all the miles I had to drive tomorrow between Forsterville and Nashville.

WE MADE IT, all of us—well, almost—through my farewell supper. Drew, Bryson, Tobias, Shelby, and Marcus. Wheezer, dressed, arrived with a cane on his own steam, Tobias hovering close behind. He had left his head bare, with its rabbit fur exposed. Drew did salmon and vegetables on the outdoor grill. There was wine for those who wanted it, iced tea for those who didn't. And a silver bowl with fresh-cut fruit waiting for dessert. Beside my plate was a book-sized gift wrapped in white-and-gold paper.

"You have to open it now," ordered Wheezer. His face had gone ashen and he had sunk down in his chair.

It was one of those too-beautiful leather notebooks with Italian endpapers, the kind you postpone using, or never use, because you don't want to spoil it. "It's from all of us," Wheezer said. "Everyone's signed the card, but I went ahead and wrote the first entry inside."

*While I am writing this,* announced his familiar childish script at the top of the first page, *we are still together under the same roof, on the same earth at the same time. As for later, don't forget!*

There was more.

While we were serving ourselves fruit, Wheezer went limp in his chair. "Listen, Tobias, I'd better lie down." Tobias all but carried him away.

"Listen, Marcus," he said later, when we had joined him round his bed. "Show Drew that photo you were telling me about. He's so much older he might recognize the face."

I went upstairs, returned with the wallet, and handed the picture over to Drew, who took one look and raised his eyebrows.

"I think I do know this person, but I want to be sure. May I borrow this for a minute, Marcus?"

We heard him rustling around in the formal living room nobody used. A book dropped. Drew cursed and sneezed three times in succession.

"Someone needs to dust those shelves once in a blue moon," he said, returning with a book under his arm. "Okay, I've checked it out. This is the picture of Uncle Henry in the 1976 Harvard yearbook. That was his sophomore year, the year he dropped out. Only someone cut it out of the yearbook."

He opened to the page.

Under the cutout space was the name *Henry Arthur Forster, Jr.*

"And look," said Drew, "Marcus's photo fits right in the space. Now, would someone please tell me what this is all about?"

"Marcus will have to tell you," said Wheezer in a near-whisper, his eyes excited, feverish, "and it's going to be an interesting ride. Look, guys, I need to snooze for a while and when I wake up I'll be good as new. Then I expect to hear everything everybody said, and I mean *everything*."

## ACKNOWLEDGMENTS

*GRIEF COTTAGE* HAS been enriched significantly by the close readings and rereadings of my editor, Nancy Miller, who has now seen me through six books, and my agent, Moses Cardona, who is all a literary agent should be—and more. Nancy is a master of her craft who has a sharp eye for what is not there yet. Moses, besides being my champion, possesses the rare gift of seeing right into the heart of a story and helping me see it, too.

Thanks to Katya Mezhibovskaya for creating a jacket design that expresses the mood and story of *Grief Cottage* so perfectly.

Thanks to Evie Preston for her guidance and encouragement.

Thanks to my astute "tough reader" of many years, Robb Forman Dew, and to her son Jack Dew, who offered an invaluable suggestion concerning the ghost.

Thanks to Lynn Goldberg, who asked the right question at the right time.

Thanks to Ehren Foley at the South Carolina Department of Archives and History for providing details about two-hundred-year-old beach cottages and their floor plans, and for his enthusiasm and cordiality.

Thanks to Lee Brockington of Hobcaw Barony for putting me in touch with the right sources. I kept her sumptuous volume, *Pawleys Island, a Century of History and Photographs*, with Photo Editor Linwood Attman, near to me throughout the writing of *Grief Cottage*.

Professor James R. Spotila's passionate guide, *Saving Sea Turtles,* introduced me and Marcus to the fascinating journey of the loggerhead turtle.

And thanks to my sister, Franchelle Millender, who invited me to share a beach cottage with her on the Isle of Palms in South Carolina, where *Grief Cottage* was first conceived.

Aunt Charlotte's island is drawn from both Pawleys Island and the Isle of Palms.

# Darth Maul
# Shadow Hunter

## By Michael Reaves

*Hell on Earth**
*Voodoo Child*
*Night Hunter*
*Street Magic*
*The Burning Realm*
*The Shattered World*
*Darkworld Detective*

With Steve Perry:
*The Omega Cage*
*Dome*
*Hellstar*

With Byron Preiss:
*Dragonworld*

*Forthcoming

# STAR WARS

## DARTH MAUL
## SHADOW HUNTER

## MICHAEL REAVES

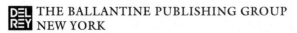

THE BALLANTINE PUBLISHING GROUP
NEW YORK

For my daughter Mallory
*"The Force is strong in this one."*

## ACKNOWLEDGMENTS

Sharecropping in someone else's field can often be an onerous task. In this case, however, it was a pleasure, and this is due in great part to the help I had from the many people who have helped create and maintain the *Star Wars* cosmos. Thanks are due to my editor, Shelly Shapiro, who got me the gig; to Sue Rostoni and the rest of the gang at Skywalker Ranch; to Ron Marz; to Brynne Chandler; to Steve Sansweet for his enormously helpful *Star Wars Encyclopedia*; to Steve and Dal Perry; and, of course, to George Lucas for creating what is without a doubt the most entertaining galaxy in the entire universe.

# AN EVEN LONGER TIME AGO
# IN A GALAXY FAR, FAR AWAY . . . .

# PART I
## MEAN STREETS

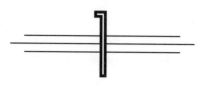

**S**pace is the perfect place to hide.

The Neimoidian freighter *Saak'ak* cruised ponderously in the uncharted deeps of Wild Space. It displayed its colors proudly, its cloaking device disabled, with no fear of detection. Here, parsecs away from the civilized Galactic Core and its surrounding systems, it could safely hide in plain sight. Even the Neimoidians, those past masters of paranoia, felt secure in the vast endless abyss between the disk and one of the spiral arms.

Yet even here the leaders of the Trade Federation could not entirely let go of their natural tendency toward subterfuge. They sought duplicity and guile the way a young grub seeks the safety and warmth of its sleeping niche in the communal hive. The *Saak'ak* was a good example of this. It was, to all appearances, merely a commercial vessel, its horseshoe shape designed to carry large amounts of cargo. Not until an unwary enemy had come within firing range would the heavy durasteel armor plating, blaster turrets, and military-strength communications arrays become visible.

By which time, of course, it would be too late.

Aboard the *Saak'ak*'s bridge all was silent save for the muted beeps and chimes of various life-support monitors and the almost inaudible susurrus of the air filtration system. Three figures stood to one side of the huge transparisteel viewport. They wore the flowing robes and mantles of the Neimoidian aristocracy, but their body language, as a fourth figure appeared in their midst, was deferential, if not outright cringing and servile.

The fourth figure was not really there with them in any physical sense. The robed and hooded form was a holograph, a three-dimensional image projected from an unknown source light-years distant. Intangible and immaterial, the mysterious stooped image nevertheless dominated the three Neimoidians. Indeed, they could not have been any more thoroughly cowed had he been physically present with a blaster in each hand.

The figure's face—what little was visible of it in the shadows of the hood—was grim and unforgiving. The cowled head moved slightly as he looked at each of the Neimoidians in turn. Then the figure spoke, his voice a dry rasp, his tone that of one accustomed to instant obedience.

"There are only three of you."

The tallest of the three, the one wearing the triple-crested tiara of a viceroy, responded in a stammering voice. "Th-that is true, Lord Sidious."

"I see you, Gunray, and your lackeys Haako and Dofine. Where is the fourth one? Where is Monchar?"

Federation Viceroy Nute Gunray clasped his hands in front of him in what was not so much a supplicating gesture as an attempt to keep them from nervously wringing each other. He had hoped he would grow used to dealing with the Sith Lord over

time, but so far that had not happened. If anything, these meetings with Darth Sidious had become even more gut-twisting and upsetting as the deadline for the embargo grew ever closer. Gunray did not know how his seconds in command, Daultay Dofine and Rune Haako, felt—discussing one's feelings was anathema in Neimoidian society—but he knew how he felt after each encounter with the Sith Lord. He felt like squirming back into his hive mother's birth chamber and pulling the cloacal flap in after him.

Especially now. Curse Hath Monchar! Where was the misbegotten rankweed sucker? Not on board the *Saak'ak*, that much was certain. The ship had been searched from the center sphere to the air locks at the outmost ends of each docking bay arm. Not only was his deputy viceroy nowhere to be found, but a scout vessel with hyperdrive capability was missing, as well. Put these two facts together, and the chances of Viceroy Gunray winding up as fodder for one of the fungus farms back on Neimoidia was beginning to look distressingly good.

The holographic image of Darth Sidious flickered slightly, then regained its none-too-stable resolution. A glitch, most likely caused by some solar flare on a star between here and whatever mysterious world the signal was originating from. Not for the first time Gunray found himself wondering on what world or ship the real Sith was standing, and not for the first time he flinched hastily away from the thought. He didn't want to know too much about the Neimoidians' ally in this undertaking. In fact, he wished he could forget what little he already knew. Collaborating with Darth Sidious was about as safe as being trapped in a cave on Tatooine with a hungry krayt dragon.

The hooded face turned to glare directly at him. "Well?" Sidious demanded.

Even as he opened his mouth, Gunray knew that it would be futile to lie. The Sith Lord was a master of the Force, that mysterious and pervasive energy field that, some said, knitted the galaxy together just as surely as did gravity. Sidious might not be able to read another's inmost thoughts, but he certainly could tell when someone was lying. Even knowing that, however, the Neimoidian could no more stop himself from dissimulating than he could stop his sweat ducts from oozing oily perspiration down the back of his neck.

"He was taken ill, my lord. Too much rich food. He—he has a delicate constitution." Gunray closed his mouth, keeping his lips firmly pressed together to stop them from trembling. Inwardly he cursed himself. Such a pathetic and obvious prevarication; even a Gamorrean would be able to see through it! He waited for Sidious to command Haako and Dofine to turn on him, to strip him of his vestments and rank. He had no doubt that they would do it. For the Neimoidians, one of the most difficult concepts to understand in the galactic lexicon of Basic was the word *loyalty*.

However, to his astonishment, Sidious merely nodded instead of showering him with vituperation. "I see. Very well, then—the four of us shall discuss the contingency plans should the trade embargo fail. Monchar can be briefed on them when he recovers." The Sith Lord continued speaking, describing his plan to hide a large secret army of battle droids in the cargo bays of the trade ships, but Gunray could hardly pay attention to the specifics. He was stunned that his desperate ruse had worked.

The viceroy's relief was short-lived, however. He knew that

at best all he had done was buy some time, and not much of that. When Sidious's hologram again materialized on the bridge of the *Saak'ak* he would once more demand to know where Monchar was—and this time he would not accept illness as an excuse.

There were no two ways about it—his errant lieutenant would have to be found, and quickly. But how to do this without arousing Sidious's suspicions? Gunray felt certain at times that the Sith Lord was somehow able to peer into every compartment, niche, and cubicle on the freighter, that he knew *everything*, no matter how trivial or inconsequential, that took place on board.

The viceroy silently commanded himself to maintain control. He took advantage of Sidious's attention being momentarily focused on Haako and Dofine to surreptitiously slip an antistress capsule between his lips. He could feel his lung pods expanding and contracting convulsively within him, on the verge of hyperventilation. An old saying characterized Neimoidians as the only sentient species with an entire organ devoted solely to the task of worrying. As Nute Gunray felt the anxiety that had been momentarily quelled threatening to build up once more in his gut sac, the adage did seem to have an unpleasant ring of truth to it.

Darth Sidious, Master of the Sith, finished relaying his instructions to the Neimoidians and made a slight, almost negligent gesture. Across the room a relay clicked and the holographic transmission ended. The flickering blue-white images of the Neimoidians and the section of their ship's bridge captured by the split-beam transceivers vanished.

Sidious stood motionless and silent on the transmission grid, his fingers steepled, his mind meditating on the eddies and

currents of the Force. Those of lesser sensitivity were oblivious to it, but to him it was like an omnipresent mist, invisible but nonetheless tangible, that swirled and drifted constantly about him. No words, no descriptions could begin to convey what it was like; the only way to understand it was to experience it.

He had learned over long years of study and meditation how to interpret each and every vagary of its restless flow, no matter how slight. Even without that ability, however, he would have known that Nute Gunray was lying about Hath Monchar's whereabouts. An old joke about the viceroy's kind summed it up nicely:

*How can you tell if a Neimoidian is lying?*
*His mouth is open.*

Sidious nodded slightly. There was no doubt of Gunray's dishonesty; the only question was *why*. It was a question that had to be answered, and soon. The Neimoidians were weaklings, true enough, but even the most cowardly creatures would rear up on their hind legs and bite if sufficiently motivated. They were plotting behind his back. To believe otherwise was to be hopelessly naive, and though a great many crimes could be laid at Darth Sidious's feet, naïveté was certainly not one of them. Given how potentially important the Naboo embargo and subsequent economic machinations could be, there was really only one thing to do.

Sidious made another slight gesture. The Force rippled in response, and the transmission grid beneath his feet glowed again. A holograph of himself was once more sent racing through the void to another remote location. It was time to bring a new player into the game—one who had trained and studied for years for precisely this kind of assignment. The one who com-

prised the other half of the Sith order. His protégé, his disciple, his myrmidon.

The one Sidious had named Darth Maul.

The dueling droids were programmed to kill.

There were four of them, top-of-the-line Duelist Elites from Trang Robotics, all armed in different ways: one with a steel rapier, one with a heavy cudgel, the third with a short length of chain, and the last with a pair of double-edged hachete fighting blades as long and wide as a human's forearm. They had been programmed with the skills of a dozen martial arts masters, and their reflexes were calibrated just a hair faster than human optimum. Their durasteel chassis were blaster-resistant. They had come factory-equipped with behavioral inhibitors that prevented them from delivering a death blow once their opponent had been beaten, but these inhibitors had been nullified by their new owner. A mistake against one would be fatal.

Darth Maul did not make mistakes.

The Sith apprentice stood in the middle of the training chamber as the four droids circled him. His breathing was calm, his heartbeat even and slow. He was aware of his body's reactions to the danger—aware and in control.

Two of the droids—Rapier and Chain, he silently named them—were within his field of vision. The other two—Cudgel and Hachete—were not, being behind him. It did not matter; through his awareness of the Force he could sense their movements as plainly as if he had eyes in the back of his head.

Maul raised his own weapon, the double-bladed lightsaber, and triggered the power control. Twin lances of pure energy boiled forth, hissing and crackling in crimson loops that began

and ended at the two flux apertures on either end of the device. Any Jedi Knight could wield a single-bladed lightsaber; only a master fighter could use the weapon first designed by the legendary Dark Lord Exar Kun millennia ago. Unless one was in perfect attunement with it, the weapon could be as deadly to the user as to the opponent.

Rapier lunged at full extension, its metal knee joint bent almost to the floor. The needle point flickered toward Maul's heart, almost too fast to see.

The dark side blossomed in Darth Maul, the power of it resonating in him like black lightning, augmenting his years of training, guiding his reactions. Time seemed to slow, to stretch.

It would have been easy to chop the blade itself in half, as few metals could resist the frictionless edge of a lightsaber. But there was no challenge to that. Maul spun toward the point, twisted around the outside, and snapped his hands horizontally at chest level. The left blade of the lightsaber sheared through Rapier's sword arm. Both arm and weapon clattered to the floor.

Maul dropped to his left knee as, from directly behind him, Cudgel's full swing whistled over his head, barely missing his dorsal horn. Without looking, guided by the vibrations of the Force, he thrust backwards with the right blade, then forward with the left—*one, two!*—skewering both Cudgel and Rapier in their abdominal compartments. Sparks spewed from shorted circuitry, and lubricating fluid sprayed in a reddish oily mist.

Using the momentum of the forward thrust, Maul dived over the collapsing droid before him, flowing smoothly into a shoulder roll. He came up twirling his lightsaber overhead, then stepped down solidly into the teräs käsi wide stance called Riding Bantha. Even as he did the movement, part of him was monitoring his body's state. His breathing was slow and even, his pulse

elevated by no more than two or three beats per minute from its resting rate.

Two down, two to go.

Chain charged, its weapon whirling over its head like the propeller of a gyrocraft. The heavy links lashed toward him. Maul spun on his right foot and shot his left leg out in a powerful side kick, slamming his boot into the droid's armored chest, stopping it cold. He dropped into a squat, spun the lightsaber like a scythe, and sickled the droid cleanly at the knees. Lower legs gone, it collapsed as Maul again twisted himself and his weapon, flowing into the form known as Rancor Rising. He brought the right blade up between Chain's mechanical thighs, hard, using his leg muscles to augment the strike as he pushed up from the squat to a standing position.

The force of his strike bisected Chain from its crotch right through the top of its head. There was a hard metallic screech as the droid came apart in two halves. Its feet and lower legs hit the floor slightly before the upper halves landed atop them.

The acrid smell of burned lubricating fluid and circuitry washed over Maul. What was, seconds ago, a functional piece of high-tech equipment was now a barely recognizable pile of scrap metal.

Three down, one to go.

Hachete moved to Maul's left, whirling its razor-edged blades in defensive movements—high, low, left, right, a blinding pattern of edged death waiting to blind the unwary and cut him down.

Maul allowed himself a twitch of his lips. He pressed the lightsaber's controls. The humming died as the energy beams blinked out. He bent, keeping his eyes on the droid as he put the weapon on the floor and shoved it away with his boot.

He settled himself into a low defensive stance, angled toward the droid at forty-five degrees, left foot forward. He watched the flickering arabesque of death as Hachete edged toward him. A droid like this knew no fear, but Darth Maul knew that to put his weapon down and face a live opponent barehanded would certainly terrify anybody brighter than a dueling droid. Fear was as potent a weapon as a lightsaber or a blaster.

The dark side raged inside him, sought to blind him with hatred, but he held it at bay. He held one open hand high, by his ear, the other by his hip, then reversed the positions, watching. Waiting.

Hachete stole forward another half step, crossing and recrossing the blades, looking for an opening.

Maul gave the droid what it was looking for. He moved his left arm wide, away from his body, exposing his side to a thrust or a cut.

Hachete saw the opening and moved in, fast, very fast, snapping one of the blades out to cut while bringing the other blade over for backup.

Maul dropped, hooked his left foot around the back of the droid's ankle, and pulled as he kicked hard at the droid's thigh with the other foot.

The droid fell backwards, unable to maintain its balance, and hit the floor. Maul sprang up, did a front flip, and came down with both boot heels driving into the droid's head. The metal skull crunched and collapsed inward. Lights flashed and the hardshell photoreceptors shattered.

Maul dived again, rolled up in a half twist into the förräderi stance, ready to spring in any direction.

But there was no need—these four were done. It would take

a technician days to repair Hachete, Cudgel, and Rapier. Chain was beyond repair, useful only for parts.

Darth Maul exhaled, relaxed his stance, and nodded. His heart rate had accelerated perhaps five beats above normal at most. There was the faintest sheen of perspiration on his forehead; otherwise his skin was dry. Perhaps sixty seconds had elapsed from start to finish. Maul frowned slightly. Not his personal best, by any means. It was one thing to face and defeat droids. Jedi were a different matter.

He would have to do better.

He picked up his lightsaber, hung it from his belt. Then, his muscles warmed up now, he went to practice his fighting exercises.

He had barely gotten more than a few meters, however, when a familiar shimmering in the air in front of him brought him to a stop. Before the hooded figure's image had time to solidify, Maul dropped to one knee and bowed his head.

"Master," he said, "what do you wish of your servant?"

The Sith Lord regarded his apprentice. "I am pleased with the way you dealt with the Black Sun assignment. The organization will be in disarray for years."

Maul nodded slightly in acknowledgment. Such offhanded praise was the most he ever got in recognition of his work, and that only rarely. But praise, even from Sidious, did not matter. All that mattered was serving his master.

"Now I have another task for you."

"Whatever my master wishes shall be done."

"Hath Monchar, one of the four Neimoidians I am dealing with, has disappeared. I suspect treachery. Find him. Make sure he has spoken to no one of the impending embargo. If he has— kill him, and everyone he has spoken to."

The holographic image faded away. Maul straightened and headed for the door. His step was firm, his manner confident. Anyone else, even a Jedi, might have protested that such an assignment was impossible. It was a big galaxy, after all. But failure was not an option to Darth Maul. It was not even a concept.

Coruscant.

The name evoked the same image in the mind of nearly every civilized being in the galaxy. Coruscant: Bright center of the universe, cynosure of all inhabited worlds, crown jewel of the Core systems. Coruscant, seat of government for the myriad worlds of an entire galaxy. Coruscant, the epitome of culture and learning, synthesis of a million different civilizations.

Coruscant.

Seeing the planet from orbit was the only way to fully appreciate the enormity of the construction. Practically all of Coruscant's landmass—which comprised almost all of its surface area, its oceans and seas having been drained or rerouted through huge subterranean caverns more than a thousand generations ago—was covered with a multitiered metropolis composed of towers, monads, ziggurats, palazzi, domes, and minarets. By day the many crosshatched levels of skycar traffic and the thousands of spaceships that entered and left its atmosphere almost blotted out views of the endless cityscape, but at night Coruscant

revealed its full splendor, outshining at close range even the spectacular nebulae and globular clusters of the nearby Galactic Core. The planet radiated so much heat energy that, were it not for thousands of strategically placed $CO_2$ reactive dampers in the upper atmosphere, it would long ago have been transformed into a lifeless rock by a rampant atmospheric degeneration.

An endless ring of titanic skyscrapers girded Coruscant around its equator, some of them tall enough to pierce the upper fringes of atmosphere. Similar, if shorter structures could be found almost anyplace on the globe. It was those rarefied upper levels, spacious and clean, that constituted most peoples' conception of the galactic capital.

But all visions of soaring beauty and wealth, no matter how stately, must be grounded somewhere, somehow. Along the equatorial strip, below the lowest stratum of air traffic, beneath the illuminated skywalks and the glittering facades, lay another view of Coruscant. There, sunlight never penetrated; the endless city night was lit only by flickering neon holoprojections advertising sleazy attractions and shady businesses. Spider-roaches and huge armored rats infested the shadows, and hawk-bats with wingspans of up to one and a half meters roosted in the rafters of deserted structures. This was the underbelly of Coruscant, unseen and unacknowledged by the wealthy, belonging solely to the disenfranchised and the damned.

This was the part of Coruscant that Lorn Pavan called home.

The meeting place had been suggested by the Toydarian; it was a dingy building at the back of a dead-end street. Lorn and his droid, I-Five, had to step over a Rodian sleeping in a pile of rags near the recessed entrance.

"I've often wondered," the protocol droid said as they entered, "if your clientele all subscribe to the same service—the one listing the most disgusting and disreputable places in the galaxy to meet."

Lorn made no reply. He had wondered the same thing on occasion himself.

Inside was a small lobby, most of its space taken up by a ticket booth made of yellowing plasteel. In the booth a balding human male lounged in a formfit chair. He looked up incuriously when they entered. "Booth five's open," he grunted, jerking his thumb at one of a series of doors lining the lobby's circular wall. "One credit for a half hour." He looked at I-Five, then said to Lorn, "If you're taking the droid in, you gotta sign a release form."

"We're here for Zippa," Lorn told him.

The proprietor glanced at them again, then shifted his bulk and pressed a button with a grimy finger. "Booth nine," he said.

The holobooth was even smaller than the lobby, which meant it was barely big enough to contain the four who were now crowded into it. Lorn and I-Five stood behind the single contour couch that faced the transmitter plate. Zippa hovered slightly above the plate, facing them, the sound of his rapidly beating wings providing a constant background buzz. The dim light darkened his mottled blue skin to an unhealthy shade of purplish-black.

Behind the Toydarian stood another, bulkier form; Lorn could tell that it was nonhuman, but the light was too faint for him to guess its species. He wished that Zippa would stop hovering: whatever the being behind the Toydarian was, it stank like a silage bin at high noon, and the breeze generated by Zippa's wings wasn't helping matters any. It was obvious that Zippa hadn't

been any too fastidious about bathing lately, as well, but fortunately the Toydarian's body odor wasn't offensive; in fact, it reminded Lorn of sweetspice.

"Lorn Pavan," Zippa said, his voice somehow sounding faintly of static, as if it were tuned just a hair off true. "Good to see you again, my friend. It has been too long."

"Good to see you again, too, Zippa," Lorn replied. Thinking, you really had to hand it to the old crook. Nobody could fake sincerity like he could. In reality, the best thing that could be said about Zippa was that he would never stab you in the back unless it was absolutely . . . expedient.

Zippa changed the angle of his wings slightly, rotating to one side as he gestured to the shadowy mass in the corner. "This is Bilk, an . . . associate of mine."

Bilk stepped forward slightly, and Lorn could now see him well enough to recognize him as a Gamorrean. That explained the stench.

"Pleased to meet you, Bilk." He gestured at I-Five. "This is my associate, I-FiveYQ. I-Five, for short."

"Charmed," I-Five said dryly. "Now, if you don't mind, I'll shut off my olfactory sensor before it overloads."

Zippa turned his bulbous gaze toward the droid. "*Chutchut!* A droid with a sense of humor! This I like. You want to sell him?" The Toydarian drifted closer and slightly higher, the better to evaluate I-Five's worth. "Looks pretty cobbled together. Are those Cybot G7 powerbus cables? Haven't seen them used in years. Still, he might be worth something as a curiosity. I'll give you fifty creds for him."

Lorn kicked the droid in his lower left servomotor coupling before I-Five could voice an indignant protest. "Thanks for the offer, but I-Five's not mine to sell. We're business partners."

Zippa stared at Lorn for a moment, then broke into a wheezing laugh. "You got a weird sense of humor, Lorn. I never know when you're kidding. Still, I like you."

Bilk suddenly narrowed his beady eyes and rumbled deep in his throat, leaning truculently toward I-Five. Probably only just now realizing that the droid's earlier remark had been an insult, Lorn surmised. Gamorreans weren't the brightest species in the galaxy, not by several decimal places.

Zippa drifted in front of his hulking bodyguard. "Relax, Bilk. We're all good friends here." He turned back toward Lorn. "My friend, this is your lucky day." The Toydarian dug knobby fingers into a pouch and pulled out a palm-sized crystal cube, which glowed a dull red in the semidarkness of the booth. "What I have here is an authentic Jedi Holocron, reliably chronon-dated to be five thousand years old. This cube contains secrets of the ancient Jedi Knights." He held the cube at Lorn's eye level. "For an artifact such as this, you must agree that no price is too great. Nevertheless, all I am asking is a measly twenty thousand credits."

Lorn made no attempt to touch the object that the fence held before him. "Most interesting, and certainly a fair price," he said. "*If* it is what you claim it is."

Zippa looked affronted. "*Nifft!* You doubt my word?"

Bilk growled and cracked one set of knuckles against the horny palm of his other hand. They sounded like bones snapping.

"No, of course not. I'm sure you believe what you say is true. But there are many unscrupulous vendors out there, and even someone with your discerning eye might conceivably be taken in. All I'm asking for is a little empirical proof."

Zippa twisted his snout into a grin, exposing teeth scrimshawed with the remnants of his last meal. "And how do you

propose we get this proof? A Jedi Holocron can be activated only by someone who can use the Force. Is there something you're not telling me, Lorn? Are you perhaps a closet Jedi?"

Lorn felt himself go cold. He stepped forward and grabbed Zippa by his fleekskin vest, jerking the surprised Toydarian toward him. Bilk growled and lunged at Lorn, then stopped cold as a hair-thin laser beam scorched his scalp between his horns.

"Settle down," I-Five said pleasantly, lowering the index finger from which the beam had fired, "and I won't have to show you the other special modifications I've had installed."

Ignoring the face-off between the droid and the Gamorrean, Lorn spoke in a low voice to Zippa. "I know that was intended as a joke—which is why I'm letting you live. But don't ever—*ever*—say anything like that to me again." He glared into the Toydarian's protruding watery eyes for a moment longer, then released him.

Zippa quickly assumed a position just behind Bilk, wings beating harder than ever. Lorn could see him swallow the surprise and anger he was undoubtedly feeling as he smoothed away the wrinkles in his vest. Inwardly, Lorn cursed himself; he knew it was a mistake to let his temper get the best of him. He needed this deal; he couldn't afford to antagonize the Toydarian fence. But Zippa's remark had taken him by surprise.

"Touched a nerve, looks like," Zippa said. During the altercation he had held on to the Holocron; now he stuffed it back into his belt pouch. "I didn't know I was dealing with someone so . . . temperamental. Maybe I should find another buyer."

"Maybe," Lorn replied. "And maybe I should just take the cube and pay you what it's worth—which I figure is about five thousand creds."

He saw Zippa's cavernous nostrils flare. The Toydarian couldn't resist bargaining, even with someone who had laid hands on him. "Five thousand? *Pfah!* First you assault me, then you insult me! Twenty thousand is a fair price. However," he continued, stroking his stubbly, practically nonexistent chin, "it's obvious that you've had some sort of bad experience with the Jedi. I am not without compassion. In recognition of your past tragedy I might be persuaded to lower my price to eighteen thousand—but not a decicred lower."

"And I am not without some remorse for my behavior. As a gesture of apology, I'll raise my offer to eight thousand. Take it or leave it."

"Fifteen thousand. I'm cutting my own throat here."

"Ten thousand."

"Twelve." Zippa leaned back in midair, folding his spindly arms in a gesture of finality.

"Done," Lorn said. He had been ready to go as high as fifteen, but of course there was no reason for Zippa to know that. He pulled a thick wad of Republic credits from a belt compartment and began counting them. Most transactions uplevels were handled by electronic credit chips, but few people used the chips down here. Zippa brought the Holocron back into view and handed it to Lorn simultaneously with Lorn handing him the bills.

Lorn accepted the cube. "Well," he said, "it's been a pleasure doing—" He left the sentence unfinished when he saw that Bilk was now pointing a blaster directly at I-Five's recharge coupling. Zippa, his smile now decidedly unpleasant, floated forward and plucked the Holocron and the remainder of the credits from Lorn's hand.

"I'm afraid in this case the pleasure is all mine," the Toydar- ian said as both Lorn and I-Five raised their hands. Then Zippa's smile vanished, and the next words came out in a sinister hiss. "No one *ever* threatens me and lives to tell about it." One three- fingered hand made a pass before a sensor plate, and the booth door slid open. "I'll tell the proprietor that booth nine will be needing some extra cleaning," he said as he exited. "Hurry up, Bilk—I want to find another buyer for this item."

The booth door closed after Zippa's departure. It was impos- sible to tell if the piglike snout of the Gamorrean was smiling, but Lorn was pretty sure it was. "What's the galaxy coming to when you can't trust a Toydarian fence," he said to I-Five.

"Disgraceful," the droid agreed. "It just makes me want to . . . *scream.*"

Lorn still had his hands raised, and now he quickly jammed his two index fingers into his ears as deeply as he could as a deafening high-pitched screech came from I-Five's vocabu- lator. Even with his ears plugged, the volume was excruciat- ingly painful. Bilk, caught with no defense, reacted exactly as they had hoped he would: he howled in pain and reflexively clapped both hands over his ears, dropping the blaster in the process.

I-Five stopped the scream, caught the weapon before it could hit the floor, and in another second was aiming it at Bilk. The Gamorrean either didn't notice this fact or was too enraged to care. Snarling, he lunged at Lorn and the droid.

The particle beam punched through Bilk's armored chest plate, seared its way through various internal organs, and exited between the shoulder blades. The beam's intense heat instantly cauterized the wound, stopping any visible bleeding—not that

that mattered much to Bilk. He dropped to the floor like a sack of meat, which was essentially what he had become.

Lorn waved his hand over the exit plate, and the panel snapped open again. "Come on—before Zippa gets away!" he shouted to the droid as he charged through the lobby. The proprietor barely glanced up as they dashed by.

They both emerged into the dim light of the dead-end street, Lorn now holding the blaster, which I-Five had tossed to him. But there was no sign of Zippa. No doubt he had heard I-Five's scream, realized Bilk's probable fate, and let his wings carry him out of sight as fast as possible.

Lorn slammed a fist against the graffiti-scarred wall. "Great," he groaned. "That's just *great*. Fifteen thousand credits *and* the cube gone. And I had someone on the hook to pay *fifty* thousand for an authentic Holocron."

"Perhaps if you hadn't committed that slight blunder earlier . . ."

Lorn turned and glared at I-Five, who continued, "But now may not be the most appropriate time to discuss it."

Lorn took a deep breath, let it out slowly. Dusk was falling fast. "Come on," he said. "We'd better get out of this sector before the Raptors find us. That would be the perfect end to the day."

"So," I-Five said as they started walking, "was it a real Jedi Holocron?"

"I didn't get a chance to examine it closely. But from the cuneiform on it, I'd say it was even rarer than that. I think it was a Sith Holocron." Lorn shook his head in disgust—mostly self-disgust. He knew I-Five was right; his burst of temper had probably precipitated Zippa's reneging. He'd dealt with the

Toydarian before and never been double-crossed. Stupid, stupid, *stupid!*

But there was no point in self-flagellation. He was out of credits, and this was a bad part of Coruscant to be in with no assets. He needed a hustle, and he needed it soon—or he might very likely wind up as dead as Bilk.

Not at all a comforting thought.

**D**arsha Assant stood before the Jedi Council. This was a moment of glory that she had dreamed about ever since she had begun her Padawan training. For nearly her entire life the world within the Jedi Temple had been, to all extents and purposes, her only world. During those years she had studied, had practiced weapon and bare-hand forms, had sat in meditation for hours on end, and—in many ways the most difficult task of all—had learned to sense and manipulate, to a small degree, the power of the Force.

And now she was close to the culmination of her training. Now she stood in the topmost chamber of the spire known as the Jedi Council, with its spectacular view of the planetary city spreading away in all directions to the far horizon. Seated in twelve chairs around the perimeter of the rotunda were the members of the council. Though she had seen them but rarely during her years of training—indeed, this was only the fourth time she had been in the Council Chamber—she knew their names and histories well from her studies. Adi Gallia. Plo Koon.

Eeth Koth. The ancient and venerable Yoda. And, of course, Mace Windu, a senior member of the council. Darsha felt more than a little giddy just being in the presence of this august company.

At least she was not standing there alone. Behind her and slightly to one side was her mentor, Anoon Bondara. Master Bondara epitomized what Darsha hoped to become one day. The Twi'lek Jedi Master lived in the Force. Always still and complacent as a pool of unknown depth, he was nevertheless one of the best fighters in the order. His skill with a lightsaber was second to none. Darsha hoped that one day she might be able to exhibit a tenth of Anoon Bondara's adeptness.

Darsha had entered the order at the age of two, so like most of her comrades she had no real memories of any place other than the cloistered hallways and chambers of the Temple. Master Bondara had been parent and teacher to her for as long as she could remember. She found it hard to conceive of a life in which her Jedi mentor was not involved.

Yet now she was taking a big step into just that sort of life. For today she would be given the final assignment of her Padawan training. If she completed it successfully, she would be deemed worthy to assume the mantle of a Jedi Knight.

It was still so hard to believe. She had been orphaned in infancy on the planet Alderaan and was being raised as a state foundling when Master Bondara happened across her in his travels. Even as an infant she had shown strong Force tendencies, so she was told, and she had been brought to Coruscant in hopes of qualifying for training. Darsha knew she had been phenomenally lucky. As an orphan raised by the state, her best hope would have been some obscure midlevel government job. She would have been just another one of the countless departmental drones necessary

to the smooth functioning of a planetary government, had she not been discovered by someone who recognized her potential.

But now—to stand on the verge of becoming a Jedi! To be one of the ancient order of protectors, one of the guardians of freedom and justice in the galaxy! Even now, after all these years of preparation, she could hardly believe it was true—

"Padawan Assant."

Master Windu was speaking to her. The dark-eyed human's mellifluous voice was quietly pitched, yet its power seemed to fill the large room. Darsha took a deep breath, reaching for the Force to calm and steady her. Now was definitely not the time to appear nervous.

The Jedi Master wasted no time in pleasantries. "You are to go alone to the area in the Zi-Kree sector known as the Crimson Corridor, where a former member of Black Sun is being kept in a safe house. He is to receive the council's protection in return for information regarding a recent shake-up in the higher echelons of that criminal organization. Your job is to bring him back to the Temple alive."

Darsha was afire with eagerness, but she knew it would be unseemly to show it. She bowed slightly. "I understand, Master Windu. I shall not fail." Evidently she was not entirely successful in maintaining her equanimity, because she saw a slight smile tug at the senior member's lips. Well, so be it—being too enthusiastic was certainly not a crime. Mace Windu raised his hand in a gesture of dismissal. Darsha turned and exited the rotunda, followed by Anoon Bondara.

As the doors slid noiselessly shut behind her, Darsha faced her mentor. The question on her lips as to how soon she could begin her mission remained unasked, however, when she saw the look of worry in Master Bondara's eyes.

"Master, what is it?" For a moment she was certain that there was disappointment in the Twi'lek's gaze, as well; that Darsha had said or done something before the council to dishonor herself and her mentor. The fear sliced through her like a lightsaber's deadly edge. But the Jedi's first words relieved her of that concern.

"It is a most . . . *arduous* mission," Master Bondara said. "I am surprised at Master Windu's choice of this particular test."

"Do you doubt my ability to accomplish it?" The thought that her mentor might lack faith in her was even more distressing than the possibility of having unknowingly embarrassed herself before the council.

Master Bondara hesitated, then looked her squarely in the eyes and smiled. "I have always taught you to be honest in your feelings," the Jedi said, "for they are the surest conduit to knowledge, both of the self and of the Force. Therefore, I cannot be less than honest with you. As part of your trials, you must go alone—and I am concerned that the mission may be too difficult and dangerous a test. The Crimson Corridor is rife with gangs, criminals, street predators, and other dangers. Also, several assassination attempts have already been made on the Black Sun member's life. But—" The Twi'lek's lekku twitched in a way that Darsha had come to recognize as a fatalistic shrug. "—the council's decision is final, and we must accept it. Be assured that my concern in no way reflects my opinion of your abilities; assign it rather to the frets and misgivings of advancing age. I am sure you will acquit yourself well. Now come—we must prepare for your departure."

Darsha followed her mentor as the latter moved down the corridor toward the turbolift. Master Bondara's words had dampened her enthusiasm slightly. What if he was right? What if this was too dangerous an assignment? She had heard stories of

the dangers in the infamous Crimson Corridor. And she would be on her own for the first time, without Master Bondara or even another Padawan as backup. Could she do it?

She squared her shoulders. Of course she could! She was a Jedi—or would be as soon as she completed this assignment. Mace Windu must have thought her capable of it; he would not have assigned it otherwise. She had to trust in the living Force, as Master Qui-Gon Jinn, another of her tutors, had often said. She was not going into danger alone; she had the Force with her. It would not make her invulnerable, but it certainly gave her an advantage few others had. With the Force she could accomplish things most people viewed as nigh unto miraculous: She could leap twice her own height in a one-gravity field, she could slow her rate of descent in a fall, she could even telekinetically move items a dozen meters and more away. And she could also cloak herself in its essence, hiding in plain sight, so to speak.

Granted, her ability to do these things weren't on the same level of expertise as her mentor's. Nevertheless, she was better off with the Force than without it, that was for sure. She would not fail. She would accomplish her mission, and when she returned to the Temple the title of Jedi Knight would be waiting for her.

The *Infiltrator* emerged from hyperspace well inside the Coruscant system and continued sublight toward the capital world. Darth Maul kept the ship cloaked, though he would drop that as he neared his destination—extended cloaking took too much power. His coordinates and entry code had been given to him by his lord and master, and would clear him through the orbital security grid to land at any spaceport on the planet. Still, the less noticeable he was, the better. Even a single raised

eyebrow at the sight of the *Infiltrator* resting on a landing pad was too much.

The ship had been provided for him by Lord Sidious only recently, and he was still getting used to it. It handled well and easily, however. He approached Coruscant over the south pole. He was not concerned about being spotted, even though Coruscant had the most sophisticated and far-reaching system of detection arrays of any world in the galaxy. The *Infiltrator* boasted a state-of-the-art stygium crystal cloaking device and thrust trace dampers capable of confounding even Coruscant's warning grids.

He chose as his landing site a rooftop pad on an abandoned monad in an area of the city awaiting urban demolition and renewal. He left the cloaking device activated and deployed his speeder bike through the cargo hatch. The bike was a stripped-down model, designed for maximum speed and maneuverability. Maul continued his journey across the cityscape on it.

Lord Sidious had been able to learn that Hath Monchar maintained an apartment on Coruscant in a well-to-do section of the city several kilometers south of the Manarai Mountains. Maul did not know the exact address, but that did not matter. He would find the missing Neimoidian, even if he had to search the entire planetary city.

It was impossible even to conceive of a time when he had not been in thrall to Darth Sidious. He knew that he had come originally from a world called Iridonia, but knowing that was like knowing that the atoms composing his body had originally been born in the primordial galactic furnaces that had forged the stars. The knowledge was interesting in a remote, academic way, but no more than that. He had no interest whatsoever in learning

any more about his past or his homeworld. As far as he was concerned, his life began with Lord Sidious. And if his master ordered an end to that life, Maul would accept that judgment with no argument.

But that would not happen as long as he served Lord Sidious to the best of his abilities. Which, of course, he would. He could not even imagine a situation or circumstance that would prevent him from doing so.

Faintly, from behind him, came the wail of a siren. Maul glanced back over his shoulder and saw he was being pursued by a police droid on a speeder similar to his own. The sight did not surprise him; he knew he was breaking several traffic laws due to his speed and course. Just as he knew there was no way the droid was going to catch him.

Maul pushed the speeder bike to maximum velocity, rocketing through the ferrocrete labyrinth on a plane between two levels of skycar traffic. The speeder had no stealth capabilities, but that did not matter; his speed and his control were more than sufficient to leave the pursuing droid behind. He knew the droid was comlinking ahead, calling for reinforcements to surround him and bring him to a stop.

He couldn't let that happen.

There was a break in the lower traffic flow ahead. Maul altered the speeder's thrust angle and dived through it, descending several stories until he dropped through a fog layer that hovered perhaps thirty meters above the ground. They could still track him, of course, but he knew that, as long as he was not endangering any lives other than his own, he would not be as high a priority to them. Besides, he had almost reached his destination.

He arrived without further incident and parked the speeder

bike in one of the local lots, paying for the rest of the day in advance. Then he stepped onto a slidewalk that carried him toward one of the many outposts of the Coruscant Customs Bureau.

Several times he noticed people looking at him; his appearance was capable of turning heads even on so cosmopolitan a planet as Coruscant. It would take considerable concentration to blind these crowds to his presence by using the Force, though it could be done. But it did not matter who saw him at this point. If all went according to plan, he would be off Coruscant in less than a day, his mission completed.

He had one thing to his advantage: Even though there was a bigger variety of alien races and species here than practically anywhere else in the galaxy, there still weren't a lot of Neimoidians to be seen, due to the recent tension between the Republic and the Trade Federation. Maul entered the imposing structure of the Customs Bureau and moved quickly to a data bank terminal. Using a password provided by Lord Sidious, he instituted a HoloNet search that turned up a record of a recently arrived Neimoidian. The image matched the one of Hath Monchar given to him by his master. The name was different, but that was not surprising.

Maul ordered a new search parameter, trying to track Monchar though debit card use. There was no record of any transactions—again, not surprising. The Neimoidian would be too canny to be caught that way. No doubt he used only cash while on Coruscant.

A line had begun to form behind him; other people wanted to use the terminal he was monopolizing. He could hear grumbling voices as citizens and tourists grew increasingly impatient. He ignored them.

He hacked into the planetwide security grid that monitored the spaceports and surrounding environs, calling up the last

twenty-four hours of a constant collage of images taken by stationary and roving holocams. He ordered the system to search its files for Neimoidians.

He found several images, one of which was promising. It wasn't much to go on—a blurred image of a Neimoidian entering a tavern not far from there, a few hours earlier—but it was better than nothing.

Maul smiled faintly. His hand brushed the grip of the double-bladed lightsaber that hung from his belt. He noted the address of the tavern, then turned and left the building.

**N**ute Gunray pushed the plate of fungus aside in irritation. It was his favorite dish: black mulch mold marinated in the alkaloid secretions of the blight beetle, seasoned to perfection, with the spores just beginning to fruit. Normally his taste and olfactory nodes would be quivering in ecstasy at the prospect of such a gastronomic experience. But he had no appetite; indeed, had not been able to look at food since the Sith Lord's last appearance on the bridge, when Sidious had noticed that Hath Monchar was missing.

"Take it away," he snapped at the service droid hovering respectfully nearby. The plate was removed, and Gunray stood, stepping away from the table. He faced one of the transparisteel ports, looking gloomily out at the infinite vista of the star field.

There was still no news of Monchar, and no clue as to where he had gone. If the viceroy had to guess—and guessing was all he had at this point—he would say that his deputy viceroy had decided to go into business for himself. There were plenty of ways

that the knowledge of the impending blockade could be converted into currency, enough currency to begin a new life on a new world. Gunray felt fairly confident that this was Monchar's plan, largely because he had thought of doing it himself more than once.

That didn't make it any less of a problem, however. Unless Monchar could be returned to the *Saak'ak* before Sidious contacted them again . . .

He heard the panel to his suite chime softly. "Come," he said.

The panel slid open, and Rune Haako entered. The settlement officer of the Trade Federation forces crossed the room, sat down, and arranged his purple raiment with meticulous precision, smoothing the pleats assiduously before looking at Gunray.

"I assume there has been no further word of Hath Monchar?"

"None."

Haako nodded. He fiddled with his collar for a moment, then adjusted his bloused sleeves. Gunray felt a flash of irritation. He could read Haako like a data file; he knew the attorney had a suggestion to make regarding the situation, and he knew also that this circuitous approach to it was designed to put Gunray on the defensive. But protocol demanded that he show nothing of what he felt; to do so would be to acknowledge that Haako had the upper hand in the situation.

At last Haako looked up, meeting Gunray's eyes. "Perhaps I might suggest a course of action."

Gunray made a slight hand gesture designed to convey no more than polite interest. "By all means."

"In my offices for the Trade Federation I have had occasion to encounter a number of people with singular attributes and abilities." He adjusted the crossed points on his cowl. "I refer

specifically to a certain human female named Mahwi Lihnn. For a prearranged fee she searches for and retrieves people who have strayed from their duties or who have committed crimes."

"You are speaking of a bounty hunter," Gunray said. He saw Haako restrain himself from smirking, and realized belatedly that by admitting knowledge of the term used for someone of such crass abilities he had lost face before his subordinate. He didn't care, however—he was too excited at the possibility the attorney's suggestion presented. "We could hire this Mahwi Lihnn to track down Monchar and bring him back before Sidious convenes with us again."

"Just so."

Gunray noted the veiled contempt in Haako's tone. He adjusted his own collar and took his time replying. His initial excitement at a potential solution to the problem had calmed slightly, and now he decided to show Rune Haako that one did not lightly play games of position with a commanding viceroy of the Federation. "And you . . . *know* this personage?" he inquired, his tone and expression conveying just the right amount of disdain that anyone of Haako's station would admit to having had actual social intercourse with such a low individual.

Haako's look of smugness wavered. His fingers plucked nervously at a bit of filigree. "As I said, in the course of my duties as attorney and diplomatic attaché for the Federation . . ."

"Of course." Gunray infused the two words with equal parts pity and haughtiness. "And the Trade Federation is most grateful to you for your willingness to fraternize with such . . . *colorful* . . . characters, in hopes that their abilities may one day somehow be of use." He watched Haako's lips purse together as though the barrister had bitten into a rotten truffle, and continued. "To be sure, desperate times call for desperate measures. Though I re-

gret having to ask this of a person of your stature, I hope you can find it within yourself to once again contact this Mahwi Lihnn, in order that we may satisfactorily resolve the Monchar situation."

Rune Haako muttered an acquiescence and left. After the door closed, Nute Gunray nodded in satisfaction. Not bad, not bad at all. He had managed to implement a possible solution to the question of Monchar's disappearance, and at the same time had taken that insufferable prig Haako down a peg. He listened in pleasure to a faint rumbling in his gut sac that signified the return of his appetite. Perhaps he would give his dinner another try.

"Had th' Hutt *primed* for this," Lorn said. "Was ready t'part with a *great deal* o' cash for a real Jedi Holocron. Would've paid *twice* as much for one from th' Sith." He gazed dejectedly into the depths of his glass, swirling the remaining blue-green Johrian whiskey that had recently filled it. "Fifty thousand credits, th' cube was worth. Now've lost it *and* the fifteen thousand. All I had."

"It does put us in somewhat desperate straits financially," I-Five said.

The two were sitting at the bar near the back of the Green Glowstone Tavern not far from one end of the infamous Crimson Corridor section of the city. They were regular patrons, and the droid's presence there no longer caused much controversy, despite the sign at the entrance that proclaimed NO DROIDS ALLOWED in Basic and several other languages.

" 'S all *my* fault," Lorn muttered, more to the drink-stained counter than to I-Five. "Hadn't lost m'temper . . ." He fixed the droid with a somewhat bleary gaze. "Dunno why y' stay partners with me."

"Ah, now we come to the maudlin stage. Will this take long? I may want to put myself in cyberostasis until it's over."

Lorn grunted and signaled for another refill. "Y'can be a real *bastard*, y'know that?" he told I-Five.

"Let's see . . . according to my data banks, the primary definition of *bastard* is 'a child born of unwed parents.' However, a secondary usage is 'something of irregular or unusual origins.' In that respect, I suppose I qualify." When the bartender came over to fill Lorn's glass again, I-Five put his hand over it. "My friend has had enough neurons destroyed by various hydroxyl compounds for today. It's not like he has an overabundant supply in the first place."

The bartender, a Bothan, glanced at Lorn, then shrugged and moved on down the bar. A Duros wearing spacer's togs and sitting nearby looked at them, seeming to register the droid's presence for the first time. "You let your *droid* decide how much you can drink?" he asked Lorn.

" 'S not *my* droid," Lorn said. "We're partners. *Business* associates." He pronounced the words carefully.

The Duros flickered nictitating membranes over his eyes in a sign of surprise and disbelief. "You're telling me that droid has citizenship status?"

"*He's* not telling you anything," I-Five said as he turned to face the Duros, "largely because he's so drunk he can barely stand. *I'm* telling you to mind your own business. My status in galactic society is not your concern."

The Duros glanced around, saw that the rest of the tavern's patrons were rather pointedly ignoring the exchange, shrugged, and went back to his drink. I-Five pulled Lorn off the bar stool and aimed him in the direction of the door. Lorn walked, weaving, across the room, then turned and faced the tavern.

"I *was* somebody, once," he told the group, most of whom didn't bother to look up. "Worked uplevels. Penthouse suite.

Could see th' *mountains*. Damn Jedi—*they* did this to me." Then he turned and walked out, I-Five following.

Outside, the air was chill, and Lorn could feel a small amount of sobriety returning. The sun had set, and the long twilight of the equatorial regions had begun.

"Guess I told 'em, didn't I?"

"Absolutely. They were riveted. I'm sure they can't wait for the next thrilling installment. In the meantime, why don't we go home before one of the colorful locals decides to see how fast alcohol-soaked human tissue burns?"

"Good idea," Lorn agreed as I-Five took his arm and started walking.

They passed sidewalk vendors offering bootleg holos, glitterstim, and other illegal items for sale. Beggars of various species, wrapped in tattered cloaks, pawed at them for alms. They entered the nearest kiosk entrance to the underground, descending a long-broken escalator that ended in a winding corridor. It had been warm on the surface; down here it was like a sauna. The mingled body odor of various unwashed beings moving through the passageway, combined with the fungal reek permeating the walls, verged on hallucinogenic. Why can't they all smell like Toydarians? Lorn wondered.

They turned down a narrow side passage, its walls and ceiling a complex pattern of pipes, conduits, and cables. Flickering luminescent strips at irregular intervals provided dim illumination. Granite slugs oozed along the floor, requiring Lorn to pay attention to where he stepped—no small task in his condition. Eventually they reached the third in a series of recessed metal doors, which he opened after several tries with his keycard.

The windowless cubicle, a cell carved from the city's massive ferrocrete foundation, was designed for single occupancy, but

since Lorn's roommate was a droid, they were not particularly cramped for space. There were a couple of chairs, an extensible wall cot, a tiny refresher, and a kitchenette barely big enough for a nanowave and food preserver. The compartment was spotlessly clean—another advantage of having a droid around.

Lorn sat on the edge of the cot and stared at the floor. "Here's all you need to know about the Jedi," he announced.

"Oh, please—not again."

"They're a bunch of self-serving, sanctimonious elitists."

"I have this entire rant recorded, you know. I could play a holo at fast speed; it would save time."

" 'Guardians of the galaxy'—don't make me laugh. All they're interested in guarding is their way of life."

"If I were you—a hypothetical situation the mere mention of which threatens to overload my logic circuits—I'd stop obsessing over the Jedi and start thinking about where my next meal is coming from. I don't require nourishment, but you do. You need something hot to peddle—fast."

Lorn glared at the droid. "I never should have disconnected your creativity damper." He brooded for a while longer, then said, "But you're right—no point dwelling in the past. Got to look ahead. What we need is a plan—right now." And with those words he fell backwards onto the cot and began to snore loudly.

I-Five stared at his recumbent companion. "Random evolution should never have been entrusted with intelligence," the droid muttered.

**D**arth Sidious was also thinking about the Jedi.

Their fire was dying in the galaxy; of that there was no doubt. For more than a thousand generations they had been the self-appointed paladins of the commonweal, but that was now coming to an end. And the pathetic fools, blinded by their own hypocrisy, could not see the truth of this.

It was right and fitting that this be so, just as it was right and fitting that the instrument of their downfall be the Sith.

The few pedants and scholars who even knew the name thought that the Sith were the "dark side" of the Jedi Knights. This was, of course, far too simplistic an evaluation. It was true that they had embraced the teachings of a group of rogue Jedi thousands of years ago, but they had taken that knowledge and philosophy far beyond the insular didacticism they had been given to start with. It was easy and convenient, as well, to demarcate the concept of the Force into light and dark; indeed, even Sidious had used such notions of duality in the training of his disciple. But the reality was that there was only the Force. It was

above such petty concepts as positive and negative, black and white, good and evil. The only difference worthy of note was this: The Jedi saw the Force as an end in itself; the Sith knew that it was a means to an end.

And that end was Power.

For all their humble posturing and protestations of abdication, the Jedi craved power as much as anyone. Sidious knew this to be true. They claimed to be the servants of the people, but over the centuries they had increasingly removed themselves from contact with the very citizens they ostensibly served. Now they prowled the cloistered hallways and chambers of their Temple, mouthing their empty ideologies while practicing hubristic machinations designed to bring them more secular power.

As one half of the entire existing order of the Sith, Darth Sidious craved power, as well. It was true that he was operating covertly toward that end, but he was doing so out of necessity, not sophistry. After the Great Sith War, the order had been decimated. The lone remaining Sith had revived the order according to a new doctrine: one master and one apprentice. Thus it had been, and thus it would be, until that glorious day that saw the fall of the Jedi and the ascendancy of their ancient enemies, the Sith.

And that day was fast approaching. After centuries of planning and collusion, it was now almost here. Sidious was confident that he would see its culmination in his lifetime. There would come a day in the not too distant future when he would stand, triumphant, over the last Jedi's body, when he would see their Temple razed, when he would take his rightful place as ruler of the galaxy.

Which was why *no* loose ends, no matter how inconsequential, could be permitted. Perhaps Hath Monchar's absence had

nothing to do with the Trade Federation's looming blockade of the planet Naboo. That was conceivable. But as long as the slightest chance existed that it did, the Neimoidian had to be found and dealt with.

Darth Sidious looked at a wall chrono. It was now slightly over fourteen standard hours since he had given Maul the assignment. He anticipated hearing from his apprentice shortly. The stakes were high, very high, but he had every confidence that Maul would perform the task with his customary ruthless efficiency. All would continue as planned, and the Sith would rise again.

Soon.

Very soon.

The Crimson Corridor was in the Third Quadrant of the Zi-Kree sector. It was one of the oldest areas of the vast planetary metropolis, overbuilt with skyscrapers and towers constructed long ago. The buildings towered so tall and so thick that some areas of the Corridor received only a few minutes of sunlight a day. Darsha remembered hearing legends of inbred subhuman tribes living in the near-total darkness of its depths for so long that they had gone genetically blind.

But darkness was the least of the dangers in the Corridor. Far worse were the things, both human and nonhuman, that lived in the darkness and preyed on the unwary.

Darsha piloted her skyhopper down through the miasmal fog that lay like a filthy blanket over the lowest levels. Why, she wondered, would anyone pick a neighborhood like this for a place in which to conceal informants? The answer was, of course, that it was the last place anyone would look.

The safe house—a barricaded block of ferrocrete and plasteel—

was in a street that was not wide enough for her to set the sky-hopper down. She landed in the closest intersection, got out, and instructed the autopilot to take the craft up twenty meters and remain in hover mode there. That way it was more likely to be there when she got back.

There were a few glow sticks in protective wired cages set here and there on the buildings, but after centuries of use they were so weak that they did little to relieve the gloom. As soon as Darsha disembarked from her vehicle she was set upon by beggars supplicating for food and money. At first she tried the ancient Jedi technique of clouding their minds, but there were too many of them, and most of them had brains too addled by privation and various illegal chemicals to respond to the suggestion. She gritted her teeth and pushed her way though the forest of filthy waving arms, tentacles, and various other appendages.

The mingled revulsion and sympathy she felt was almost overwhelming. For nearly as long as she could remember, Darsha had been coddled and cozened in the Jedi Temple, protected from direct contact with the dregs of society—an ironic situation, since the Jedi were supposed to be the protectors of all levels of civilization, even those considered untouchable by most of the upper classes. True, elements of her training had taken her to various rough neighborhoods, but nowhere else had she seen anything that even remotely compared with this. It horrified her that such poverty and neglect could exist anywhere, let alone on Coruscant.

She made it to the recessed entrance of the safe house and pounded on the reinforced door. A slit opened, and a sentry cam extruded from it. "Your name and business?" it asked in a rasping voice.

"Darsha Assant, on the Jedi Council's business."

An emaciated Kubaz sought to pluck her lightsaber from its hook on her utility belt. She seized his hand and bent the thumb backwards. He squealed and backed hastily away, but others took his place immediately. The only reason they did not drag her back into the street was that there were too many to crowd into the narrow aperture where she stood.

The security cam quickly ran a laser scan over her face. "Identity confirmed. Please hold your breath."

Darsha did so—whereupon hidden nozzles surrounding the door sprayed a pink mist at the crowd of mendicants. A chorus of indignant shouts, squeals, bleats, and other protests rose from them as the airborne irritant drove them momentarily back. The door slid quickly up, and a metallic arm grabbed Darsha and pulled her inside.

She found herself in a narrow corridor that was almost as dark as the street. The security droid who had taken her arm now led her down this passageway and around a corner, into a small, windowless room. The light was not much better here; Darsha could barely make out a hunched form sitting on a chair. Bald and humanoid, he looked like a Fondorian to her.

The droid said, "This is the Jedi who will take you to safety, Oolth."

Though she knew it was foolish, Darsha felt a little thrill at being called a Jedi, even by a droid.

"About time," the Fondorian said. He stood quickly. "Let's get out of here before it gets dark—not that it ever really *stops* getting dark around here." He moved toward the room's entrance, than stopped and looked back at Darsha. "Well, come on," he said testily. "What're you waiting for?"

"I'm just trying to decide how best to get back to my sky-hopper," Darsha replied. "I don't relish the idea of wading through those poor beings out there again."

"*We'll* be the 'poor beings' if we don't get moving. This is Raptor territory. They make those scum out there look like the Republic Senate. Now let's go!"

Darsha moved toward the hallway; Oolth stood aside to let her pass. "I'm the one who needs protecting; you go first."

Whatever good he was to the council, Darsha was sure Oolth the Fondorian wasn't valued for his bravery. She pushed past him and strode back to the outside door.

The cam's monitor was mounted by the door; it showed a few street people still loitering around the area. Most of them, however, had apparently gone looking for someone else to importune. If Darsha and Oolth moved quickly, they could probably get back to the intersection where her vehicle was without too much trouble.

"All right," Darsha said. She took a deep breath and reached for the Force to calm herself. She was a Jedi Padawan with a job to do. Time to get on with it. "Let's move out."

The door panel slid open. Darsha quested with the Force and felt no sense of anybody nearby who posed a danger. Thus reassured, she started down the street with Oolth. The vagrants seemed to materialize from out of the shadows, clustering around them again. Oolth shoved at them as they crowded in. "Get away from me! Filthy creatures!"

"Just keep moving," Darsha said to him. She had refused the droid's offer of escort because she didn't want to draw any more attention than absolutely necessary. If she had to, she could activate her lightsaber; she had no doubt that just the sight of the energy blade would send the majority of the street people fleeing.

But she hoped it wouldn't be necessary. They were almost to the intersection.

And then her heart, already pounding from nervous tension, suddenly tried to batter its way up her throat.

Her skyhopper was still where she had parked it, hovering twenty meters up in the air. Clustered on the street beneath it was a heterogeneous assortment of beings, about a dozen in all. Among the species Darsha recognized were humans, Kubaz, H'nemthe, Gotals, Snivvians, Trandoshans, and Bith. All of them appeared to be in the late adolescent stage of their particular species, all were dressed in colorful and motley styles, and all looked extremely dangerous.

Oolth the Fondorian gasped, and whispered in a strangled tone, "The Raptors."

Darsha had heard tales of the street gangs that terrorized many of the more run-down sectors of Coruscant's surface. The Raptors were reputed to be the worst, by far. She had hoped to complete her mission quickly enough to avoid an encounter with them. So much for that idea.

Several grappling hooks had snagged into the two-person craft, and from them dangled ropes. Three members of the gang—a human female and two male Bith—had climbed aboard and were busily ransacking the vehicle. They tossed down various items—a holoprojector, an aquata breather, a pouch of food capsules, and medical supplies—to the gang members below. Even as Darsha watched, one of them managed to disable the autopilot, causing the craft to settle gently to the street. This was greeted by a cheer from the rest of the gang.

Oolth grabbed her robe and tried to pull her into the shadows of the narrow street. "Quick—before they see us!"

She shook off his grasp. "I can't let them strip the skyhopper.

It's our only way out of here. Wait here until I've dealt with them." Then, forcing herself to project a confidence she did not in any way feel, Darsha strode toward the Raptors.

She hadn't taken more than a few steps before her approach was noted. The raucous chatter and laughter quickly subsided; no doubt, Darsha thought, because they were having a hard time believing someone could be this suicidal.

She stopped a few meters from them. There was no one else on the street now, save for the Fondorian cowering somewhere behind her. No one in their right mind wanted to be around when the Raptors were on the prowl.

"That's my skyhopper," she said, relieved to find that her voice was not shaking. "Please return the things you stole and move away from it."

The Raptors looked at each other in astonishment before breaking into the various sounds that constituted laughter for each species. One of the human males—lean and wiry, sporting an improbable mane of green hair standing straight up in an electrostatic field—swaggered toward her.

"New around here, I'm guessing," he said, causing more sniggering—this time with a distinctly unpleasant edge—to erupt from his compatriots.

Darsha reviewed her options quickly. There weren't many. She was one against a dozen, and while her knowledge of the Jedi fighting arts improved the odds somewhat, she was still not at all confident in her ability to come out ahead in a battle. She was on their turf, after all, and for all she knew, there might be a dozen more of them lurking in the shadows.

But there were alternatives to fighting. The mind trick she had tried earlier on the beggars hadn't been completely success-ful, but it had turned away a few of them. It might serve now to

confuse the Raptors long enough to allow her to reach the vehicle. Of course, she still had to get Oolth in the craft with her, but
one problem at a time.

She raised her right hand, fanning the fingers in a gesture designed to focus their attention while she reached out mentally for
the Force. "You're not interested in me," she said, using the soft
but compelling tone she had been taught, "or my vehicle." She
could see by their confused and uncertain expressions that it was
working, could feel their wills beginning to vibrate in resonance
with hers.

Green Hair was either the leader or something close to it, because when he nodded and said slowly, "We're not interested in
her, or her vehicle," the rest of the gang mumbled the same
words in ragged unison.

Darsha took a few steps forward, making the hypnotic gesture again. "You might as well go now," she told Green Hair.
"There's nothing interesting going on here."

"We might as well go now. There's nothing interesting going
on here." The rest of the gang again echoed him.

Darsha kept moving slowly but steadily forward. She stepped
past Green Hair and was now in the midst of them, only a step or
two away from her craft. She had them now; she could feel their
minds, some struggling feebly, others willingly surrendering to
her suggestive power amplified by the Force. Another moment
and she would be in the skyhopper.

A scream echoed down the dark street.

Startled, Darsha whipped around, staring back toward the
source of the cry. It was Oolth the Fondorian, staggering out
into the middle of the narrow thoroughfare, shaking and kicking his leg frantically to dislodge a large armored rat that had
clamped its jaws onto his shin. Even as she realized who it was,

she realized, as well, that her tenuous mind-lock on the Raptors had been shattered by the unexpected sound. Blinking and shaking their heads as if awakening from slumber, the Raptors realized that their prey had obligingly delivered itself right into their midst.

Darsha had no choice now but to fight. She reached for her lightsaber, but before she could seize it they were upon her.

# 6

Hath Monchar was afraid.

This was not a particularly surprising state of affairs to anyone who knew the deputy viceroy of the Trade Federation. Even among Neimoidians, Monchar was considered remarkably timid. Which made it all the more amazing that he had done what he had done.

Monchar was afraid, yes, but underneath that was another emotion, one far less familiar to him than fear. This emotion was pride—a nervous and fragile pride, it was true, but pride nevertheless. He had taken a chance—a big chance. He had dared to steer his life in a new and, with any luck, more profitable direction. He had a right to feel proud of that, he told himself.

He glanced around at the patrons of the tavern he was sitting in. It was a different establishment than the one he usually frequented when on Coruscant. That tavern was in the affluent Kaldani Spires monad, where he had an apartment. He was not staying in his apartment on this visit, however. That would make him too easy to find. Instead he had rented a cheap domicile

near the Galactic Museum under an assumed name. He had seriously considered buying a holographic image disguiser that could change his appearance to that of another species, as well. His paranoia had warred with his parsimony for quite some time on that one, and finally the stinginess had won out, though just barely.

Hath Monchar had come to Coruscant because the capital world was the best place to move information quickly and anonymously. That was what he had to sell—information. Specifically, information about the upcoming blockade of Naboo and the fact that the man behind it all was a Sith Lord.

It was a dangerous scheme, to be sure. If his coconspirators found him, Monchar knew they would quickly give him up to Darth Sidious's tender mercies. The mere thought of being in the Sith Lord's clutches was enough to make the Neimoidian start to hyperventilate. Even so, Monchar couldn't resist the opportunity to make a quick fortune.

He took another gulp of the agaric ale he was drinking. Yes, the risks were high, but so was the potential for profit. All he needed was to contact the right person as an intermediary—someone who knew the people who would pay handsomely for the news he had. All it would take was a bit more fortitude on his part. He had come this far; he was not going to stop now, not with his goal nearly in sight.

Hath Monchar signaled the Baragwin bartender. One more flagon of ale ought to give him the fortitude he needed.

Mahwi Lihnn had been a bounty hunter for going on ten standard years, ever since she had been forced to leave her homeworld after killing a corrupt government official. During that time she had traveled nearly the length and breadth of the galaxy

on various assignments. She had pursued fugitives from justice on such diverse worlds as Ord Mantell, Roon, Tatooine, and dozens of others. Oddly enough, however, she had never been to Coruscant, and she was looking forward to seeing the capital of the galaxy.

The assignment from the Neimoidian viceroy's lieutenant seemed straightforward enough. Lihnn did not anticipate any great trouble in finding the missing Hath Monchar, even on a crowded world like Coruscant. As her ship descended on auto-pilot toward the landing pad at the eastern spaceport, she reviewed her equipment and weaponry. Her garb looked like no more than a simple utilitarian tunic and pants, but they were made of densely woven shell spider silk, a material capable of resisting even a vibroblade's thrust, as well as reflecting low-power parti-cle beams and lasers. It was armor that did not look like armor—to the uninitiated. Experts would spot it, of course, but she didn't expect to run into any opposition. She wore twin DL-44 blasters on each hip, and a small disruptor pistol in a concealed ankle holster. Strapped to each wrist was an MM9 wrist rocket, and in her right hand she wore a palm flechette shooter. On her utility belt she carried, among other things, a set of stun cuffs, a stun baton, and three glop grenades.

Mahwi Lihnn believed in being prepared.

Her first stop after disembarking from her ship was the Kaldani Spires Residential Apartments. She seriously doubted that Monchar would be foolish enough to stay in an apartment registered to him, but one never knew. More than once Lihnn had saved herself needless trouble and time by looking in the most obvious places for her quarry.

As she entered the lobby the security droid on duty asked whom she wished to see. "Hath Monchar," Lihnn told him. The

droid checked a monitor screen, then informed her that Monchar was not in; indeed, was not even on Coruscant. Lihnn nodded pleasantly and clapped the circuit disruptor she had pulled from her belt onto the droid's chassis. The droid stuttered for an instant before its photoreceptors went dark.

Lihnn took the lift tube up to the five hundredth floor and strolled down the corridor to Monchar's apartment, where she used an electronic lock breaker to void the security system. Once inside, she quickly checked the rooms. The droid had been telling the truth; Monchar was not there. Furthermore, the apartment appeared to have been vacant for some time.

The large suite was decorated in what was, to a Neimoidian, the epitome of tasteful decor; to Lihnn it looked and smelled like a fetid swamp. She did some more investigating, hoping to find a clue to Monchar's whereabouts. In this she was disappointed.

At last she left, going back down to the lobby and pulling the circuit disruptor off the security droid. Before it could reaccess its memory banks sufficiently to realize what had happened, Mahwi Lihnn had left and was strolling along one of the skywalks fifty stories above the surface.

It would certainly take some time to search a city the size of a planet for one person. Fortunately, Lihnn felt fairly sure that such a search wouldn't be necessary. Even though Monchar was smart enough not to stay in his apartment, she was willing to bet that the Neimoidian was somewhere in the general vicinity. This was the part of Coruscant with which he was most familiar, so it made sense that he would be holed up not too far away.

Lihnn stopped at an observation deck and enjoyed the view for a few minutes. The descriptions she had read and the holos she had seen did not do justice to the stupendousness of the real

thing. The last census put the population of Coruscant at some-where in the neighborhood of a trillion living beings. Even if she could investigate one person every second, she would still need the life span of a hundred Tatooine Sarlaccs to get to them all. But there were ways to narrow the search.

Paranoid as Monchar no doubt was, he still had to eat. Lihnn pulled a portable HoloNet link from a pocket and consulted it, entering search parameters for restaurants in the area that spe-cialized in the disgusting swill Neimoidians called food. As she had thought, there were not all that many. She glanced at her chrono and saw that it was almost the hour when most species eat their evening meal. She would go check out a few of these restaurants. It was worth putting up with the smell if it meant an early resolution to this case.

Darth Maul signaled for an air taxi. Even though his speeder was not far away, he did not wish to risk anyone connecting him to it, now that he was close to his quarry. The taxi pilot—a Quarren—looked somewhat dubiously at his passenger as Maul got into the backseat, but said nothing as he was given the ad-dress. The taxi rose rapidly straight up through two strata of traf-fic, its lift repulsors humming barely within the threshold of Maul's hearing, then veered north in a long arc toward a cluster of tow-ers in the distance.

The taxi landed gently at a terminal within fifty meters of the tavern. Maul entered, stepping immediately to the shadows near the door while he looked about. His vision adjusted far more quickly to extremes of light and darkness than did most species; he was able almost at once to see the tavern's dim interior and its customers.

He saw humans, Bith, Devaronians, Nikto, Snivvians, Arcona—a cornucopia of species, all drinking or otherwise imbibing various substances capable of altering their brain chemistry. He did not see Hath Monchar. For that matter, he did not see any Neimoidians at all.

Maul approached the bar. The bartender was a tall gaunt Baragwin, his folds of facial dewlaps as leathery and creased as a bantha's skin. "I am looking for a Neimoidian," Maul said to him. "He would have been in here within the last few hours."

The Baragwin sent a ripple running through his dewlaps from top to bottom—the equivalent of a human shaking his head. "Many beings come in here," he said, his voice absurdly high and flutelike coming from such a massive head. "They come, they drink, they talk, they go. I do not recall seeing a Neimoidian recently."

Darth Maul leaned forward. "Think again," he said softly. He could easily use the Force to get whatever information might be had from this weak-willed creature, but there was no need. He knew he could get what he wanted by intimidation.

The Baragwin's nasal polyps began to quiver—a sign of nervousness. "Upon further reflection I do seem to remember a representative of that species imbibing here perhaps an hour ago."

"Did he speak to you or anyone else?"

The Baragwin's polyps were vibrating almost too fast to see now. "No. That is . . . he—he ordered agaric ale."

"And did he speak of anything else?"

"Yes. He inquired of me how one might contact someone proficient in the buying and selling of sensitive information."

Maul leaned back. "And you told him—what?"

"I gave him a name."

"You will now give me that name."

The Baragwin rippled his dewlaps from bottom to top in acquiescence. "Lorn Pavan. A human—Corellian, I believe. He is well known in this city sector as one who traffics in such merchandise."

"And where might I find this Lorn Pavan?"

"I do not know."

Maul leaned forward again, his yellow eyes blazing. The Baragwin backed up hastily. "I speak the truth! He comes in here occasionally, always accompanied by a protocol droid called I-Five. I know nothing more."

That was interesting news, Maul reflected. It should help to narrow the search; personal droids were not that common in this area of Coruscant. "Describe this Lorn Pavan."

"Tall. Muscular. Black filamentous cilia on his scalp, but none on his face. Brown ocular pigmentation. The females of his species would probably characterize him as 'handsome.' "

Maul nodded, then raised his right hand in a focusing gesture as he mentally reached for the Force. He had to make sure that this next question was answered truthfully, because the answer would determine whether or not he had to kill the Baragwin.

"Did the Neimoidian speak at all to you about the nature of the information he wished to sell?"

The dewlaps quickly undulated downward. "He did not. I have told you all that I know."

Maul sensed no negative vibration in the Force as the Baragwin spoke. He turned away without another word and exited the tavern.

He was glad that he did not have to kill the Baragwin—not out of any moral sense, or even out of pity for the pathetic creature; his relief stemmed purely from having avoided the inevitable difficulties brought on by killing someone in a public place. Nevertheless, if the Force had told him the Baragwin was

lying, he would have struck him down without a second thought and dealt with the consequences. Darth Sidious had told him to kill everyone with whom Hath Monchar had shared knowledge of the blockade, and Maul would follow his master's commands, as always.

He strode along the outdoor concourse, pondering his next move. Though the walkway was crowded, his passage was not impeded, as most of the pedestrians gave him a wide berth. Which was as it should be. Darth Maul had nothing but contempt for the masses. Of all the uncounted trillions of sentient beings that populated the galaxy, only one was deserving of respect: Darth Sidious. The only man who dared to dream of conquering not just a world or a star system, but an entire galaxy. The man who had taken the young Maul from a backwater planet and raised him to be his successor. He owed Darth Sidious everything.

It had not been an easy path that he had been set upon. To be a truly superior being, apart from and above the senseless herd, required absolute devotion and dedication. He had had to learn self-sufficiency, both in body and in mind, almost from the time he had learned to walk. His master would accept nothing less than the absolute best that Maul could offer. When he was younger, if he had flinched during his training when the edge of a weapon found his flesh, or when an incorrect block or defensive maneuver resulted in a cracked bone, his punishments had always been swift and inevitable.

He had soon learned to think of pain as his teacher. From fearing it, he had actually come to welcome it, because he knew it would test his willpower and his courage; it would make him stronger. To be content, to be comfortable, was to be compla-

cent. No one learned anything from pleasure. Pain, on the other hand, was a most efficient instructor.

He returned to the problem at hand. Perhaps tracking down the human Lorn Pavan would lead him in turn to his primary target. In all probability the Corellian would have to be killed, as well. The longer the Neimoidian was alive, the more likely his information would be disseminated. Still, Maul was not worried. If he had to wipe out this entire city sector in order to contain the news about the blockade, he would do it without a qualm. Lives, even hundreds of lives, did not matter.

The first blow came from behind, half stunning Darsha and causing her to drop to her knees. A booted foot impacted against her side, driving her breath from her. Half-blinded by pain, Darsha reached for the Force as the Raptors closed in, felt its power enfold her, cloak her like an invisible shield. She stood, thrusting out one arm in a warding gesture, and felt the reverberating ripples flowing outward, hurling back her surprised attackers. For a brief moment she stood clear of them, and she used that moment to draw and activate her lightsaber. The yellow energy blade boiled out from the hilt's projector, extending to its full length.

"She's a Jedi!" one of the Raptors, a Trandoshan, shouted. He seemed surprised, but not particularly awed or impressed.

"She's still dead meat," Green Hair said. But none of his gang seemed particularly anxious to be the first within reach of the lightsaber.

"You should have listened to me," Darsha said as she moved slowly until her back was against the skyhopper. "I don't want to hurt any of you. Walk away now, while you can."

She saw Green Hair and the Trandoshan exchange a glance—just a flicker of eye movement. It was enough to warn her, however, and even if it had not been, she had already sensed the disturbance in the Force coming from behind her. Darsha spun and raised the blade in a high defensive movement just in time to intercept a stocky Gotal who had leapt over the craft, aiming a vibroblade at her. The lightsaber sheered effortlessly through the Gotal's wrist, sending the blade, still clutched in the severed hand, arcing back to land in the empty vehicle. The Gotal shrieked and fell in a heap on the pavement, clutching his cauterized stump.

There was a moment of utter stillness, save for the Gotal's whimpers. Events hung in delicate balance, Darsha knew. Would they swarm over her to avenge their comrade, or flee in fear?

It was Green Hair who decided which course to take: He turned and ran up the street. The rest of the gang members promptly followed his lead, two of them dragging the wounded Gotal with them. In a matter of seconds the street was completely deserted save for Darsha and Oolth the Fondorian.

Darsha moved quickly to Oolth, who was lying on his back, moaning and still kicking feebly in an effort to dislodge the armored rat. Darsha touched the tip of the lightsaber's blade to the creature's neck, right at the soft juncture between the head and body carapaces, and the rat released its grip and bolted toward the shadows.

Darsha deactivated the lightsaber and pulled Oolth to his feet. "Let's go—before they come back with reinforcements."

"What took you so long? That blasted rat nearly gnawed my leg off!"

*A pity it wasn't your head,* Darsha thought. "Just be grateful I was able to chase them away. Now let's get out of here." She

helped him climb into the passenger side of the skyhopper, then settled herself behind the controls.

And realized that they weren't going anywhere.

"Come on—what're you waiting for? Lift off!"

"I can't." She pointed at the console, where the activated vibroblade, still gripped by the Gotal's severed hand, had sunk to the hilt in the panel. Sparks and smoke were still faintly visible, and she could hear the faint hum of the weapon's high-frequency oscillation. "It's cut through the controls for the stabilizer vanes. We'll spin like a corkscrew if we try to fly in this."

Oolth stared at the blade, then at her. "I don't *believe* this. Some Jedi you are! You managed to disable your own ship!"

Darsha bit back on several scathing replies that came to mind, saying instead, "It's just a setback. I've got my comlink; I'll just call the Temple for—"

She left the sentence unfinished, for as she was speaking she was reaching into her tunic for her comlink. The moment her fingers touched it she realized it was unusable, as well. The plaek-lite casing was shattered, no doubt by that kick she had received from one of the Raptors. It had probably protected her from a broken rib; although, all things considered, at this point she would rather have had the injury.

Before she could explain this latest reversal to Oolth, the windshield in front of her suddenly cracked in a starburst. Simultaneously she heard the muffled report of a projectile weapon. Someone, most likely one of the Raptors, was shooting at them.

Darsha made a quick decision. They would have to abandon the skyhopper. They had to get uplevels as quickly as possible. She glanced about them and realized that such an action was easier said than done. Most of the buildings were blocked off

above levels ten or twelve; the inhabitants of the upper stories didn't even acknowledge the existence of those lower floors. But they couldn't stay here. As if to underscore that fact, another bolt from the hidden sniper whistled past her ear. They couldn't even take the risk of trying to get back to the safe house.

The last light of day was fading fast; soon it would be full night. Darsha stood up. "Out of the ship—fast!" She jumped to the pavement, pulling her ascension gun from her utility belt. She fired the grappling hook straight up at maximum length, hoping to strike a ledge or projection above the fog layer.

Another blast struck the windshield. Oolth screeched in fear and leapt out of the skyhopper. "What are you doing? We have to get out of here!"

"That's exactly what we're doing," Darsha said as she felt the vibration down the length of the cable, which meant the hook had found purchase. "Hang on to me!" She grabbed the Fondorian around his waist and thumbed the winding mechanism.

The liquid cable reservoir was good for a maximum of two hundred meters, and the tensile strength of the monofilament line would easily support them both. Darsha knew that if they could make it up to the first traffic skylane—around level twenty—they could find an air taxi and get back to the Temple, or at least find a working comm station from which to call for help.

Another bolt caromed off the wall directly beneath them as they rose quickly up past the first level, then the second, then the third. Darsha's arm felt like it was being pulled from its socket. She looked up and estimated that the fog was hovering at around level ten. Once they were enveloped, they would be safe enough from the sniper.

A massive shadow flitted past her, followed by several more.

In the dimming light she wasn't sure what they were at first. Then she saw one clearly, and recognition sent a chill of fear through her.

Hawk-bats.

She had never seen one this close before. Their eggs were considered a delicacy; she'd eaten them more than once for the morning meal in the Temple. Ordinarily hawk-bats weren't considered dangerous, but she had heard stories of people occasionally being attacked by flocks of the creatures. Evidently they were very territorial, and danger fell to anyone who ventured too close to one of their rookeries.

Which, apparently, was just what she had done.

Suddenly they were enveloped in a shrieking, flapping nightmare of wings, beaks, and talons. Distracted, Darsha buried her head in her shoulder as best she could to protect her eyes. She tried to summon the Force, to use it as a shield against the creatures, but the fierce buffeting of their wings made holding on to the ascension gun the best she could manage.

She kept her thumb pressed on the winding control—their best hope now was to get past the hawk-bats' territory.

Oolth tightened his grip around her chest until she felt in danger of suffocating. He shouted with pain and fear as the winged furies strafed the two of them. The claws on the edges of their leathery wings tore at Darsha's clothes; her vision was full of beaks and angry ruby eyes.

Oolth screamed again, louder this time. She glanced down and saw that one of the hawk-bats had landed on his shoulder and was savagely pecking at his face. The beak scored his cheek, drawing a line of dark blood across his skin.

Darsha felt his grip lessen. She saw another hawk-bat clinging to Oolth's arm, stabbing at his hand with its beak.

"Hang on!" she shouted. "We're almost through this!"

Oolth cried out again, louder than all his previous cries. Darsha looked down at him, saw that one of the hawk-bats had hooked its cruel beak into his right eye. Mad with pain, the Fondorian let go of her, raising both hands to push away his winged tormentor.

"*No!*" Darsha shouted, trying to hang on to him with her free hand. But his weight was too much; his shirt tore, leaving a swatch of it in her grip as he dropped with a trailing cry down into the darkness.

Darsha knew there was no point in trying to go after him, even if there was any way it could be accomplished; she was seven or eight levels up now, and the fall had undoubtedly been fatal. A moment later she entered the fog level, but the hawk-bats showed no sign of lessening their attack. Already her skin was cut and torn in a score of wounds. At this rate she wouldn't survive to reach the upper levels.

Only one course of action promised even a faint hope of survival. Each level that slipped by her had a line of dark windows. Darsha released the winding control and drew her lightsaber. As her ascent slowed and then stopped, she swung the energy blade, melting a large hole through the transparisteel of the window next to her. She got a foot on the ledge beneath it and tumbled through, releasing the ascension gun as she fell forward into darkness.

She turned the fall into a shoulder roll, holding the lightsaber away from her as she had been taught to avoid self-inflicted injury. She came to her feet, the weapon held ready to defend herself against the hawk-bats.

But apparently there was no need; none of them pursued her into the building. Slowly Darsha abandoned her fighting stance. She looked around, trying to take stock of her surroundings.

It was fully dark outside now; the broken window was merely a patch of lesser darkness. The lightsaber's coherent light beam didn't vouchsafe much in the way of illumination. Darsha listened, both with her ears and with the Force. No sound, and no sense of danger. For the moment she seemed to be safe.

Of course, that depended on one's definition of *safe*. She was trapped in the abandoned lower levels of a building in the infamous Crimson Corridor. She had no comlink and no transportation. Worse still, she had failed in her mission. The man she had been sent to save now lay dead in the street far below.

If this was "safe," Darsha thought grimly, maybe she ought to consider another line of work.

Assuming she made it back alive.

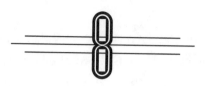

L orn awoke feeling like a herd of banthas had stampeded over him.

He risked opening one eye. The light in the cubicle was very dim, but even so it felt like a blaster beam had fired straight into his eye and up the optic nerve to his brain. He groaned, hastily shut the eye, and wrapped both arms around his head for good measure.

Somewhere in the darkness he heard I-Five say, "Ah, the beast awakes."

"Stop shouting," he mumbled.

"My vocabulator is modulated at a median level of sixty decibels, which is standard for normal human conversation. Of course, your hearing *might* be a trifle oversensitive, given the amount of alcohol still in your bloodstream."

Lorn groaned and tried, unsuccessfully, to burrow into the sleeping pad.

"If you're going to continue such behavior," I-Five went on remorselessly, "I suggest having a few healthy liver cells

removed—if indeed you have any left—and cryogenically stored, since you may need that particular organ cloned in the near future. I can recommend a very good MD-5 medical droid of my acquaintance—"

"All right, all *right!*" Lorn sat up, cradling his aching head in his hands, and glared at the droid. "You've had your fun. Now make it go away."

The droid feigned polite incomprehension. "Make it go away? I'm just a lowly droid, how could *I* possibly—"

"*Do* it—or I'll reprogram your cognitive module with Bilk's blaster."

I-Five gave a remarkably humanlike sigh. "Of course. I live to serve." The droid paused for a moment; then there issued from his vocabulator a low trilling tone. It warbled up and down the scale, seeming to resonate in the small cubicle.

Lorn sat on the bed and let the sound wash over him, let it reverberate in his head. After a few minutes the headache began to lessen its iron grip, as did his nausea and general malaise. He wasn't sure exactly how the wordless song of the droid accomplished it, but something about the vibrations made it the best hangover cure he had ever come across. But no cure comes without a price, and Lorn knew that the price of this one would be having to put up with I-Five's smug superiority for most of the day.

It was still worth it. When I-Five finally let the sound trail off, Lorn felt remarkably better. He wouldn't be doing any zero-g calisthenics at the null-grav spa over at Trantor Center today, but at least he could think of doing them someday soon without feeling like throwing up.

He looked at I-Five and found himself wondering once again

how a droid with only one fixed facial expression and limited body language could manage to look so disapproving.

"And are we all better now?" I-Five inquired with mock solicitousness.

"Let's just say I'm willing to hold off on that reprogramming—for today at least." Lorn stood up, somewhat carefully, as his head still felt like it might topple off his neck if he moved too quickly.

"Your gratitude overwhelms me."

"And your sarcasm underwhelms me." Lorn went into the refresher, splashed cold water on his face, and ran an ultrasound cleaner over his teeth. "I might actually be able to be in the same room with some food," he said as he came out.

"Time enough for that. First I think you should have a look at these messages that came in while you were comatose."

"What messages?" It was too much to hope that Zippa had decided to sell him the Holocron after all. Nevertheless, he knew I-Five wouldn't have bothered keeping the communication unless it was important.

"*These* messages," the droid replied patiently, and activated the message unit.

A flickering image of an enormous, blubbery body formed in midair over the unit. Lorn recognized Yanth the Hutt.

"Lorn," the image said in a deep voice, "I thought we were going to meet sometime today, to discuss a certain Holocron you wished me to look at. It's not polite to keep buyers waiting, you know."

The image dissolved. "Thanks," Lorn said to I-Five. "If you're not too busy later, I've got a scraped knuckle you could rub some salt into."

"I think your attitude may change when you see the next message."

The second image materialized above the projector. It wasn't Zippa or Yanth; that much was immediately evident. After a moment Lorn recognized the species—a Neimoidian. That in itself was surprising; the masters of the Trade Federation were rarely seen on Coruscant, given the current strained relationship between their organization and the Republic Senate.

The Neimoidian glanced around furtively before leaning in close and speaking softly. "Lorn Pavan—your name was mentioned to me as someone who can be . . . discreet in handling sensitive information," he said in the gurgling tones of his kind. "I wish to discuss a matter that could be very profitable to both of us. If you are interested, meet me at the Dewback Inn at 0900. Tell no one of this." The three-dimensional image winked out.

"Play it again," Lorn said.

I-Five complied, and Lorn watched the message a second time, paying more attention to the Neimoidian's body language than to what he was saying. He wasn't all that familiar with Neimoidian mannerisms, but it didn't take an interplanetary psychoanalyst to see that the alien was as nervous as a H'nemthe groom. Which could mean trouble, but which could also mean profit. In his present line of work Lorn seldom saw the second happen without having to wade through the first.

He pressed a button that deleted the second message, and glanced at I-Five. "What do you think?"

"I think we have seventeen Republic decicreds in the bank, and whatever change might have fallen under the sleeping pad. I think the rent is due in a week. I think," I-Five said, "that we should talk to this Neimoidian."

"I think so, too," Lorn said.

\*     \*     \*

The time of the evening meal was almost over. Mahwi Lihnn had by now investigated four restaurants whose menus included Neimoidian cuisine. Only one of them was occupied by a Neimoidian at table—a female. Lihnn had questioned her, but she had professed no knowledge of a countryman named Hath Monchar. She had, however, told Lihnn of another eatery in the area that her kind had been known to frequent. It was a small tavern called the Dewback Inn, one of the few drinking establishments in the sector that featured agaric ale, a beverage most Neimoidians were extremely fond of.

Lihnn decided to check it out.

It had not been terribly difficult to find Lorn Pavan's dwelling cubicle. As Darth Maul approached it, he saw the door open. A human and a droid—the latter one of the protocol series—emerged. Maul quickly faded back into the shadows of the underground thoroughfare and watched them pass. Both matched the descriptions he had been given by the Baragwin bartender.

Excellent. With any luck, they would lead him to his prey.

He followed them at a safe distance, making use of shadows and concealment when it was available and trusting to the cloaking power of the Force when it was not. The human and his droid had no idea they were being followed. He would tail them until they contacted the Neimoidian, and then he would take what action was appropriate.

Maul could feel the dark side surging within him, filling him with impatience, urging him to complete this assignment as quickly as possible. *This is not what you were trained for,* he thought. *These are not prey worthy of your abilities.*

He tried to dismiss these thoughts, for they were heretical.

His master had given him this assignment; that was all that mattered. But he could not help chafing at this duty. There was no real challenge to his abilities in it. He had been bred and trained to fight and kill Jedi, after all, not rank-and-file beings like these.

The Jedi—how he hated them! How he loathed their hollow sanctimoniousness, their pretense of piety, their hypocrisy. How he longed for the day when their Temple would be a ruin of smoking rubble, littered with their crushed corpses. If he closed his eyes, he could see the apocalypse of the order as vividly as if it were reality. It *was* reality, after all—a future reality, but nonetheless valid. It was destined, ordained, predetermined. And he would be instrumental in bringing it about. It was what his entire life had been designed for.

Not tracking some pathetic failure through the slums of Coruscant.

Maul shook his head and snarled silently. His purpose was to serve his master, no matter what the assignment was. If Darth Sidious knew he was having such doubts, the Sith Lord would severely punish him, such as he had not been punished since he was a child. And Maul would not resist, even though he was now a grown man. Because Sidious would be right to do so.

The human and his droid emerged from the underground thoroughfare and proceeded along the narrow surface streets. It was late at night, but the planetary city never slept. The streets were crowded no matter what time of day or night it was. This was fortunate, in that it made it easier for Maul to keep his quarry in sight without being noticed.

It would not be much longer, Maul told himself. He would bring this job to a successful conclusion—and then, perhaps, Darth Sidious would reward him with a task more worthy of his

abilities. Something like the Black Sun assignment. That had been a challenge he had enjoyed.

Pavan and his droid turned down another street, this one so narrow and bounded by tall structures that there was barely room for two lanes of foot traffic. They entered a doorway under a hanging sign decorated with a rampant dewback.

This was their destination, then. Despite his near-perfect control of his nervous system, Maul felt his pulse quicken slightly in anticipation. If all went as planned, soon this onerous chore would be over. He entered the tavern.

Lorn looked around the dingy, ill-lit interior. The Dewback Inn was even less reputable looking than the Glowstone, and that was saying something. There weren't many customers, but each one that he noticed looked like he or she or it had seen their share of combat. Lorn noticed a Devaronian with one horn missing, a piebald Wookiee—half of whose hair had apparently been singed off—and a Sakiyan whose bald head was stitched with ridged keloid tissue, among others.

I-Five surveyed the room, as well. "It just keeps getting better," the droid said.

Lorn noticed a sign above the bar that read NO DROIDS ALLOWED in Basic. He also noticed several of the patrons looking suspiciously at I-Five. "I think you'd better wait outside," he told the droid. "Sorry."

"I think I can deal with the rejection." I-Five went back outside.

Lorn saw a Neimoidian sitting alone at a corner table, looking very uncomfortable. As he started to make his way through

the tables he heard the door open behind him, and out of the corner of his eye he glimpsed a cloaked and hooded form entering. The newcomer had a sinister aspect about him—but then, with the possible exception of the Neimoidian, so did everyone else in the room, so Lorn didn't give the new arrival much thought.

As he drew near the Neimoidian's table he felt his arms seized abruptly in an iron grasp. "Hey!" He tried to pull free, but his assailant—a Trandoshan—was far stronger than he was. His struggles alerted the Neimoidian, who looked up.

"Are you Lorn Pavan?" he asked.

"That's me. Call off your bullyboy."

The Neimoidian made a gesture. "Release him, Gorth."

The Trandoshan let Lorn go. Lorn pulled back a chair and sat down, rubbing his arms, both of which had gone somewhat numb from the reptilian being's grip.

"I do apologize," the Neimoidian said, his gaze darting here and there about the bar as he spoke. "You can understand my desire to have some protection in a place like this. Gorth comes highly recommended."

"I can see why," Lorn said. "Let's get down to business. What do you have?"

As Darth Maul slipped into the rathole called the Dewback Inn, he kept his cowl up and moved to the darkest corner. When one of the weak minds surrounding him caused its owner to idly cast a glance in his direction, he used the Force to squelch or redirect that interest. As always when he wished it in such dens of mental weakness, he was effectively invisible.

He had spotted his prey immediately. The urge to simply step up and sever the Neimoidian's head from his body was tempting,

but he knew that would be foolishness. He would have to kill the big Trandoshan bodyguard first, and probably the Corellian, as well. Slaying three people, even in a pit such as this, would not go unnoticed. Calling attention to one's self in a public place would be bad; his master had impressed that upon Maul at an early age. The Sith were powerful, but there were only two of them. Stealth was therefore one of their greatest strengths. Even as weak-minded and chemically besotted as most of the patrons of this place were, there were simply too many to control completely. He could not wipe the memories of a cold-blooded assassination from several dozen heads, nor could he be sure of destroying all of them. And here and there burned an intellect too strong to be swayed by simple mind-control techniques. These he could feel; they stood out like photonic lamps on a darkling plain.

And besides all that, he had to question the Neimoidian thoroughly to find any others the traitor might have tainted in his flight.

Nevertheless, Maul had his target in sight now. That was what was important, and it would now be only a matter of time before he was able to close the assignment. He would wait for a propitious moment to deal with him.

The human dealer in information was speaking with the doomed Neimoidian, and likely that sealed the man's fate, as well. Later, when he questioned Hath Monchar, Maul would determine precisely what had passed between the man and the Neimoidian. If this Lorn Pavan had come to discuss other matters and knew nothing of Monchar's treachery, he would be allowed to keep his insignificant life. But if he had become party to the subversion, then the human would die. Quite simple.

*　　*　　*

Mahwi Lihnn trekked through the back streets and alleys, searching for the Dewback Inn. She was certainly not over-impressed with this area of Coruscant. The surface streets in this sector were all twisted turnings and narrow byways, teeming with gutter scum looking for an easy mark. Lihnn, armed to the teeth as she was, did not present such an easy target, and the strong-arm thieves and head-bashers watched her pass but stayed on their own ground, smart enough to recognize danger when they saw it. Lihnn wasn't particularly worried about her safety; she had been in much worse places than this and survived. It was largely a matter of attitude. She projected confidence and an air of danger as she walked, an aura that made it clear that, at the first sign of trouble from any of this riffraff, the troublemaker would find his-, her-, or itself a smoking corpse on the greasy walkway, to be quickly picked over by the rest of them.

She came to an intersection, hesitated briefly, then chose the right fork. Another person could easily get lost and stay lost in this maze, but Mahwi Lihnn had honed her sense of direction in scores of such places around the galaxy, and she knew she would eventually arrive at her destination. She always got where she was supposed to go, and she always came out on top when she got there. She was, quite simply, the best at what she did.

As Hath Monchar would soon find out.

After climbing a few flights of stairs Darsha Assant reached the lowest inhabited levels of the building. Here she found what passed for a pharmacy at the end of a squalid corridor. She had lost her regular credit tab along the way, though she still had her emergency tab. It was good for only a small amount—not nearly enough to rent a speeder, unfortunately, but sufficient to purchase enough antibiotic synthflesh bandage to treat and seal her wounds

and even hire a taxi, if it didn't have to go far. Her robes were in pretty sad shape, as well, but the emergency fund was not up to covering replacements for those. No matter—she had more important things to worry about than her wardrobe.

Feeling somewhat better after she smoothed the healing synthflesh into place, she looked for a quiet spot—preferably one with walls to protect her back and sides—to ponder what she should do next.

There was no way to sugarcoat her situation. She was, quite simply, ruined. She had lost her charge; the hawk-bats were no doubt picking clean the Fondorian's bones by now. She had lost her transportation to a common street gang. Her comlink was shattered. The mission, in short, had been a complete and utter disaster. Master Bondara had been right to wonder about her ability.

Darsha sat down on a graffiti-scarred bench and sought to center herself as she had been taught. It was no use; the stillness that a Jedi should always operate from was nowhere to be found. Instead she felt grief, sadness, anger—but most of all, she felt shame. She had disgraced herself, her mentor, and her heritage. She would never become a Jedi Knight now. Her life as she had known it, as she had expected it to be, was over.

Maybe it would have been better to have died, to have been eaten by the hawk-bats. At least she would not have to face Master Bondara, not have to see the disappointment in her mentor's eyes.

What was she going to do?

She could find a public comm station—some of them would work, even down here—and call for help. The council would send a Jedi—a *real* Jedi, she thought bitterly—to come and fetch her. She would be escorted back as if she were a child, taken into custody so that she could do no more damage.

She envisioned entering the Temple with such an escort. That would be all that was needed to make her shame complete.

Darsha clenched her jaw muscles. No. That wasn't how it was going to go. She had failed her mission, true enough, but she still had her lightsaber, and she still had some pride, if only a trace of what it had been. She would *not* call for help. She could find some way to return to the council under her own power. She owed that much at least to Master Bondara—and to herself.

She took a deep breath, let it escape slowly, and once again sought calmness in the Force. Her path as a Jedi Knight was done. There was no way to change that. But she could deliver herself to that judgment without begging for help.

She stood, took another deep breath, and blew it out. Yes. At the very least, she could do that much.

Lorn could not believe his luck. Finally, it looked like things were taking a turn for the better. Carefully, so as not to reveal his enthusiasm, he said to the Neimoidian, "And you say you have recorded all this information—the details of the impending blockade, and the fact that the Sith are behind it—on a holocron?"

"That is correct," Monchar replied.

"And may I, ah, see this crystal?"

Monchar gave Lorn a look that was plain to read, even given the differences between Neimoidian and human facial expressions: *What am I, stupid?* Aloud, he said, "I would not carry it around on my person in such places, even with Gorth as a protector. The holocron is safely stored and guarded elsewhere."

Lorn leaned back. "I see. And you would want to sell it for— how much?"

"Half a million Republic credits."

Lorn grinned. The way to play this was cool and easy. "Half a million? Why, sure. You have change for a million-cred note?"

The Neimoidian gave Lorn a fishy smile in return. "I'm afraid not."

Lorn had played this game before, and he knew it was time to palaver. "All right," he said. "If it is what you say it is, I might be willing to go two hundred and fifty thousand."

"Don't insult me," Monchar replied. "If it is what I say it is—and I assure you, it is—the information on that crystal is worth twice what I am asking—more, in the right hands. We will not dicker like a couple of bantha traders, human. Half a million credits, period. You'll stand to make that much and more off it if you have the wits of a Sarconian green flea."

That was true, Lorn knew. Of course, if he could lay his hands on half a million creds, he wouldn't be sitting in this dive trying to negotiate stolen data. But there was no way he could let a deal like this pass. He might never see another like it. "All right. Half a million. Where shall we make the exchange?"

The Neimoidian touched a button on a wristband, and a small holographic projection lit up just above the surface of the table, no bigger than Lorn's thumb.

"Here is the address of my cubicle," Monchar said. "Meet me there in an hour. Come alone."

One hour! Lorn kept his expression carefully noncommittal. "I, ah, might need a little longer than that to raise the funds."

"One hour," Monchar repeated. "If you cannot procure funding by then, I will seek others who are more capable. I am told there is a Hutt, Yanth by name, who would be most interested in this commodity."

"I know Yanth. You don't want to deal with him. He's shiftier than a crystal snake."

"Then bring me the money and we will consummate this transaction."

Lorn memorized the address and nodded. Monchar shut the holo off.

"Okay. No problem," Lorn said. "I'll see you in an hour." He stood and wended his way toward the door.

Outside, I-Five was waiting. "Well?" the droid said, as they walked down the narrow street.

Lorn explained quickly as they walked. "So we've got an hour—actually, fifty-five minutes—to raise five hundred thousand credits." He looked at the droid. "Any thoughts?"

"It is an excellent opportunity, to be sure. In fact, it might well be the chance of your lifetime, though I expect to have better opportunities myself, since I will probably outlive you by a factor of seven-point-four to seven-point-six, at a conservative estimate, disallowing major accidents, natural disasters, or acts of war—"

"We're on the chrono and you're discussing actuarial tables. The big question is, where are we going to get half a million credits in less than an hour?"

"That is indeed the question."

"We could find a card game. I'm good at sabacc."

"But not consistently—if you were, we wouldn't be in this situation. And since we have no money of which to speak, who in all of the underground would give us enough of a marker to buy into a sufficiently high-stakes game?"

"Offhand, I'd say . . . nobody," Lorn admitted.

"And how long would it take to win such an amount, assuming you could get into such a game? Even if you cheated and were not caught, could you do it in fifty-two minutes—not counting, of course, transit time to the Neimoidian's domicile?"

"All right, sabacc is not a viable option. I assume you've got a better idea?"

I-Five cleared his speaking circuits in what sounded almost like a human cough. "There is only one viable option: Bank fraud."

Lorn stopped to stare at I-Five. A Givin blundered into him, muttered an apology, and kept going. Without taking his gaze from I-Five, Lorn grabbed the Givin's exoskeleton, pulled him back, and retrieved his wallet. He then shoved the pickpocket away. "I'm listening," he told the droid.

"I have been considering this idea for some time," I-Five said. "Keeping it in reserve as a final contingency plan. If we effect it, we will be forced to flee Coruscant, and it would be unlikely that we could ever return, unless we wished to radically change our appearances and spend the rest of our lives looking over our shoulders."

"If we had a million credits in our account, that would take us a long, long way from here," Lorn said. "And I'd be happy to leave. We could set up shop on some outlier world where the Republic doesn't have a presence, make a few smart investments, live like kings. Tell me about this plan."

They continued to walk while I-Five elaborated. They wouldn't really be able to steal the money, but the droid was confident he could jack into the data flow of one of Coruscant's many banking firms and manage a phantom transfer of funds into their personal account. The auditor droids would catch it almost immediately, so timing would be critical. But if all went well, Lorn would be able to show Hath Monchar an unencumbered credit tab that was worth half a million. Much more than that, the droid explained, would kick in automatic inquiries, and

if they tried to transfer the funds after the audit, the bank would catch that, too. The real trick would be to have the Neimoidian accept the credit tab as payment and make the transfer to his account before time ran out.

"The window will be narrow, and it will close quickly," I-Five concluded. "But in theory it can be done."

Lorn felt a warm rush of excitement. They might actually pull this off. And if they did, they could walk away with a holocron worth a million creds and leave the Neimoidian holding an empty bag. Which would be too bad for him, but that's how life was in the real galaxy. Lorn wouldn't stay awake nights worrying about it, that was for sure.

"Let's do it," he said. "If it doesn't work, we won't be any worse off than we are now."

"Save for the distinct possibility of you occupying a cell in a Republic asteroid prison for thirty years, and me having a complete memory wipe."

"You worry too much."

"And you don't worry enough."

But Lorn knew I-Five would take the risk. Droids were supposed to be programmed with more integrity and honesty than humans or other natural-born species, but it didn't always work quite like that. I-Five had somehow evolved a greed circuit along the way, and the glitter of credits called to him as much as it did Lorn. Which was one of the reasons they got along so well.

Lorn felt an excitement he hadn't known in years as he contemplated it. It *would* work, and they would use the money to build a new life out on the Rim. There were plenty of worlds where, with enough money, one could disappear into a new identity and live a life of ease with no questions asked.

A new life—a *real* life this time. Maybe not the one he had before, but certainly a better one than this hardscrabble existence he was suffering through now.

Of course, it would mean leaving behind any possibility of ever seeing Jax again.

*So what?* a savage voice in the back of his head asked. *Like there's any chance at all of that now? That's in the past. It's time you started living again.*

Yes. Far past time, in fact.

He looked at I-Five, and though there was no expression on the droid's metallic countenance, he felt certain that I-Five knew exactly what he was thinking.

"What are we waiting for?" he asked the droid. "The Hutt's still expecting us to bring him a holocron; why disappoint him? Let's find a dataport and make it happen."

The gods of fortune smiled upon Mahwi Lihnn. Just as she arrived at the Dewback Inn she saw the Neimoidian depart in the company of a hulking brute of a Trandoshan. The big reptiloid with Monchar sported a pair of blasters, one on each hip, and moved like a bodyguard, which undoubtedly he was.

Lihnn reviewed her options. This was too public a place to take out the guard and collect Monchar, so she'd just have to follow them until circumstances were more viable. She stepped into a narrow aperture between two buildings and let them pass. She was about to fall in behind at a safe distance when someone else emerged from the inn—a robed and cowled figure, bipedal and human-sized, who slipped into the shadow of a doorway across the alley. Lihnn didn't get a look at the face, but whoever he was, he was obviously interested in Monchar.

Lihnn quickly moved behind a stanchion and out of sight.

A footpad bent on robbery? she wondered as she watched. Whoever he was, he had to be pretty sure of himself if he was willing to take on an armed bodyguard.

Sure enough, the robed figure followed the Neimoidian and the Trandoshan, keeping to the dimly lit areas and moving with a stealth that Lihnn had to admire. If this fellow could shoot half as well as he could tail, he could drill the Trandoshan and be on the Neimoidian in a hurry.

Lihnn frowned and loosened her own DL-44s in their holsters. This job was threatening to become complicated. She decided the best course was to take out the bodyguard and the mysterious robed tracker as quickly as possible. If she had to, she could use a glop grenade on Monchar, seal him up in a gel bubble, and haul him back to Gunray like that, though she didn't think it would be necessary. She'd never met a brave Neimoidian, never even heard of one, and she didn't think Hath Monchar would prove the exception to the rule.

Darth Maul melded with the darkness, becoming a shade among shadows, a ghost in the fetid gloom. It was always night this deep in the ferrocrete canyons. Artificial lights were few and far between at best, and there were many places where lights were burned out, stolen, or shattered by vandals. He had plenty of cover, and the lumbering pair in front of him had no idea they were being followed. Now and again the bodyguard would glance around to assure himself that no threat drew close, but it was obvious that he was an oaf, without skill or much training. Maul did not need to use the dark side to hide from such a being.

As he surveilled the Neimoidian and his guard, however, Maul felt a small prickling of something—not real danger, but a kind of disquiet—touch his awareness. He looked about and listened carefully, but did not see any cause for this. He expanded

his consciousness, let the dark currents of the Force extend outward from him—and became aware of another presence behind
him, hidden from normal sight and hearing.

Probably just another of the many predators in this dreary
place, looking for prey. Now that he was aware of the presence,
Maul dismissed it. He felt no real concentrations of the Force
emanating from the hidden watcher, and thus whoever he was
and whatever his reasons for being here, he did not pose a threat.

The Neimoidian and his guard took a convoluted path, turning and twisting back, until finally they arrived at a block of small
cubic living units stacked a dozen high and twenty wide, and
probably that many deep. The pair entered the building through a
locked durasteel door that Monchar opened with his thumbprint.

Maul waited a few moments, then approached the door.

Mahwi Lihnn was a bit slow in arriving at the domicile.
Though she couldn't put her finger on the exact reason why, she
felt sure the robed stalker tailing the Neimoidian had somehow
known he was being tailed in turn. Lihnn didn't think she'd been
seen, and she'd moved with as much stealth as she could muster,
which was considerable. But the feeling had persisted, and as a
result she had dropped back. She was trusting that the lurker in
the cowl wouldn't lose Monchar, and so she let the Neimoidian
and his bodyguard get far enough ahead that she couldn't see
them. It was risky business to track a tracker and not the primary
subject, but she didn't see that she had much choice.

Given all that, by the time she got closer, the Neimoidian and
the bodyguard were already inside—or so she assumed—and the
tracker in the cowl was just arriving at the door.

There came a sudden flash of light, the source of which was

hidden by the tracker's body. Lihnn ducked back behind a garbage bin as the light strobed. When she looked again the door was wide open and the cowled figure was nowhere in sight.

Lihnn pulled her left blaster, keeping her right hand clear to use the palm flechette shooter—the quieter, and therefore preferable, weapon. She hurried across the dim street.

When she reached the door she paused in surprise. Where the locking mechanism had been on the durasteel plate was a still-smoking semicircular hole, its glowing edges carved as cleanly as if done by laser surgery. The lock and handle lay on the ground, also smoldering from whatever tool had cut them free. Lihnn knew of only a couple of devices that could excise a thick slab of durasteel so fast and smoothly: a plasma torch, which was much too big to hide under a cloak and haul around, or a lightsaber.

And the only people she knew of who used lightsabers were Jedi.

Lihnn swallowed dryly, her belly suddenly roiling. If the Jedi were somehow involved, the risk factor had just shot off the scale. A Jedi Knight was nobody to mess with. You'd get only one shot at taking out a Jedi who was paying attention; after that you'd likely be sliced apart real quick. Lihnn had once seen a Jedi knock a blaster bolt out of the air using a lightsaber. That required inhumanly fast reflexes.

For a second she seriously considered turning around and heading for the spaceport. Haako hadn't said anything about Jedi.

But—no. She was a professional, trained and adept. She couldn't have word getting around that she had backed away from a job, no matter what the reason. She didn't know for certain that the cowled stalker was a Jedi. Besides, for all their battle skill, she had heard that Jedi did not kill unless there was ab-

solutely no alternative—although she would hate to be in a position where she had to rely on that.

She was just going to have to take it very slowly and carefully from here on.

*Very* slowly and carefully.

Lorn and I-Five walked down the narrow street toward their destination, keeping to the middle so as to avoid being surprised by a robber looking for a quick knockover. Lorn had a small blaster in his tunic's pocket, gripped in his right hand—which, he noticed, was somewhat sweaty. The idea of living on a planet where you didn't have to worry about such things every time you stepped outside was most appealing. And seeing things under the natural light of a sun was a novel concept, too. They'd been down here far too long. It was definitely time for a change.

"So the scam-transfer went all right?" he asked I-Five.

"For the seventh time, yes, it went all right. We have precisely one hour and twenty-six minutes before it's discovered and rectified by the auditor droids. Perhaps another four minutes before they are able to pinpoint the location of the credit tab and, depending on how busy the local police are, anywhere from six to fourteen minutes before they arrive to take the bearer of the tab into custody for attempted grand theft and illegal use of communication protocols THX-one-one-three—"

"Spare me the details. We have less than an hour and forty-five minutes to get this deal done and be on our way. How much farther is this place?"

"At our present rate of speed we'll arrive in two-point-six minutes. Plenty of time to accomplish our task, as well as fence the holocron to the Hutt."

"Assuming the Neimoidian doesn't want to have a drink and chat about Republic politics and the latest hi-lo ball scores."

"Since you are to negotiate alone, I trust you will find some way to skip the small talk. Time's running out and the fake ID I utilized on the transfer won't slow the authorities for more than another few minutes after they collect the credit tab. That's assuming Hath Monchar doesn't give your name to the arresting officers—which would be a dangerous assumption, for if I were him, I would do so instantly, and so would you to anybody who cheated you thus. In which case we will be in bantha excrement up to our eyeballs and photoreceptors, respectively. So decline liquid refreshment and idle chitchat and get the deal done; that's my considered advice."

Finding the Neimoidian was child's play for Maul. Walls could not stop the dark questing fingers of the Force. When he arrived at the correct domicile, he sensed that there were four beings behind the door. Monchar, of course, and the bodyguard he had seen accompanying him. The dull ripples of the other two rumbled with suppressed violence. More guards, no doubt.

No matter. Be there three guards or thirty, the result would be the same. It was time for Hath Monchar to pay the penalty for attempting to double-cross Lord Sidious.

Darth Maul pulled his double lightsaber from his belt and held his thumb upon the ignition button. He took a deep breath and centered himself in the swirls and eddies of the dark side. Then, his power and concentration thus augmented, he thrust forward his free hand as though hurling an invisible ball.

The door shattered inward.

\*　　\*　　\*

Mahwi Lihnn moved through the building's dimly lit halls with great care, ready to shoot anything that moved. A door opened and an old human woman started to step out, saw Lihnn with her finger tightening on the trigger, and launched herself back into the room, slamming the hinged door behind her.

Lihnn managed to keep from blasting her, though just barely.

This could be a problem, she reflected. There were hundreds of rooms in this hive, and no way that she could search them all. Her plan had been to follow the cowled one to their common destination, but her few moments of shock at discovering the way the other had breached the entrance had been enough to let her quarry vanish into the warren. Lihnn knew she could wander around here for days and not find the Neimoidian. Maybe she should go back outside and set up a watch on the building's exit?

The problem with that was she wasn't sure of the cowled one's intent in pursuing Monchar. Lihnn's mandate from the Trade Federation was clear: Bring Hath Monchar back alive. If she didn't find the Neimoidian soon, she might wind up with a corpse on her hands, which would not make Haako at all happy.

There didn't seem to be much choice but to continue her search.

As soon as he was through the door, Maul triggered his lightsaber. The bright beams lanced out to their full lengths.

He took in the room: The Neimoidian sat in a chair against the far wall. A pair of Squid Heads scrabbled for their holstered blasters. The Trandoshan bodyguard already had his out, and now he fired it.

Maul spun the lightsaber and angled it slightly. Stopping the

blasterfire was easy. Redirecting it properly was a bit more difficult, but certainly not impossible. The bolt bounced from the
potent energy lance and ricocheted into the nearest Squid Head,
striking him on the thorax. The Quarren collapsed.

Maul allowed himself a slight frown. The deflected beam
was two centimeters lower than he had aimed. Poor control on
his part.

A second blaster bolt from the Trandoshan seared its way at
him, and another quick shift, guided by the dark side, caught
that bolt and returned it to the sender. The Trandoshan took the
deflected beam in the face. He went down, twitching in his death
throes, his face a blackened ruin of flesh and scales, at the horrified Neimoidian's feet.

Better.

Maul leapt at the remaining Quarren, who had his blaster
halfway up. The Squid Head fired a panicked round, far too low
to do any damage save to the floor. Then the lightsaber arced,
and with a snap of his wrists, Maul lopped the Quarren's tentacled head from his neck.

The battle had begun and ended far too quickly for the
Neimoidian to even think about running. He cowered in the
chair, hands uselessly raised to ward off danger. He didn't even
have a weapon.

Maul shut the lightsaber off and hooked it back on his
belt. He spared a contemptuous glance at the three corpses. His
dueling droids had given him a better fight than these three had.
Pitiful.

He turned toward the terrified Neimoidian. Slowly he raised
his gloved hands and slipped his cowl back and off, revealing his
frightening visage. He smiled, showing his teeth, adding to the
effect.

A pungent reek became noticeable over the stench of death in the room. The Neimoidian's bladder sac had let go its contents.

"Hath Monchar," Darth Maul said. "We have things to discuss, you and I."

As Lorn and I-Five reached the cube complex, the droid said, "Approximately one hour and thirty-three minutes left. Speed is of the essence. As it is, even assuming the meeting with the Hutt goes smoothly, the police will probably be searching for us while we're en route to the spaceport."

"Don't worry about me, just you be ready to—Hey, what happened to the door?"

"It appears to have had a disagreement with somebody," I-Five said. "Not a big surprise in this neighborhood. In any event, that's not our concern, is it? Now hurry!"

Lorn nodded and entered the building. In the small lobby he paged the lift tube to take him to the fourth level, where the Neimoidian supposedly had a residence. Monchar must be low on funds to be staying in a dive such as this—or perhaps trying very hard not to be noticed. Either way, the quicker Lorn could make the exchange and leave, the happier he'd be. He kept his grip on the blaster in his pocket and tried to look nonchalant as he waited for the lift tube to arrive. Nonchalant was hard to pull off at this juncture. The credit tab in his wallet felt like it was made of fissionable material. It wasn't every day he tried to scam a million-credit deal.

Caught in the power of the dark side, the Neimoidian struggled to breathe. Maul's left hand, raised before him, tightened into a fist, and the Neimoidian's throat constricted even more.

"Ready to talk?" Maul asked.

The Neimoidian could not speak, but he managed a nod. The crimson sclera of his eyes had darkened several shades due to blood congestion.

Maul relaxed his fist and his concentration. Hath Monchar collapsed on the floor, wheezing as he tried to suck in a breath.

"Who else knows?"

"No—no one, except a human, Lorn Pavan."

Maul sensed the truth of Monchar's words. This was good. All he had to do was kill the Neimoidian, then find the human and kill him. And then this dreary chore would be at an end.

"Where can I find the human now?"

"I don't know."

Maul's hand clenched again. Monchar choked, gasping once more for air. Maul released him.

"*Where?*"

"He—he's coming here to buy the holocron!"

"When?"

"Any time now!"

Maul smiled. He had all the information he needed.

"Excellent. You have been most cooperative, Hath Monchar."

Monchar looked up from his supine position. There was an instant of hope in his eyes, but it died when he read his fate in Maul's expression.

Maul drew his lightsaber. "Time to die," he said.

"Wait!" The Neimoidian's voice was a bleat of fear. "I can pay you—every credit the human gives me will be yours! *Please*—"

"Stand up," Maul said. "You can at least meet your fate without groveling."

But Monchar was too palsied with terror to comply. Maul felt a wave of disgust for the cringing creature. With his free hand he made a sharp upward gesture, and the Neimoidian was lifted like a puppet on strings. He hung, helpless, in the Force's grasp.

"*Nooo—*"

Darth Maul lit one blade of the lightsaber and swung it laterally, cutting off the Neimoidian's final wail, along with his head. He then released the lines of Force that held the twitching body and watched it crumple.

There was a durasteel safe on the floor behind the body. Maul opened it with a careful swipe of his lightsaber. Ah—there was the holocron crystal of which Monchar had spoken. He extinguished his lightsaber, hung it on his belt, and bent to pick up the holocron. Before his fingers touched it, however, he sensed that he was not alone.

"Don't move!" came a voice from the door even as he realized this. "You so much as breathe deep and I'll fry you where you stand!"

Maul glanced at the doorway. A tall human female in shell spider silk armor stood there, aiming a pair of blasters at him.

Maul realized that this was the same being he had sensed following him earlier. His lips twitched in annoyance. He tried a quick mental probe, but the bounty hunter—for surely that was what she was—was too sharp, her attention too focused, to fall for mind tricks.

Maul considered his options. He would never reach his lightsaber fast enough, even as quick as he was. He might be able to dodge a single blast, maybe even two, but hemmed in as he was in this small cubicle against a woman who could likely put a

dozen bolts into the air from two semiautomatic blasters in half a second, he would have to have a distraction.

Near his feet lay the Trandoshan's blaster. It would serve nicely.

Using his control of the Force, Darth Maul gripped the weapon in a dark tentacle of energy and hurled it at the bounty hunter's face, hard.

The woman was fast. She dodged the blaster, firing a bolt at it. She missed and recovered, but the distraction had served its purpose. Before the weapon had bounced off the wall and landed on the floor, Maul had the lightsaber in his grasp. He thumbed on both blades as the next blaster bolt and half a dozen more came his way in rapid succession. The Sith apprentice's hands were a blur as he let the dark side take him over completely, giving in to its power and allowing it to control and manipulate him.

Blaster bolts struck the lightsaber's spinning blades and were deflected into the walls, the ceiling, the floor. No time to aim, though a bolt or two did hit the bounty hunter without apparent effect. Her armor was apparently state-of-the-art.

The bounty hunter dropped her useless blasters and reached for one wrist, where she wore a rocket launcher. The fool! Maul thought grimly. If a rocket exploded in here, it would kill them both!

There was no time to try to stop her. Maul slipped along the lines of the Force, moving at unnatural speed as he spun toward the nearest wall, a cheap plastic panel, twirling the lightsaber in a cutting pattern. The plastic shredded easily before the blades' superhot plasmatic edges, and Maul ran through the wall, leapt over a chair in the next room—which, fortunately for its tenants, was deserted at the moment—and stabbed downward

with one blade of his lightsaber, shearing a ragged oval in the floor. He dropped through the ceiling of the cubicle below just as the rocket struck the wall of the Neimoidian's room and exploded.

Lihnn had never seen anybody move like the man with the horned and tattooed head. He wasn't dressed like a Jedi, but his expertise with the double-bladed lightsaber far exceeded the skill of any Jedi Lihnn had ever heard of. He knocked blaster bolts away as if swatting flies! And if he could do that, Lihnn couldn't stop him. He would use that double-bladed lightsaber to slice her apart.

Desperate, she reached for her wrist launcher. Her only chance was to hit the horned one squarely and hope that the explosion would be contained enough by the other's body to allow Lihnn to survive. But as she triggered the launcher the tattooed man seemed to disappear in a blur. All of a sudden there was a hole in the wall where an instant ago it had been solid.

Too late, Lihnn tried to stop the rocket from firing, but the reactionless motor flared and the missile leapt from her wrist. She tried to jump back into the hallway.

Lorn was almost to the room where he was supposed to meet the Neimoidian when a sudden explosion hurled him backwards a good three meters, impacting against the wall of a T intersection. As the shock wave lifted him he caught a glimpse of what looked like an armored human flying across the hall just ahead of him and smashing halfway through the wall. Then he hit the far wall himself and didn't think about anything for a time.

He was out for only a minute or two; when the corridor swam back into focus the smoke was still swirling and debris

was still settling. There was a ringing in his ears that was a result of either the blast or the dozens of residential alarms activated by it, or both. Lorn managed to get to his feet, pulled his blaster, and edged unsteadily forward. All he could see of the body was a pair of legs, unmistakably female, sticking out of a hole in the wall, so thinking of her as dead seemed a pretty safe bet.

He turned and peered into the blackened cube. What looked like the remains of four bodies lay scorched and smoking on the floor. He took a few steps into the chamber. One of the smoldering corpses looked like Monchar, but it was hard to be sure— given that it was headless.

Lorn felt his guts churn, both at what he saw and what it meant: Hath Monchar wouldn't be making any more deals with anybody. He was quite seriously dead, and Lorn and I-Five might as well be, too, if they didn't get off Coruscant in the next hour or so. The whole bank-fraud escapade had been for nothing!

Damn!

Lorn turned to run. Even in this sector an explosion like the one that had just happened would bring the security forces in to investigate. He had to get out of there, and fast. But as he started to move he noticed a glimmer of light in a corner of the room and reflexively glanced at it.

What he saw brought him skidding to a stop.

Could it be? It seemed too much to hope for. But when he bent down and looked closer, he realized that maybe the game wasn't over yet.

The holocron crystal lay in the half-open safe, which had no doubt protected it from being destroyed by the explosion. Lorn grabbed it up, holding it tightly in one hand and the blaster in

the other, and now he did run, as fast as he could, down the corridor, past the confused and frightened faces of tenants who had cautiously emerged to investigate, and toward the stairwell. There was still a chance—a very slim chance—that he and I-Five could yet turn this fiasco into a winning situation. But doing so meant getting far away from here as fast as possible.

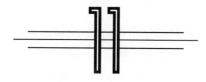

The building Darsha had entered was a monad—a kilometer-high, totally self-contained habitat. More than just an apartment complex, the huge structure, like countless others sprouting from the surface of Coruscant, contained virtually everything its tenants needed: living quarters, shops, hydroponic gardens, and even indoor parks. Many people, she knew, literally lived their entire lives in buildings like these, in some cases holo-commuting to offices halfway around the planet without ever venturing outside.

She had never understood the attraction of such a life before. Now, however, she found herself in sympathy with such people in at least one respect: she had no desire to leave the building either. But her reluctance did not rise out of nascent agoraphobia; rather, it stemmed from the fact that to leave meant returning to the Jedi Temple, where she would have to face the council and admit her failure.

However, there was no other alternative. The council had to

know of the Fondorian's death, and quickly. It was her duty to report her failure, no matter how shameful it was.

She had to climb four more flights of stairs before she reached a level that had a working lift tube. This she took up another ten levels, where she encountered a border checkpoint, complete with an armed guard droid, separating the downlevels ghetto from the functioning upper section of the monad. The droid eyed her disreputable appearance with some suspicion, but let her pass when it realized she was a Jedi.

When Darsha emerged from the building, she was in a much more familiar world. She walked out onto a transparent skybridge and looked down through the permacrete floor. The sleek sides of the buildings all around her fell away into darkness and fog. Beneath that fog was the abyss she had just escaped. If she was given a choice between returning to it or returning to the Temple to admit her defeat, she honestly wasn't sure which she would take.

But there was no choice, was there? Not really.

She made her way to an air taxi stand, aware of the stares that her torn clothing and bandaged wounds drew. *Truly I am still trapped between worlds,* she thought.

Just enough credit was left on her emergency tab to hire an air taxi that would take her back to the Temple. As Darsha settled into the vehicle's backseat, she felt suddenly overcome by lassitude. It was all she could do not to fall asleep as the taxi made its short journey. She recognized the drowsiness as not so much a reaction to the trials she had just undergone but as an attempt to escape what lay ahead.

All too soon the commute was over. Darsha paid the driver and entered the Temple. As far back as she could remember,

passing through the doors had been a source of comfort to her. It meant a return to sanctuary, to safety, to a place where the cares and worries of the rest of the world were left behind. She did not feel this way now. Now the high walls and soft lighting induced anxiety and claustrophobia.

She shook her head and squared her shoulders. Might as well get it over with. At this time of day she would most likely find Master Bondara in his quarters. She would report to her mentor first; then, in all likelihood, they would both go to the council.

Darth Maul had made an error.

The enormity of that knowledge weighed upon him like a giant planetoid. He had underestimated the bounty hunter because the woman had not been strong in the Force. Such a mistake had almost cost him his life—and how ignominious would *that* have been, to die at the hands of a common bounty hunter, he who had been trained to fight and slay Jedi!

He could not make such dangerous assumptions.

He would not make them again.

He knew what his next move had to be. Hath Monchar was dead, but there was still the human to deal with. As Maul emerged from the building the police and firefighting droids were already starting to arrive. He could not cloud the cognitive circuits of droids as easily as he could organic brains, and so he had to move quickly into the shadowy surface streets to avoid questioning.

He found a deserted blind alley a few blocks away and activated his wrist comm. A moment later the image of Darth Sidious appeared before him.

"Tell me what progress you have made," Sidious said.

"The tergiversator Hath Monchar has been killed. He has shared his knowledge with one other—a human named Lorn Pavan. I know where the human lives. I go now to find him and kill him."

"Excellent. Do so as quickly as possible. You are certain that no one else knows of this?"

"Yes, Master. I—" Maul stopped suddenly in shocked realization. The holocron!

As always, Sidious immediately knew that something was wrong. "What is it?" the Sith Lord demanded.

Darth Maul knew he would have to admit failure. He did not hesitate. The concept of lying to his master never even occurred to him. "Monchar possessed a holocron that he said contains the information. I had an opportunity to acquire it, but I—failed to do so." It would be pointless to try to exculpate himself by telling Sidious of the bounty hunter's unexpected appearance and the subsequent explosion that he had barely escaped. The only important fact was that the holocron was not in his possession.

Maul saw Darth Sidious's eyes narrow in disapproval. "You disappoint me, Lord Maul."

He felt that censure spear him like an icy shaft. No trace of it showed on his face. "I am sorry, my master."

"Your tasks are now twofold: Destroy this Lorn Pavan and find the crystal."

"Yes, my master."

Sidious regarded Maul steadily for a moment. "Do not fail me again." The hologram vanished.

Darth Maul stood silently for a moment in the perennial darkness of the city's surface. His breathing was steady and even, his body motionless. Only one trained to sense the whorls and

verticils of the Force would get a sense of the dark storm that raged within him.

His master had *rebuked* him. And rightly so. That crystal could be the ruination of all Darth Sidious's carefully laid plans. And he, Darth Maul, heir to the Sith, had left it behind when he had fled for his life.

*Fool!*

Maul's nostrils flared as he drew in a deep, shuddering breath. He had no time for self-recrimination. The Neimoidian's cubicle was no doubt already overrun with police droids searching for a clue to the explosion. They would hardly overlook an information crystal lying in an opened safe.

There was, of course, the possibility that it had been destroyed in the explosion, but he couldn't count on that. He would have to go back and find out what had happened to it, even if every police droid on Coruscant was packed into that tiny room.

And after he had found the holocron and disposed of the human, then he would have to face whatever punishment Darth Sidious would undoubtedly devise for his lamentable failure.

Maul strode out of the alley and back toward the domicile.

Lorn found I-Five just venturing into the first floor of the building—or trying to, as the stampede of panicked tenants had filled all the exits. Though the droid's metallic face was expressionless as always, he still somehow managed to project concern, followed by relief as he saw Lorn.

"Let's get out of here," Lorn muttered to the droid. "Fast."

"That sounds like a remarkably astute idea."

Walking quickly, they soon put several city blocks between

themselves and the debacle. Then I-Five said, "It appears that all did not go entirely according to plan."

"Ever a master of the understatement." Lorn explained what had happened. "I have no idea who the dead woman was. I have no idea what caused the explosion. I have no idea who killed the Neimoidian and his goons. What I *do* have is this." He pulled the holocron from a pocket.

I-Five took it and looked closely at it. "It appears to be encoded," the droid said. "It definitely contains some sort of information. Whether it's the details of the trade embargo of Naboo or a recipe for Alderaan stew is impossible to tell without activating it."

"It better well be what Monchar said it is." Lorn glanced at his wrist chrono. "We've got barely enough time to make the meeting with the Hutt and then get to the spaceport."

"I would predict another half hour or so of grace. Most of the local law enforcement will be more interested in the explosion than in catching us. Nevertheless, I agree that a hasty retreat is called for. I took the liberty of using our temporary wealth to secure two berths on the next spice transport bound for the Rim. Once we have the money from the Hutt we can pay the fare in cash."

Lorn nodded. I-Five was right; the important thing was to unload the holocron and get offworld as quickly as possible. It was likely that whoever had terminated Hath Monchar was looking for the crystal, and Lorn most definitely did not want to make his acquaintance. In his mind's eye he could still vividly see the Neimoidian's headless body lying on the floor of the apartment, along with his bodyguards. One of them had been decapitated, as well.

He stopped abruptly, paralyzed by shock. I-Five looked at his

face, then quickly dragged him out of the stream of foot traffic. "What is it?"

"No blood," Lorn said.

I-Five said nothing. He waited.

"Whoever did Monchar cut off his head. One of the Quarren bodyguards got the same treatment. But there was no blood to speak of. You understand? No blood. That means—"

"Cauterization. Fusion of the tissues by sudden intense heat." I-Five paused, and Lorn knew the droid had reached the same conclusion that he had. "Perhaps a quick lateral movement of a blaster on continuous fire—"

"The particle beam from a hand blaster—even a DL-44— isn't that hot, and you know it. On a straight line, yeah, it can seal as it burns, but to cauterize something the size of a neck would take several seconds. It would have to have been done after Monchar was dead, and what's the sense of that?

"There's only one weapon capable of doing it instantaneously. The same weapon that was used to cut the lock out of the dura-steel door."

"A lightsaber." I-Five glanced about as if to assure himself that no one was listening. "Are you saying a Jedi killed Monchar?"

"Much as I hate to admit it, executions aren't their style." Lorn's mouth was suddenly very dry; he had to swallow several times before he could continue. "Which leaves only one other logical choice."

"The Sith? Impossible. The last one died over a thousand years ago."

"That's what everyone believes. But it's the only conclusion that makes any sense. The Jedi have kept the details of lightsaber manufacture secret for millennia. To create and use one, you

have to be adept in the Force. And the Sith were the only other order of Force-sensitives the galaxy has ever known."

"And why couldn't it just as easily be a rogue Jedi? One who has succumbed to some kind of psychosis—a failing organic beings are often prone to, I've noticed. I think you're jumping to conclusions," I-Five said.

"No, I'm not." Lorn grabbed the droid and pulled him along as he started to walk faster. "I'm jumping on that spice transport and getting off this overbuilt rock—and so are you." He spied a public trash disintegrator across the street and changed course, with I-Five still in tow. "And we're getting rid of this holocron, right now."

They stopped before the disintegrator receptacle. Lorn pulled the information crystal from a pocket, but before he could throw it in, I-Five grabbed his arm.

"Now I *know* you're crazy," the droid said. "That holocron is our only chance to build a new life. And how will we pay our passage on the spice freighter? We can't just—"

Lorn shoved the droid up against the graffiti-frescoed wall of a large hydro-reclamation processor. Pedestrians of various and sundry species passed them, paying little or no attention to the altercation.

"Listen to me," Lorn said through clenched teeth. "If I'm right, there's a Sith out there. He's probably looking for this." He held up the holocron. "He can't be bought off, scared off, or thrown off the trail, and he'll stop at nothing to get it. I don't fancy having *my* neck cauterized."

"Let's say you're right," I-Five said. "Let's say Monchar's mysterious assassin is a Sith. Let's say he wants the crystal, and he knows we have it. Let's say he corners us before we reach the

Hutt and demands we give it to him. Which will make him happier with us—handing him the crystal, or telling him we destroyed it?"

Lorn paused, trying to quell his panic. He knew he wasn't using his brain—at least, not the part parked directly behind his forehead. He was thinking with the organ's hindquarters, the primal fight-or-flight component.

But fight-or-flight—or, more precisely, just *flight*—was the only option that made any sense in this case. In his previous life Lorn had researched the Sith thoroughly, and he knew they were fanatics, pure and simple. If a Sith was on their trail, the only prudent thing to do was to put half a galaxy between them and their stalker as quickly as possible.

Nevertheless, he had to admit that I-Five's argument about keeping the holocron had a certain logic. After all, fencing it to the Hutt might be sufficient to throw the Sith off their trail. It was reasonable to assume he was after the holocron, not them.

And all this was based on the assumption that Monchar's killer was in fact a Sith. It was a big galaxy, after all, and Coruscant was the biggest melting pot of all the inhabited worlds. It was possible that there existed someone, neither Jedi nor Sith, who had somehow gotten hold of a lightsaber and could make it work. After all, it probably didn't require being a master of the Force to simply slice an energy blade through someone's neck.

But none of this made Lorn feel any easier. Neither he nor I-Five had managed to survive these past four years in the rancid underbelly of Coruscant by taking chances. As he had told the droid more than once, it wasn't a question of being paranoid, it was a question of being paranoid *enough*.

Still, there wasn't a whole lot of choice. They could keep the holocron and stay on Coruscant in the hope that giving it up would dissuade Monchar's murderer from beheading them, as well. Or they could sell it and use the credits to flee—and hope they were not pursued.

Neither alternative seemed to offer much in the way of living to a ripe old age.

Lorn sighed and released the droid. "All right," he said. "Let's go meet the Hutt."

**A**lone in his secret chambers, Darth Sidious meditated on this latest set of circumstances.

In many ways Darth Maul was an exemplary acolyte. His loyalty was unquestionable and unshakable; Sidious knew that, if he were to command it, Maul would sacrifice his life without a second's hesitation. And his skills as a warrior were nonpareil.

Nevertheless, Maul had his flaws, and by far the largest of these was hubris. Though he had said nothing when given the assignment, Sidious knew Maul felt that such a job was beneath his skills. There were times—many times—when Sidious could see Maul's aura pulsing with the dark stain of impatience. He wondered sometimes if he had inculcated too much hatred of the Jedi and their ways in his apprentice. Maul did tend to focus on their destruction at the expense of the larger picture.

Even so, Sidious had every confidence that Maul would accomplish the task he had been set. Complications and setbacks were to be expected, and would be dealt with. All that mattered was the grand design, and it was proceeding apace. Soon the Jedi

would be put to the slaughter. That should make his impetuous subordinate happy.

Soon. Very soon.

Master Anoon Bondara sat in silence for several minutes after Darsha finished her report. They were, quite possibly, the longest minutes of the Padawan's life. The Twi'lek Jedi sat with head bowed and fingers steepled, looking at the floor between them. There was no way to read his body language, to tell what he was thinking. Even his lekku were motionless. But Darsha had a pretty good idea that, whatever her mentor's thoughts were, they did not bode well for her continued career as a Jedi.

At last Master Bondara sighed and raised his gaze to meet Darsha's. "I am glad you are still alive," he said, and Darsha felt a surge of gratitude and love for her mentor that was almost overwhelming in its intensity. Her safety had been more important to Master Bondara than the mission.

"Now tell me," the Twi'lek continued, "did you see the Fondorian die?"

"No. But there was no way he could have survived such a fall—"

Master Bondara held up a hand to stop her. "You did not see him die, and I assume you did not feel any upheaval in the Force that could have meant his death."

Darsha thought back to the nightmarish events of several hours previous. Scanning the waves of the Force for such a ripple of disturbance hadn't exactly been uppermost in her mind at that moment. Would she have felt such an agitation, preoccupied as she had been with trying to save her own life? Her mentor would have, of that she was sure. But was she that finely attuned to the Force?

"I did not," she said slowly, then felt compelled to add, "but, given the circumstances—"

"The circumstances were hardly optimal, I'm sure," Master Bondara said. "But as long as the slightest chance exists that Oolth is still alive, we must pursue it. The information he had is that important."

"You want me to go back and verify his death?" The thought of returning to the Crimson Corridor was enough to make her dizzy with revulsion. Nevertheless, if that was what had to be done, she would do it.

Master Bondara stood, his attitude and posture decisive. "We shall go together. Come." He strode toward the door of his quarters, and Darsha hastened to follow.

"But what about the council? Should we not tell them—"

The Jedi stopped before reaching the door and looked back at the Padawan. "Tell them what? There is nothing definitive to report as yet. Once we know for certain whether the Fondorian is alive or dead, then shall we make our report." He turned back to the panel, which slid open before him, and started down the corridor. Darsha followed, only gradually beginning to realize that there might be a chance, however infinitesimal, that her mission had not ended in failure. It was the lightest and most frangible of straws; nevertheless, as long as it hovered before her, she could do nothing else but grasp at it.

Maul kept his cowl up and his lightsaber clipped as he reentered the building. Fortunately there was a human officer at the checkpoint, asking those coming and going to state their business. It was ridiculously easy for Maul to cloak himself in the Force and thus slip by the dim-witted fellow.

The forensics droids were laser-scanning the cubicle when he

arrived. There were a couple of criminologists, one Mrlssi and one Sullustan, as well. He stayed in the hallway and listened to what scraps of conversation he could. He heard no mention of a holocron being found. Carefully he probed and prodded first the Mrlssi's mind, then the Sullustan's, and detected nothing about the crystal in their thoughts. Still cloaked in the dark side, he stole past the entrance of the cubicle, glancing at the open safe as he did so. The holocron was not there. Maul pondered the possibilities. If it was gone, then someone other than the security forces must have taken it. And who might that have been? Obviously, the buyer Monchar had been expecting momentarily—the human known as Lorn Pavan. He was going to enjoy taking that one's head.

Darth Maul turned and headed for the exit.

Now he had a double incentive to find the human and his droid. The first place to check, of course, would be their pathetic subterranean cubicle. It was not far from here; only a few minutes' walk.

Which, with any luck, would be the same few minutes Pavan had left of his life.

On the whole, Lorn did not consider himself to be overly xenophobic—after all, given the way he had been making his living for the last half decade, to be prejudiced against other species was not only bad for business, it could be downright dangerous.

But he hated dealing with Hutts.

On a purely physical level, everything about the giant invertebrates repulsed him: their huge, reptilian eyes, their slithering method of locomotion, and, most of all, their slimy mucosal skin. Just having to be in a room with Yanth sent a wave of horripilation over him that he was hard put to quell.

Yanth was young as Hutts go—less than five hundred standard years old. Even so, he was smart and cagey, and working his way up through the underworld ranks rapidly. Though Lorn could barely stand to be in the same room with the overgrown slug, he had to admit a reluctant admiration for the young Hutt's amoral cunning and craftiness. No one could figure the angles as quickly and completely as Yanth could.

Now he reclined on a dais in his subterranean headquarters, desultorily puffing on a chakroot hookah while he examined the holocron crystal. A couple of Gamorrean bodyguards stood nearby, watching Lorn and I-Five.

"Why did you not go directly to the Jedi with this?" he asked Lorn, his rumbling basso profundo setting off unpleasant vibrations in the human's gut. "They would seem the logical ones to approach."

Lorn saw no reason to elaborate on his own personal distaste for the Jedi to Yanth. "They claim to have very little discretionary funds for this sort of thing," he said. "Besides, I wouldn't put it past them to use their mind tricks to force me into handing it over for free." He glanced surreptitiously at his chrono and said, "So, are you interested or not? I can always take it directly to the Naboo representative here on Coruscant."

Yanth waved a pudgy hand in a placating gesture. "Patience, my friend. Yes, I am interested. But—and please don't take this as a reflection on you—I would be a fool not to test its authenticity before handing you a stack of credits."

Lorn kept his face carefully expressionless. If Yanth suspected the time crunch they were in, the Hutt would have no compunctions about using it as leverage to gouge a cheaper price. On the other hand, time was most definitely running out. "And just how do you plan on doing that?" he asked the Hutt.

Yanth simply smiled and slid several facets of the crystal aside at various angles, manipulating it much as one might a child's geometric puzzle. After a moment a beam projected from the holocron's uppermost surface, resolving into a midair display of glowing words and images that slowly curtained up the length of the holographic frame before vanishing. Lorn was too far away to read the text—not only that, but he was behind the display, so that the words and alphanumerics appeared reversed to him. The text seemed to be in Basic, however, and the images looked like schematics for Naboo N-1 starfighters and Trade Federation ships.

Yanth rotated a facet, and the images cut off. "Opening one of these holocrons can be somewhat tricky," he said. "Neimoidians as a species are not overly clever."

I-Five said, "Excellent. Now you know the article is genuine. We are asking a million credits."

"Done," Yanth replied, much to Lorn's surprise. "It is worth ten times that." The Hutt turned to a control console near at hand and pressed a button.

Lorn permitted himself another glance at his timepiece. They could still reach the spaceport, if everything continued to proceed smoothly. In another hour Coruscant, the mysterious Sith killer, and the police would be vanishing into the void behind them.

Darth Maul neatly and quickly excised the lock on the underground cubicle with one blade of his lightsaber, as he had earlier at Hath Monchar's building. He stepped inside quickly, letting the door slide closed behind him. Harsh glow lamps flickered on automatically, illuminating a living space even smaller and tawdrier than the one the Neimoidian had rented. The compartment

was empty; the only possible place where someone might hide was the refresher, and it was the work of only a few seconds to make sure that was empty, as well.

Maul stepped to a section of wall that held a vidscreen and message unit. He activated the latter. An image formed in midair; the image of a Hutt. He recognized the creature: Yanth, an up-and-coming gangster in the Black Sun organization—one of the few who had survived the slaughter Maul had recently unleashed.

The Hutt's image spoke. "Lorn, I thought we were going to meet sometime today, to discuss a certain Holocron you wished me to look at. It's not polite to keep buyers waiting, you know."

Maul turned and strode out of the cubicle, moving quickly.

All too soon, Darsha Assant found herself back in the underbelly of Coruscant.

When she had escaped the area earlier that day, she had estimated that by now she would have been stripped of her rank and reassigned to the agricultural corps. She had envisioned herself in the process of packing her belongings and saying her good-byes. That she might instead be returning to the scene of her disgrace with her mentor had certainly never occurred to her.

And yet, here she was, seated beside Anoon Bondara in the latter's four-person skycar, heading back toward the Crimson Corridor and the monad where she had lost the Fondorian and nearly lost her life, as well.

The ways of the Force were nothing if not unpredictable.

"That's the one," she said, pointing toward the tower that rose up ahead, stark against the afternoon sun. "Down there."

Master Bondara said nothing as he angled the skycar out of the flow of traffic. They slipped into a vertical descent lane and began dropping.

The mist that seemed always present around the hundred-meter mark, demarcating the thriving upper levels from the slums below, wrapped around them momentarily and then faded away, to be replaced with an aerial view of the dark streets. Though it was still daylight above, down here it was at best a dim perpetual twilight.

She watched the wall of the building slip past, and pointed out to her mentor the ascension gun's grapnel, still hooked to a ledge. They followed the cable into the miasmic depths.

When they were ten meters above the pavement, Master Bondara turned on the landing lights. The section of street below them was illuminated. Darsha, looking over the side, could see shadowy figures, long conditioned to prefer darkness to light, scuttling away.

There was no sign of the Fondorian. In all probability his body had been dragged away by scavengers. There was, however, a smear of purplish blood on the pavement and, nearby, the body of a hawk-bat, its neck broken in the fall. Master Bondara trained one of the lights on that and looked at it. His lekku slumped slightly, along with his shoulders. And, watching him, Darsha realized that her last hope of salvaging the mission was finally, irrevocably dead.

"What shall we do now?" she asked him softly.

He was silent for a long moment. Then he sighed and said, "Return to the Temple. We must report what has happened to the council."

So there it was, she thought. Oddly enough, now that she knew hope was dead, she did not feel the crushing sorrow that she had anticipated. Instead she felt a surprising sense of relief. The worst had happened, and now she would find a way to deal

with it. As with most looming disasters, the reality was almost anti-climactic compared to the dreadful anticipation.

Up to this point her concern about the mission had left little room for her to feel sympathy for Oolth the Fondorian. Now, however, looking at the stain of his blood on the walkway, she felt compassion well within her. He had been an obnoxious poltroon, and no doubt a conscienceless criminal, but few people deserved a death as horrible as his had been.

Master Bondara fed power to the repulsors, and the skycar began to rise.

Lorn watched as one of the Hutt's flunkies delivered a large case to his master. Yanth opened it, and Lorn grew dizzy at the sight. It was filled with crisp Republic credit standards in thousand-denomination notes. Yanth turned the case toward him, displaying the wealth, and Lorn could feel his fingers twitching with the desire to take possession of it. He hadn't seen that much hard cash in—he had *never* seen that much cash in one place before.

"One million nonsequential Republic credits," Yanth said, as casually as if he was discussing the weather. "You take them—I keep this." He held up the holocron. "Everybody's happy."

Lorn didn't know or care about everybody, but he was sure of one thing—*he* was happy. He watched, still hardly able to believe this was happening, as I-Five stepped forward to take possession of the money that would transform their lives. He glanced at his chrono. Just enough time to get to the spaceport, if they left now.

I-Five was reaching for the case when the door behind them suddenly flew open. A Chevin bodyguard staggered backwards into Yanth's sanctum, a force pike dropping from his nerveless

fingers. It clattered across the floor to the foot of the dais. The leathery-skinned being looked down at his chest, in the middle of which was a smoking hole, and then collapsed.

Through the door stepped a nightmare.

Lorn stared in shock at the apparition. The Chevin's killer was almost two meters tall and dressed entirely in black, including hooded cloak, boots, and heavy gauntlets. He carried a lightsaber unlike any Lorn had ever seen: It boasted not one but two energy blades, emanating from either end of the hilt. But as intimidating as his weapon was, it was his face that struck true horror into Lorn's heart. The killer pulled back his hood, revealing a countenance that was a sinister variegation of red and black tattoos around gleaming yellow eyes and blackened teeth. From the bald scalp sprouted ten short horns, like a demonic crown. He stared balefully at the others in the room, then spoke in a guttural voice.

"None shall survive."

Lorn was completely frozen to the spot, unable to offer any resistance, as the killer stepped toward him. His eyes shone like twin suns as he raised the lightsaber.

I-Five grabbed the case full of money from Yanth and hurled it between Lorn and his attacker just as the latter swung the lightsaber in a flat arc that would have separated the Corellian's head from his neck. The case intercepted the blade's swing; the plasmatic edge sliced through the case, scattering burning credits everywhere. The force of the blow was so strong that it probably would still have decapitated Lorn, but its momentum was slowed just enough to give the droid time to dive forward, knocking his friend out of harm's way. Lorn felt the heat as the blade's incandescent tip seared through his hair.

The Sith—for there was no doubt in Lorn's mind that he was

facing one of those legendary Dark Lords out of the mists of the past—recovered almost instantly and swung around to attack again. But by this time both Gamorrean guards had pulled their blasters and were firing. The Sith spun the double-bladed weapon before him, deflecting the blasterfire back at the guards. That was all Lorn had time to see before I-Five yanked him to his feet and pulled him through the doorway.

They fled down the narrow corridor that led from Yanth's sanctum, passing several more dead guards and two piles of melted, twisted metal that had once been droids. Yanth's head-quarters was beneath a nightclub he owned called the Tusken Oasis; Lorn and I-Five stumbled up a short flight of stairs and burst out into a blue-lit chamber full of sabacc tables, dejarik game boards, and scantily clad females of various species danc-ing on pedestals. They hurtled through the room and out the entrance.

"Where are we going?!" Lorn shouted as they ran down the street.

"Away from there!" I-Five shouted back.

Lorn wanted to protest that it wouldn't make any difference; he had looked into the eyes of the Sith, and he had seen his doom there, as plainly as the tattooed whorls that surrounded those eyes—an implacable fate that would hunt him down no matter how far and how fast he ran. But he had no breath in him to speak, no breath left for running either, but the fear of what he had seen in those eyes kept him running anyway.

Maul saw his quarry slip past him, but could do nothing to stop their flight while his attention was occupied by the two Gamorreans. Using one hand to spin the lightsaber in a blazing pattern that blocked the particle beam bursts, he gestured with

his free hand, plucking the invisible lines of the Force and sending reverberations that caused the blasters to fly from the surprised guards' grips.

Before they had time to recover from their surprise, Maul
leapt forward, skewering first one and then the other with quick,
deadly thrusts. The lifeless Gamorreans sagged to the floor, and
Maul wheeled quickly about to deal with the Hutt.

Despite his bulk, Yanth could move quickly when he had to.
He slithered off the dais and grabbed up the force pike dropped
by the Chevin. He hurled it at Maul, who slashed it in two with a
sweep of his own weapon. The generator in the pike's shaft
shorted out in a shower of sparks.

Yanth had not waited to see the results of his attack. His massive bulk moved rapidly, slithering through the singed and blackened credit notes that littered the floor, the holocron crystal still
clutched in one hand. He had almost reached the exit when
Maul leapt, executing a twisting forward flip that covered the
length of the large chamber and deposited him directly in front
of the Hutt.

Before Yanth could recover from his surprise, Darth Maul
plunged one of the lightsaber's blades deep into the Hutt's
chest. The stench of burning flesh and blubber filled the room.
Yanth died with a croaking gurgle, the gelid mass of his body
sagging bonelessly to the floor.

Maul deactivated both blades. He reached out with his free
hand, and the holocron leapt from the dead Hutt's grasp into his
own. Stuffing it into a belt compartment, he turned and ran from
the room. At the top of the stairs he plunged recklessly through
the gambling chamber, hurling guests and workers aside with
savage Force-laden gestures.

He reached the street and paused, looking first one way, then another for his prey. Pavan and the droid were not in sight. Maul gritted his teeth. They would *not* be permitted to slip away again! One way or another, he was determined to end this chore. It had already gone on far too long.

He sought the dark side once more, bade it illuminate the path his quarry had taken. Then he began to move, shoving his way through the hapless press of street people.

Though his appearance alone was enough to cause most of the hard cases on the street to give him a wide berth, his progress was still too slow. *Enough of this!* Maul thought. He unleashed the dark side, using the Force like a battering ram against those who got in his way.

Maul angled to the middle of the narrow avenue. His speeder bike was parked not far away; he could activate the slave circuit by remote control and have it here within a few minutes at most. But there was an even quicker way to overtake them. He called upon the Force, moving easily five times faster than a human could travel at a dead run. There was no way they could escape him now.

Within moments he was in sight of his quarry. Another few seconds and he would catch up to them—and then the lightsaber would do its work once more, slashing through metal and flesh, and at last bringing this dreary task to an end.

He grinned and lengthened his gargantuan stride even further, sailing over the fire-blackened husk of a parked landspeeder. Pavan and the droid looked back and saw him coming; he could see the fear in the human's face. It was most satisfying to witness.

One more leap, and both of them would be his.

And then an invisible hammer struck him in midleap, pounding

him to the ground. What was this? Who *dared* to interfere? Maul looked up, saw a skycar settling to the ground alongside Pavan and the droid. The repulsor beams from its undercarriage had struck him down when the vehicle passed directly over him. The skycar was less than five meters away; he could see the driver and his passenger clearly.

They were Jedi.

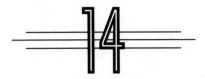

**D**arsha had sensed the disturbance in the Force at the same time as Master Bondara. They had almost reached the cloud level when they felt the dark vibrations from below; they stared at each other simultaneously in shock, and then the Twi'lek put the sky-car in a steep dive back down toward the street.

Neither spoke; Darsha wasn't sure how the blast of hatred and destruction reverberating from below had affected her mentor, but she had been left shaken and nauseated by the intensity of the empathic burst. Someone down there was well-versed in the use of the Force and powerful to boot. There had been several deaths already, and more intended, no question about it. She didn't know who had died or who was in danger, but they could not ignore such a strong and savage use of the Force. They had to find out who was responsible, and stop him, her, or it if they could.

Master Bondara leveled off at twenty meters above street level, moving as fast as was prudent through the urban maze. The skycar's headlights illuminated the narrow thoroughfare,

and as they rounded a corner they saw, perhaps a hundred meters ahead, the one who had to be responsible for the pulsation they had felt: a tall biped in dark robes, covering ground in a series of gigantic strides that had to be Force-assisted.

Who—or what—could he be? Not a Jedi, that much was certain. He wielded the Force with the surety of a Master, but no Jedi ever gave off such darksome emanations.

There was only one explanation—but even as the thought occurred to her, Darsha felt her mind flinching away from it. It *couldn't* be. It was impossible.

She had no time to wonder about it. Up ahead they could see the two who were the dark one's targets; that much would be obvious from their terror-stricken flight.

The dark one would reach his prey in one more gargantuan leap. Darsha could think of only one way to stop him, and it was evident from the direction in which Master Bondara was taking the skycar that he had thought of the same tactic.

The skycar passed right over the robed figure at a height carefully calculated to deliver a force from the repulsors sufficient to stun but not kill. It worked; as the vehicle lurched and moved on, Darsha looked behind them and saw the mysterious assailant lying in the street, the fuliginous robes a darker blot against the general darkness. Then Master Bondara brought the skycar to a stop near the two fugitives. Darsha noted with surprise that one of them was a droid.

"Get in," Master Bondara said to the human. "He's unconscious, but I don't know how long he'll be—"

"Not long," the droid said, and pointed back toward the pursuer.

Darsha glanced back and saw to her astonishment that the

dark one was already rising to his feet. She could scarcely believe he had recovered from the repulsors' hammering so fast.

"Get in!" Master Bondara shouted. "Now!"

The human, who had been staring at Darsha and her mentor with a strange expression—mingled relief and revulsion—seemed to wisely decide that they were by far the lesser of two evils. He vaulted into the skycar's backseat, followed by the droid. Darsha cast another glance behind her and saw the dark one leaping toward them. This close, she could see his face, and a more fearsome visage she could not recall ever having encountered. Then her neck was jerked painfully as Master Bondara hit the ascent control and the skycar rocketed upward.

But not swiftly enough. The vehicle shuddered from a blow delivered to the stern undercarriage, and then lurched to one side. As Master Bondara fought the controls, Darsha saw a black-gloved hand catch the cockpit's rear gunwale.

He must have used the Force to help him jump, she thought, as the skycar was already a good ten meters off the ground. Even as the thought went through her mind, she thrust out both hands in a pushing gesture, hurling an invisible but nonetheless powerful blow concentrated at that hand. It lost its grip, and the craft jerked again as the dark one fell back to the street.

"Let's get back uplevels!" she shouted. But even as the words left her, she saw the look on Master Bondara's face.

"We can't," he said.

Darth Maul's fury at seeing Pavan and his droid snatched from his clutches yet again was almost mitigated by the realization that the Jedi had entered the picture. Finally, a foe that might be worthy of his attention—someone who could truly test

his mettle! Shrugging off the effects of the repulsor field, he charged after the rising skycar, igniting his lightsaber and slashing at the drive mechanism that made up part of the vehicle's undercarriage. His blow did some damage—that he could tell by the way the craft pitched to one side. Gathering the Force around him, Maul leapt and managed to seize the gunwale with one hand. Before he could heave himself into the cockpit, however, he felt the younger Jedi strike out at him with considerable power, enough to cause him to lose his hold and plummet back to the street.

He landed lightly, the Force cushioning his fall. Even before his boots touched the ground he had his wrist comm activated and was speaking into it the code command that would activate his speeder bike and bring it homing in on his signal. As he did this, he watched the skycar stabilize and then shoot forward. In the space of a second it had rounded a corner and disappeared from view.

No matter, he told himself as he awaited the speeder bike's arrival; the skycar would be easy enough to track via the Force, especially with the Jedi on board. Pavan and his droid had had more than their share of luck this day. But now their luck had most definitely run out.

"The vertical adjustment on the repulsor array has been damaged," the Jedi piloting the craft said.

"What does that mean?" the woman asked. She was younger than her companion; younger than Lorn, too.

"It means," I-Five said, before the Jedi could answer, "that while we can move laterally and descend, we can't rise above this level."

Lorn glanced over the side. It was hard to estimate their alti-

tude in the pervasive gloom, but it looked to him that they were about twenty meters above the street. The skycar was moving at a fast clip. There was little air traffic at this level, which was fortunate, given the limited room for maneuverability granted by the narrow, twisting streets.

He looked at the Jedi. He was a Twi'lek who appeared to be in his mid to late forties. Lorn could not recall having seen him around the Temple. Of course, that meant nothing; there were plenty of Jedi with whom he had had little or no contact.

The irony of it all would have made him laugh, if it wasn't still so blasted terrifying. To be rescued from the deadly grasp of a Sith by a Jedi! Still, he had to admit it was providential that they had come along when they did. Since it looked like he and I-Five wouldn't be heading offworld any time soon, the Jedi Temple was probably the safest place for them now—though it galled him to admit that, even to himself.

So much had happened within the last few minutes—and practically all of it disastrous—that he hadn't even begun to come to grips with it yet. The Jedi shot around another corner, and Lorn felt inertia press his body against the low-powered tractor field designed to prevent injury in the case of accidents.

"Take it easy!" he said. "There's no way he can catch up with us on foot now."

"He's not on foot," the woman said tensely.

Darth Maul leapt onto the speeder bike as it flashed past him. He wrapped both hands around the acceleration grips on the handlebar and opened them up. The repulsor engine's hum climbed as the speeder shot forward. Maul leaned into the turns as the speeder zoomed around corners.

There was no need to activate the heads-up tracking display.

The Jedi and his quarry gleamed like twin beacons in his mind; he could feel them in the skycar ahead of him. The speeder bike was moving at half again their speed. He would overtake them in mere minutes.

Maul grinned savagely. It would be the work of a moment to dispose of Pavan and the droid. Then he would see just how good the Jedi were. It had been far too long since he had felt his lightsaber clash against another, had heard the grating scream of energy blades in conflict, had smelled the ozone tang. Far too long.

"Why is the Sith after you?" Master Bondara shouted over the slipstream's howl.

Though Darsha had come to the same conclusion, it was still shocking on a very deep level to hear Master Bondara articulate her thoughts. She had learned much about the Sith during her studies, of course, but all of the lectures and data seemed unanimous in the conclusion that the ancient dark order was no more. And yet, what else could he be, this creature of the night who even now pursued them? He was adept in the use of the Force, but it was quite obvious he was not a Jedi. That didn't leave a whole lot of choices.

She saw the human and the droid look at each other, and realized they had come to a silent agreement about something. Then the droid spoke.

"We are information brokers," he said, and something—or rather, the absence of something—in the timbre of his voice surprised Darsha. She could hear none of the built-in obsequiousness that droids, particularly those of the protocol series, evidenced as a rule. He had a confidence in his tone and manner

that was startling enough for her to notice, even given the duress of the moment.

"I am known as I-Five, and my associate is Lorn Pavan," the droid continued. Darsha saw Master Bondara glance quickly at Pavan, and then return his attention to piloting.

*He knows the name,* she thought.

"We were recently contacted by a Neimoidian named Hath Monchar, who wished to sell us a holocron containing details of a trade embargo to be imposed on the planet Naboo by the Trade Federation."

Master Bondara said nothing in reply for a moment. Then he asked, "Is this in retaliation for the new tax recently imposed by the Republic Senate on the Trade Federation?"

"Yes," Pavan replied. "The Federation fears the new tax will cut into their profits."

"Naboo is highly dependent on imports to maintain its way of life," Master Bondara said. "Such sanctions could prove devastating to its people." He steered the skycar around another corner. Pedestrians, knowing the potential danger from the repulsor beams of a vehicle traveling this low, scattered left and right. "That doesn't explain why the Sith is trying to kill you," Master Bondara continued.

Darsha admired the Jedi's equanimity; he might have been having this conversation in one of the quiet, comfortable reading chambers of the Temple instead of in a damaged skycar traveling a dangerous route at maximum velocity.

"You can see why the Neimoidians don't want this information to get out," I-Five said. "We're not sure why or how the Sith are involved. But Hath Monchar was killed by the one who's now pursuing us."

"What happened to the holocron?" Darsha asked.

"We were in the process of selling it to a Hutt named Yanth," Pavan replied, "when the Sith broke in. My guess is that the Hutt is dead, and the Sith either destroyed the crystal or has it with him."

"This information must be brought to the council immediately," Master Bondara said. "You two will be kept safe until the threat of the Sith has been dealt with."

Darsha glanced at Lorn Pavan and saw mingled frustration and resignation in his expression.

"Jedi," he muttered to himself. "Why did it have to be Jedi?"

She looked behind them. Their circuitous route had brought them into a somewhat less dark area of the city now, and she could plainly make out the shape of a speeder bike behind them. Even without the Force to confirm it, she would have been sure that it was the Sith pursuing them.

"Here he comes," she said. "He's gaining fast." She saw that Pavan's face had gone pale, but that he didn't seem to be panicking. Good; the last thing they needed to deal with was another Oolth the Fondorian.

She looked at Master Bondara and saw his jaw muscles clench in determination.

"Take the controls," he told her.

His order surprised her, but his tone of voice brooked no questioning. She slid over as Master Bondara pushed himself up and back, then swung his feet over the back of the padded crossbar separating the front and rear seats. She looked at the rear vidscreen and saw that the Sith was not more than five meters behind her. He drew his lightsaber, activating the twin crimson beams.

"Get them back to the Temple!" Master Bondara shouted at her. Then, before Darsha could even realize what he intended, much less protest or try to stop him, the Jedi stood up on the rear seat between Pavan and I-Five. He activated his lightsaber, took two steps up onto the rear engine compartment—and leapt from the speeding skycar.

The Twi'lek Jedi's leap, guided by the Force, landed him squarely behind Maul on the rear engine housing of the T-shaped bike. The action took Maul by surprise; he had not expected such a courageous, if foolhardy, deed.

Unexpected as the move was, however, Maul was still able to block the slash of the other's lightsaber with his own energy blade. He quickly activated the speeder's autopilot, then twisted around in the saddle, thrusting his weapon at the Jedi's chest. The Jedi blocked the blow and countered with another.

Maul knew the battle could not continue this way. The speeder bike's autopilot was not sophisticated enough to chart a safe course at high speed through the torturous windings of the surface streets. He grabbed the handlebar and jerked the speeder toward a docking platform on a nearby building, about thirty meters above the street. They shot by the skycar, which had slowed after the Jedi left it, and rose toward the shelf. As the ledge came within range of the autopilot's sensors, the speeder

slowed, then settled down to a landing on the extruded slab of ferrocrete.

The Sith and the Jedi leapt from the speeder bike onto the platform to continue their battle. The docking ledge was only about ten meters by fifteen, barely enough room to maneuver in. Maul knew he had to dispatch the Jedi quickly, before Pavan once again vanished into the labyrinth of Coruscant's downlevels. He pressed the attack viciously, blocking and thrusting, the twin radiant blades spinning a web of light about him.

The Jedi was obviously a master of the teräs käsi fighting arts, as well, judging by the smooth way he parried and counterattacked. Still, within the first few moments of the engagement, Darth Maul knew that he himself was the superior fighter. He could tell that the Jedi knew it, too, but Maul also knew that it didn't matter. The Jedi was committed to stopping the Sith, or at the very least slowing him down enough to let the others get away, even if it meant giving his own life to do so.

Maul bared his teeth. He would *not* lose his quarry again! He doubled his efforts, pressing the attack hard, hammering away at the Twi'lek's defenses. The Jedi gave ground, but Maul was still unable to slash through his guard.

Then he heard something: the distinctive sound of the skycar's damaged engine. He let his awareness expand on the ripples of the Force, and what he sensed brought a dark smile of satisfaction to his face.

The skycar—with his prey—was returning.

Darsha could not believe it at first when Master Bondara leapt from the skycar onto the Sith's speeder bike. Her first

action was reflexive; she slowed the skycar, intending to go to her mentor's aid.

"What are you doing?" Pavan shouted. "He said head for the Temple!"

"I'm not going to abandon him to that monster!" Darsha shouted back. She saw the speeder bike shoot past them, then rise and head for a docking ledge that protruded from a dilapidated building.

"He knows what he's doing," the droid told her. "Are you prepared to make his sacrifice meaningless?"

Darsha knew the droid's words made sense, but she didn't care. After all, she had made one mistake after another in the past several hours; why stop now? She had gone far past the point of worrying about the consequences of her actions; all she knew was that she could not leave Master Bondara to battle the Sith alone. It was hard for her to conceive of a situation in which her mentor could be bested in combat, but if anyone was capable of it, she had the feeling the Sith was that one.

She slowed the skycar and brought it around, heading back toward the landing ledge—and realized she had a problem. The damaged repulsor array had fixed the vehicle's ceiling, and the platform was a good ten meters above them. Her ascension gun was still, as far as she knew, attached to the monad, nearly a kilometer from her present position.

It would be no problem to leap ten meters straight up; in training exercises she had used the Force to help her perform jumps higher than that. To assay such a leap onto a narrow platform and into the midst of a raging lightsaber duel was a considerably more complex undertaking, however. It would do Master Bondara no good for her to get herself killed by the Sith.

Still, there was no other choice. Her mentor might sense the skycar's presence and leap back into it, but there was no guarantee he would be able to do so in the heat of battle. Darsha brought the skycar to a hovering stop below and to one side of the ledge. Above her, the two dueling figures were hidden by the ferrocrete slab, but she could see the variegated flashes and hear the angry buzzing and screeching of the lightsabers as they clashed. She had to take action, now. She stood, pulled her lightsaber from its belt hook, and prepared to leap.

And the world suddenly dissolved in a burst of blinding light and a deafening roar.

Darth Maul had seen the grim realization in the eyes of his foe: the knowledge that the Twi'lek could not defeat his adversary. Once defeat was conceded in the mind, its reality was inevitable. It was only a matter of time.

He pressed his attack to an even higher intensity, driving the Jedi back toward his speeder bike, intending to pin him between the dual-bladed lightsaber and the bike. With his movements thus constricted, it would be mere moments before the Twi'lek's tentacled head was separated from his neck.

But then he saw the desperation in the other's face suddenly give way to realization, and then to triumph. Quickly, before Maul could intuit what was intended, the Jedi whirled toward the speeder bike, raised his lightsaber—and plunged it to the hilt into the bike's repulsor drive housing.

Maul realized his suicidal intention, but too late. The superheated energy blade melted with lightning swiftness through the housing and sank into the bike's power cell core. Maul turned and leapt from the platform, reaching for the dark side, enfolding

himself in it even as the power cell exploded, the heat and pressure wave vaporizing the Jedi in a microsecond and then expanding, reaching hungrily for him, as well.

The landing platform shielded the skycar from the main force of the explosion; otherwise the three passengers would not have survived. Even so, the shock wave hurled Darsha from her standing position back over the rear of the craft. She would have plunged to the street below had Lorn not grabbed her wrist as she fell past him. I-Five lunged for the controls and fought to stabilize the vehicle, which was pitching and yawing wildly. For an instant that felt like an eternity Darsha hung over the abyss, too stunned to use the Force to help lift herself to safety—and then Lorn managed to pull her back into the rear seat compartment.

But the danger was not yet over; the explosion had caused the platform to break free of its supports. It began to collapse, sagging away from the building wall. As it did so, Darsha caught a glimpse of the Sith's dark form hurtling from the ledge into the darkness below. The buckling platform clipped the skycar's side, sending it spinning out of control toward the street, as well.

I-Five fought with the controls and managed to level out as the vehicle reached the ground. The spectators drawn to the scene by the explosion scattered in panic as the skycar pancaked to a rough landing.

Darsha, half-stunned, was vaguely aware of an insistent beeping that was rising in frequency and tone. Even as realization of what the beeping signified penetrated her dazed brain, she felt herself seized in a powerful grip and pulled from the wrecked skycar. As she stumbled across the litter-strewn pavement she realized the droid was dragging her and Lorn Pavan away from the vehicle.

"Hurry," she mumbled. "Power cell's on overload . . ."

"A fact of which I am quite aware," I-Five replied. He stopped before a kiosk. A sign on the door read KEEP OUT in Basic, but the droid ignored this and blasted the lock with a laser beam that shot from his left index finger.

Within the kiosk was a narrow, dimly lit stairwell. The three of them hurried down it as, behind them, the alarm beeps reached a crescendo. A moment later a second, more powerful explosion rocked the area. Darsha felt the stairwell shift and shudder as if in the throes of a temblor. The light went out, she felt herself falling—and then she knew no more.

PART II

# PART II
## Labyrinth

**N**ute Gunray was in his suite on board the *Saak'ak*, trying to enjoy a mildew rubdown and failing utterly, when his private comlink chimed. His masseuse had slathered his naked form with liquefied green mold and was industriously kneading the muscle nodules of his upper back, which were so tight with tension that he could hear them crackle.

At his grunted acknowledgment, the image of Rune Haako formed near the massage table. The barrister did not look happy, but that in itself meant little; Neimoidians as a species rarely looked happy.

"I have news," Haako said in a low voice.

"Come to my quarters," Gunray replied, and the holoimage flickered out.

Whatever news Haako had for him was best heard in person, in the privacy of his sanctum. Even though there was supposedly no one on board the freighter who was not loyal to him and his cause, the viceroy was taking no chances. He knew very well just

how easily the allegiance of his cohorts and underlings could be bought.

He dismissed the masseuse, donned a vermilion robe, and paced restlessly, awaiting Haako's arrival. The intricacies of protocol dictated that he be sitting at ease in a couch or chair, his nonchalant attitude conveying the impression that, no matter what news Haako might be bearing, it could not possibly be important enough to cause him any concern. But he was beyond caring about such formalities at this point. There had been no word for nearly forty-eight hours from the bounty hunter they had engaged, and no news of Hath Monchar's whereabouts or plans. At any moment he expected to see the holographic presence of Darth Sidious materialize again before him, demanding that he once more assemble his gang of four to continue discussions concerning the Naboo blockade. And what would happen when Gunray was still not able to account for Monchar's absence? He winced as the mere thought of such a conversation with Sidious caused his gut sac to fill with acidic bile. He knew he was building a world-class ulcer in his lower abdomen, but there didn't seem to be much he could do to stop it.

The door panel slid open, and Haako entered. A moment later Daultay Dofine entered, as well. Gunray steeled himself; one look at his compatriots' hunched postures and furtive miens assured him that he was not about to hear good news.

"I have just heard from the consular representative at our embassy on Coruscant," Haako said. His willingness to skip the preamble of verbal fencing and get right to the subject was ample evidence that his concern was just as great as Gunray's. "One of our people has been killed there."

Gunray had to will his salivary glands to moisten his palate before he was able to speak. "Was it Monchar?"

"At this point, we don't know for certain," Dofine said. "There was evidently an explosion, although the investigation is unclear as to whether that was the cause of death. Genetic ID verification is pending."

"However," Haako continued, lowering his voice and peering about as if he expected Darth Sidious to appear at any moment, "a piece of singed cloth that was once part of a miter of the office of deputy viceroy was found at the scene."

Nute Gunray closed his eyes and tried to imagine what life as a mulch farmer back on Neimoidia would be like.

"In addition," Dofine said, "several other bodies were discovered at the scene of the explosion. One has been conclusively identified: the bounty hunter Mahwi Lihnn."

Mulch farming probably had its good points, Gunray told himself. For one thing, the possibility of having to deal with the Sith in his new occupation was very unlikely.

"I think we must admit the conclusion that Hath Monchar is no longer among the living," Rune Haako said. He began to wring his hands as though he was twisting the life out of a swamp toad he planned to have for a snack.

"This is a disaster," Dofine whined. "What will we tell Lord Sidious?"

What indeed? the viceroy of the Federation wondered. Oh, there was no shortage of lies that they could come up with—but would Sidious believe any of them? That was the all-important question. And the answer, much as Gunray hated to admit it, was, almost certainly not. The Sith Lord's cowled face rose unbidden before his mental vision, and he could not help but shudder. Those eyes, hidden deep in that hooded cloak, could penetrate subterfuge and dissimulation as easily as X rays penetrated flesh and illuminated the bones within for all to see.

But what other option was there? Though the thought of doing so galled him on a very fundamental level, Gunray knew that they could simply admit the truth: that Monchar had absconded, to where and for what reason they did not know—although anyone with the brains of an oxygen-starved Gamorrean could extrapolate *that* fairly quickly. But the truth had its own built-in hazards, chief among which was the fact that it had not been presented when Sidious first noticed Monchar's absence.

Veracity and prevarication seemed equally dangerous here. It was a Neimoidian's worst nightmare: a situation from which it was impossible to worm one's way out. Gunray looked down and saw that he was wringing his own hands every bit as industriously as were Rune Haako and Daultay Dofine.

Only one thing was certain. Soon—very soon—they would have to tell the Sith Lord *something*.

Jedi Master Yoda entered the conference antechamber, a smaller room off to one side of the Council Chamber. Mace Windu and Qui-Gon Jinn were already seated at the pleekwood table. Behind them a floor-to-ceiling transparisteel window offered a panoramic view of the endless architectural welter that was Coruscant and its continuous streams of air traffic.

Yoda moved slowly toward one of the chairs. He leaned on his gimer-stick cane as he walked, and Windu had to suppress a smile as he watched Yoda's progress. While Yoda was easily the oldest member of the council, being well over 800 standard years of age, he was by no means as decrepit as he sometimes pretended to be. Though it was true that he had slowed slightly in the years that Windu had known him, Yoda's skill with a lightsaber was still second to none on the council.

Windu waited until his colleague was seated before he spoke.

"I have not deemed it necessary to call a general meeting of the council concerning this yet," he said. "Nevertheless, it is a problem that in my opinion warrants discussion."

Yoda nodded. "Of the Black Sun matter you speak."

"Yes—specifically of Oolth the Fondorian, and the Padawan Darsha Assant, who was sent to bring him here."

"Has there been any word at all from her?" Qui-Gon Jinn asked.

"None. It has been almost forty-eight hours. The mission should not have taken more than four or five at the most."

"Anoon Bondara is missing, as well," Yoda said reflectively. "Coincidence I doubt it is."

"You think Bondara has gone in search of Assant?" Windu asked. Yoda nodded.

"Understandable," Jinn said. "Assant is his Padawan. If he felt she was in danger, he would look into it."

"Of course he would," Windu replied. "But why did he not inform any of us as to his intentions? And why has there been no communication from either of them?"

There was silence for a moment as the three Jedi Masters pondered the questions. Then Yoda said, "Some infraction on her part, perhaps he knew or suspected. Want to protect her from repercussions, he would."

Jinn nodded. "Anoon has always been one to chafe at rules and restrictions."

Mace Windu glanced at Jinn and raised an eyebrow. Jinn smiled slightly and shrugged.

"This makes sense to me," Windu said. "It feels right. But, however noble Anoon Bondara's intentions, we cannot have him and Assant acting without the knowledge or consent of the council."

"Agreed we are on this matter," Yoda said. "Send an investigator we must."

"Yes," Windu said. "But who? With the current state of affairs in the Republic Senate, all our senior members are on standby alert, and may continue to be for some time."

"I have a suggestion," Qui-Gon Jinn said. "Dispatch my Padawan. If Black Sun is involved, he will be able to sense it."

"Obi-Wan Kenobi? Potentially strong in the Force he is," Yoda mused. "A good choice he would be."

Mace Windu nodded slowly. Yoda was right. Though not yet a full-fledged Jedi Knight, Kenobi had amply demonstrated his skills in battle and in negotiation. If anyone could find out what had happened to Bondara and Assant, he could.

The senior member of the council stood. "We are decided, then. Qui-Gon, you will explain the situation to Kenobi and send him on his way as soon as possible. There is something about all this . . ." Windu was silent for a moment.

"Yes," Yoda said soberly. "No accident this was."

Qui-Gon Jinn said nothing; he merely nodded his agreement, then stood. "Obi-Wan will leave for the Crimson Corridor immediately," he told Windu and Yoda.

"May the Force be with him," Yoda said softly.

*There is no emotion; there is peace.*
*There is no ignorance; there is knowledge.*
*There is no passion; there is serenity.*
*There is no death; there is the Force.*

The Jedi Code was one of the first things Darsha Assant had learned in the Jedi Temple. As a child, she would sit cross-legged on the cold floor for hours at a time, repeating the words over and over, meditating on their meaning, letting that meaning seep into her bones.

*There is no emotion; there is peace.*

Master Bondara had taught her that this did not mean one should repress one's emotions. "One of the few things that all intelligent species in the galaxy share is the ability to have feelings. We are creatures of emotion, and to deny those emotions is profoundly unhealthy. But one can feel anger, for example, without being controlled by it. One can grieve without being crippled by

grief. The peace of the Force is the foundation upon which the structures of our feelings are built."

*There is no ignorance; there is knowledge.*

"Chance," the Twi'lek Jedi had told her, "favors the prepared mind." Certainly the Jedi were among the most prepared in the galaxy as far as that went. She had never seen anyone as awesomely well-educated as Masters Windu, Bondara, Yoda, Jinn, and the many others she had studied under or otherwise come in contact with. She had doubted her ability to hold her own in conversations with them, or even with her fellow Padawans like Obi-Wan and Bant. So she had studied assiduously, almost obsessively, taking advantage of the incredible wealth of wisdom and lore available in the Temple's libraries and data banks. And she had found that the more she knew, the more she wanted to know. Knowledge was as addictive in its own way as glitterstim.

*There is no passion; there is serenity.*

At first she had thought this was merely a restating of the code's first precept. But Master Bondara had explained the difference. Passion, in this context, meant obsession, compulsion, an overweening fixation on something or someone. And serenity was not merely a synonym for peace; rather, it was the state of tranquility that could be reached when one was able to let go of such fixations, when one could be at peace with one's emotions and had replaced ignorance with knowledge.

Master Bondara had taught her so many things, had helped her forge her life into something far beyond anything she had thought it was her potential and destiny to be. She owed him so much, and now she would never be able to repay him.

*There is no death; there is the Force.*

Darsha knew that if she had truly internalized the first three maxims of the Jedi Code, she would be able to take comfort from this last one, as well. But it was obvious that she had not reached that stage yet. Because she could find no peace, no serenity, in the knowledge that her mentor was dead.

All she could do was grieve.

She had been in a state of half awareness, her only real emotion that of sorrow, for an unknown amount of time before she was jolted back to consciousness by a building vibration and roar that seemed to be hurtling toward her. She opened her eyes in time to see a huge transport vehicle thunder by, only a meter or so from where she lay. The sound of its passing was deafening; then it was gone, the roar dopplering swiftly away to silence.

Or rather, relative silence; there was an omnipresent background drone of machinery and ventilation equipment. She looked around, saw Lorn Pavan seated against a wall about a meter away, and I-Five standing next to him. They were in a large tunnel, dimly illuminated by photonic wall sconces set at wide intervals.

She realized where they were—in one of the countless service conduits that stitched Coruscant's lowest levels, like the skein of blood vessels under living skin. Through these tunnels flowed an endless automated stream of vehicles hauling goods and materials from spaceports and factories to millions of destinations all over the planetwide metropolis.

"How did we get down here?" she asked. Even as the question left her lips she dimly recalled being dragged from the wreckage of the skycar and down the stairwell by the droid as the

craft's power cell exploded. He had undoubtedly saved both of their lives.

Pavan jerked a thumb at I-Five. "Thank Wonder Droid here," he said. "Hadn't been for him, we'd both be hash for the armored rats. Sometimes he's almost worth having around."

"Please, don't gush," the droid said. "It's embarrassing."

Darsha struggled to her feet. The planet skewed nastily on its axis for a moment, and the lights dimmed even more than they already were, but then things steadied again. She checked for her lightsaber and was relieved to find it hanging where it should be from her utility belt.

"Where's the stairwell?" she asked. "I have to see if . . ." *If Master Bondara is still alive,* she finished to herself. She could not bring herself to say it out loud, for fear that one of them might tell her what she already knew.

Pavan pointed to an alcove about two meters away. "But the stairwell won't do you any good. The skycar's explosion brought about a ton of real estate down on it. We'll have to find another way out."

Darsha nodded. "Then we'd better get going. There has to be another access stairwell along this route."

"Why not just call for help?" Pavan asked. "You've got a comlink, haven't you?"

"I had one, but it was damaged earlier." It occurred to her only now that she should have replaced it when she had been back at the Temple.

Pavan raised an eyebrow. "First time I've seen a Jedi who wasn't prepared for everything." There was a faint note of sarcasm in his voice.

Darsha bit back the retort that rose to her lips. It wouldn't

take much to put him on her list of least favorite people; after all, he was indirectly responsible for Master Bondara's death. On the other hand, he had saved her from falling out of the skycar. "Don't *you* have a comlink?" she asked.

Pavan looked uncomfortable and didn't reply.

"Yes, he does," I-Five said. "It's in fine working order, too—except that the power pack is depleted and he can't afford to replace it."

Darsha said nothing to that; her silence was ample indication of how she felt.

Pavan stood up. "Might as well get moving," he said, "before another—"

His words were drowned out by the passage of another transport. They shrank back against the curved wall of the tunnel as it hurtled by them. The automated conveyances were sleek, massive bullets that all but filled the shaft, moving in excess of a hundred kilometers an hour, propelled by repulsor drives.

As it disappeared into the distance Darsha said, "Let's hurry. We'll be deaf inside of an hour if we stay here."

They moved quickly, single file, down the narrow sidewalk. It didn't matter which direction they went at this point; the goal was just to get out of the transport tube as fast as possible. The droid led the way, as his photoreceptors were best able to adjust to the dim light.

They saw another recessed doorway ahead as the rumbling approach of a third transport began to build behind them. The door was locked, but I-Five's finger blaster quickly removed that obstacle, and they hurried through it just as the freight vehicle blasted by.

Other than the fact that there were now no convoys

thundering past, their new location was not much of an improvement. The transport tube had at least been reasonably clean and lit. Best of all, while it hadn't led back to the surface, it had remained horizontal.

Now, however, they found themselves in another stairwell, only this one led down rather than up. There seemed to be little choice but to follow it. There were no lights; the only illumination came from a phosphorescent lichenlike growth on the walls, and this light was barely enough to let them see each other and the next few steps. The ferrocrete walls wept with a slimy discharge, and there was a faint scent of decay in the air.

At last they reached the bottom of the stairwell, which opened into a small chamber lit by one flickering photonic sconce. In the wall opposite the stairwell were openings to three branching tunnels. Signs mounted above each one supposedly gave directions, but they had been reduced to illegibility by successive layers of graffiti.

"My locator was in my comlink," Darsha said. "I have no idea which way to go."

"Fortunately, I have a built-in global positioner," I-Five said. "To orient ourselves toward the Jedi Temple, we would be best served by taking that one." He pointed to the leftmost tunnel.

"That's a good argument for taking the right-hand tunnel," Pavan muttered. Darsha looked at him; he met her eyes for a moment and then looked away.

"I'm trying to get you back to a safe haven," she told him. "If you'd rather take your chances with our friend up there, that's fine with me. I can tell the council about the impending blockade as easily as you can."

He turned back to look at her again. "Hey, the Sith was

probably vaporized along with your Jedi buddy," he said. "And good riddance to both of 'em."

Darsha felt herself go cold with anger. Without taking her gaze away from his, she said, "I-Five, what do you think the chances are that the Sith's dead?"

"Given the fact that, in our brief peripheral acquaintance with him, he has already survived several attempts on his life and killed quite a few beings, as well, I wouldn't count him out until I saw his dead body," the droid said. "And even then I'd want him frozen in carbonite just to make sure."

Darsha nodded. "I agree. But you're entitled to your opinion, Pavan. Maybe it'll be safer if we all go our separate ways; after all, *you* seem to be the one he's looking for."

Even as she said this, she realized it was a mistake. She didn't need to see the look that passed between the droid and Pavan to know that she couldn't play one off against the other. Whatever bond they had was strong enough to unite them, even in a situation like this.

I-Five said to Pavan, "She's right about you being the primary target. Sanctuary from the Jedi may be your only option. Are you willing to accept that?"

"Of course," Pavan replied with a scowl. "I'm not stupid. But that doesn't mean I have to be happy about the situation."

"True," Darsha said. "But you could at least try being congenial. If we're going to be stuck with each other for a while, we might as well try to make it pleasant." She turned to face the left-hand tunnel, took a few steps toward it, then turned back to him and added, "Anoon Bondara died saving your life. I don't want to hear any more disparaging remarks about him."

Neither Pavan nor I-Five made any reply to that as she

started down the tunnel. After she had taken a few steps they fell in behind her.

*There is no emotion; there is peace.* Well, maybe someday. After all, she wasn't a full-fledged Jedi yet, and the way things were going, it didn't look like she ever would be. But some truths you didn't need the Force to see. Like the fact that one Anoon Bondara was worth a fleet of Lorn Pavans.

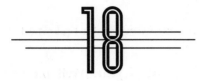

Lorn didn't like the Jedi Padawan. This fact would hardly be surprising to anyone who knew him even casually—which was how pretty much everybody knew him, these days—as he was not reticent about his feelings when the subject of the Jedi Knights arose. He had stated on more than one occasion to anyone who would listen that he considered them on a par with mynocks in terms of parasitic opportunism, and a notch or two beneath those energy-sucking space bats on the general scale of galactic evolution.

"Shooting's too good for them," he once told I-Five. "In fact, dumping them all in a Sarlacc's pit to marinate in gastric juices for a thousand years is too good for them, but it'll do until something worse comes along."

He had never told anyone why he felt this way. In his present circle of acquaintances only I-Five knew, and the droid would never divulge the secret of Lorn's bitterness to anyone.

And now, thanks to a truly ironic twist of fate, here he was al-most literally stun-cuffed to a Jedi and dependent on her to save

him from the murderous intentions of a Sith—a member of an order sprung from the Jedi millennia ago. It seemed that, no matter which way he turned, the self-styled galactic guardians were there to complete the ruination of his life that they had started.

Lorn felt the bitterness growing within his breast as he trudged along through the subterranean tunnel following I-Five and Darsha Assant. It certainly hadn't taken her long at all to settle into that sanctimonious holier-than-thou attitude that he despised so much. They were all alike, with their sackcloth fashion sense and their austere asceticism, mouthing empty platitudes about the greater good. He much preferred dealing with the street scum; they at least were villains without the taint of hypocrisy.

Lorn was under no illusions about the treatment he would receive when he once again entered the Jedi Temple. Forget about any sort of reward; he and I-Five would be lucky to get protection against the Sith while the council debated how they could best make use of this windfall of information. He had no doubt that they would find a way to make it serve their purposes, as they were able to do with everything they came in contact with.

Everything and *everyone*.

This underground passage they were traveling was no more dark and torturous than the labyrinth of his memories and hatred. He wondered for the dozenth time why he hadn't just let Assant fall when the speeder bike explosion had hurled her from the skycar. He couldn't even excuse it on the grounds that he had needed her to pilot the vehicle; I-Five was perfectly capable of that. No, it had been that most pernicious of impulses, one

that Lorn thought he'd managed to eradicate within himself long ago: a humanitarian motive.

The memory of what he had done bothered him immensely. He had made it a policy during the last five years to stick his neck out for nobody, with the exception of I-Five. The mordant droid was the closest thing to a friend that he had. What made him such a good friend, in Lorn's opinion, was very simple: he asked for nothing back. Which was good, because Lorn had nothing to give. Everything that had made him human had been taken from him five years ago. In a very real way, he realized, he was no more human than the droid who was his companion.

He forced his thoughts away from memories; he knew of no more certain way to plunge himself into a black depression. This he could not afford to do; he had to keep his wits about him if he was going to get out of this situation alive. He couldn't count on the Jedi for help; he trusted them about as far as he could throw a ronto. He refocused his attention, not without some effort.

The weak glow of the ancient photonic sconces had petered out about half a kilometer back. The only light source they had now was the droid's illuminated photoreceptors, which were capable of casting twin bright beams as strong as vehicle headlights. They revealed what was directly before or behind them, depending on where I-Five turned his head, but from all other sides the darkness pressed in avidly. Lorn was becoming claustrophobic. It wasn't just the pervasive gloom; he could *feel* the incalculable weight of the structures overhead pressing down on him. Coruscant was a tectonically stable planet—that and its location had been the main reasons for it having been chosen the galactic capital—but even though there had not been a major quake anywhere on it for thousands of years, he found himself

vividly imagining his probable fate should one occur while he was wandering around in the bowels of the planet.

It was hard to tell in the gloomy murk, but judging by the echoes of their footsteps, the tunnel seemed to be widening out somewhat. For the last couple of hundred meters they had been passing what seemed to be branching passageways—nothing more than clots of darkness in the walls—and Lorn's imagination had no problem supplying those side tunnels with all kinds of nasty inhabitants. Armored rats the size of skycars was one image he could happily have done without. Life on the upper levels of Coruscant was a joy to experience, because such problems as environmental pollution had been largely eradicated centuries before. But there was always a price to be paid for the benefits of technology, and while the upper levels didn't have to pay it, the lower levels did. Down here below the planet's city scape it was one huge, pulsing malignancy of industrial waste and carcinogenic chemicals. The more sensational news programs on the HoloNet were always full of stories about dangerous mutations being found in the sewers and drainage systems—stories that, at the moment, Lorn had no problem whatsoever believing. He was sure he could hear ominous slithering sounds from either side, the slow step-and-drag of some murderous bipedal beast following them, the stealthy breathing of something huge and hungry about to pounce. *Stop it*, he told himself sternly. *It's nothing but your imagination.*

"Did you hear that?" Assant asked.

The three stopped. I-Five probed the darkness in various directions with his eye beams, which revealed nothing more than ancient, moss-covered walls. "My audioreceptors are set at maximum. I hear nothing that might indicate danger. In addition, my radar detects no movement in the vicinity."

"Maybe you've got radar," Assant said, "but I've got the Force, and right now it's telling me that we're not alone."

"Impossible," Lorn said. The Jedi were always playing the Force as a hole card, using it as an excuse to justify all kinds of actions and opinions. Not that Lorn had any doubt that the Force existed and could be manipulated by them; he'd seen too many examples of it. But he felt that their use of it was largely just another way to justify questionable actions.

He continued, "You think something that lives down here could have access to a radar jammer?" He was about to enumerate several sarcastic reasons why this was a ludicrous idea when something whistled out of the darkness and struck him in the head, and he lost interest in the conversation for a while.

Darsha jerked her lightsaber from its clip and activated it. She had no idea what sort of threat was impending, but whatever it was, it was all around them. She and the droid positioned themselves back-to-back, with Pavan's unconscious form lying between them. I-Five had both hands up, the index fingers extended, like a child pretending to point a pair of blasters. He swiveled his head slowly through 360 degrees, illuminating their surroundings. There was a branch corridor on their left and two more on their right. Nothing moved. There was no indication of where the weapon that had laid Pavan low had come from. It was a curved throwing stick; she could see it lying on the floor at her feet.

"We're too exposed here," she said in a low voice. "Pick up your friend and let's at least get our backs against a wall."

The droid did not answer. Keeping his left finger blaster extended, he reached down with the other arm and hooked it around Pavan's waist, lifting the unconscious human as easily as

Darsha might lift a small child. They began to move cautiously toward the nearest wall.

The attack came from the one direction they had not expected: above.

Without warning, a net of fine mesh dropped down on them. Darsha sensed it settling from overhead and slashed at it, only to have the lightsaber's blade screech and emit a shower of sparks. She realized too late that the net was charged with some kind of power field. She felt a bolt of energy slam through her, and then for the second time in as many hours darkness engulfed her.

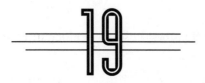

**D**iscipline.

Discipline is all. It conquers pain. It conquers fear.

Most important of all, it conquers failure.

Discipline is what allowed Darth Maul to survive a thirty-meter fall into a pile of rubble and debris: the discipline of his teräs käsi fighting skills, which gave him complete control over his body, allowing him to utilize midair acrobatics to direct his fall and so avoid striking ornamental projections, ledges, and other potentially lethal obstructions; the discipline of the dark side, which let him manipulate gravity itself, slowing his descent enough to hit the ground without becoming a lifeless bag of broken bones and ruptured organs. Even half stunned by the unexpected explosion of his speeder bike, Maul was able to aim his falling body in such a way as to survive.

But even someone in as superb shape as Maul could not come out of such an explosion and a fall completely unscathed. After the impact he lay, semiconscious, in the debris, remotely

aware of a second explosion some distance away as the skycar blew up.

He lay there, and he remembered.

*There is no pain where strength lies.*

To Darth Maul, it seemed that his master had always been there, a part of his life—implacable, indomitable, inexorable. Since before Maul learned to walk, discipline had been his guiding beacon. Darth Sidious had molded him from a weak, puling child into the ultimate warrior, sculpting his body and his mind as a seamless weapon. Maul was willing to die for him, without question and without hesitation. Lord Sidious's goals were the goals of the Sith, and they would be achieved, no matter what the cost.

Maul's entire existence had consisted of training, of exercise and instruction. Early in his life, before his voice had deepened, Maul had learned the intricate movements and forms of the teräs käsi fighting style, the patterns of movements based on the hunting characteristics of various beasts throughout the galaxy: Charging Wampa, Rancor Rising, Dancing Dragonsnake, and many more. He had practiced gymnastics in environments ranging from zero-g to gravity fields twice that of Coruscant's. He had mastered the intricate and dangerous use of the double-bladed lightsaber. And all for one purpose: to be the best possible tool of his master's will.

But he had not learned just how to fight. His master's teaching had encompassed far more than that. He had also learned stealth, subterfuge, intrigue.

*What is done in secret has great power.*

One of his earliest memories was that of being taken to the Jedi Temple. Both he and Sidious had been disguised as tourists.

His master's command of the dark side had been sufficient to cloak them from being sensed by their enemies, as long as they did not enter the building. That had been unlikely anyway—the Jedi Temple was not open for tourism. They had stood there for the better part of the day, Darth Sidious pointing out to him the various faces of their foes as the latter came and went. It had been thrilling to Maul to realize that he could stand in the presence of the Jedi, could listen to his master whisper to him of their ultimate downfall, without them having any inkling of the fate that ultimately awaited them.

That was the great glory and hidden strength of the Sith: the fact that there were only two, master and apprentice. Their clandestine operations could take place practically under the very noses of the Jedi, and the fools would not suspect until it was too late. The day of the Jedi's downfall would be soon—very soon.

It could not happen soon enough for him.

*Anger is a living thing. Feed it and it will grow.*

The Twi'lek he had fought had not been the first Jedi he had crossed lightsabers with, but he was not far from having that honor. It had been exhilarating to know that he, Darth Maul, was better in combat than his hated foes. He longed to battle one of the truly great Jedi warriors: Plo Koon, perhaps, or Mace Windu. That would be a true test of his skill. And he had no doubt that such an opportunity would come to him. His hatred of the Jedi was strong enough that it alone would bring such a confrontation into existence.

Soon.

He came to his senses, realizing he was lying in a pile of trash not far from where the Jedi had engineered his own doom and nearly that of Maul's, as well. A Devaronian scavenger was about

to appropriate his lightsaber, which lay nearby. Maul glared at the encroacher, who lost no time in making himself scarce.

Maul seized his lightsaber and rose to his feet. His muscles, bones, and tendons screamed in pain, but pain meant nothing. The only important question was, was his mission finally complete?

A hundred meters down the street lay the wrecked remains of the skycar. Maul investigated it. It had been smashed beneath large chunks of ferrocrete and durasteel that would take too long to move, even with the aid of the Force. He opened his senses, trying to determine if his enemies' bodies lay beneath the rubble. What the Force told him made him clench a fist in fury.

The skycar was empty.

It was possible that the explosion had flung them clear before the debris collapsed. If so, their bodies might have been dragged away by those who scrounged the streets. But he wasn't certain that was what had happened. Given the kind of luck the Corellian had had so far, Maul knew he would have to see Pavan's dead body—preferably after his head had parted company with his shoulders, thanks to Maul's lightsaber—before he would feel comfortable reporting to Lord Sidious that the problem was at last resolved.

Maul was actually starting to feel something of a grudging respect for this Lorn Pavan. Although some of the hustler's continued avoidance of his fate could be ascribed to luck, some, the Sith apprentice had to admit, was due to Pavan's survival instincts. Of course, he would not have lasted as long as he had downlevels if he had not had a roachlike ability to sense and avoid danger. Nevertheless, Maul was slightly impressed. Not that it mattered. His quarry's skill at staying alive would just make Maul's inevitable triumph all the more satisfying.

He began to search the area, questing along the filaments of the dark side, seeking the route they had taken. He saw the kiosk almost immediately. Even without the Force to guide him to it, he knew this could be the only logical escape route. Unfortunately, the skycar's explosion had covered the underground entrance with debris.

Maul was running out of patience. Five meters farther up the street he spied a ventilation grid that appeared to open onto the same underground conduit as the kiosk. He lit one end of his lightsaber and jabbed it into the grid. The blade sliced easily through the metal slats. In a second the grate had dropped down into the conduit, and Darth Maul followed it.

He landed lightly. The entire tunnel was shaking as with the roar of some titanic beast. Maul looked up to see a driverless freight transport bearing down on him at better than one hundred kilometers an hour.

Anyone else, even a trained athlete raised in a heavier gravity field, would have been crushed to paste. But Maul seized the Force, let it whip him up and to the side as if he were attached to a giant elastic band. The metal behemoth missed him by millimeters.

Maul found himself standing on the narrow lip of a walkway that ran along one side of the conduit. He looked about, questing with his eyes and his mind. Yes—they had escaped down here. The trail still remained.

They could run, but they couldn't hide.

Darth Maul resumed the hunt.

Lorn's first thought as he returned to partial consciousness was to wonder why someone had gone to the trouble to kidnap him off Coruscant and drop him on one of the galaxy's gas giant worlds—Yavin, possibly. Obviously this was what had happened,

because gravity and atmospheric pressure were slowly crushing him into a boneless putty. His head, particularly. And whatever it was that he was breathing, it wasn't anything close to a comfortable oxygen-nitrogen mixture.

Or maybe he'd been parked in a too-close orbit around the event horizon of a black hole, and the tidal forces were pulling him apart. That would explain why his head hurt so abominably, and why he couldn't feel his hands and feet.

Lorn blinked, then saw dim light the color of verdigris. He realized he was lying on a cold stone floor, his arms and legs bound. The light, faint and sickly though it was, was still too much for his headache to deal with. *Must've* really *tied one on this time,* he thought. *Maybe I-Five's right about those liver cells, not that I'd ever admit it to him.*

But something was still wrong with this picture. He knew he could be a fairly obstreperous drunk on occasion, but he'd never reached the point of obnoxiousness where he'd had to be trussed up. Hmm. Maybe he'd better open just one eye again—carefully, of course—and take another look around.

Staring at him from no more than a handbreadth away was a face unimagined in his worst nightmares.

Lorn gasped and instinctively jerked backwards, trying to get away from the monstrous apparition. The sudden movement set off a thermal detonator that someone had unkindly implanted in his skull, and the pain was so amazingly intense that for a moment he forgot about the *thing* that had been inspecting him.

But only for a moment.

It moved closer to him, staring at him—no, Lorn corrected himself, not staring: you had to have eyes to stare. Just about every component of its face was repulsive in the extreme, but the

eyes were unquestionably the worst. Worse than the dead bluish-white skin and the stringy, mosslike hair, worse than the wide lip-less gash of a mouth, like a cavern entrance filled with yellowed stalagmites and stalactites, worse even than the skull-like nub of a nose, with two vertical slits for nostrils.

The eyes were definitely worse than all that.

Because it didn't seem to have any. From the heavy ridges at the sloping base of the forehead down to the gaunt cheekbones, there was nothing but albino skin. Behind that skin, where the orbital sockets should have been, Lorn could see two egg-shaped organs moving restlessly, swiveling independently of one another. Occasionally they were occluded by darker hues, as if membranes beneath the skin were sliding over them.

Lorn had dealt with a large variety of alien species in the past few years. One grew used to seeing all kinds of creatures on the streets and skywalks of Coruscant. But something was terribly, obscenely *wrong* about this monster's appearance—him and the others like him, for now that Lorn's eyes had adjusted to the wan light, he saw that there were at least a dozen, maybe more, hunkered down in a semicircle around him.

He backed up still farther, scrabbling on his heels and elbows—not an easy task considering that his head still felt large enough to warrant its own orbit. The creatures moved closer to him, shambling grotesquely on bent legs and knuckles. Lorn glanced around desperately, looking for I-Five, feeling the beginnings of a scream welling in his throat. He saw Darsha Assant lying about two meters away from him on the filthy stone floor, and I-Five an equal distance on the other side. The Padawan seemed to be unconscious, but she was breathing normally as far as he could tell. He noticed with no great surprise that her

lightsaber no longer dangled from her utility belt. I-Five was lying with his face turned toward Lorn, and the human could see that the droid's photoreceptors were dark. His master control switch had been turned off.

They were in a large chamber, the ceiling supported by groined pillars. The light—what there was of it—emanated from more of that phosphorescent lichen covering the walls. The place looked like a junkyard; pieces of broken equipment and machinery were lying here and there. It smelled like a charnel house.

Looking closer, he saw that scattered among the technological debris were what looked like gnawed bones of various species.

Lorn carefully adjusted his position, getting his legs underneath him. His head was still screaming like a Corellian banshee bird, but he tried to ignore the pain. If he could reach I-Five and flip the master switch on the back of his neck, the droid could probably make short work of these subterranean horrors. Their ears seemed to be abnormally large; no doubt they relied primarily on hearing to guide them through the darkness. One good screech from I-Five's vocabulator should send them stampeding back into the shadows where they belonged.

He was fairly certain he knew what they were now, although the knowledge gave him little comfort. Quite the opposite, in fact. Occasionally, since his fall from grace had landed him on the mean streets of Coruscant, he had heard rumors of devolved humanoid creatures called Cthons, lurking deep within the underground labyrinths of the planetary city. Dwelling in darkness for thousands of generations had robbed them of their eyes, so the story went. Supposedly they retained some rudimentary working knowledge of technology, which would explain the electroshock net they had used to capture Lorn and his comrades.

Supposedly also they were cannibals.

Lorn had never given any credence to the stories before now. He had assumed they were just tales used to scare recalcitrant children into obedience, just another of the many stories that sprouted like mushrooms on the downlevels streets. But now it was obvious that this particular rumor was all too real.

The Cthons moved closer. One of them positioned himself— or herself; though they were all naked save for ragged loincloths, their skins were so loose and flabby that it was hard to determine what sex any individual was—between Lorn and I-Five.

*This is the way it ends,* Lorn thought, feeling surprisingly little fear. *What a unique career arc: To go from being a prosperous business affairs clerk in the employ of the Jedi to a fugitive about to be devoured by mutant cannibals in the bowels of Coruscant. Didn't see that one coming.*

The Cthons moved closer still. One reached out a pale, hirsute arm toward him. Lorn tensed. He would fight, of course. He would not be led like a nerf to the slaughter. He could at least do that much.

*I'm sorry, Jax,* he thought as they closed in on him.

**O**bi-Wan Kenobi activated the descent repulsor array and dropped out of the airstream traffic flow. As his skycar descended in a tight spiral down toward the blanket of mist that marked the inversion layer, the young Padawan watched the lights in the monads and skyscrapers all around him blinking on. It was just before sunset, and the cerise light faded fast as he descended.

He glanced at the instrument panel, reassuring himself that he was homing in on the coordinates for the safe house in the Crimson Corridor. He noted some deterioration in the appearance of the buildings as the skycar dropped deeper—peeling paint, a few broken windows—but it wasn't until he passed through the mist that he noticed a real change. Now shattered and lightless windows gaped like wounds on all sides, and the few skywalks stretching between the structures were deserted, their railings sagging or broken.

*It's a different world,* he thought. Descending through the cloud layer was almost like making a hyperspace jump to some decrepit outlying planet. Obi-Wan had known that slums like

this existed here and there on Coruscant's surface, of course; he just hadn't realized that one lay this close to the Jedi Temple— less than ten kilometers away.

Once through the mist, the skycar's head- and groundlights activated, and he could see fairly clearly. The vehicle came to a hovering stop a few centimeters from the cracked surface of the street. The area was relatively deserted, save for a dozen or so mendicants of various species who fled as his skycar touched down. That was odd, Obi-Wan thought; one would expect them to crowd around, begging, instead. Perhaps it had to do with the fact that this was Raptor territory after dark.

He looked around and saw Darsha's skyhopper parked not far away, in the shadow of a building. He deactivated the safety field and vaulted over the skycar's edge.

When Master Qui-Gon had told Obi-Wan that Darsha Assant was missing, the Padawan had volunteered to search for her before his mentor could tell him to. He and Darsha were not close friends, but she had been in several of his classes and he had been quite impressed with the way she had excelled in her studies. He had mock-dueled with her twice: he had won one match, she the other. They had even shared a mission once. She was bright, and she knew it; she was quick-witted, and she knew that, too. But she didn't come across as conceited. Obi-Wan thought that Darsha had the makings of a fine Jedi Knight in her. And it wouldn't take much coaxing to get him to admit that she was pleasant to look at, as well.

Even if she had been someone he couldn't stand to be around, he would have accepted without question the assignment to search for her. It was, after all, his duty. But Darsha, he felt, was special, even among the Jedi. He hoped she had not come into harm's way. Now, however, looking at her skyhopper, he found that hope fading fast.

For the craft had been gutted. There was little left of it except the frame; the drive turbines, the power generators, the repulsor engines, and just about everything else that wasn't too heavy to carry had been stolen. The instrument panel had a huge gash in it, as if some kind of vibroblade had punched through it, although there was no weapon in sight.

Obi-Wan checked the craft's interior carefully, using a small but powerful glow light. He found no evidence of foul play in the vehicle, but he did see a few spots of blood on the ground nearby. It was impossible to tell if it was human blood or not.

Something flickered at the edge of his vision.

Obi-Wan froze, then slowly turned to look. He saw nothing threatening in the vespertine shadows. Nevertheless, there had definitely been movement—stealthy, furtive movement. He had been thoroughly briefed on the dangers of street gangs and predators, both human and nonhuman, in the Crimson Corridor. It did not take an overactive imagination to assume that one of these threats might be lurking nearby, ready to strike. If there was a whole gang of footpads sizing him up, he would be hard put to defend himself, even with a lightsaber.

Fortunately, the lightsaber was not the only defense at his disposal.

Obi-Wan Kenobi reached out for the Force. It was there for him, as it always was. He let his awareness expand outward along its invisible corrugations, a psychic radar that searched and probed the darkness. If danger existed, the Force would find it.

His mind touched that of another: a will that felt weak and serpentine, more used to striking furtively from the shadows than in direct confrontation. A human mind.

Before the lurker was fully aware that he was being probed, Obi-Wan seized his will. The Force, Master Qui-Gon had told

him more than once, can have a strong influence on the weak-minded. Though Obi-Wan was by no means anywhere near as accomplished a practitioner as his tutor, it didn't take much more than the skill of a novice to influence a mind as weak as this one.

"Come here," he said, his tone quiet and authoritative.

From out of the dusk emerged a young human male—probably around sixteen or seventeen standard years old, Obi-Wan estimated. He was wearing mostly rags and leather, topped by a ten-centimeter-high thatch of green hair held in place by an electrostatic field. The Padawan could feel the sullen guilt and fear in the other's mind—the fear that his captor somehow knew that he and his gang had assaulted the other Jedi.

"Where is she?" Obi-Wan asked.

"I—I don't know who you're—"

"Yes, you do. The Jedi Padawan who owned this skyhopper. Tell me quickly, or—" Obi-Wan let his hand drop, to rest suggestively on the lightsaber hilt hanging at his belt. He wouldn't go so far as to actually use it, but even a veiled threat could work wonders.

He could feel Green Hair's fear and hatred, like an acid in his brain. It was difficult to keep his composure.

"All *right*—we messed with her a little, but we took the hint when she chopped off Nig's hand, y'know? I mean, she wanted the ship so bad, she could have it, right?"

"Where did she go?"

Green Hair shook his head and shrugged. Obi-Wan listened to the Force and knew he was telling the truth.

"Was there a Fondorian male with her?"

"Him?" Green Hair grinned crookedly. "The hawk-bats got *him*. What was left, the street trash dragged off."

Obi-Wan felt despair pushing in on him, as bleak as the

downlevels darkness that surrounded them. It appeared that Darsha's mission had been a total failure that might very well have culminated in her death. He would, of course, comb the area, ask any other locals he could find, and try to sense her through the Force, but given the time that had passed and the inhospitable environment he was searching . . .

"There was some more Jedi," Green Hair said abruptly. "I didn't see it, but I heard about it."

"Heard about what?"

"Some o' my bloods saw somebody on a speeder bike chasin' another in a skycar. He caught up with 'em and there was this big brawl. The speeder blew up an' the 'car crashed over on Barsoom Boulevard. Big blowup. That's what I heard."

Obi-Wan frowned in puzzlement. The Jedi Green Hair spoke of could only be Darsha and her mentor, Anoon Bondara.

He questioned Green Hair more thoroughly, making sure he would be able to find the crash site, then released him from thrall. The boy lost no time in making himself scarce. Obi-Wan got back in his skycar and headed for the location, more puzzled than ever. Even under careful questioning and mind-probing, Green Hair had stuck to his story: Two robed and cowled figures had been seen first in a high-speed pursuit and subsequently on a docking ledge, battling each other with all the ferocity of a couple of Tyrusian manglers. The battle had culminated in two big explosions as both the speeder bike and the skycar had blown up.

Obi-Wan shook his head as he piloted the skycar down the dark and narrow streets. Speculation was fruitless at this point. With any luck, all would be made clear when he reached the crash site.

\*　　\*　　\*

Very little had been disturbed since the crash of the skycar; in this part of town it might be months before a droid cleanup crew was assigned to deal with the wreckage. But few of Obi-Wan's questions were answered by investigating the torn and twisted hulk of the skycar, or the nearby pile of debris that was once a docking ledge. So much rubble was piled on Master Bondara's vehicle that Obi-Wan couldn't even tell if bodies were still in it or not. The Force did not seem to indicate that a Jedi had died here, but it had been several hours since the occurrence, and what perturbation remained in the energy field was subtle and hard to read. Possibly Master Qui-Gon Jinn could read it, but Obi-Wan was not that skilled yet.

Still, he sensed something disturbing here. The sense of a powerful evil, a corruption. Obi-Wan glanced about him nervously. The street was mostly deserted and quiet, but it wasn't a peaceful silence. Instead it bore a feeling of trepidation, of lurking danger. The temptation to snatch his lightsaber up and activate it was almost overwhelming. The combination of few street lights, towering buildings, and omnipresent cloud cover made it impossible to see more than a meter or two in any direction. An entire army could be surrounding him, invisible in the breathing darkness, poised to attack.

Obi-Wan shook his head, attempting to banish the sudden surge of uneasiness. *There is no emotion; there is peace.* Giving in to paranoia would not further his mission. He had to operate from the assumption that either Darsha or Master Bondara or both were still alive. Based on that assumption, he had to find an eyewitness to the battle who could give him a better account of what had happened. Facts were what he needed, not speculation and hearsay. *There is no ignorance; there is knowledge.*

He knew this was true. Nevertheless, it was hard to quell the anxiety he felt as he started toward a nearby tavern to ask some questions of the locals.

Two hours later Obi-Wan was more baffled than ever.

He had found few people who were willing to talk with him without being prodded by the Force, and what little he had learned was confusing and contradictory. One thing was for certain: A lot had been happening in this neighborhood recently, even by the rough-and-tumble standards of the Crimson Corridor.

He had found no one who would admit to being an eyewitness to the battle, but several had seen the high-speed chase between the skycar and the speeder bike. Some had said there were Jedi involved, some said one or none. Some swore a droid was piloting the skycar. Some were certain a Jedi had been riding the bike, others were not. He had also learned that a black-clad figure—possibly, according to one, the figure who had been on the speeder bike—had been somehow implicated in yet another explosion, this one in a block of cubicles a few streets away. Several people had been killed in that blast, including a human bounty hunter. There had also been a fracas at a nightclub owned by a local Black Sun vigo, one Yanth the Hutt, in which a cowled character had been somehow implicated.

None of this seemed to make any kind of sense.

He had spoken to one witness who seemed certain that the two Jedi in the skycar had been a Twi'lek male and a human female. That would be Anoon Bondara and Darsha, Obi-Wan surmised. But he still had no clue as to whether they had survived the explosions. His informant said they had been riding with a human male and a droid.

After some consideration, Obi-Wan decided his best bet would be to investigate the nightclub. If Yanth, the owner, was a member of Black Sun, he might know more about all this than the street rabble.

"I've got a bad feeling about this," he murmured to himself as he headed for the nightclub.

**A**s from a far distance, Darsha heard the sounds of a struggle. It seemed to rise and fall, the sounds breaking over her like oceanic waves as her mind struggled to find its way back to consciousness. She wished dimly that whatever was going on would stop, so that she could slip back down into the depths of the black well out of which she was reluctantly rising. She had been through a lot of pain and fear lately, and she felt she deserved a rest.

But the altercation didn't subside; instead it grew louder. Now she recognized one of the voices: it was Lorn Pavan's. The other voices seemed to be nonhuman—mostly grunts and guttural bellows.

It was obvious that he was in some kind of trouble. In her semiconscious state Darsha didn't see any real reason why she should come to his aid. She didn't like him, and he'd made it perfectly clear that he wasn't overly fond of her. There didn't seem to be any personal animosity involved on his part; he just despised Jedi in general. In a way, that was even more insulting.

Darsha would rather someone base their dislike on her personality, not on an abstract that she represented. She could deal with enmity easier than bigotry.

It was becoming painfully obvious, however, that the struggle she was hearing wouldn't resolve itself anytime soon. And suddenly, in a rush of returning wakefulness, Darsha remembered what had happened: the attack by unseen foes in the tunnels, the electroshock net that had trapped them. She had been knocked out by the net's power field. Wherever she was now, it couldn't be any place healthy.

Darsha opened her eyes and managed to raise her head enough to see what was going on, even though doing so sent a stab of pain like a blaster bolt through her skull. What she saw kicked her adrenal glands into overdrive. Pavan was struggling with several creatures—hard to tell in the dim light exactly what they were, other than bipedal and definitely subhuman. He had apparently managed to knock one of them unconscious; the limp form lay on the mossy stone floor next to the droid, who seemed to be out of commission, as well.

Darsha pushed herself up to a kneeling position. The movement attracted the attention of several of the creatures who were circling Pavan, looking for an opening. They turned and shambled toward her, their snarling mouths stretched wide. She saw the undulating skin that covered their eye sockets, and the horror of the sight caused her heart to stutter.

Darsha gathered the Force to her. Still on her knees, she thrust out both arms, fingers splayed wide, hurling twin waves of invisible power toward them. The unexpected surges struck them, causing them to stagger back. They howled in mingled fear and anger, an eerie ululation that reverberated in the chamber.

Darsha took advantage of the momentary respite to stagger

to her feet. She reached instinctively for her lightsaber, and wasn't really surprised to find it missing from its belt clip. She had no time to look for it, because now several more of the subhumans were lumbering her way. Though they moved slowly, it was hard to avoid them, given how many there were in the relatively small chamber.

Pavan, who had two of them hanging on to each arm, saw she was awake. "Cthons!" he shouted to her. "They're cannibals!"

His words sent a chill of fear and repugnance down Darsha's spine. Like most people who lived on Coruscant, she had heard the legends of the sightless subhumans, but had never considered them based in reality. Fear gave her new strength and focus, and once again she drove them back by throwing Force waves at them. But they were stronger than they looked, and extremely tenacious; though battered off their feet by her power, they picked themselves up and came back for more, moaning and howling.

Pavan was doing worse than she was, having only his fists and feet to fight with. The Cthons were dragging him toward one of the darker recesses of the chamber.

"I-Five's been deactivated!" he called to her. "He can help us!"

*Yes, of course!* Darsha thought. She'd had firsthand experience of how strong the droid was when he'd carried both her and Pavan to safety after the skycar's crash. She looked at I-Five and could just see in the dim light that the master switch on the back of his head was in the off position.

Could she reactivate him? She wasn't sure. There was no way she could reach him physically, and she wasn't at all confident in her control of the Force, particularly under these circumstances.

It was one thing to use it like a bludgeon against an enemy, but quite another to flip a small switch several meters away.

She pushed the doubts away. She *had* to do it—or she and Pavan were quite literally dead meat.

She focused her mind on the droid, felt the tenuous, intangible connection between her thoughts and the cool metal of the control switch. She pushed against it with her mind, feeling the resistance.

A Cthon grabbed her from behind.

Darsha bit back a cry of shock and surprise. She felt her attenuated mental grip on the tiny nub of durasteel almost slip free, and with all the power of her will she *thrust* the Force tendril against it. Then the Cthon yanked her backwards, and she felt its clammy fingers, like the hands of a corpse, reach up and close about her neck.

A shrill screech, unlike anything she had ever heard before, suddenly filled the air. It was more than just unpleasant; it was actively painful. It drilled into both ears and expanded in the center of Darsha's head like something alive and voracious. The Cthon released her and she staggered forward, clapping her hands over her ears. That helped somewhat, but not nearly enough.

But it was obvious that the stridency was causing the Cthons far more pain than she was feeling. Which made sense, certainly; here in the eternal darkness the creatures would have grown over generations to depend on their ears far more than their vestigial eyes. Their shrieks and moans of agony were barely audible above the continuing screech, which Darsha now realized was coming from I-Five.

The reactivated droid was standing. He moved quickly, pushing through the dazed group of subhumans toward Lorn Pavan

while the earsplitting sound continued to emanate from his vocabulator. The Cthons who had been dragging Pavan away were writhing in pain like their comrades, leaving him free.

Darsha followed in the droid's wake. I-Five grabbed Pavan and headed for the dark aperture of a tunnel in the chamber's far wall. No matter where it led, it had to be someplace better than where they were now.

But the chances of their reaching it were not looking good. Though obviously still in pain, the Cthons were starting to rally, no doubt motivated by the sight of their dinner making an escape. Darsha hurled more invisible blows to either side, clearing a path for the three of them. But a large group was gathering ahead to block their escape.

Darsha looked about desperately for something to use as a weapon—and saw her lightsaber lying perhaps five meters away on a mound of mingled offal and techno-trash. With a gasp of surprise and gratitude, she reached out for it with her hand and her mind. The device flew from its position across the intervening space. A Cthon somehow sensed it sailing through the air and made a clumsy leap that almost intercepted it. He sprawled on the ground at her feet, and Darsha felt the lightsaber smack into her hand. She thumbed the activator button and heard the satisfying *thrum* as the yellow blade boiled out to its full length.

She gripped the weapon in both hands, weaving it in a figure-eight defensive pattern. It was hard to concentrate, as I-Five was still emitting his painful siren cry and her head was feeling like it would come apart at any minute. She hoped that some of the Cthons would at least get hit by the shrapnel.

Against the combined threats of her lightsaber and the droid's howl, the subhumans had no choice but to fall back. The three entered the tunnel at a dead run, I-Five in the lead and

Darsha bringing up the rear. Their former captors' enraged cries followed them, but that was all.

The phosphorescent lichen that covered the chamber's walls continued only a short way into the underground passage and then died out, save for sporadic patches that did little or nothing to relieve the darkness. I-Five illuminated his photoreceptors, revealing a brick-lined tunnel barely high enough for Lorn to stand upright. It did not run in a straight line, but instead meandered gently, first left, then right.

I-Five shut off the screeching sound once they were out of sight of the Cthons' chamber. They dropped from a run to a fast walk. Darsha had to hustle to keep up with the long-legged strides of the other two, and each time her boots contacted the hard pavestones she felt a new spear of pain go through her head. She wished devoutly that one of the Force's attributes was an ability to cure headaches.

As if reading her mind, the droid began making another sound: a low trilling that was as unlike the discordant noise of before as it was possible to be. It seemed to somehow penetrate her bones and muscles—indeed, her very cells—and subtly vibrate them, flushing away the toxins and pains that had filled them. After a few minutes the sound ceased, leaving her feeling, if not in top shape, at least markedly better.

After walking for another few minutes, I-Five stopped. Pavan and Darsha stopped, as well, the latter deactivating her lightsaber as she did so.

"My sensors indicate no one is following us," the droid said.

"Let's keep moving anyway," Pavan replied. "You were wrong before, remember?"

"Don't be so hard on him," Darsha said. "After all, he just saved our lives again."

"Much as I crave validation, I feel constrained to point out that you saved us this time," said I-Five. "I couldn't have done anything if you hadn't reactivated me." Though the droid was speaking to Darsha, he was looking at Lorn Pavan.

Pavan hesitated a moment, scowling. Then he looked at Darsha and said, "He's right. Thanks."

It obviously had taken a herd of wild banthas to drag the words out of him. Why did he hate Jedi so much? Darsha wondered. Aloud, she said, "No problem. You saved my life back in the skycar. Now we're even."

Pavan gave her a look that seemed equal parts gratitude and resentment. He said to I-Five, "Let's find the fastest route back to the surface. Even the Raptors look friendly compared to what lives down here."

The droid nodded and started walking again. The two humans followed. Neither of her companions spoke further, which suited Darsha just fine. She strode along behind Lorn Pavan, wondering once again what caused his intense antipathy toward her and her order.

She could simply ask him, of course. The only reason she hadn't done so yet was because there hadn't been any time to; they'd been on the run from the moment they'd met. But her instincts told her that now would not be a good time to bring it up, so she kept quiet. Maybe after they emerged from these labyrinthine catacombs—if they ever did—she would broach the subject. For now it seemed best to just let it lie.

"I'm surprised the Cthons gave up so easily," Pavan said abruptly to the droid. "They didn't even follow us into this tunnel."

"I've been wondering about that, as well," I-Five said. "Two possibilities come to mind—neither of them particularly pleasant

to contemplate. The first is that they may be planning another trap of some sort."

"That's what I was thinking," Pavan replied. "What's your second scenario?"

"That there may be something up ahead that even the Cthons fear."

Pavan did not reply. They trudged on through the bowels of the planetary city, and Darsha mulled over the droid's words. They certainly didn't paint a cheerful picture of the immediate future. Something even worse than the Cthons?

Darth Maul followed his instincts. They led him a short distance along the transit tube and down a stairwell, and from there into a dark tunnel. He moved swiftly but cautiously. He knew that this deep in the guts of the planet there lived creatures that even a Sith Lord would have a hard time dealing with. But they would not keep him from overtaking his quarry and completing his mission.

He would kill Pavan first, for two reasons: because he was the primary target, of course, but also because Maul would then be free to take his time killing the Jedi. He did not anticipate her putting up much of a fight. His impression was that she had been naught but an apprentice to the Twi'lek he had killed, and thus not much of a potential opponent. But she was still a Jedi, and he could toy with her for a bit before delivering the fatal blow. He felt he deserved some entertainment as partial recompense for all the trouble they had put him to.

The subterranean course he followed was as dark as a coal sack nebula. Even Maul, whose eyes were far more sensitive to

light than a human's, could barely see enough to make his way. But he was not depending on vision so much as on the perturbations in the Force to guide him. Now he could sense them ahead—he would not go astray.

Nevertheless, he felt impatient. He wanted to run, to rapidly close the distance to his prey, to be done with all this. But only fools rush into unknown and hostile territory, and Darth Maul was no fool.

He had pushed his hood back the better to hear anything that might warn him of a threat. Then he paused abruptly, listening to faint vibrations.

He knew he was not alone.

The dank and miasmal air was still, and even the disturbance he sensed in the Force was of the most subtle nature. Still, he had no doubt that he was being watched. The almost nonexistent light told him that he was standing in a wide part of the tunnel, with several side passages opening into it. It was from these that he suspected the attack would come.

Moving very slowly, he dropped his gloved hand to the lightsaber dangling at his belt.

He did not expect the assault to come from above, but he was not taken by surprise when it did. He sensed the electroshock net dropping down from overhead, and knew that if he tried to slash it with his energy blade, the power surge would reverberate back down his arm and through him with devastating effect. So instead he dived forward, executing a smooth shoulder roll that carried him beyond the reach of the mesh. He came to his feet and spun about, lighting both ends of his weapon as he did so.

And then they were upon him.

Darth Maul once again abandoned himself to the dark side,

letting it guide his movements and power his strikes. He stood in the center of a maelstrom of hulking silhouettes, visible only in brief stroboscopic flashes as the whirling energy blades struck them down. He recognized them from his studies of Coruscant's indigenes: Cthons, degenerate subterranean humanoids, considered by many scholars to be apocryphal. His master would be most interested to learn that they actually existed. Assuming, of course, he did not slay them all.

By the time they broke off the attack and retreated, howling, into the side tunnels, there were several fewer in existence than had been moments before. Maul had killed, as best he could count in the darkness, nine of the loathsome creatures.

He moved on, continuing to follow the trail and wondering if Pavan and the Jedi had encountered the Cthons, as well. If they had, he felt it strongly possible that they had not survived. Perhaps his job had been done for him. That would be a disappointment, as he would then be deprived of the pleasure of the kill, but at least the mission would be at an end.

Of course, he could not assume that this was the case, not until he found definite evidence. The human had certainly proven harder to kill than he had anticipated so far.

He pressed ahead through the everlasting night, alert for the possibility of more attacks.

As Lorn followed I-Five through the dark tunnel, he considered various possible solutions to his situation. There didn't seem a lot of them. In all his years as a businessman, information broker, and even working for the Jedi, he certainly hadn't come across anything this challenging before. Pursued by the Sith—who weren't even supposed to exist—into the deepest pits of the

city where flesh-eating cannibals stalked him . . . it was a challenge, no doubt about it.

Assuming that they made it back aboveground and were able to return to the civilized levels of society, what should his next move be?

He knew that the Padawan planned on taking him straight to the Jedi Temple so that he could share his information with Mace Windu and the other council members. But that event was not anywhere near the top of Lorn's list of desires. Certainly the Jedi would be best at protecting him from the Sith—assuming their tracker had not been killed in the explosion—but as far as he was concerned it would be a solution almost as bad as the problem. To be a resource held and *used* by the Jedi? It was a sickening thought, one that awoke far too many memories Lorn had worked hard to put away. So instead of giving in to the feelings that threatened to overwhelm him, he considered his other obvious option: *Run.*

The key question was how to get on board a ship that could take him and I-Five far enough away to avoid being tracked by both the Sith and the Jedi. The spice transport I-Five had arranged passage on had already left, but there was certainly no dearth of ships at the spaceports. Once they were off Coruscant it would be easier. It was a big galaxy, after all. There couldn't be that many Sith out there, or there would have been rumors that the Jedi would have picked up by now. And if there were only a few, Lorn reasoned, it wouldn't really be in the Sith's interests to spend much time tracking down one low-life information broker.

So that was the plan: get on a fast ship, maybe a smuggler, and leave Coruscant behind. He didn't know how he was going to pay for passage yet, but he would figure something out. They

could hightail it out to some backwater planet like Tatooine, hole up in the Dune Sea or the Jundland Wastes for a while, become part of the scenery. After a few years he could maybe open a tavern in some place like Mos Eisley. It wasn't a particularly thrilling life to contemplate, but at least it was a life.

Of course, I-Five might not be too happy about all that sand. Droids tended to need a lot of oil baths in environments like Tatooine's. Lorn looked thoughtfully at his partner walking ahead of him, the droid's metallic shell catching the reflected light from his photoreceptors. He would need to discuss this plan with him, see if I-Five had any new angles about the money end of it. The droid always seemed to have the right idea to complement Lorn's own. Of course, to do this he would have to get a few moments away from the Jedi.

Darsha. Her name was Darsha.

With an uncomfortable start, Lorn realized that he was feeling a little guilty at the thought of running out on her. He'd hated the Jedi with an all-inclusive passion for so long, it was hard to see any of them as individuals. After all, she had saved his life. It was difficult to get past the fact that she was a Jedi, but deep down he knew she was more than that: she was a person. Even likable, hard though that was to believe. And admirable in a number of ways, as well. Considering that her mentor had been killed in that explosion, she was carrying her grief fairly well. She'd saved all of them back there from the Cthons, too, no question about that.

*But not because she liked you. Only for the information.*

Lorn nodded to himself. He had to keep in mind that the Jedi did nothing that did not serve their own interests. Nothing. He would be doing himself no favors to walk into their clutches.

No, the best way out was to run. But to book passage on even a garbage scow was financially out of the question at this point.

And then he remembered—Tuden Sal! A few months past he'd given the owner of a successful chain of restaurants a tidbit of data that had helped the Sakiyan keep his liquor license. At the time Lorn had been flush and had charged only a few drinks—well, more than a few—but Sal had promised him a favor if the day ever came that he needed one.

As far as Lorn was concerned, that day was here. Tuden Sal was known to have strong contacts with several smuggling organizations, including Black Sun. He would know how to get them off Coruscant. Lorn felt revitalized by the possibility. This was a good plan—if he could just stay alive long enough to make it happen.

Ahead of him the droid slowed down. There was a change that Lorn could feel in the air. The echoes of their footsteps seemed to be hollower, more distant.

I-Five confirmed it.

"For those of you who are interested, the cavern we have just entered is roughly seven hundred standard meters wide, two hundred meters across, and festooned with stalactites starting forty or fifty meters above our heads. The ledge we are on, unfortunately, ends within seven meters, culminating in a drop that is—" The droid paused. "—currently not measurable with my modest sensory capabilities."

Terrific, Lorn thought.

Darsha heard Lorn Pavan release a long-suffering sigh. "Let me guess," he said, "we have to jump across."

"Not unless you've suddenly gained greater levitation powers than our Sith friend," the droid replied.

Darsha reached out with the Force. She sensed nothing other than the usual low-level life signs found everywhere.

"It feels empty," she said.

"Well, thank you, Mistress of the Force, but pardon me if I don't stop worrying," Pavan replied sarcastically. "It seems like your track record with that skill is still a little on the nebulous side."

She glared at Pavan. "It so happens that even Jedi Masters—which I am not—can be taken by surprise by things that are not Force-sensitive. Creatures who make very little ripples in the psychic flow are sometimes as good as invisible." Abruptly she remembered Bondara's leap toward the Sith, and fell silent.

After a moment, I-Five said, "The good news is that there seems to be a bridge."

Darsha moved forward to stand next to the droid. To keep her balance, she inadvertently put her hand on Pavan's shoulder, felt him tense and move away.

What was it with him? she wondered. What did he feel the Jedi had done to him to make him hate her and her kind so? Darsha remembered the look on Master Bondara's face when Pavan had introduced himself. Her mentor had known the man's name. What did that mean? She wasn't usually the prying type, but as soon as she got back to the Temple she'd do her best to find out.

Sure, she thought. As if there would still be a place for her in the Temple after all this. Fail the graduation exercise, get her Master killed, and wind up nearly eaten by a bunch of blind monsters. What kind of Jedi was that?

Not a very good one, she had to admit.

Darsha shook her head slightly, trying to banish encroaching despair. *There is no emotion, there is peace.* She had made mistakes, that was for sure, had probably lost any chance of ever becoming a Jedi. But until Master Windu or another member of the council officially reassigned her, she would continue to do her duty as best she saw it. She would get Lorn Pavan to the Temple because his information would be valuable to the council, could help maintain order against the misuse of power. It was what a Jedi would do, and so it was what she would do.

Thankfully, Pavan was not at all like Oolth the Fondorian. That one had been nothing but bluster and cowardice. Pavan was hard to read, but his actions so far had been those of a loyal, brave individual. The only thing that made him difficult to get along with was his hatred of the Jedi.

I-Five turned his photoreceptors up a few notches brighter and aimed them down at the bridge.

Several large ropes, gray and dusty with age, stretched out from the end of the tunnel beyond the limited light put out by the droid. Across the ropes had been laid an odd assortment of flat objects: boards, pieces of sheet metal, and other odds and ends. About the only thing they had in common was that they were all more or less flat and laid out in the direction the group wanted to go.

Lorn stepped out and jumped on one of the ropes. His balance was excellent, she noted, and he seemed to have a natural grace as he leapt. He saw her watching and pushed off extra hard on the last bounce, doing a quick somersault in midair.

"Ropes seem strong enough to me," he said, landing in a perfect double-foot plant. He waited a moment before answering her

unasked question. "I used to dabble in zero-g sports when I, uh, had a better lifestyle."

The droid broke in. "If you two are finished playing primitive mating games, maybe we could see about traversing this bridge. There may be a Sith pursuing us, if you recall."

"Excuse me?" Lorn said. *"Mating games?"*

Darsha felt indignant as well. "Your droid has a point. We need to keep moving." *Mating games, indeed,* she thought as she stepped onto the bridge. Not likely.

**L**orn wished he had a weapon.

Ahead of him, I-Five was armed with his finger blasters, as well as a few other tricks, and behind him Darsha had her lightsaber.

It wasn't that he felt they were in any particular danger at the moment, but a weapon—any weapon—would have given him a better sense of control over his own safety. While it was true that being unarmed did make him very alert, that didn't count for much with a sensor-equipped droid and a Force-sensitive Jedi for companions. Lorn felt he might as well be blind compared to them.

The going was slow; there were no handrails on the bridge, and it didn't look like the planks, lids, and other objects they were walking on had been attached very firmly to the support ropes. Indeed, he got the opinion that they had been added *after* the trestle had been formed. By the Cthons, perhaps? It was impossible to say. The bridge, Lorn noted, was of a very strange construction. In addition to the thick support cables that ran

along either side of the odd planks they walked on, there were vertical cables every few meters, some coming from the roof of the cavern, as might be expected, but others stretching from the bridge supports down into the darkness below.

What could all this be for?

He voiced the question.

"Based on the depth of the excavation," I-Five said, "I postulate that this could have been used as an access point for the underground oceans."

Possible, Lorn thought. Most of Coruscant, except for a few park areas, was built-over landmass. The water had to go somewhere.

"But why this bridge? I mean, it's a pretty primitive construction. Why not have a better way of getting around?"

The droid paused and looked over its shoulder, photoreceptors gleaming. "Perhaps the Cthons are responsible. Why can't you just be grateful that it's here where and when we need it?" I-Five resumed his progress forward.

Lorn raised an eyebrow. "Who pissed in *your* power supply?" he muttered.

He heard a chuckle from behind him. Great. Shot down by his own droid, and a *Jedi* got the laugh.

"I've got to ask," Darsha said. "How did you two wind up working together?"

"I'm impressed. You managed to come up with a topic even less interesting than his," I-Five said.

"Perhaps *you* aren't in need of a distraction," Darsha said, "but I sure could use one after the last few hours."

The woman had a point. Lorn, somewhat to his surprise, was the one who answered.

"I acquired I-Five a few years back when I first got started selling information. He was a protocol droid belonging to a rich family who left him with the children. The children were spoiled. They used to do things like make him jump off the roof to see how high he would bounce."

The memory surprised him with its intensity. He recalled the smell of the junk dealer's shop, a mixture of hydraulic fluid and the ozone of cooking circuits. It had been a humid day, and he was tired. He'd been fired from the Jedi Temple only a few days previously—not that *they* had called it that, of course.

*There is no emotion; there is peace.*

He'd read the words a thousand times when he had studied his enemies, fought their power over his life and Jax's. The words had never made sense before, and they didn't now.

"I figured that he might have some interesting secrets tucked away that I could use, so I bought him and brought him back on-line."

Lorn remembered the first words the droid had spoken. They had hit him with their utter hopelessness and helplessness, reminding him of his own.

"I am I-FiveYQ, programmed for protocol." There had been a pause after the initial main sequence had activated, and then the droid had asked, "Are you going to hurt me?"

Fury had blossomed in Lorn when he heard those words. He, too, had been broken into pieces recently, hurt savagely by those he had always been told would protect him.

The Jedi.

Darsha watched Lorn go quiet. Something seemed to have disturbed the man in the telling of his story, something that

she felt reticent to press him on. She decided to ask the droid instead.

"So he fixed you up, and you talked him into being your partner?"

I-Five answered after a pause.

"Lorn had been treated badly recently by his . . . employers. He felt that I was a kindred spirit, at least in potential. He had a friend who was handy at reprogramming droids install a top-of-the-line AI cognitive module, and deactivated my creativity damper, as well. As a result, I am as close to full sentience as any droid can be."

Intrigued, Darsha had to ask. "Who were his employers?"

I-Five glanced at Lorn before replying. "The Jedi."

She had suspected as much. That explained Master Bondara's recognition of the name. But why and how had the order treated Lorn so terribly? As far as she knew, they always dealt fairly with all employees who were non-Jedi. It didn't make any sense.

"How long have you trained at the Temple, Padawan Assant?"

It was plain, at least, that I-Five was a better droid than the one assigned to watch over the Fondorian in the safe house. That one hadn't recognized her as a Padawan.

"I've lived at the temple practically all my life. My formal training started when I was four," she said. And probably ended as of today, she added silently.

"I have been in business with Lorn Pavan for five standard years."

Then the droid went silent and left Darsha to her own thoughts. She realized that he had given her a clue to the mystery of Lorn's past.

She cast her thoughts back five years earlier. A new student had come to the temple back then, a two-year-old. Darsha remembered it because of the boy's high midi-chlorian count. She hadn't heard all the details of course, but the temple was a small pond, and ripples of any discord traveled quickly across its surface. Apparently the boy had been the son of a temple employee, who had been fired after he agreed to let his son be trained—why, she wasn't sure.

She gave Lorn a measuring look. If he were that student's father, and if his son had been taken from him without his consent, to be raised by the order—well, then it was certainly no wonder that he hated the Jedi.

She tried to imagine how she would feel in his place, but could not.

She looked at Lorn again and knew her suspicion was right. It certainly explained the man's attitude toward her and Master Bondara. She felt a great upsurge of pity for him then, so much so that she had to look away from him lest he read it in her expression.

She turned her focus back to their surroundings. It still rankled her that she hadn't noticed the Cthons before they had attacked, and she had vowed to herself not to let something like that happen again. Seeking out life-forms around her with the Force was a task with varying degrees of difficulty. Intelligent, Force-sensitive beings were usually easy to spot, of course, while lower-level forms—insects and animals, for example—did not broadcast nearly much of a blip on her mental radar. It was true that her mastery of the Force was nowhere near perfect, but that was no excuse for not doing the best she could. Her Twi'lek Master had once explained to her that sensitivity and fine-tuning came with time. "As a Padawan," he had said, "I

could push boulders around with ease, but seeds were next to impossible."

The thought reminded Darsha that it was time to check on possible pursuit again. Ever since they had entered the underground tunnels she had periodically scanned behind them for any signs of the Sith. She had not sensed his approach before the Cthon attack and was still hoping that he had been killed along with Master Bondara. But she couldn't take the chance of becoming complacent. She closed her eyes, keeping a slight cognizance of her immediate surroundings with the Force, and cast her awareness backwards, along the path they had traced across the old bridge, across the ledge, back into the tunnel.

A cold pillar of darkness formed in her mind as her awareness reached the tunnel. Power and energy seemed to radiate off of it like electricity from a thundercloud.

He was right behind them!

"Lorn, I-Five—the Sith is behind us, almost to the bridge!"

There was no response from either of them. Darsha opened her eyes and for a moment forgot about the imminent threat of the Sith.

They had found the reason why the Cthons had not pursued them.

Darth Maul advanced along the dark passage as fast as he dared. His sense of the Jedi and her companions grew stronger. Events had stretched out much longer than they should have; it was well past time to put an end to this.

Even so, he realized he was letting his eagerness overcome his caution. He deliberately slowed his pace, forcing patience. It would not do to be caught in some trap deep underground, to have half of the Sith in the galaxy lost due to carelessness.

He probed the darkness with renewed caution, sensing nothing dangerous ahead. The path of the Jedi was very fresh now; he could sense her presence. Not much farther.

And then he felt her find him. A clumsy probe it was, weak and hesitant. He was disappointed by it. It would be no real challenge to face someone so little steeped in the ways of the Force. Definitely not in the same class as her Master, the Twi'lek who had destroyed his speeder bike. He had been a worthy adversary. Not as good as Maul, of course, but that was to be expected.

He saw a faint light up ahead as he came around a curve in the tunnel. The echoes of his footsteps changed, and he realized he had reached a larger open space. He sent mental investigative tendrils of the Force outward, finding the boundaries of the ledge he stood on and the bridge just ahead. He sensed the Jedi on the bridge, perhaps halfway across, with Lorn Pavan and his droid just ahead of her, and beyond them.

Maul frowned. There was an odd quality ahead of them in the darkness—an empty spot in the mental topography of his probe. The light, which he now realized had to be from the droid's photoreceptors, gave him a brief glimpse of something huge and oddly insubstantial, like a weaving pillar of smoke ahead of the three on the middle of the bridge. Whatever it was he saw produced no corresponding vibration in the Force.

This was most odd.

Curious, he tried again. And again his probe met with nothingness. No, not exactly nothingness—the sensation was almost like encountering a surface so slick that one could find no purchase on it. It was like trying to see something that radiated only ultraviolet light. A strange phenomenon, but one he paid little attention to, because he now noted that the Jedi and Pavan were coming back along the bridge toward him.

He was surprised—pleased, but surprised. Surely the Padawan knew she could not defeat him. What, then, was her purpose? Had the other human continued ahead he would have been certain it was a delaying tactic, such as the Twi'lek had attempted earlier. But no—Pavan was accompanying the Jedi, along with his droid.

Once again Darth Maul admitted to being impressed by his prey. They were brave enough to come back and face him, and

smart enough to realize, finally, that it was pointless to keep running. Naturally they would die, but perhaps he would grant them some small measure of mercy, would be a trifle quicker in killing them than he had originally planned.

The woman had activated her lightsaber. As if that would make the slightest bit of difference, he thought.

He stepped forward onto the bridge and walked out to meet them.

Darsha had never seen anything like the creature that faced them on the bridge. It was *huge*, a great long body that stretched back at least as far as a hoverbus. As she watched, segment after segment wound over the side of the bridge, which shuddered in response as the motion brought the creature up from underneath and onto the structure with them. Its skin was composed of segmented overlapping plates, dotted here and there with small nodules that were perhaps two centimeters in diameter. Its head was capped by two great black eyes and a pair of curved mandibles, each easily as long as her leg. Below them were an array of small, clawed arms, and below that a series of short, thick legs.

The most amazing thing about it, however, was that its chitinous exoskeleton and internal organs seemed to be completely *transparent*. Apparently it had no internal skeletal structure, though how a creature that size could exist without the support of bones in a one-gravity field was beyond her understanding. Darsha saw a flash of reflected light from within its midsection, a few segments back from the head, and stared in disbelief. Momentarily illuminated by I-Five's photoreceptors was a pile of bones—human bones—that shifted in the thing's gut as it heaved

more of its quaking mass up onto the bridge. Also in the monster's digestive tract was a more recent acquisition—a partially digested Cthon. Thankfully, the droid's light failed to show it in great detail.

"Why didn't this thing show up on your sensors?" Lorn hissed at I-Five as the two backed hastily away from the giant beast.

"Perhaps you forget it was the *less*-expensive unit you had installed? Not the one with the extra sensitivity hi-band—something about saving money, as I recall . . ."

Those two would probably die arguing, Darsha thought as she backpedaled carefully, trying to keep her balance on the swaying bridge. The big question as far as she was concerned was why the Force hadn't warned her of this thing's presence. While it was true that sentient beings were on the whole easier to sense than nonsentient ones, a living creature this size and this close would have made a noticeable dent in the energy field even if it had a brain the size of a jakka seed.

As she retreated, Darsha sent a questing mental beam toward the creature—and felt it disappear. There was no psychic reverberation at all.

How could that be?

Her surprise nearly caused her to topple into the abyss. Her eyes told her the monster was there before them, her body felt the bridge swing and vibrate as it raised more of its bulk up out of the depths, but as far as sensing it via the Force, she felt nothing.

This was *impossible*. Maybe she wasn't an adept in the same league as Masters Yoda or Jinn, but she'd have to have zero-point-zero midi-chlorians in her bloodstream not to get some kind of reading on something that huge!

The creature reared up, some of its legs quivering in the light of I-Five's photoreceptors. There was a sound, a kind of dry rasping, which it seemed to make by rattling its segmented chitinous plates. It towered over them and opened its mouth.

Darsha activated her lightsaber as the droid fired both finger blasters, hitting several pairs of legs and scarring the creature's torso. It shrieked and slammed the upper length of its body back down on the bridge, nearly shaking the group off. They had to drop prone to keep from falling—which was lucky, because the stream of fluid that arced from the dark rictus of its mouth passed over their heads instead of coating them. Even as she clung to the metal plank beneath her, it was clear to Darsha that the stuff being spat by the monster was the same substance that made up the gray silken material of the bridge.

This thing had made the bridge.

Something about all this seemed familiar, but she couldn't recall how or why. A vagrant stream of the silk drifted toward the Padawan, and without thinking, she moved her lightsaber to intercept it. The silk burned as it hit the yellow energy beam, vaporizing into a cloud of smelly vapor.

The three got to their feet and started moving quickly back down the bridge toward the tunnel. Behind them the monster hitched itself forward, its multiple legs clinging to the silken bridge.

Well, I-Five's blasters hadn't worked, Darsha told herself. Let's see how well it stands up to a lightsaber.

Lorn was *really* wishing he had a weapon right about now. Forget hand blasters—he was far past desiring something that small. Maybe a tripod-mounted V-90, or a few plasma grenades. As long

as he was wishing, how about a ship-mounted turbolaser—with him safely inside the ship.

Where had this creature come from? One minute they were walking along the bridge, the next it was just *there*.

Retreat was the obvious choice. But just before this thing reared its ugly head, hadn't he heard Darsha say something about the Sith being right behind them?

Talk about being trapped between the Black Hole of Nakat and the Magataran Maelstrom.

At that moment he realized what the creature was.

When Lorn had worked for the Jedi he'd had access to a lot of literature about them and many related topics. After he'd learned that Jax was off-limits to him he'd spent weeks studying everything he could about the Jedi: their history, their powers, their strengths and weaknesses. He hadn't found anything that could help him, but he had come across some interesting and esoteric bits of knowledge—including, in one old text, stories about a supposedly extinct species of giant invertebrates that could, after a fashion, hide from the Force. What had it been called?

*Taozin*—that was it.

Apparently they *weren't* extinct.

At that moment Darsha dived past him and I-Five toward the monster, her lightsaber flashing.

"Darsha! Stop! It's a taozin!"

Darsha came out of her forward roll near the base of the creature, lightsaber extended. She thrust forward, angling the cut of the weapon to carve out a huge chunk of the monster's belly. *Let's see how hungry you are after your prey bites back,* she thought.

She executed the move as perfectly as she ever had in practice; Master Bondara would have been proud. The only problem was that it didn't work.

She watched in disbelieving shock as the yellow glow of her blade *diffused* as she sank it into the creature, losing its coherency and radiating in all directions. Darsha dodged back, narrowly avoiding the backsplash of her own weapon. The blade regained its congruency as she withdrew it from the creature's abdomen. The beast spasmed and roared angrily, its translucent flesh rippling in reaction; the strike had evidently hurt it, though not nearly as much as she had anticipated.

Darsha was so astonished by the result of her attack that she almost let the beast seize her with those sharp mandibles and pull her into the mouth that gaped overhead. At the last moment she scrambled back, waving the lightsaber to evaporate the gout of wet silk that it vomited toward her. At least the energy blade was good against that. She noted that the silk expellant became opaque only after it left the thing's mouth.

She realized belatedly that Lorn had called out something to her a moment ago. It hadn't registered at first, but now it did.

A taozin?

She remembered a few references to the beasts in her first history class. Thought to be extinct, they had been one of the few living creatures ever encountered that could not be perceived through the Force. Apparently someone had imported one to Coruscant some time in the past.

There was an old Jedi adage that Master Bondara had been fond of quoting: Any enemy may be defeated—at the right time.

This, Darsha realized, was not the right time.

She retreated toward Lorn and I-Five, who had gained another few meters. The taozin sprayed more webbing at them. Darsha pushed with the Force, deflecting the flow of sticky fluid when she could and vaporizing it with her lightsaber when she couldn't. There was nothing else to do but keep retreating—back into the clutches of the Sith.

Lorn, I-Five, and Darsha moved away from the taozin as fast as they could without dislodging the planks and plates that made up the bridge. These were held in place only by the stickiness of the web support cables, so the three couldn't break into a full run.

Fortunately, for all its many feet, the creature wasn't terribly fast. It lurched along behind them, launching webbing from time to time, which Darsha managed for the most part to deflect. As they retreated, I-Five spoke to Lorn in a low voice, pointing at the varied surfaces they were walking on.

"Help me remove some of these."

Lorn blinked. Did I-Five think the taozin might fall through the cracks? He started to question the droid's instructions, but then shrugged. Apparently his companion had a plan, which was more than Lorn had at the moment. It wasn't like he had anything better to do; why not spend the last few minutes of his life dismantling a bridge?

Darsha saw what they were doing and slowed her pace slightly, giving them more time to work. It went surprisingly quickly, considering that Lorn had no tools. I-Five used his finger blasters to sever the largest connecting points between each item and the supporting web, and they began tossing the various pieces over the side.

Lorn estimated that they were about three-quarters of the way back to the ledge. For an instant he entertained the crazy hope that maybe Darsha was wrong and the Sith actually wasn't behind them. Which would give them a little more space in which to retreat, although eventually they would reencounter the Cthons. That hope was quickly extinguished, however, when he glanced over his shoulder and saw the twin crimson blades of the Sith's lightsaber glowing behind them. So much for that idea. Their nemesis was there waiting for them.

He turned back to I-Five. "If you're going to do something, now would be a good time."

The droid glanced back at the Sith and shook his head. "Not yet. We need to be closer to the edge."

Lorn resisted the temptation to point out that he personally was already far closer to the edge than he cared to be. Instead he grabbed the corner of the next support piece—it looked like the cowling of a vaporator unit—and tugged it free of the bridge. Maybe he would jump before he let the Sith get him. He tossed the cowling over the bridge and watched it sail out of range of I-Five's photoreceptors. There was no sound of it hitting bottom. A plethora of ways to die were available here, none of them pleasant: eaten by a monster, decapitated by a lightsaber, or falling to smash against the planet's bedrock.

Lorn gritted his teeth and pulled another support free.

\*       \*       \*

Even with the aid of the Force, Darsha could barely manage to keep dodging fast enough as the taozin fired barrage after barrage of silken webbing at her. She had given up trying to influence it with the Force; its eerie invulnerability to that form of attack was evidently quite complete.

Despite the desperate straits she found herself in, however, Darsha had never felt so deeply *in* the Force. So much at peace, so . . . *calm.* The logical, rational side of her mind kept reminding her that she was trapped in a tightening vise, but for some reason that just didn't bother her. All that mattered was reacting to the monster's attack, letting the Force guide her movements, letting it fill the vessel that she had become. A constant current of challenge and opposition, attack and defense. As insane as it sounded, given the situation, she felt good. Better than good, in fact; she felt *great.*

Master Bondara had told her it would be like this. "When you are one with the Force," he had once said, "you are as nothing. A calm in the storm, a pivot to the lever. Chaos may rage around you, yet you are still. You will experience it someday, Darsha, and you will understand."

A distant part of her mind was sad that she could not tell him now, could not share the joy of discovery with him—but another part of her was somehow certain that he already knew.

She kept the lightsaber moving, keeping the taozin at bay. Although the blade was less than fully effective against the creature, it still respected the weapon's incandescent bite. She swung it again, grazing the thing's exoskeleton and shaving a couple of those small skin nodules off. They hit the bridge's surface and stuck to the webbing.

Whatever the droid's idea was, it had better be quick. Darsha could feel the presence of the Sith without seeking him now.

Darth Maul felt surprise as the Padawan and Pavan approached closer. Neither was facing him; instead, they were backing away from some huge, incredible creature.

Once it was close enough for him to see clearly, he recognized what it was. Darth Sidious had insisted that he read and reread every scrap of information available on the Jedi, as well as all data that related to them, no matter how obscurely. Knowledge of the enemy was power, his master had told him, and the Sith are the acme of power. An obscure HoloNet article on beasts that had, through various quirks of mutation and natural selection, become invisible in the Force had told him about the taozin.

They were supposed to be extinct—but then, so were the Sith. Sidious's apprentice sent a strong tendril of power molded from the dark side toward the creature—and felt the mental probe pass *through* it, as light penetrates transparisteel.

Fascinating.

Darth Maul stepped back a pace; his presence had drawn the creature's attention. It fired a thin runnel of webbing at him, and he let his connection to the Force take over, his lightsaber easily vaporizing the stream.

The creature paused and spat webbing at the Sith, who was just a few meters behind them now. I-Five pulled a final object from the bridge's surface, then spoke to Lorn and Darsha. "Now is the time," he said. "Hold on tightly to me."

The droid waited to be sure both humans had done as he

said, and then jumped over the side of the bridge, hooking one of his arms around the main support rope nearest him.

"Cut the support," he said to Darsha.

Darsha understood what his plan was now. It was a bold one, she had to give him that. He and Pavan had ripped away enough of the detritus that coated the bridge's webbing to render its supports unstable. When the Padawan's lightsaber bit through the thick support cable, the section of the structure they were clinging to collapsed. As the three began falling, I-Five fired upward, his finger blasters striking the juncture of every remaining plate and the support rope they were clinging to. Their momentum increased, and suddenly they were past the tail of the taozin, swinging in a very long arc toward the opposite side of the chasm.

In the distance they heard the Sith shout—in rage, it sounded like—as they kept falling. After a second or two I-Five no longer had to shoot to separate the support cable from the bridge decking. Their weight and momentum ripped the strand away for them as they fell.

"If you can slow our acceleration," the droid said to Darsha, "it will perhaps make this fall survivable."

Darsha closed her eyes, knitting her brow in concentration, and reached out for the Force once more. After a few seconds she could feel their speed decrease.

I-Five said, "I calculate that we will reach the other side of the cavern in about—"

The trio hit the rock wall on the opposite side of the cavern. Even with Darsha's use of the Force to slow them, the impact was considerable. Darsha gasped, the wind knocked out of her. She barely managed to keep her grip.

"Well, about now," I-Five finished.

"Thanks," Lorn managed, "for your accurate-as-usual timing."

"You're welcome."

They'd made it across. Now all they had to do was climb up the cable.

As he fanned the vaporized webbing away from his vision with one gloved hand, Darth Maul saw his quarry jump over the side of the bridge and cut the support strand away, turning it into an escape route. For a moment the Sith apprentice stood absolutely still, realizing how he had been outwitted. He let his rage boil out of him in a frustrated shout. The Force-dampening energy of the taozin had prevented his sensing their escape until they were already gone. It was astounding, the amount of good fortune his prey were experiencing.

He was really going to enjoy completing this mission.

Just now, however, he had more pressing matters to attend to. Between the weight of the taozin and the dismantling by his quarry, the bridge was beginning to fall apart. The Sith jumped nimbly over to the remaining support cable and began to move toward the opposite side of the cavern. He could easily cross the remaining distance before his prey climbed up out of the chasm. His athletic skills and connection to the Force made the thin support rope seem as wide as a walkway.

But the taozin had other ideas. It wound around the remaining support cable, blocking his path. Its head—now below the cable—fired another stream of webbing up at him.

Again he vaporized the arcing reticulation. The creature attacked again, but in a different way this time, using its legs to vibrate the strand on which the Sith stood.

Darth Maul began to fall backwards, but he did not panic. He reached out, grabbing the support cable with his free hand,

careful to keep his lightsaber away from it. He now hung directly in front of the creature, only a couple of meters away from its sharp mandibles.

He knew now that he wouldn't be catching up to Pavan and the others within the next few minutes. He spun his lightsaber over in a perfect execution of Slashing Wampa and cut the remaining bridge support that he clung to. He and the taozin fell away in opposite directions, he slamming against the wall on the opposite side from the three fugitives while the taozin disappeared into the abyss.

Unfortunately, disposing of the creature had also disposed of his only route across the cavern. Darth Maul climbed up the support cable to the ledge from whence he had come.

He gritted his teeth. Even with the Force to aid him he could not leap across a chasm this wide. He would have to retrace his route back up to the surface, which was frustrating beyond bearing. He knew he would find them again. There was no place in the galaxy he could not follow them, and he would not fail, however long it took. But to be so close and to fail yet again—it enraged him.

They would pay for this in full.

**O**bi-Wan Kenobi shouldered through the doors of the Tusken Oasis and for a few seconds felt as though he had returned uplevels. The club was lavishly decorated and well kept. Statues of beasts from various galactic mythologies intertwined in a lusty wall frieze that stretched around the big room, and photonic crystal fixtures glowed with multicolored lights, offsetting the overall darkness. The predominant color at the moment was blue, but as the Padawan watched, it cycled higher up the spectrum toward violet. A quartet of Bith musicians were playing something lively in the corner, their large, bulbous heads bobbing in time to a melody from their leader's omni box.

Only after looking more closely at the patrons of the club was he reminded that he was still below levels in the Crimson Corridor. Gamorrean bodyguards carrying blasters mingled with their gambling clients, and many patrons without paid protection carried their own weapons. There was enough firepower in the room to start a small revolution.

As Obi-Wan let his senses ride the currents of the Force and

expand into the club—feeling its pulse, so to speak—he sensed a wrongness, an out-of-step sequence. *Something* had happened here not too long ago, of that he was sure. He spotted a Twi'lek's lekku wiggling over the heads of some of the patrons near the band, and for a moment he thought he'd found Anoon Bondara, but a closer look told him it was not the Jedi after all.

He moved toward the large bar at the back of the room and noticed that he was being watched. Several Rodians at the end of the bar followed him with their black, featureless gaze, snouts quivering. Each wore cut-down versions of Stalker armor suits and might as well have been stamped with the words *Black Sun Enforcer.* As he neared the back of the room a Kubaz crunching on still-wriggling insects from a bowl on the bar looked up, noticed the cowled figure approaching, and promptly hopped off his barstool, heading for one of the exits.

The bartender was of a species that Obi-Wan did not recognize. Its dark blue head had no neck, instead flowing smoothly into large shoulders from which draped six muscular arms resembling serpents. At the end of each arm was a pair of digits. Two arms were currently mixing a large drink while another tapped information into a datapad. As Obi-Wan approached the bar, he saw the remaining three arms drop down below the level of the bar.

It didn't take the skills of someone like Yoda to guess that a weapon was being readied down there. His source regarding the Hutt's establishment had apparently been correct. He faced the bartender and slowly moved his hands up to slide back the cowl covering his face. The bartender looked at him with an expression that, on a human face, would have been called a scowl. "Whar' ya wan'?" it croaked in thickly accented Basic.

"I'm looking for some information."

"Don' hav'ny," the bartender rumbled, a fourth arm slithering furtively down under the bar to join the other three. Obi-Wan could feel the tension building.

*Be in the moment; be aware only of the present.*

He had heard Master Qui-Gon's admonition so many times, it seemed almost as though his Jedi mentor was standing next to him. The Padawan knew that his tendency to look to the future sometimes blinded him to the present. In his current situation, he felt it prudent to take Qui-Gon's advice.

Obi-Wan reached out with his mind and felt what could not be seen. The bartender was close to activating a blaster under the bar, which was pointed straight at the Padawan's abdomen. The two Rodians had split up and were flanking him now, just out of lightsaber range. He could sense their weapons being readied, as well.

What were they waiting for?

Then he noticed the bartender's four eyes glance over at a tiny pair of crystals inset in the bar's surface near the datapad, seemingly part of the design. One was lit; it glowed red. Near it was a green crystal, unlit. As he watched, the red crystal winked out and the green crystal lit up.

Events slowed and perception stretched then, as Obi-Wan Kenobi reached for the Force and his lightsaber simultaneously. He dropped flat to the floor as the bartender fired its weapon, sending pieces of the beautiful wooden bar exploding outward to shower the apprentice with splinters. He ignited his lightsaber and swung it up in a shallow arc, the superhot blade slicing almost without resistance through the bar and the blaster it concealed without touching the bartender's prehensile limbs. He rose to his feet quickly, almost levitating with the aid of the

Force, and continued the arc, twisting to face the Rodians, who had raised their weapons. He gestured, and one of the blasters leapt out of its surprised owner's hand and seemingly flung itself across the room. His partner fired, a particle beam burst that was deflected by the cobalt-hued energy blade, sending its trajectory off into the ceiling somewhere. Obi-Wan gestured again, and the second Rodian's blaster flew over to land at his feet.

All around him, the club's habitués had stopped their gambling to watch, many dropping instinctively into defensive postures, weapons ready, or hiding behind their bodyguards. Sensing the immediate danger was over, they turned back to their games of sabacc, dejarik, and other pursuits.

Obi-Wan turned around and faced the bartender, his lightsaber already deactivated.

"Like I said—I just want some information. No trouble."

Although he couldn't read the being's face, Obi-Wan noted that the color of the bartender's head had altered to a much lighter shade of blue and that it seemed to be having trouble with its respiration. He sensed movement behind him: the Rodians were moving in again. He turned to face them.

"That's enough, boys," someone said. "Our Jedi guest isn't here to cause a problem. Are you, friend? . . ."

"Kenobi. Obi-Wan Kenobi. And, as I mentioned to your bartender, all I'm looking for is information." The Padawan turned to face the new arrival, who was a short, muscular human with a large braid of hair trailing down his back. There was an aura of power about him—not Force related, just sheer animal prepotency.

"I'm looking for information, too, Jedi Kenobi," the man said. "Perhaps we can help each other. My name is Dal Perhi."

\*    \*    \*

Perhi led Obi-Wan down a short flight of stairs and along a corridor, apologizing as they walked.

"Sorry about the rough stuff—but we had to be sure you really were a Jedi. The fact that you didn't even have to harm any of our boys speaks for itself. The Jedi are known, after all, for valuing life."

There was more than a touch of sarcasm to his tone. Obi-Wan smiled tightly.

"And the Black Sun are not. You realize if I hadn't been a Jedi, I would likely be dead now."

The gangster nodded. "As I said, a simple precaution. You'll see why in a minute. Just part of doing business, Jedi Kenobi."

"Are you taking me to see Yanth the Hutt?"

The gangster glanced at the Padawan. "Good guess."

They reached the end of the corridor and passed through a pair of wide doors that looked as if they had been melted in the center. As they entered the room, Obi-Wan immediately noted several Gamorrean guards lying on the floor. He was no forensic specialist, but it seemed as though they had been shot with blasters. He stepped over a broken force pike and followed Perhi toward a large shape on the floor ahead.

He knelt down and examined the wound that had killed the Hutt. It looked almost as if it might have come from a lightsaber. That wasn't possible, of course. It had to be a blaster burn.

He looked over at the Black Sun representative. Could it be that his organization was having one of its periodic in-fighting episodes? A coup in the making?

"I was hoping, Jedi Kenobi, that you might be able to shed a little light here. Isn't there some—" Perhi gestured vaguely. "—mystic way you can tell who did this?"

It was interesting, Obi-Wan thought, the mythologies of various organizations. Among the Jedi there might well be those who wondered about the mysterious Black Sun, exaggerating their reach, their connections, their dangerousness. Certainly the opposite was true here. Perhi obviously felt there was some cabalistic way his Jedi guest could learn what had happened here.

"Give me a minute," Obi-Wan said.

The gangster nodded and stepped back.

Obi-Wan knelt on the floor and allowed his senses to expand, meditating on the apparent events. The sense of corruption he'd felt before on the street came back strongly, as did the disturbances caused by many other beings—but it was all too muddled. Too much time had passed, too many people had been in and out. A Master such as Mace Windu could probably make sense of it—but Obi-Wan was not a Master. He wasn't even a Jedi Knight yet.

He shook his head. "I'm sorry. Perhaps if I'd been here earlier—"

The gangster nodded. Obi-Wan sensed his disappointment, though Perhi hid it well. "Not your fault. Thanks anyway."

Obi-Wan was surprised to find that he felt slightly relieved. After all, if he'd found it was Darsha or Master Bondara who had perpetrated this carnage . . . But in all probability it was not.

But who could it have been?

"No one saw who did this?" he asked Perhi.

"No. You'd think there'd be at least one witness, but everyone says they couldn't get a good look at him, even when he ran right by them."

Obi-Wan nodded. That could be the natural reticence to get involved usually found in people on the far side of the law—or in fear of retribution.

He walked toward the exit, followed by Perhi.

"Jedi Kenobi?"

"Yes?"

"I've never had the pleasure of seeing one of you work until today. What you did up there in the bar—are all Jedi that good?"

Obi-Wan stopped and turned to face Perhi. "No, they're not."

The gangster seemed to relax slightly—but his expression changed as Obi-Wan continued.

"I'm only an apprentice. I have yet to take the Jedi trials. My Master is far more skilled than I. As a student, I'm afraid I'm a bit of a disappointment to him. In terms of fighting skills, I'm probably least among the Jedi."

The Padawan had the satisfaction of watching the gangster pale slightly. Then he turned and left Yanth's underground office, and the Tusken Oasis. With any luck, he had given Dal Perhi something to think about.

As he returned to the street, Obi-Wan mentally reviewed what he knew so far. Not much, unfortunately. He debated reporting back to the council, but decided to wait until he had something more than hearsay and supposition to offer. So far, all he knew for certain was that Darsha Assant had lost the informant she was assigned to protect. Her skyhopper had been gutted by a street gang, and her Master's skycar had been destroyed after a supposed brawl with a cowled figure. He had seen the vehicles, but no body for the informant, no Darsha, and no Master Bondara.

Add to that the fact that a Black Sun vigo, Yanth the Hutt, had been killed by a cowled figure. There had been a sense of corrup-

tion pervading the location, similar to what he had experienced at the crash site of Bondara's skycar.

Obi-Wan had two theories, which unfortunately were mutually contradictory. Theory number one: Darsha loses her informant to Black Sun attackers and trails them to the Tusken Oasis, where she is attacked and defeats an entire roomful of guards, along with Yanth the Hutt. She calls for help, and her master comes to aid her. They flee and . . . vanish.

There were holes in that theory that he could fly a Dreadnought through. Darsha was good in a fight, but if she was *that* good, she would never have lost her informant in the first place. Also, it didn't explain the sense of wrongness that lingered over the site of the skycar crash and the murders.

Theory number two was that there was some other entity— most likely connected somehow with Black Sun—involved who had killed Yanth the Hutt and his bodyguards. Obi-Wan liked the second theory better for several reasons, not the least of which was that he didn't want to believe any Jedi capable of the crimes he'd been investigating. But neither theory explained where Darsha and her Master were, or why they hadn't been heard from for so long.

Obi-Wan sighed. He hadn't exhausted all his leads yet. There was still the block of cubicles to investigate. He checked the address he had been given and started to walk. With any luck at all, he might learn something there that would shed some light on the entire mess.

No such luck.

At the site of the cubicle explosion Obi-Wan had learned some very interesting news—but it was news that served only to

muddy the waters further. One of the local police investigating the incident had told him that Hath Monchar, the Neimoidian deputy viceroy of the Trade Federation, had been the tenant of the blasted cubicle, and that he, too, had been killed.

It seemed obvious that Black Sun was somehow mixed up in all this. There was no evidence anywhere to suggest that the crime cartel was in bed with the Trade Federation, but it was possible, certainly.

Too many questions, Obi-Wan thought. Too many questions, and not nearly enough answers.

There was light at the end of the tunnel.

Lorn, I-Five, and Darsha hurried toward it. They reached a doorway—the partially boarded-over entrance to another kiosk similar to the one by which they had entered the underground—and emerged into the tenebrous shadows of Coruscant's Crimson Corridor section.

It was like stepping into bright sunlight compared to the labyrinth they'd been trapped in for so long.

Lorn breathed a sigh of relief. It had taken longer than they had expected to find a path back to the surface, involving several dead ends and retracing of their routes, but at least they had not suffered any further attacks by more underground denizens. Apparently the only Cthons on the other side of the bridge had been the ones in the taozin's belly.

Which was fortunate, because after the effort of climbing the long silken rope to the top of the underground chasm, the two humans were exhausted. But they couldn't afford to rest, or even

slow down. They had to assume that the Sith was still somewhere behind them, still pursuing them.

Which was the worst of their problems, but by no means the only one. Lorn figured that in all likelihood the bank's security personnel were after him and I-Five by now, as well. The transaction fraud they had committed would probably have also attracted the notice of the planetary police, and very possibly a few Republic treasury agents.

It had also occurred to Lorn that Black Sun might have a few questions for him, depending on what kind of records Yanth had left of his business dealings and what the eyewitnesses at the Tusken Oasis had pieced together. In short, probably just about every organized power on the planet was looking for him and I-Five.

Of course, the only pursuit he knew of for certain was the Sith's. The rest I-Five would probably characterize as paranoia. So what? Lorn told himself. Downlevels, paranoia wasn't a disorder; it was a lifestyle.

Darsha spoke. "My people will no doubt have sent out searchers by now. If we can get to a comm station, all we have to do is alert them to come pick us up."

Right—the Jedi. He'd forgotten about them. That made one more at the party.

I-Five said, "We are in an area with very few operating public comm stations. It's likely there will be a higher quantity of functional ones some levels up."

Sharp, Lorn thought. There were stations to be found if you knew where to look, but he didn't want to give Darsha a chance to drag them back to the Temple just yet. Back there in the tunnels, during the endless search for a way out, he'd managed to

whisper a few instructions to the droid without Darsha hearing him. I-Five knew Lorn wanted to get to Tuden Sal as quickly as possible—without the Jedi Padawan.

"So we're back to the question of the day: How do we get uplevels?" Darsha asked. "Climbing is risky. I had a bad experience earlier with some hawk-bats. I found my way up a monad, but I don't see any of those nearby."

It was true: without some kind of transportation, the problem of getting uplevels in this area was a sticky one. Of course, if he could contact Tuden Sal, the man would send a transport—but the problem was circular. First he had to get to a comm station.

It was extremely frustrating. They had never been more than half a kilometer from one of the most cosmopolitan areas in the galaxy. The only problem was, it was half a kilometer *straight up*. The possibility of freedom lay only a score of levels over their heads, and yet it might as well be on one of the orbiting space stations for all that they could reach it. All things considered, Lorn thought, it was hard to see how things could get any worse.

"We are being watched," the droid said.

Even as the droid spoke, Darsha could feel them—more than one, of different species, and with unmistakably malign intent.

"Why am I not surprised?" Lorn said. "Any way to tell exactly *who* is watching us?"

Darsha reached out with her senses and felt familiar signatures. She was sure she had come across them before recently.

"It's not the Sith," she said, and saw the broker relax. And then she recognized the vibration in the Force. "It's—"

"Hey, lady—still slumming?"

It was Green Hair, the leader of the Raptor gang that had

attacked her when she first touched down in the Corridor. Three of his cronies—the Trandoshan, a Saurin, and a Devaronian—were with him. Darsha almost smiled in relief. Compared to the creatures she'd faced under the surface, these punks were nothing.

Lorn seemed to feel the same way. He said, "Slide off, boys—we're more trouble than you're worth."

She could tell from the look on Green Hair's face that this was not the script he had planned on running. His purported victims were showing no fear. She had to give him credit, though—he tried again, speaking as if he hadn't heard Lorn.

"You're in our territory, and you gotta pay the toll."

Darsha almost laughed. It seemed like years ago that she'd been nervous about facing this riffraff. Her perspective had radically changed in the last thirty-six hours. Something of what she felt must have gotten across to the Raptor leader, because he looked worried for a few seconds.

"I said—" he began.

Lorn interrupted him. "What you said and what you're gonna get are two entirely separate things. Listen up—this is how it's gonna play. You give us your money now—*all* of you. And you—" He pointed at the leader. "—are taking us on a tour."

Green Hair could not have looked more shocked if Lorn had shoved a power prod against his chest. He stood there like a statue for a few moments, his electrostatic hairdo quivering slightly in the low breeze. His mates looked uneasy, as well; this kind of confidence was not something they encountered often on their turf. They glanced at Green Hair, and Darsha did not need the Force to read what was in that look. They were waiting for him to make a decision.

It was equally obvious that Green Hair knew what was ex-

pected of him. He looked back at his crew, then at Darsha, Lorn, and I-Five. "Take 'em!" he shouted, jumping toward Lorn.

Lorn sidestepped, tripping the youth as he rushed by. I-Five hammered the green head with one metal fist, and the boy went down. The Trandoshan lunged forward, a vibroblade extended. The droid used his finger blaster to heat the vibrating blade to incandescence. With a scream, the Trandoshan dropped the blistering metal and bolted into the shadows, cradling his burned hand with his other one.

Darsha was deep in the Force, knowing what her attackers were going to do before they did it. It was far easier than facing the taozin. Before she was even aware of reaching for it, the lightsaber was in her grasp, its blade gleaming in the shadows as she deflected the blaster bolts that whizzed from the Devaronian's weapon toward her and her friends. She thrust out her free hand, and the Saurin's blaster leapt from his hand toward Lorn, who caught it. He thumbed the setting to stun and fired twice. The remaining two gang members collapsed on the street's cracked ferrocrete alongside their stunned leader.

The skirmish had taken no more than a few seconds. Lorn and I-Five began searching the three unconscious bodies.

"What are you doing?" the Padawan asked.

"What does it look like?" Lorn replied. "We're taking from those who don't need and giving to those who do—namely us. We've got to have credits to get uplevels."

Darsha started to say something, then thought better of it. She didn't like scavenging off the bodies, but she could see the necessity.

Green Hair stirred and moaned. Lorn prodded him with the blaster. "Up," he said. Green Hair got to his feet, not looking too happy.

"I'm sure you boys have a way uplevels," Lorn said to him. "Let's go find it."

Darsha could feel the boy's resistance. She started to make a hand motion to focus the Force on him and give Lorn's suggestion a better chance of working, but Lorn held out a palm to her. "No mind tricks, Darsha—I want him alert."

She started to say something, then shrugged. He seemed to have a plan, which was more than she had at the moment.

Lorn prodded the Raptor with his newly acquired blaster. He felt much better now that he had a weapon. True, it wasn't much—only a BlasTech DH-17, without optical sighting arrays and with its power charge nearly depleted, but it had made a satisfying sizzle when he'd fired it during the short battle. He'd also picked up a vibroblade. These weapons might not help him if the Sith caught up with them, but they were better than facing his nemesis empty-handed.

There was another reason to celebrate. Since he and I-Five had been the only ones to check the unconscious bodies of the Raptors, Darsha had missed I-Five's find. The droid had flashed it at Lorn when she had been watching Green Hair. It was a small comlink—no doubt keyed to the Raptor who had owned it, but both Lorn and I-Five had hacked comlinks often enough that he knew getting around basic security would be no problem at all.

The three of them set out, following their unwilling guide, alert for any deception on his part. He led them toward an alley about two hundred meters from the direction he'd come.

Now if I-Five could just get a few minutes away, or have a chance to socket the comlink into his data plug, he could call Tuden Sal and set up a meeting. Things were looking better and

better, Lorn told himself. He and his partner just might be able to get themselves safely offplanet after all.

Of course, it would mean dropping Darsha—a prospect that, he had to admit, he wasn't looking forward to nearly as much as he thought he would. After all, she had helped keep him alive through this nightmare. He tried to remind himself that she was doing it purely to get the Neimoidian's information into the hands of the Jedi—but at this point she knew practically as much as he did. While he might be able to supply some more details, Darsha was as capable of delivering the gist of the data to the Jedi Council as he was.

Though it galled him to admit it, the truth was that he was growing somewhat fond of her. True, she was younger than he was by a considerable factor, but there was still a certain attractive quality to her.

*Remember,* he told himself sternly, *she's a Jedi.*

Or a Padawan, to be pedantic. A Padawan on her first solo mission—that much he'd gleaned from listening to conversations she'd had with I-Five. Tough cut of the cards, Lorn thought, to lose her Master, her mission, and even her informants on the first trip out. Why did she keep going? What made her want to bring them back to the Temple? Couldn't she see what manipulators the Jedi were?

Lorn wanted to find out. As they walked, he dropped back a couple of paces until he was alongside her, leaving I-Five to keep tabs on Green Hair.

"Padawan Assant," he said, somewhat stiffly, "I hope you don't mind my asking, but—just what made you choose the Jedi path? They're not—I mean—" He stopped, unsure how to continue. He glanced at her and saw her watching him.

Even in this dim light, her eyes were so incredibly blue.

"Never mind," he said gruffly. He started to walk faster, to bring himself back up to I-Five, but she put her hand on his arm. He looked at it, then at her.

"I was chosen," she said. "Chosen by the Force." She told him that she had never been part of a family. "When the Jedi came and told me I could be a part of theirs, it all made perfect sense."

*Of course it did,* he thought. *You weren't taken from a father who loved you by an order who then fired him because they thought it best that his son have no attachments.*

He felt angry at her answer. He wanted to somehow break that composure, shatter that maddening calm, that sanctimonious righteousness she shared with all the others of her order.

"But now you might not be able to keep on being a Jedi," he said. "Doesn't that make you angry? These people, this order that you consider your family, casting you out?"

"Do you know of the Jedi Code?"

Lorn nodded. "Yes. I've heard it plenty of times."

" 'There is no emotion; there is peace,' " she quoted. "This doesn't mean I won't be upset if I can't stay at the Temple—just that emotion does not rule me. I am joined with the Force for my entire life. Down there, facing the taozin, I had a chance to really understand what that means.

"Whether or not I become a Jedi doesn't matter now. I have felt the balance of the Force at a deeper level, and I know that I have done—and will continue to do—what I can to help maintain that balance. I'll do it with the Jedi, or on my own—but I will do it. I am at peace, even though I may suffer disappointment."

His confusion must have shown on his face, because she

smiled. There was a time when a smile like that on the face of a Jedi would have infuriated him, probably would have even made him try to wipe it off with his fists.

He didn't feel that way now.

"Let me put it another way," Darsha continued. "I have achieved my goals, even if I do not complete my mission."

Lorn nodded, but did not reply. It sounded like just the kind of ambiguity all the Jedi Knights were so fond of spouting—but like the smile, it didn't anger him to hear it coming from her. He wasn't sure what that meant.

He wasn't sure he wanted to find out.

**D**arth Maul stalked the underground passage back the way he had come, his rage boiling into the darkness like superheated steam. His power in the Force was magnified by this; unlike the foolish Jedi, the Sith harnessed the intensity of their emotions, refusing to pretend that such things did not exist. Any creature foolish enough to impede his speedy progress to the surface would be sorry indeed.

He passed through the Cthons' cavern and saw no sign of the subterraneans. Doubtless his previous passage through their domain had given them ample cause to make themselves scarce. Which was just as well—though he would have welcomed the opportunity to mow some of them down given the mood he was in, time was of the essence.

The intensity of his connection to the Force brought back a memory: another day of intense focus of his power. The day he had constructed his lightsaber. Maul was not wont to revisit his past, unless doing so somehow served his master, but the satisfaction of the creation, the perfection of focus and the highly

charged connection to the Force that had wrought his weapon stood out now in his memory.

The specialized furnace, which he had created from plans taken from his master's Sith Holocron, had radiated an intense heat as it shaped the synthetic crystals needed for his lightsaber. But rather than leaving the kiln chamber and allowing them to form on their own, he had remained near the device, concentrating on the metamorphosing gems, using the Force to purify and refine the lattice of the molecular matrices.

Most Jedi used natural crystals in their lightsabers; Adegan crystals were the gems of choice. Most of the other components of a lightsaber were easily obtained—power cells, field energizers, stabilizing rings, flux apertures—but not the crystals themselves. They had to be mined in the Adega System, deep within the Outer Rim Territories. The difficulty of using natural materials meant that the alignment process could take a long time—and the calibration had to be perfect, because mismatched crystals could destroy not only the lightsaber, but its creator. Finding and aligning the crystals was a Jedi test, but it was not the way of the Sith. The dark masters of the Force preferred to create their own synthetic crystals, to match the harmonics in the searing heat of a crucible and thus take their creation of the weapon to a deeper level.

Maul had sat by the furnace, focusing his hatred of the Jedi to a fiery peak and expanding his control of the Force, which he used to manipulate the molecular structures of the four gems required for his double-bladed weapon. The choice to make two blades instead of one had been an easy one. Only an expert would even think of trying to handle a double-bladed weapon, and he would be no less than an expert. The glory of the Sith required it, as did his master.

Not even the compressed ferrocrete walls of the pressurized chamber could entirely contain the intense temperature required to form the crystals. Hour after hour had passed, the searing heat washing over the apprentice. But his control had not wavered; the pain had not swayed his focus. Layer after countless layer of the crystals had been laid down, aligned, and perfected. It had taken days, days without food or water or sleep, but eventually he had sensed their readiness. Then he had deactivated the furnace and cracked it open. There, sitting in the formation crucibles, had been his four perfect crystals.

Maul grinned into the darkness. Yes, it was a good memory, an attainment that reminded him of his powers, that reassured him of his eventual and inevitable triumph. He had been thwarted thus far by an odd chain of events, but that would change soon.

He was back in the transport tube now. Ahead of him he could see light shining down from overhead, where he'd cut through the ventilation grid. Maul gathered the Force to himself and jumped straight up, rising several body lengths to shoot through the opening. A derelict human, deep in the throes of some narcotic delusion, was lying on the street nearby. He saw the Sith rise from the depths, gave out a little gasp, and passed out as Maul's boots touched the pavement.

Not far away, the wreckage of the Twi'lek Jedi's skycar and its attendant debris still partially blocked the streets. The Sith Lord considered how he might best locate his quarry. Once he reacquired their trail he could easily locate them. The weakness of that strategy was that he would still be following them. There

had been far too much of that. Much better to get ahead of them somehow and be waiting for them.

Maul recalled the method by which he'd located the Neimoidian earlier. Perhaps the planetary net cams would be useful to him again; if he could find the most recent location where the humans had been seen, he could save time tracking them by going straight to it.

But to begin his search he needed a data terminal, and there were none to be found in this urban jungle. He was reminded of something Lord Sidious had once told him: "For every solution there are two problems."

Darth Maul considered for a moment, then activated his wrist comm and holoscreen monitor. He commed the *Infiltrator*, tapped into its main computer, and used that to access the port datalink, bypassing the regular navigation request screens until he located a menu offering access to other networks. His master's password again opened locked doors, and within a few seconds he had called up several data sources.

The first was a holomap of this section of the Crimson Corridor. Maul located his current position and tapped in the last known vectors for the humans and the droid.

The planetary data bank gave him the information he wanted. It was as he had suspected; they were heading in the direction of the Jedi Temple, using the droid's global positioner to guide them. Fortunately they still had a long way to go, not only toward the Temple, but uplevels, as well. He zeroed down to street level and identified several exits from the subterranean passages that they might have used.

Next he tapped into Coruscant's security network and called up a listing of surveillance cams near those exits. He flashed

through hundreds of images from the last few minutes, finding nothing that would help him. He left the link open and shifted to check recent crimes in the area. Not surprisingly, hundreds of incidents popped up for the last few hours in the Crimson Corridor: street fights, petty theft, other common crimes. He noted in passing an oddity: a droid was being sought for scamming the banking system. But he found nothing recent that had happened in the target areas that would serve him.

Darth Maul scowled. He needed transportation; that way he could get nearer his target zones. He considered the problem.

As he did so, his comm flashed that he had an incoming message. He felt a finger of worry touch him. It could be only his master. The thought of not answering did not occur to the Sith. He toggled the secure communications mode, dumping his connection to the security net, and waited for the readout to confirm his scrambled signal.

Sidious's voice crackled over the comlink. "Time grows short, my apprentice. What is the state of your current project?"

"My master, I have obtained the holocron. I am holding it for your inspection. There have been . . . delays in finding the human whom the Neimoidian spoke with, but they are now within my grasp. I shall not fail you."

Darth Sidious was silent for a second before he replied.

"See that you do not. When they are dead, contact me, and I will instruct you in how to deliver the holocron. Be very careful not to reveal our presence, Lord Maul—it is not yet time."

"Yes, my master."

Darth Maul moved toward the clearing where the Jedi's sky-car had crashed. It would be a good location to try what he had planned. He reached out with his senses. There was no sign of Jedi anywhere close now.

Cautiously Maul shielded his strength, hooding his power in the Force lest any approaching Jedi notice. It was sensible that those of the Temple would investigate the crash of one of their transports, but it was still cause for discretion. He had little doubt that he could defeat any living Jedi, but there were many of them here on the capital of the Republic. Even he was not foolish enough to try to take them on all at once. With the Jedi searching, events were complicated that much more.

It had certainly turned out to be a much more interesting mission than he had thought it would be.

Maul settled himself in the shadows beyond the area where the skycar had crashed, and reaccessed the planetary security grid, using the same technique he had before. Few taxi drivers could be enticed to enter the Crimson Corridor, and even the security forces did not enter the zone without good cause. But good cause was something he could supply.

This time, instead of activating the menu, he scanned the current patrol routes for this quarter of the city. High above, still several kilometers away, were a pair of patrol officers on speeder bikes, circling on their regular beat. Maul noted their designations and then accessed the dispatch queue for emergency calls. He fed data directly into the dispatch computer. Eventually an audit might reveal his call to be a ruse, with no comlink recording, but it would serve for now.

The bait he chose was the droid banking crime. The police

would be wary of any dangerous call-outs for the area, but they would perhaps be less concerned with a white-collar crime conducted by someone's mechanical servant. It was the best inticement he could come up with on short notice.

Having set out his lures, the Sith apprentice waited to see what he might catch. He did not have to wait long. A few minutes after he'd entered the data into the security net, two police speeder bikes came roaring in from uplevels, strobe lights flashing. From the shadows in which he crouched, Darth Maul prepared to move.

Abruptly he halted. At the edge of his perceptions was something else. He reached for it, projecting jagged tendrils of the Force to discover what lay unseen. And then, as his probe reached it, it swung lower into view, hovering above the crash site.

It was a PCBU—a droid-piloted police cruiser backup unit. The Crimson Corridor had been the site of a number of officer murders over the years, which was why the PCBU had been developed. It carried two state-of-the-art swivel laser cannons mounted on the top and bottom of the unit, as well as a variety of sensors, scanners, and disruptors. Maul watched it approach. He had not expected the arrival of such a heavily armed craft, but it would delay his plans only slightly.

He waited until the unit had passed him, following the two speeder bikes, and then acted. He seized the Force and used it to propel himself high into the air, to land on the top of the PCBU. His lightsaber blades ignited as his feet hit the surface of the craft, and he quickly sheared the upper gun free of its mount, spinning the double-ended blade after this to cleave through the transparisteel cockpit bubble and the droid pilot. The PCBU be-

gan to descend, its autopilot taking over now that the droid was no longer activated.

Either the speeder bike patrol officers had noted the descent of the craft, or the driver of the PCBU had had time to get off a signal, because they spun their bikes around and flew toward him.

Excellent.

One speeder bike was ahead of the other. Maul deactivated one of his lightsaber's blades and hurled it toward the first of the oncoming speeders like a spear. It pierced the officer's armored chest while the Sith, again assisted by the Force, jumped from the descending PCBU toward the other officer.

By the time he had landed on the speeder his lightsaber had rejoined him, snatched back to him by a feathery runner of the Force. Within moments the second police officer was dead, and Darth Maul had his transportation. With no witnesses, there was little chance of anyone suspecting the use of the Force, and the entire operation had been accomplished quickly enough that, in all probability, neither of the two officers had had a chance to send a distress signal.

Immediately he lifted off on one of the speeder bikes, heading uplevels to get ahead of his quarry. He set the speeder into a vertical spiral and checked his wrist comm as he rose. Again, he noted nothing unusual in the target area. However, one of the cam pickup sites seemed unusually devoid of traffic. Something about it . . .

Darth Maul replayed the scene again at a slower speed. Yes, right there—a flicker of something. He watched the security cam footage play again, slowing it even more. Nothing, nothing . . . and then, abruptly, there he was.

It was unmistakably his target: the information broker known as Lorn Pavan.

The Sith checked the time stamp on the data. The image had been recorded only about twenty minutes ago. He accelerated the speeder toward the location given on the screen.

He had them now.

Lorn poked the Raptor leader in the back with the barrel of his blaster as they reached the alley. "Hold it," Lorn said. He turned to I-Five and Darsha. "Any warnings from the science and sorcery team?" he asked. "And don't start whining again about the cheap sensor suite I had installed in you," he added to the droid.

"Well, it *was* less expensive than the Mark Ten."

"But more expensive than the other five choices. A *lot* more expensive." Lorn glanced at Darsha as he spoke, intending to ask her if she was receiving anything on the Force bandwidth, and was somewhat surprised to see that she was smiling. What was even more surprising—downright shocking, actually—was the way he found himself reacting to that smile.

He liked it.

He liked her.

This was bad.

He knew he would soon have to break clear of her. There was just no way he was going back to the Temple. Sure, she was

nice-looking, but he'd had nice-looking before, lots of times since Siena had left him. This was definitely not the direction in which his best interests lay. It was best to cut this off, right here and right now. Raise the blast shields, secure the air locks, bolt the hatches.

But instead, to his horror, Lorn realized he was smiling back.

As they walked toward the alley, Darsha enjoyed the patter between Lorn and I-Five. It was clear that they cared as much for each other as two friends would, two equals. Unusual, but at the same time it seemed quite natural.

She'd rarely had the opportunity to develop that kind of bond. The Jedi didn't discourage friendships, of course, but the intensity of her studies and the time they demanded made it difficult to cultivate anything more than casual friendships with the other Padawans. Probably the closest she had to a friend at the Temple—aside from her Master, of course—was Obi-Wan Kenobi, and if she had the opportunity to speak with him more than once a week, she counted herself lucky.

As she listened to Lorn and I-Five, she kept her senses alert for any potential dangers ahead or behind. The only obvious latent trouble was Green Hair; the Raptor was brimming with hatred that he had been so easily captured, and that he was being made to lead enemies to his gang's secret exit route uplevels. He would bear very close watching, but I-Five and Lorn seemed to have the situation in hand.

Behind them, she could feel no sign of the Sith, which either meant that they had finally made a successful escape, or was merely evidence of the fact that she still had a long way to go before she could stay in the Force at all times. Earlier, while fighting

the Raptors, she'd stepped back into a full communion with it, every sense sharpened and honed, as she had done with the taozin. But she was not yet to a point where she could remain there. She had many years to go before she could be anywhere as good as Master Bondara had consistently been.

Lorn was arguing with I-Five about the latter's sensors. Darsha quested outward with the Force, feeling only the minimal vibrations of animal life in the alley—a few spider-roaches, armored rats, those sorts of creatures. Certainly nothing that represented much of a threat.

". . . more expensive than the other five choices. A *lot* more expensive," Lorn was saying to the droid. He glanced at her as she finished the sentence. She grinned, and was very surprised to feel a depth to his answering smile. Could he possibly be attracted to her? There was certainly no hostility in him at the moment, which was a far cry from his attitude toward her when they had first been thrown together.

It was tempting to probe his emotions, to use the Force on an empathic level to see if she was right. But even as the urge to do so came over her, she quelled it. It would be taking unfair advantage. Besides, looking at him now, Darsha realized that she didn't need to use the Force. The attraction was definitely there on his end, obvious to anyone.

How interesting.

Which begged the question: How did she feel in response?

Lorn suddenly looked away, and Darsha knew he was uncomfortable, unsure of how to deal with this new dynamic between them. A strong sense of guilt came from him: this wasn't a question of probing; she'd have to be blind to the Force not to notice. She could certainly understand where the guilt was

coming from. After years of hating the Jedi, to find himself attracted to one would have to be a considerable shock.

Now was neither the time nor the place to explore this, Darsha told herself. With any luck, there would be better opportunities later. For now, she decided to save face—his and hers.

"I don't sense any large life-forms in the alley, for what it's worth," she told him.

Lorn nodded, still looking away, and prodded the Raptor again with his blaster. "Okay, killer—lead on."

Off balance a bit, still focused on the fact that she'd just noticed his attraction, Darsha almost missed the Raptor's sudden surge of anger. It reminded her that they were by no means out of the woods yet.

Lorn followed Green Hair into the alley, his mind still very much on the wordless interchange that had just taken place between him and Darsha. Had she somehow felt what he was thinking, used the Force to peer at his naked emotions? He hoped not. But let's face it, he told himself, she was a Jedi. She certainly had the ability to do such a thing, and in Lorn's experience, people who had skills tended to use them.

He tried to feel angry, to feel invaded by her action, but all he felt was curiosity—curiosity as to whether there was any attraction on her side. And *that* bothered him even more than the invasion of privacy.

I-Five broke into his thoughts. "I concur with Padawan Assant's conclusions about life-forms, but you might be interested to know that there are two active power relays in the first fifteen meters of—"

"Lorn, watch it! He's going to try something!" Darsha shouted from behind.

Sure enough, the Raptor dived toward a pile of trash just under a small architectural overhang on the left side of the alley. Lorn leapt after him, trying to see what the gang member was reaching for under the garbage. Green Hair hit the ground first, however, tearing into the trash. His palm slammed toward a large yellow activation reader. Lorn had seen readers like these before; they were capable of being utilized only when someone with the right identification pattern touched them. That pattern could be the user's DNA, a subcutaneous chip, or sometimes a skin decoration, like a tattoo. Whatever the activation mode, Lorn knew that if he didn't move fast, he would very shortly find out what the switch was for.

Lorn caught the boy's wrist and pulled his arm up behind his back, hard. Green Hair let out a cry, and Lorn grabbed his other hand, as well. He dragged the struggling youth back to where I-Five and Darsha stood.

"Got anything we can use to immobilize him?" he asked the droid.

"What a clever idea," I-Five said, handing Lorn a length of rope he had picked out of the trash. "Too bad it didn't occur to you before we were nearly vaporized."

Lorn secured Green Hair's wrists, then turned the youth around to face him. "All right, what's the switch for?"

Green Hair just stared at him, mouth defiantly clamped shut.

Lorn glanced at I-Five, who said, "I traced the circuit to an energy source high on the alley wall—about there." The droid pointed up at a rusty vent about three meters above the group. Abruptly his pointing finger deformed, the end irising open. A beam fired four times, each hair-thin line of ruby light striking a corner of the vent. Lorn smelled the tang of vaporized metal faintly over the ripe organic scents that filled the alley.

The vent cover fell off and hit the ground below with a clang, and he could see the harsh end of a tripod-mounted blaster just inside the hole. Motorized, no doubt, and cued to zap anyone not near the activation switch.

Wouldn't *that* have been a nasty surprise.

Lorn shook his head, then glanced at Darsha. "Here's a thought," he said. "Maybe we ought to try one of those mind tricks you wanted to use earlier."

Darsha gave him a wry look, then turned her attention to Green Hair. She made a subtle gesture with one hand as she said, "You will show us the way uplevels, with no more tricks."

Fascinated, Lorn watched as the Raptor's eyes defocused and he repeated, "I will show you the way uplevels, with no more tricks."

It was eerie, seeing the ease with which she controlled the boy, and Lorn found himself wondering, not for the first time, if she could do the same thing to him.

Their prisoner pointed deeper into the dark alley. "This is the way," he said woodenly.

Lorn glanced at Darsha. She nodded. Lorn took the lead.

Darsha couldn't believe she'd missed the relays. She'd been so focused on the idea of living enemies that it hadn't occurred to her to check for mechanical ones. She had to make sure that it didn't happen again.

She sent her senses questing out ahead of them, feeling for living and nonliving eyes. Just around the corner was a security cam. Lorn stepped around the bend before she could call out, but it didn't matter—she had it handled. It took a little more concentration to defeat a mechanical device, but it certainly wasn't beyond her abilities. She simply jammed the lens aperture control shut.

She, the Raptor, and I-Five caught up to Lorn in short order. He was looking at the security cam.

"Don't worry," she said, "I rascaled it."

He glanced at her. "It was live? I figured it was a dummy they'd set out to keep their trail clear."

"There were, you'll remember, two active power relays back there," I-Five said.

Lorn glanced at him, shrugged, then nodded thanks to Darsha. The gesture came from him easily and naturally. It was hard to believe that less than a day ago he'd resented her for saving his life.

They continued on. It was a twisty path that Green Hair led them down, even for Coruscant—through dark alleys and back utility routes grown vermicularly complex over the centuries. At times the way was so narrow and the darkness so complete, it was hard to believe that they had returned to the surface. Darsha kept her senses sharp, but other than an occasional mendicant or vagrant huddled shapelessly in dark corners, they met no one on the route. After another ten minutes they came to a large round tube, identified as a thermal conduit. Faded signs all around it gave warnings in various Republic languages as well as universal pictograms about the dangers of the pipeline.

Green Hair indicated an access hatch on the side of the pipe. "Through there," he said.

Lorn stared at the access hatch on the side of the conduit, then at Green Hair. "You're sure the whammy you put on him is still working?" he asked Darsha.

Darsha nodded. "He's not lying," she said. "He believes this is the route. Unless he's delusional, this is the way they use to go uplevels."

I-Five tapped the pipe. It rang hollow. "My sensors can't penetrate the insulation. It could be safe, though."

"Fine," Lorn said. "*You* open it." He stepped back and let I-Five take his place.

"I live to serve," the droid said sarcastically, gripping the access wheel. He twirled it easily and popped the hatch. No clouds of boiling steam poured out, and the droid looked inside.

"It appears to go up ten levels, at least. There's a ladder on the inside. Anyone ready?"

Lorn glanced at Darsha. Green Hair waited placidly beside them. "Do we bring Fashion Plate here with us, or leave him?" he asked her.

Darsha turned to the youth. "Are there any other traps or codes we need to know to get through the tube?"

The Raptor nodded. "Only the door access code at the other end. One-one-three-four-oh."

The Padawan looked at Lorn. "Leave him."

Lorn nodded and untied their captive. Darsha laid her hand on the youth's shoulder and spoke to him one more time. "You will forget all about us."

"I will forget all about you."

"Be on your way. If danger threatens, you will come to your senses immediately. Otherwise, you will become yourself again after an hour. Go. And," Darsha added as he turned to leave, "get a haircut."

Green Hair nodded and wandered off, still in his Jedi-induced daze. Lorn couldn't help smiling at the Padawan again. Not bad, not bad at all. He glanced at I-Five and saw the droid watching him, his blank expression somehow even more non-committal than usual. Lorn cleared his throat and motioned the

droid into the pipe. He wasn't looking forward to climbing a ladder ten stories.

Darsha followed Lorn and I-Five up the ladder. It was a long, claustrophobia-inducing climb, and on top of all the other exertions she had been through, it was fairly grueling. But the thought of finally leaving the lawless abyss that was the Crimson Corridor helped propel her upward.

There was another access hatch at the top, which I-Five popped open easily. They followed him through.

They were in a large chamber that, by the look of it, once had been a central power-dispensing agency for several blocks' worth of buildings. It was two stories high and filled with conduits of all types, a bewildering array of catwalks, and what looked like several old thermal generators. At some point the plant must have been closed down and turned into a storage facility. At the far end of the room was a thick durasteel storage chamber designed for hazardous wastes. I-Five took a look inside it.

"More junk," he reported, "including a small carbon-freezing chamber." The droid looked around the room, noticing the various containers of fuel and tanks of gas for welding stacked all over the place. "I wouldn't fire any blasters if I were you," I-Five said to Lorn.

"If I have anything to say about it," Lorn said with heartfelt intensity, "I'll never fire a blaster again."

Darsha looked at I-Five and would have sworn the droid was smiling. Across the room was a door. There were several windows in the upper walls, and through them streamed bright sunlight. She grabbed Lorn and hugged him.

"We made it!"

He looked surprised, then uncertain—then surrendered to the moment and returned the hug. Before he could say anything, however, Darsha felt her joy wash away in a flood of dread.

She could feel him before she could see him. She let go of Lorn and spun toward the door, lightsaber already in her hand.

The door opened.

The Sith was there.

**D**arth Maul stood in the doorway and gazed upon his quarry, feeling the surprise and horror of the two facing him ripple across the room. They were trapped. He knew it and so did they, and it made this moment all the more glorious. He grinned slowly.

He had arrived at the lower end of the conduit quickly, using the patrol speeder's strobes to clear a path through the traffic. He had missed them, of course, but a quick reconnaissance of the conduit had revealed the only logical destination of the group. All the while he had acted with just the barest awareness of the Force, cloaking himself from its embrace. He had lived within the powerful boundaries of the dark side for so long that to not do so had left him feeling naked and blind at first, but it was necessary in order to not provide any warning to the Jedi apprentice who had sided with his quarry. He had circled the building, seeing only a few high transparisteel windows and one main doorway to the interior. He could not have devised a better trap had he tried.

Still further removed from the Force than he had been in years, he had extended the tiniest tendril of awareness to the edge of the door leading into the building. There he had stood, waiting for confirmation that his prey was at its final destination.

After a time, it had come, and he had stepped back into the Force, enjoying the sensation as the dark side enfolded him. Immediately he had felt the Padawan react, and then he had opened the door.

Now Darth Maul stepped forward, igniting both blades of his lightsaber. The moment had been perfect, but like all such, it was fleeting, already over. It was time to create another, far more satisfying one: the triumph of finally completing his mission.

For a few incredibly long heartbeats Darsha was paralyzed by shock, defeated by her emotions. Fear, despair, and hopelessness clawed at her, sapping her will. She faced the ultimate enemy; the Sith was far more powerful than she in the Force. He had slain Master Bondara, one of the Jedi's best fighters.

*Give up,* an insistent voice in the back of her mind whispered. *Drop your weapon. Give up . . .*

But as the Sith activated his lightsaber's twin blades, years of training that had grown almost into instinct flared within her. The council of despair in her head was stilled.

She embraced the Force.

*There is no emotion; there is peace.*

Her fear evaporated and was replaced by quietude. She was still conscious of the fact that the Sith was well capable of killing her, but it was a distant concern. If death was inevitable, then what mattered was how she faced it.

*There is no ignorance; there is knowledge.*

She had attended a lecture on battle techniques given by

Master Yoda earlier this year, and the memory of it came back to her now.

Yoda had faced the assembled students and spoken, his thin reedy voice somehow carrying to the far corners of the lecture hall without benefit of amplifiers.

"Better than training, the Force is. More than experience or speed it gives."

And he had given a demonstration. Three members of the council—Plo Koon, Saesee Tiin, and Depa Billaba, excellent fighters all—had come forward and attacked him. Master Yoda had not been armed, and had not seemed to move more than a meter or so, his tread slow and measured. Nevertheless, none of the three had been able to lay a finger on him. The lesson had struck powerfully home: Knowledge of the Force was infinitely better than technique.

Now Darsha let herself sink into the Force, not trying to maintain any control over it, letting it take over as she had when facing the taozin and the Raptors. How many times had Master Bondara told her to simply relax, to let go? She did so now, feeling herself reach a deeper place in the Force than she had ever been before. How she knew this she could not say—it simply *was*. She felt her senses heighten to diamond sharpness, and every feature of the abandoned power station came into focus, both the visible and the invisible. She knew every wall, door, and piece of machinery, each particle of dust.

And she knew what she had to do.

All this, in less than a second's time.

With a small wave of her hand behind her, Darsha telekinetically pushed Lorn and I-Five backwards, sending them shooting dozens of meters into the storage chamber that she knew had been designed to be strong enough to hold dangerous, volatile

waste. The hatch slammed shut. The Sith would not be able to reach them immediately, which would give her time. With a thought she scrambled the lock mechanism so that the door could not be opened, then ignited her lightsaber, its golden glow shining in the dimness of the old power station.

The twin ruby blades of the Sith's lightsaber spun as he leapt toward her, and she stepped forward to meet him.

Lorn pounded on the door of the waste-containment chamber, but it would not open.

"Darsha! Open the door!"

He tugged frantically at the latch, but the lock mechanism had been scrambled. There was a small port of yellowed transparisteel in the hatch, and through it he could see Darsha and the Sith battling, the energy blades colliding in showers of sparks.

This was madness! What had she done? She had to know she had no chance against the demon who had killed her Master. The three of them together, with I-Five's finger blasters and his own blaster, might possibly be able to take him. But there was no way she could face him alone.

She was going to die.

After her, in all probability, he would be next—but Lorn barely thought about that. All that mattered was getting that hatch open so that he could reach her, somehow help her!

He pulled the vibroblade from his pocket and tried it on the locking mechanism. No good.

"I-Five, get us out of here!" he shouted. When the droid did not respond, he turned to see why.

I-Five had powered up the carbon-freezing unit. A cloud of bilious smoke—carbonite vapor—misted the small chamber.

"What are you doing? She's going to die out there!"

"Yes," the droid said. "She is."

Darth Maul felt a change in the Force as the woman stepped forward. Interesting—she was more powerful than he had thought. It did not matter, of course. He, who had trained his entire life to kill Jedi, could certainly not fail to kill a mere Padawan. But a more challenging opponent would take more time. Still, there were no other exits from the building; his target and the droid weren't going anywhere.

He might as well enjoy himself.

Maul twirled his twin blades in an overhand arc, the better to separate her upper body from her lower.

And she caught the strike on her weapon's yellow length of plasma, deflecting the first blade, then sparking on the second to twist it past.

He changed direction, stabbing forward in the form known as Striking Sarlacc to pierce her heart.

Which was deflected by her in a downward stroke, the tip of her blade then arcing out to gut him.

But he wasn't there, having backflipped to land in a defensive posture.

Darth Maul bared his teeth at her. For a Padawan, she was a worthy opponent. No Jedi Master lived within the Force more fully than she did at this moment.

But he was going to kill her. He knew it, and so did she.

The Sith apprentice launched a simultaneous attack, using the Force to throw a rusty power-wrench and a bucket of old fasteners from a worktable at her as he launched himself forward, lightsaber dancing a variant of a teräs käsi Death Weave.

This entertainment was beginning to pall. Time to kill her and move on to his primary target.

*There is no passion; there is serenity.*

It was true. Every action she took was committed and well defined, but there was no emotion, no conscious thought preceding it. The Force guided her, helped her make the lightning-fast movements necessary to deflect the Sith, and even to counterattack.

But it was not enough. The Sith was the best fighter Darsha had ever seen. His movement was precise, his control of the Force that of a musician playing an intricate solo. All of which made it even more mandatory that information about him reach the Temple.

Using the Force, she deflected the tool and bucket of parts he hurled at her. Several of the latter got through, striking her legs and torso as she leapt five meters up and onto a catwalk that ran the length of the chamber. As she landed, she caught a glimpse of Lorn's stricken face, framed in the viewport of the containment unit's hatch. She barely had time to catch her breath before the Sith was there in front of her. His eyes were hypnotic, their golden hue an eerie counterpart to the bloodred and black tattoos covering his face. But they did not prevent her from deflecting his strikes as he again moved within range, his twin blades spinning so fast they seemed to merge into a crimson shield.

There was a sizzle as her blade intersected his, a flash of sparks as they separated, she to deflect, he to attack with the blade opposite.

Darsha slashed backhand, feeling a weakness in his defense.

But it was a trap, carefully laid, and he spun a ruby shaft to intersect, which would have hit her at the same time.

But she wasn't there, having propelled herself sideways to a new position a meter away, her lightsaber pointed at his chest.

And the Sith dived forward, striking left-right-left in a series of attacks that left her winded, even assisted as she was by the Force. She deflected, forcing her mind to disengage from following his technique, to relax and maintain her deep connection to the Force. Thoughts were a hazard.

He did not share that weakness; she could feel the truth of that. He had more conscious control of the power at his command, and that gave him the edge. If she tried to increase her control of the Force, she would reduce her ability to simply react—but if she did not, she could only defend.

The problem reverberated within her as she maintained her connection with the environment, her senses reaching out, her mind searching for answers.

When she found one, she tested it and realized it was her only chance.

Lorn grabbed the droid's arms and tried to pull him away from the unit's controls. He might as well have tried to pull a skyhook down from orbit. "What are you *doing*?"

I-Five did not stop working as he answered. "Trying to ensure that her sacrifice is not a futile one."

"It won't be, if you'll just blast that damned door open!"

I-Five kept talking, his voice maddeningly even. "Even my reactions are no match for the Sith's—and I am far faster than you and Padawan Assant. She is doing for us what her Master did for her—buying time."

"What good will that do? We're trapped in this chamber—"

"With a carbon-freezing unit that can be adapted to put us both in cryostasis."

Sheer surprise kept Lorn from protesting for a moment. The droid continued, "It's theoretically possible for living beings to be frozen in a carbonite block and later revived. I read an interesting treatise on the subject once in *Scientific Galactica*—"

Lorn turned, a snarl building deep in his throat, and aimed the Saurin's blaster at the hatch lock. One way or another he was going to reach her.

"Stop!" I-Five commanded. "This chamber's magnetically sealed. The ricochet would most likely destroy us both."

Lorn spun about and pointed the blaster at I-Five. "Get over there and open that door," he said, in a voice that did not sound remotely like his own, "or I'll blow you to scrap metal."

I-Five turned his head and looked at him for a moment. Then the droid reached out and grabbed the blaster, taking it away from Lorn before the latter had time to pull the trigger.

"Now listen to me," I-Five said as he returned to his work. "We have one chance to survive this, and it's not a very good one. The Padawan has no chance. She knows this." He finished entering a final bit of data on the unit's control panel. "Get into the unit."

Lorn stared at him, then turned and looked back out of the hatch window. He couldn't see Darsha or the Sith directly, but he could see their shadows moving on the floor, cast by the light from the high windows. He realized they had taken the battle to one of the overhead catwalks.

*She is doing for us what her Master did for her—buying time.*

He had known her for barely forty-eight hours, and in that

time he had gone from hating her and everything she stood for, to—this. This frantic pain, this frustration, this welter of emotions he had not allowed himself to feel for years. He did not love her; there hadn't been enough time for that. But he had come to feel fondness for her, to deeply respect and admire her. If all the Jedi were like her . . .

He didn't want to finish the thought. He forced himself to.

*If all Jedi are like her, then what happened to Jax was the best thing for him.*

"Hurry!" I-Five said. "The unit's on a timer. We have less than a minute."

Lorn pressed his face to the transparisteel, trying to get a last look at her. He failed. He could dimly hear the crackling and buzzing of the lightsabers, could see the flashes and cascades of sparks as they clashed against each other or sliced through metal as though it were flimsiplast. But he could not see her.

I-Five took him gently but firmly by the shoulders and turned him away from the hatch. Lorn let the droid lead him over to the carbon-freezing unit. He felt no fear as he stepped into it. The temptation was to not feel anything at all, to just be numb.

No, he told himself. He had lived too long that way. If these were to be his final moments—which they could very well be; the odds of the droid's plan succeeding were slim indeed—he would not live them in an emotional void.

It was the very least he could do in acknowledgment of her sacrifice.

He stepped into the open cylinder of the device. I-Five crowded in beside him. There was barely enough room for both.

Lorn looked at the droid.

"If we come out of this alive," he said, "I'm going to kill that Sith."

I-Five did not reply; there was no time. Lorn felt freezing-cold steam boiling up around him. His vision was obscured by mist, which turned to darkness—a darkness as deep and complete as death.

**D**arth Maul felt a slight disappointment as he realized that the Jedi was not truly as powerful as she had first appeared. Her depth in the Force was impressive, but her methodology did not match it. Both of them knew it was only a matter of time now. He focused his attacks, forcing her to use a more technique-based defense.

She leapt down to the floor, and he followed her. He felt a Force-powered pressure move toward him and deflected it, sensing several large tanks and canisters being shoved around behind him. She was growing weak. Such an attack was a sign of desperation. Soon it would be over.

He dived forward, rolling to come up alongside her, deflecting her attack as he did so. Another invisible pressure wave knocked over more equipment behind where he had been.

Pitiful.

Maul thrust upward with his blade and was met with hers, thwarted for the moment. A deliberately left weakness in his attack was not exploited, and again he felt a loss of respect for her.

It was too bad, but there would be other missions, other challenges more worthy of his skills. Someday the Jedi Temple would be in ruins, and he would be there to see it, after having killed many of the Jedi himself. But now it was time to end this.

Darth Maul readied himself for the final strike.

Darsha sent a second wave of the Force outward, tumbling over yet another tank of fuel. She had managed to move several welding cylinders and fuel cells toward each other. They were heaped together now, an extremely explosive accident waiting to happen.

How appropriate, she thought, to use Master Bondara's sacrifice as an example.

Darsha let herself think of Lorn for a moment. She hoped the droid had figured out the potential for escape that the carbon-freezing unit represented. If not, then her sacrifice would be in vain.

She had seen Lorn's face in the hatch window, his expression full of desperation and concern—not for himself, but for her. It had most definitely not been the expression of someone who hated her, or was even indifferent to her fate.

It was too bad, she thought. If they had had more time . . . If they'd been able to see this through to the end, reach the Jedi Temple together . . .

But that was not the way it was fated to be.

*There is no passion; there is serenity.*

She thrust at the Sith, her lightsaber thrumming, and moved into a better position. She had to get this just right, make it look like it wasn't deliberate.

She left herself open. The Sith immediately took advantage of it.

His blade pierced her side, a fiery hot jet of pain that caused her to cry out.

Darsha Assant released her lightsaber, using the Force to send it forward, still lit, to pierce one of the gas cylinders.

She had time for one last thought.

*There is no death; there is the Force.*

She knew it was the truth.


Darth Maul saw his opponent's strategy, realizing what she planned to do nearly too late. He jumped, using the Force to propel him upward toward one of the high windows. He smashed through it easily and landed on a nearby walkway as the explosive canisters within detonated.

Fortunately, the strong walls of the structure contained the explosion. The Padawan had been truly devious at the end; he now realized she'd been preparing the trap with her feeble Force attacks. A far more worthy opponent than he'd realized.

Her actions had cost him the pleasure of killing his primary target. Maul offered a smile to her memory. Not all could fight so well; this was to be honored.

A crowd was beginning to gather. He had to make sure his mission was complete, and that was best done quickly. He leapt back to the window he had just broken through. Smoke was pouring from it now; through it he could dimly make out the inferno that the chamber had become. He used the Force to momentarily dissipate the clouds and saw below him the waste-containment unit that his target had hidden in. The contained pressure wave of the explosion had ripped it open; Maul could see shattered and twisted pieces of equipment.

Nothing could have survived that. He saw no trace whatsoever

of either the Padawan's or Lorn Pavan's bodies; the explosion had vaporized them.

His mission at last was complete.

Still, it behooved him to be absolutely certain. After all, Pavan had proved extraordinarily hard to kill, had even survived a previous explosion. Maul had to make sure.

He asked the dark side, sending investigatory vibrations throughout the chamber, searching for any signs of life.

There were none.

Excellent.

Darth Maul dropped back down to the walkway. Paying no attention to the milling onlookers, he pulled his cowl up and walked away from the burning building.

It was time to inform his master of his success. At last.

Obi-Wan Kenobi sensed death as he once more neared the site of Master Bondara's wrecked skycar. It wasn't the Jedi's passing that he had noticed earlier; this was something new.

As he drew closer he saw smoke rising from the street and noticed strobes flashing from police cruisers surrounding the area. Obviously some new disaster had occurred here—one important enough to bring the local law enforcement out.

After leaving the Tusken Oasis, he had decided to return to the last place that Darsha and Master Bondara had been seen, which was in the latter's skycar. A floating barricade warned the Padawan to stay back, and for a second Obi-Wan considered doing so. This was the Crimson Corridor, after all. No doubt some unconnected crime was being investigated here, and if that was the case, he would only get in the way.

But then he felt it again—the sense of foreboding that had so unnerved him when he'd been at the site before.

Obi-Wan maneuvered his vehicle past the barricade. A forensics droid was ready to warn him off, but when it saw that he was

a Jedi Padawan, it let him through. The Jedi did not like to use their secular powers, but within the structures of the Republic they were legally empowered to cross police lines on any investigation that touched on their own.

As he landed just outside the scanning line of police lasers, two plainclothes investigators—a Mrlssi and a Sullustan, both of whom looked like they'd rather be anywhere but here—made their way to intercept him. The Mrlssi spoke first.

"Can we help you?"

Obi-Wan decided to see what response he got with part of the truth. There was no reason for them to know that two Jedi Knights had gone missing.

"I've been following reports of a criminal who has been reported operating in the area. Apparently there have been some assaults . . ." He let his statement taper off, focusing on the reactions of the pair, hoping to provoke a response. "I was led to believe that there might be some connection here."

The Sullustan looked at the Mrlssi. "Well, yeah, there might be. Come have a look."

Obi-Wan followed the two over toward a new piece of wreckage, perhaps half a block from Master Bondara's vehicle. Although it had been badly burned and the metal twisted in the heat of the fire, it was plain that a large section of the police unit had been sheared away, and there was a cut through the canopy where the pilot droid would have sat.

"Any ideas, Padawan? . . ."

"Kenobi. Obi-Wan Kenobi."

The Sullustan spoke. "Recognize the skycar type?"

Obi-Wan shook his head. "Is there any significance to it?"

The investigator nodded. "This is—or was—a PCBU: police

cruiser backup unit. They're specifically designed to aid officers answering calls in places like the Crimson Corridor. SOP is to hover back ten meters, up fifteen meters from answering units."

Obi-Wan could see the problem they were wrestling with. How could someone get fifteen meters into the air to reach the PCBU without getting shot?

"Was anyone killed?" he asked, although he already knew the answer.

"Two patrol officers," the Mrlssi said.

Obi-Wan nodded to the two investigators. "This may be the work of Black Sun operatives. I will contact the Temple regarding this. You will have the full cooperation of the Jedi in this matter." So saying, he turned away, heading back to his skycar.

This matter had now grown too large to be dealt with by one Jedi Padawan. Given possible involvement with Black Sun, and now the death of two Coruscant officers, Obi-Wan knew that the only prudent thing to do was to report back to his superiors. A full-scale investigation would have to be launched, in cooperation with the security forces.

He raised his skycar up to around the tenth level—below the lowest stratum of traffic, but high enough to ensure a relatively straight course back to the Temple. Whatever was going on, he was certain now that it involved far more than just the disappearance of Master Bondara and Darsha.

Darth Sidious could feel a slight disturbance in the Force before his scrambled comlink chimed, and knew by this that his apprentice was about to contact him. He stepped to the holo-projector and activated the grid. Privacy failsafes glowed green before he spoke.

"My apprentice. Your mission is complete."

It was a statement, not a question. Sidious knew Darth Maul would not call to report failure, and there were no untoward signs in the energies that surrounded his image.

"Yes, my master. The Jedi Padawan died in combat. She fought well, for a neophyte. An explosion generated from our battle destroyed Lorn Pavan and his droid."

Darth Sidious nodded. He could feel the truth of the statement even at this distance. This was excellent news. Any leaks that could impact his plans had been sealed. Certainly there would be other challenges—he didn't trust the Neimoidians' abilities in combat any more than he did their veracity—but such obstacles would come only after his plan was too far along to be stopped.

"I will require you to bring the holocron to this location." Sidious gave Maul the coordinates and the specialized instructions his apprentice would require to get past the security droids. Darth Maul acknowledged the instructions.

"Be most wary, my apprentice. Our stealth is vital. The Jedi will be most unhappy at the loss of two of their number, and will be searching for answers. You must see that they find none."

Darth Sidious did not wait for a response; none was necessary. With a gesture he closed the relay, breaking the connection.

It was time to make other preparations. Time to finally put into motion the plan that had taken decades to set up. The strategy that would culminate in the final destruction of the Jedi.

Soon.

Very soon.


Obi-Wan pushed the skycar to the maximum safe speed, swooping through the narrow maze of streets and buildings.

Suddenly his attention was distracted by a rumble and a flash of orange light two streets over.

Yet another explosion, he thought wonderingly as he headed toward its source. He didn't know what was going on, but if it didn't stop soon, this sector of the city was going to look like it had been bombed from orbit.

He brought his skycar to a stop on a landing platform and walked cautiously closer to the inferno, using the Force once more to try to discern what had happened. His senses expanded into the building, detecting no life, but picking up the residual disturbances of a powerful struggle. He could sense Darsha's presence and the same tendrils of evil that had plagued him all day. Looking around, the Padawan noticed a section of burned rubble that had been blasted from the entrance. Something gleamed in the debris, and he stepped forward to see what it was.

Shock sent waves of jangling sensations up his body, and he had to still himself, force his mind to unclench and accept what he was seeing.

He used the Force to grasp the shiny bit of metal, pulling it out of the rubble, bringing it to his hand.

It was the twisted, melted hilt of a lightsaber, its body scorched almost beyond recognition.

Almost.

In practice duels at the Temple, two Padawans traditionally exchanged salutes prior to their match, raising their lightsaber hilts to their foreheads before igniting the energy coils. Obi-Wan had noted more than once the carefully wound wire grip on Darsha's weapon, a unique design.

The same design he was looking at now.

The Force confirmed it, as if there were any doubt. Darsha Assant was dead.

Obi-Wan Kenobi stood quietly, looking at the hilt in his hand.

*There is no emotion; there is peace.*

How he wished it were so.

Lorn stared up at the brightest light he had ever seen.

He felt . . . *brittle,* as though he might crack into countless pieces if he tried to move. There was a strange ringing in his ears, an odd smell in his nostrils. His eyes refused to focus. Everything seemed dreamlike. He had no idea where he was or how he had gotten there.

Abruptly the light—which he now realized was the sun—was blotted out by a familiar face.

"Good—you're awake. How do you feel?"

Lorn moved his jaw experimentally, found that he could speak without too much difficulty. "Like a battle dog's chew-toy." He sat up, his vision still blurred, a multitude of aches trying to drag him down. "What happened?"

I-Five didn't reply for a moment. "You don't remember our recent . . . situation?"

Lorn looked around him. He and the droid were on a small setback roof about halfway up the side of a building. The last thing he remembered . . .

He turned and looked in another direction. Perhaps fifty meters away was the building they had been trapped in by the Sith. He remembered Darsha opening the door, remembered seeing the Sith framed in the doorway—but nothing more than that. He said as much to I-Five.

The droid nodded. "Loss of short-term memory. Not surprising, given the trauma of recent events and the carbon-freezing." He helped Lorn to his feet. "Can you walk?"

Lorn tested his balance. "I think so."

"Good. The authorities will no doubt be here soon, but with any luck Tuden Sal will arrive before they do."

Tuden Sal. For some reason the name triggered more flashes of memory. "You froze us in carbonite."

I-Five nodded. "The waste-treatment chamber we were in was set up to contain volatile materials for transport. It was simply a matter of readjusting the parameters for—"

It hit him then, like a stun grenade at close range. "Darsha!"

The sunlight, so much brighter than he was accustomed to, faded momentarily back to the grayness of downlevels. I-Five's mechanical hand gripped his upper arm, steadying him.

Darsha, the Jedi Padawan, the woman with whom he'd shared the last tumultuous forty-eight hours—the woman who'd come to mean, in that short and intense time, more to him than anyone except Jax and I-Five—Darsha was dead.

No. It couldn't be. The droid and he had managed to cheat certain death; surely there had been some way that she, too, might have.

He looked desperately at I-Five. Saw that the droid knew what was going through his head. And read, somehow, in the other's metallic, expressionless face, the truth.

They had escaped because she had bought them time—had bought it with her own heart's blood.

That part came back, too. She was . . . gone.

"What happened?" he asked dully.

"She managed to stack some of the flammable containers together during her battle and ignited them as she was struck down."

*Struck down.*

Lorn was quiet as they made their way to the roof's edge.

"Why aren't we dead?"

"Carbonite is extremely dense. It survived the explosion, and since we were encysted within it, so did we. There was a process timer, which I set to thaw us after a half hour. Then I thought it prudent for us to relocate."

Lorn nodded slowly. "What about the Sith? Did he survive, or did he die with—" He could not bring himself to finish the sentence.

"Unknown. If he did survive—which, were we dealing with anyone else, I would deem extremely unlikely—then in all probability he thinks we're dead. The carbon-freezing lowered all biological and electronic processes to a level far too faint for even a master of the Force to detect."

Lorn stretched his arms and twisted cautiously from side to side. Other than a major headache, he seemed to be experiencing no adverse effects. All in all, he'd had hangovers that were worse.

A pinging sound came from I-Five's midsection. "That would be our ride," the droid said, pulling the comlink out of his torso compartment and activating it. He confirmed their location and toggled it off.

Within seconds a large black skycar with a canopied roof and

dark windows dropped toward them, its side doors opening when it reached their level. Lorn looked in and saw that Tuden Sal himself had come to pick them up.

"I'm wondering what you two have gotten yourselves involved in this time," Sal said as the chauffeured skycar lifted away from the scene. He glanced out the tinted window at the destruction below. "But given what I see down there, I'm not sure I want to know."

"A wise decision," I-Five said, as he leaned over to look out the side window. "The less you know, the less they can indict you for."

The skycar was drifting higher, heading toward a traffic lane that would take them to Eastport, where one of Sal's restaurants was located. I-Five tapped Lorn on the arm and pointed out the side window.

"You may not want to see this," he said.

Lorn looked out the window and saw a tiny figure in black striding along one of the elevated walkways below. He felt his insides ice over as if he'd been plunged once more into carbonite. He got only a glimpse of the figure, who was pretty far away, but it looked like—

His throat was dry; he had to swallow twice before he could speak. "Got enhancers on this crate?" he asked Tuden Sal, who was slouched on the cushioned bench across from him.

The restaurateur was a Sakiyan—short, stocky, and possessed of skin that looked like burnished metal. He nodded and tapped a control alongside the window panel. The aircar was the epitome of plushness: tiny drink dispenser, high-powered comlink, and an interspecies climate control. Instantly, in response to Sal's command, the tiny figure below became much larger, zooming to fill up half the window. His cowl was up, covering his

face, and the enhancement threatened to break up the image into component blocks of digital artifacting, but Lorn recognized him nonetheless.

It was the Sith.

As he watched, the cowled killer pulled something from his belt compartment and held it up to look at. A request to Sal caused the enhancer to focus on it. Lorn wasn't surprised to see the holocron in the Sith's hand.

"Friend of yours?" Sal asked.

Lorn shook his head. "Not at all. But I'd like to keep track of him. Do you mind if we take a little detour?"

"No problem. I owe you, Lorn."

"Keep the enhancers at full, and stay as far back as you can," I-Five advised.

Sal toggled a switch and gave the droid chauffeur the instructions. They began to follow the cowled figure at the maximum visible distance, just barely keeping him in sight.

Darth Maul reined in his connection to the dark side and made his shadow within it as small as he could. His master was right: it would not do to succeed in silencing the enemies of the Sith only to reveal himself to others of them through a mistake.

The apprentice hailed a cab. With his speeder bike destroyed and the one he'd taken from the patrol no doubt dangerous to use by now, he needed transportation to take him nearer to the abandoned monad where his ship was located.

As the air taxi lifted off, its driver having been given directions, Maul kept an eye out for followers. It was unlikely there would be any, since almost all who had seen him had died, or were ten or more levels below—but his master had ordered stealth, and thus it would be.

*   *   *

Lorn and I-Five watched the dark figure alight from the cab and walk toward the upper entrance of an abandoned monad. They watched for a few more minutes until the Sith reappeared on the rooftop.

A few seconds later they saw him step into thin air and vanish.

"Nice trick," Tuden Sal said.

Lorn just stared, completely baffled for the moment, not sure whether to believe his eyes. Was this some new arcane power of the murdering Sith? But then he heard I-Five say, in answer to Sal's comment, "He must have a high-grade cloaking device. Probably crystal based."

Of course. Their nemesis had gotten into a cloaked spaceship. It made perfect sense, Lorn thought. The Sith had accomplished his mission; he had gotten the holocron and, as far as he was concerned, killed everyone who knew anything about it. He was no doubt preparing to leave Coruscant.

*Only I'm not dead, you murderer. You think I am, but I'm not.*

The question was, what was he going to do now?

For the first time since this nightmare had begun, he was safe. The Sith thought he was dead. All Lorn had to do was lie low and the demonic killer would pass out of his life forever. He and I-Five could get off Coruscant and pile as many parsecs between them and the hub of the galaxy as they deemed necessary. They wouldn't be rich, but they'd be alive.

And the rankweed sucker who had killed Darsha would get away with his crime.

Lorn knew he could go to the Jedi and tell them what had happened. They would no doubt mobilize their ranks and start hunting for the one who had killed two of their order. Even though Lorn and they had some bad history, there would be no

problem convincing them to believe him—one of the few advantages of dealing with a fraternity of Force users.

But the wheels of any organization, no matter how self-consciously benign, turn slowly and ponderously. Even now, the Sith was no doubt getting ready to raise ship. Could even the Jedi find him once he fled this world?

Lorn stared out the window. Before him, spread from horizon to horizon, lay Coruscant in all its tessellated splendor. More than just about anybody else, he felt he could say that he had seen the best and the worst the capital planet had to offer. He had led a life that had been by turns dangerous, frustrating, terrifying, and heartbreaking. There had been little joy in it. Still, he was reluctant to do anything that might result in his losing it.

He had never wanted to be a hero. All he had wanted was to live a quiet, normal life with his wife and son. But his wife had left him, and the Jedi—those whom the galaxy looked upon as heroes—had seduced him into giving them his son.

He would never have called any Jedi a hero—until he met Darsha Assant.

He took a deep breath and looked at Tuden Sal. "We need a spaceship," he said.

His friend nodded. "I-Five told me. No problem. Where do you want to go?"

Lorn looked back down at the roof of the monad, where the Sith had been visible until a moment ago.

"Wherever he's going."

**D**arth Maul settled into the pilot's chair. He pressed his hand to a sensor plate on the console before him, and the hemispheric control chamber filled with various hums, tones, and vibrations as the *Infiltrator* powered up. A quick outside scan revealed nothing in the immediate area that would interfere with his launch. Maul nodded in satisfaction.

His mission was nearly over at last. It had taken far longer than anticipated and had led him into dark corners of Coruscant he had not even known existed. But now his assignment was almost accomplished. Everyone whom Hath Monchar had spoken to, every potential information leak, had been stilled. Darth Sidious's plan for the trade embargo, and eventually the destruction of the Republic, could now proceed unchallenged.

Maul pulled the holocron from one of his belt compartments and looked at it. Such a small item, and yet the repository of so much potential power. He returned it to the compartment, then activated the vertical repulsor array. He watched on the overhead

monitors as the monad's rooftop fell away from the ship. The *Infiltrator*'s nav computer began plotting directional and velocity vectors that would take him to the rendezvous point specified by his master. There he would deliver the holocron to Darth Sidious, and then his mission would be complete.

Within a matter of minutes he was high above the clouds, the curve of the planet revealing itself. It would take a little time to reach his destination; the orbital shells surrounding Coruscant were nearly as congested as the traffic strata on or near the surface. Once he was in orbit he would have to disable his invisibility field; otherwise it would be too difficult to avoid a collision with one of the myriad satellites, space stations, and ships that circled the planet.

Maul took the ship off autopilot and fed minimal power to the ion drive. The autopilot was more than capable of delivering him to his destination, but he preferred to be in control.

As he settled the *Infiltrator* into low orbit, barely skimming the tenuous gases of the upper ionosphere, Maul thought about his battle with the Jedi Padawan. She had certainly been smarter and more resourceful than he had given her credit for. So had her companion, for that matter. They had led him on quite a merry chase. He mentally saluted them both. He admired courage, skill, and brains, even in an enemy. They had been doomed from the start, of course, but at least they had fought their fate instead of submitting meekly to it, like that cowardly Neimoidian who had caused all this trouble to begin with.

He wondered what his master had in mind for his next mission. Something relating to the Naboo blockade, most likely. He hoped there would be more Jedi involved. Killing the Padawan had only whetted his appetite.

\*     \*     \*

The ship Tuden Sal provided for Lorn and I-Five was an ARE Thixian Seven—a four-passenger modified cruiser. The craft had definitely seen better days, Lorn thought as the skycar settled down next to the ship's berth at Eastport, but that didn't matter. As long as it could fly and shoot, that was all he cared about.

As Tuden Sal arranged for launch clearance via his comlink, Lorn turned to I-Five and said, "Give me the blaster."

I-Five returned the Raptor's weapon to him. "As long as you're not planning on trying to shoot me with it again," the droid said.

"I wouldn't have shot you."

I-Five made no reply to that.

"Listen," Lorn continued, "I don't expect you to go with me. In fact, it makes more sense for you to go to the Temple and tell the Jedi what's been happening. That way there'll be a backup plan if I fail."

"Oh, please," I-Five said. "You take on the Sith alone? You've got about as much chance as a snowball in a supernova."

"It's not your fight."

"Finally, something we agree on. Nevertheless, I'm not letting you go up there alone. You're going to need all the help you can get. Which reminds me—" The droid pulled from his chest compartment what looked like a small white ball. He handed it to Lorn, who looked closely at it. It was semitransparent, roughly spherical, about half the length of his thumb in diameter, and apparently made of some organic material.

"What is it?"

"A skin nodule from the taozin. They're made of specially adapted cells that block receptivity to the Force."

Lorn regarded the ball askance. Now that he knew what it was, he felt revulsed by its touch. "You're saying if I have this, the Sith can't use the Force on me?"

"I'm saying it may shroud your presence long enough for you to sneak up on him unnoticed. It won't protect you from his telekinetic powers, and it certainly won't do anything about his fighting skills. But it's better than nothing. Now I suggest we raise ship." So saying, the droid turned toward the ramp of the Thixian Seven.

Lorn let him get two paces ahead of him, then reached out and deactivated the master switch on the back of I-Five's neck. The droid collapsed, and Lorn caught him, settling him to the ground. He turned to see Tuden Sal watching.

"Family squabble?"

"Something like that. I need one more favor," Lorn said. "Deliver this bucket of bolts to the Jedi Temple. He's got information they'll want to hear."

Sal nodded. He picked I-Five up under the arms and dragged him over to his skycar. Lorn watched for a minute, then turned and boarded the ship.

Lorn could honestly say that he wasn't frightened at the thought of facing the Sith alone. *Frightened* was far too mild a word. He was *terrified*, paralyzed, totally unmanned by what he was contemplating. He knew he was pursuing a suicidal course of action, and for what? Some quixotic notion of revenge for the death of a woman he barely knew? It was madness. I-Five was right: his chances for survival were so long that the odds were up in the purely theoretical number range.

As the Thixian Seven lifted away from the spaceport, Lorn

felt himself on the verge of hyperventilation. Every nerve in his trembling body was on fire with adrenaline; every brain cell still functioning after his periodic bouts of alcohol abuse was screaming at him to leave orbit and just keep on going. Instead, he instructed the nav computer to plot the possible trajectories of a ship coming from the surface grid containing the abandoned monad.

Within far too short a time the computer had identified a craft in low orbit, thirty-five kilometers away. Lorn put it on visual, since the readout said that the stealth mechanism had been deactivated. He stared at the computer-enhanced image of the Sith's vessel. With long nose and bent wings, it was a sleek craft, nearly thirty meters long; the scan readout didn't specify armament, but it looked mean.

Below him, Coruscant looked like a gigantic circuit board laid across the planet's surface. It was a spectacular sight, but Lorn wasn't in any mood for sightseeing. He settled into an orbit below and well behind his enemy's ship. He didn't know how much protection—if any—the taozin nodule would grant him, and he wasn't going to press his luck. He was going to need plenty of luck as it was.

Lorn wished I-Five was with him. He was painfully aware that since this nightmare had begun, every time his life had been in peril it had been either the droid or Darsha who had saved him. Some hero, he thought.

He missed Darsha, as well, although he didn't wish she was with him. He wished she were still alive and far away from here, safe on some friendly planet that had never heard of either the Sith or the Jedi. He wished he was there with her.

The nav computer beeped softly to get his attention, and displayed a course vector overlay on one of the monitors. The Sith's

ship had changed course; it was now headed for a large space station in geosynchronous orbit over the equator.

His mouth dry as paper, Lorn instructed the autopilot to follow. He had no idea what he was going to do when he got there. All he knew was he had to try, somehow, to stop the Sith.

For Darsha's sake.

And for his own.

Tuden Sal loaded the deactivated I-Five into his skycar and instructed the droid chauffeur as to their destination. The vehicle lifted away from the spaceport, sliding smoothly into the airborne traffic lanes.

He felt sorry for Lorn. His friend hadn't told him very much about the situation he was in, but from the few hints he had dropped and from the look of the goon he was chasing, Sal figured his chances of survival were not great. That was too bad. He'd always thought Lorn had potential, even though he came across as a chronic underachiever. One rogue can always recognize another.

But in all probability, Lorn was going to die on this crazy quest of his. A shame, but it really wasn't any of Sal's business. He was far more concerned about the droid.

The Sakiyan had never really understood how Lorn could treat I-Five as an equal—even going so far as to call him a "business partner." Droids were machines—clever ones, to be sure, and able in some cases to mimic human behavior to a startling

degree. But that's all it was: mimicry. Legally they were property. Though he'd become somewhat accustomed to it during the year or so he'd known Lorn and I-Five, Sal had never completely gotten over the vaguely creepy feeling it gave him to see the two of them interacting as peers.

Well, there would be no more of that. He'd had his eye on this droid for some time; the weapons modifications alone would make him a valuable asset. Since Sal occasionally had dealings with Black Sun, it was not a bad idea at all to have a bodyguard, and he was certain that I-Five would make a very good one— once the droid's memory had been wiped, of course.

He wasn't overly concerned with how Lorn might feel about this. After all, he fully expected never to see Lorn again. And even if he did, it wasn't a capital crime to steal and reprogram a droid. The most he could expect in terms of legal repercussions might be a fine, which wouldn't be nearly as much as the cost of a new droid with I-Five's special features.

No matter how you looked at it, even throwing in that clunker of a ship, it was good business.

The Temple's roof sparkled in the afternoon sun as Sal's sky-car shot by it. Soon it was lost to sight among the countless other flying craft that filled the skies of Coruscant.

The *Infiltrator* settled into one of the space station's docking sleeves, and Maul heard the muffled metallic sounds of the air lock's outer hatch sealing with the station's. He deactivated the life support and artificial gravity systems—then, weightless, he made his way through the ship's dark interior to the air lock.

This point of egress to the station was in one of the outlying service modules. Darth Sidious had promised him that there would be neither human nor droid to interfere with his progress,

and as Maul emerged from the air lock he saw that this was so. The lock opened into what appeared to be a service corridor— narrow and low, the walls and ceiling covered with pipes, conduits, and the like. The artificial gravity was not on in this region of the station, no doubt for budgetary reasons. No matter; Maul had operated in zero-g environments before. He pushed himself away from the lock and floated down the corridor, using the impedimenta that festooned the walls to pull himself along.

The directions Darth Sidious had given him were clear in his head; he was to proceed down this passageway to the module proper, and then take a vertical shaft up to one of the larger habitation modules. At a prearranged time—less than fifteen minutes away—he would rendezvous with Maul. Maul would then hand him the crystal.

And then his mission would be complete.

Lorn let the autopilot take care of the docking procedure; he wasn't all that good of a pilot. *I'm not all that good at anything,* he thought bitterly, except *getting those I care about in trouble.* He still had the blaster he had taken from the Raptor, but he only now remembered its power pack wasn't good for more than a few shots. Of course, a few shots would probably be all he would have time for, one way or another.

After the green light flashed, Lorn crossed into the service shaft. It had been some time since he'd experienced zero-g. When he could afford to, he used to work out fairly regularly at a spa that featured null-grav sports. He'd enjoyed the workouts; feeling like he could fly, even if only within the small confines of the spa's structure, had always been good for taking some of the weight of his existence off him.

He was under no illusions, however, that his familiarity with weightlessness gave him any kind of edge over the Sith. He had no doubt that his opponent could handle himself with consummate and deadly skill in any kind of environment. He would need an enormous amount of luck to pull this off.

Once inside the corridor, he moved very cautiously and slowly. There was no sign of his enemy anywhere ahead, and it didn't look like there was anyplace to hide here. Nevertheless, he was taking no chances. Lorn wouldn't have been surprised if the Sith suddenly materialized out of thin air in front of him at this point.

He had no idea what he was going to do once he spotted him; he hadn't had time to formulate a plan. If the taozin nodule let him get close enough to get off a shot, he had absolutely no compunctions about shooting his adversary in the back—assuming he didn't pass out from sheer terror once he had him in his sights.

He reached the end of the corridor. An access shaft led up from here. Before following it, Lorn pulled out the blaster and checked its power supply.

What he found was not good. The weapon had enough power left for one shot at maximum setting, or three shots at the low-level stun setting. After a moment's thought, Lorn adjusted the setting to the lower level, figuring it would be better to have three chances of incapacitating the Sith rather than one chance of killing him. Assuming the stun setting would in fact stun him. By now Lorn wasn't at all persuaded that anything could harm his nemesis.

He eased himself into the shaft. It led to a larger, better-lit chamber, perhaps ten meters by ten, and fairly empty save for some equipment bins anchored to the walls.

At the other end of the chamber was the Sith.

His back was to Lorn; he was entering a code on a wall panel, preparing to open a hatch in the far wall.

Lorn rose quietly out of the tube and gripped the blaster in both hands. He braced his feet against the edge of the shaft; there would be a slight recoil in zero-g.

The taozin nodule seemed to be doing its job: the Sith was apparently unaware that Lorn was ten meters behind him and drawing a bead right between his shoulder blades. His hands were trembling, but not so much that he shouldn't be able to hit a target as broad as his enemy's back, especially with three shots at his disposal. Once the Sith was stunned, Lorn would finish him off with the lightsaber and then grab the information crystal.

The Sith pressed a wall button. A light glowed green, and the hatch started to open.

Now. It had to be now. Lorn drew a deep breath, opening his mouth wide so that the Sith wouldn't hear the intake of air. He exhaled the same way, then drew in another breath and held it.

He pulled the trigger.

The shot was true. The stun bolt nailed the Sith squarely in the middle of his back, hurling him forward to slam against the bulkhead. Lorn fired one more, which hit the Sith's lower back.

Lorn couldn't believe it. He shoved himself forward, shooting the length of the chamber toward his adversary, who was now floating limply back toward him in a slow rebound from the impact. Blaster held ready—he had one shot left—Lorn grabbed the Sith's robes, pulling the latter around to face him. As he was reaching for the lightsaber he noticed a sparkle of reflected light coming from a half-open compartment on the utility belt.

It was the holocron crystal. Lorn grabbed it and shoved it in his pocket. Then he reached for the lightsaber.

He was staring directly into the sinister tattooed face when the Sith's yellow eyes opened.

Lorn froze, mesmerized by that ferocious glare. He forgot about the lightsaber he was reaching for, forgot about the blaster still in his other hand. Then he was hurled back by a blast, unseen but nonetheless powerful, that left him gasping for air.

The Sith's lightsaber leapt into a black-gloved fist, both blades flashing into existence. One of them flickered toward him like crimson lightning. Lorn felt a blow to his right hand, saw the hand, still clutching the blaster, go spinning away in slow motion, a few globules of blood following it. He didn't feel any pain, did not in fact realize what had happened until he saw the blackened, cauterized stump at the end of his arm.

And now the Sith was spinning around, using the energy of the last blow to rotate himself into attack position again. The moment stretched for Lorn, unbelievably clear and sharp. The Sith's teeth were bared in a rictus of animal hatred. The lightsaber started a horizontal arc that would, in less than a second, shear through his neck.

He was floating in front of the open hatch. His left leg was bent, his foot grazing the side of one of the storage canisters. Lorn kicked against it, propelling himself backwards through the hatch. The energy blade slashed through the empty space his neck had occupied a moment previously.

He brought his legs up as he sailed through the hatchway. He flipped over in a back somersault, his head coming up and his left arm reaching out for the hatch controls. He saw the Sith hurtling toward him, framed in the opening. His hand slapped the button, and the hatch swung shut in the Sith's face. A red light glowed, indicating the hatchway was sealed. Lorn raked his fingers over the access panel keypad, scrambling the code.

Through the hatch's port he could see the Sith's face—a sight to chill the blood. Then, faintly, he heard the sound of metal beginning to melt and saw a faint blush of red building in the hatch's center.

The Sith was using his lightsaber to melt through the hatch.

Lorn turned and started pulling himself frantically along the corridor he was in. He didn't know where he was going, or how he was going to escape the vengeance of the monster behind him. There was no room in his head for anything—not even the pain of his severed wrist as the shock began to wear off—except raw red panic.

For possibly the first time in his life, Darth Maul had been taken completely by surprise.

He had felt no warning vibration of the Force before being hit by the blaster bolts. The astonishment this caused him was almost equaled by the shock of realizing that the attack had come from Lorn Pavan. He had been so certain of the Corellian's death back on Coruscant that awakening to see him alive and looting his utility belt had caused Maul to momentarily question his own sanity.

It was the combined shock of these two events—plus the confusing fact that, even though he could see Pavan before him, he could not sense his presence with the Force—that had slowed his reaction time just enough to let the Corellian get through the hatchway and lock it in Maul's face. Now he had to burn his way through the lock mechanism. As soon as the hatch came loose, he savagely hurled it open and shot after Pavan, using the Force to propel his weightless self in pursuit. There was no time to lose. He did not know how Pavan had escaped the explosion back in the storage facility, or how he was able to block his presence in the Force—and he did not care. In a few minutes his master would be at the rendezvous point, and Maul intended to be

there, as well, holding the holocron in one hand and Pavan's severed head in the other.

This had gone on long enough.

Lorn hauled himself up another vertical shaft, moving as fast as he could with only one hand to aid him. It seemed he could feel the hot breath of the Sith on the back of his neck; he dared not look behind him in case he actually did see the latter's demonic face. To look into those yellow eyes one more time would, he felt sure, utterly paralyze him.

His one hope was to reach the space station's main section, where he could find some kind of security personnel. Surely, with enough blasters between him and the Sith, he would be safe.

It seemed impossible now that he had ever seriously intended, even for a moment, to kill the black-robed creature. That he had even managed to take the holocron away from him now seemed a miracle. Not that he would keep it for very long if he didn't find help fast.

And then he shouldered his way through one final access port and found himself in a large solarium. As he passed through the entry, Lorn felt weightfulness return with a rush.

He looked around. Plants and dwarf trees were tastefully arranged in a small garden setting. Half of the domed ceiling was made of polarized transparisteel, affording a magnificent view of the stars and a huge crescent of the planet. And standing in the garden were several people of various species, some of whom were wearing the robes of Republic Senate members, and others dressed in the dark, formfitting attire of Coruscant guards.

He recognized one of the senators. When he had worked for

the Jedi, Lorn had heard him spoken of many times, always as a man of clear-minded practicality, a stranger to corruption and intrigue. If anyone could be counted on to protect the information on the holocron and see it safely reach the sanctuary of the Jedi Temple, it would be him.

Lorn staggered forward. One of the senators, a Gran, saw him coming and reacted with a bleat of fright. Several of the guards moved in to protect their charges, drawing blasters.

"Wait!"

The command came from the senator whom Lorn had recognized. He stepped forward, his expression one of concern.

"What's the matter, my good fellow? What brings you here in this extreme state?"

Lorn pulled the crystal from his pocket and held it out. He saw the other's eyes narrow as he recognized it.

"A holocron crystal?"

"Yes," Lorn gasped, dropping it into the senator's outstretched hand. "It must reach the Jedi. Very important."

The senator nodded, and quickly tucked the holocron away in a fold of his robe. Then he noticed the stump where Lorn's other hand had been. "You're injured!" He turned to one of the guards, summoning him with a quick, imperious gesture. "This man requires hospitalization immediately! And protection from assassins, as well, by the look of it."

Lorn sagged into a chair. As the others came forward he risked a glance over his shoulder at the service port where he had entered. There was no sign of the Sith.

Relief flooded over him. The nightmare was over, at last.

He felt his consciousness starting to slip away and realized that for the first time in days he could allow himself the luxury of

exhaustion. "Make sure . . . the holocron . . . ," he mumbled, but was too tired to finish the sentence.

His benefactor leaned over him and smiled. "Don't worry, my brave friend. I'll take care of it. Everything will be all right now."

Lorn managed to mumble, "Thank you, . . . Senator Palpatine." And then everything faded.

When Obi-Wan Kenobi reached the Temple he could tell immediately that something was wrong. It wasn't just the ominous reverberations in the Force that pulsed invisibly all around him; the Padawans and messengers he passed in the hallways all wore looks of concern and concentration. One of them saw him and stopped.

"Padawan Kenobi, you are to report to your Master immediately." Then he continued on his way before Obi-Wan could ask what was causing the palpable air of tension.

He found the door to Master Qui-Gon's domicile open. The Jedi was inside, loading his utility belt with field items such as an ascension gun and food capsules. He evidenced relief when he saw Obi-Wan standing in the doorway.

"Excellent. You have returned just in time."

"What's happened, Master?"

"The Trade Federation has blockaded Naboo. You and I have been selected as ambassadors to the Trade Federation flagship to settle this."

Obi-Wan felt stunned at the magnitude of this news. "Surely the Republic Senate will condemn such an action!"

"I suspect the Neimoidians are counting on the senate's past record of being . . . less than effective in such matters. In any event, we must leave immediately."

"I understand. But I must tell you—Master Anoon Bondara and his Padawan, Darsha Assant, are both dead. There is no doubt of this."

Master Qui-Gon paused in his packing and looked at Obi-Wan. The Padawan could see the sadness in his mentor's eyes.

"And the cause of this tragedy?"

"I'm still not certain, although I suspect Black Sun involvement."

"I want to hear all about it," Master Qui-Gon said, "and so will the council. But speed is of the essence now. You will make your report to them via holo transmission once we are on our way."

"Yes, Master." Obi-Wan followed Qui-Gon Jinn as the latter strapped his belt around his waist and left the room.

He would do as his Master said, of course. Obviously this new crisis superceded the events that had taken place in the Crimson Corridor. As he followed Master Qui-Gon, Obi-Wan wondered if he would ever know the complete story of what happened to Darsha and Master Bondara. She had had the potential to be a good Jedi Knight, and he grieved for her passing.

*The Sith lunged for him, twin energy blades flashing.*

Lorn awoke with a gasp. He stared about him, still feeling for

a moment the panic of his nightmare. Then, slowly, as his eyes took in his surroundings, he began to relax.

He was in a private room in a hotel—nothing fancy, but far superior to what he had been used to for the past five years. His severed wrist had been treated with synthflesh, and he had been told by Senator Palpatine that within a few days a prosthetic replacement would be grafted on. More important, Palpatine had also told him that the information crystal had been delivered to the Jedi Temple and the assassin captured.

In short, Lorn had won.

Not completely, of course. He still mourned the death of Darsha. He was also concerned about I-Five's whereabouts: apparently the droid had never made it to the Temple. A Pyrrhic victory—but a victory nonetheless.

He had been given his choice of futures: relocation to a colony world somewhere in the Outer Rim, or a permanent address in a monad on Coruscant. Either way, he had been assured that the bank fraud charges had been dropped, and he would be awarded a stipend that would allow him and I-Five to live comfortably. He hadn't decided yet what to do, although he was leaning toward staying on Coruscant. By staying he could possibly reestablish some form of relationship with Jax. The Jedi owed him that much, at least.

Also, he owed it to himself. It was time he started to live again—a real life, not the empty mockery he had been trapped in for so long downlevels. It might take a long time for the nightmares to subside, but eventually they would. Eventually he would know peace.

Lorn got out of the bed. In the closet was a new set of clothes, which he put on. He had no place in particular to go,

but he felt like getting outside. He needed to feel the sun on his face, to breathe clean air. It had been a long time since he had enjoyed those simple pleasures.

He opened the door.

The Sith stood before him.

Lorn was too stunned to even be afraid. His enemy stepped forward, implacable, unstoppable, and activated his lightsaber. Lorn knew there was nothing he could do. The hotel room was small, barren of weapons, with only the one door.

This time there was no escape.

Surprisingly, in that moment—the final moment of his life— he found he was not afraid. Found, in fact, that he was in a place similar to that which Darsha had described when she was deep in the embrace of the Force.

He was at peace.

The information about the Sith had been given to the Jedi. The fact that the assassin was able to escape his incarceration couldn't change that. His death, Lorn realized, was in the service of a higher purpose.

He was content that it be so.

The lightsaber's blade shimmered toward him. His last thought was of his son; his last emotion was pride that someday Jax would be a Jedi Knight.

Looking into Pavan's eyes, Darth Maul knew what the man was thinking. Even were he not Force-sensitive, he could have read it clearly in his enemy's eyes and expression.

He said nothing.

Though Maul had no compunctions about killing anyone who stood in his or his master's way, he was not without a sense of honor. Lorn Pavan had managed, against all odds, to be more

of a challenge to Maul than many of the professional killers of Black Sun. He was a worthy opponent and had earned the right to die quickly.

The lightsaber sizzled through air, through flesh, through bone.

Darth Maul turned and walked away, his mission at last complete.

## About the Author

MICHAEL REAVES received an Emmy Award for his work on the *Batman* animated TV series. He has worked for Spielberg's DreamWorks, among other studios, and is the author of several fantasy novels and supernatural thrillers. His novel *Hell on Earth* will be published by Del Rey in the Summer of 2001. Reaves lives in Los Angeles.

# Also Available from Gail Godwin

## *Publishing*

**From three-time National Book Award finalist and *New York Times* bestselling author Gail Godwin, a vibrant portrait of her writing and publishing life.**

*Publishing* is a personal story of a writer's hunger to be published, the pursuit of that goal, and then the long haul. Recollecting her long and storied career—which includes three National Book Award finalists and five *New York Times* bestsellers— Godwin maps the publishing industry over the last fifty years, a time of great upheaval and ingenuity. Her eloquent memoir is illuminated by Frances Halsband's evocative black-and-white line drawings throughout. There have been memoirs about writing and memoirs about being an editor, but there is no other book quite like *Publishing* for aspiring writers and book lovers everywhere.

"You don't have to have followed Godwin's career as a reader either, though the millions who have will be treated to a look behind the scenes." —*The New York Times Book Review*

# Also Available from Gail Godwin

## *Flora*

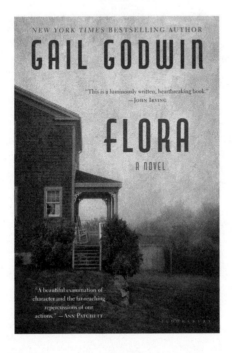

**From three-time National Book Award finalist and *New York Times* bestselling author Gail Godwin, "a luminously written, heartbreaking book"**
**(JOHN IRVING)**

Ten-year-old Helen and her summer guardian, Flora, are isolated together in Helen's decaying family house while her father is doing secret war work in Oak Ridge during the final months of World War II. A fiercely imaginative child, Helen is desperate to keep her house intact with all its ghosts and stories. Flora, her late mother's twenty-two-year-old first cousin, who cries at the drop of a hat, is ardently determined to do her best for Helen. Their relationship and its fallout, played against a backdrop of a lost America, will haunt Helen for the rest of her life. A story of love, regret, and the things we can't undo.

"*Flora* is a beautiful examination of character and the far-reaching repercussions of our actions. Gail Godwin brings grace, honesty, and enormous intelligence to every page." —*Ann Patchett*